T0325322

The Teeth
of the Souls

Praise for *Morkan's Quarry: A Novel*

You'll almost feel yourself breathing in the lime dust that coated everything the Morkan family held dear. You'll smell the heating oil, the gunpowder…and the ever-present death and decay. "Morkan's Quarry" is essential reading for anyone with an interest in the Civil War. It's a gripping family saga that entertains and educates on a grand scale. It's a lesson not only in tragedy and suffering, but in all that's good about the human spirit and the refusal to surrender one's principles.

—Joe Lee

Praise for *Some Kinds of Love: Stories*

The language is totally unlike anything used by myself or any other writer of Ozarks fiction. Is it possible that Niangua will become your Stay More? Your 'new' style is magic realism at its best.

—Donald Harington, author of
The Architecture of the Arkansas Ozarks,
The Choiring of the Trees, Enduring, and many others

Yates is one tremendous writer.

—Steve Yarbrough, author of
Safe from the Neighbors, Visible Spirits, Prisoners of War,
The End of California, and many others

Some Kinds of Love is nothing short of masterful. In Steve Yates's stories, pigs really do fly. He is a brilliant, and brilliantly inventive writer, and this book is sheer delight from beginning to end.

—Ben Fountain, author of *Brief Encounters with Che Guevara:*
Stories and *Billy Lynn's Long Halftime Walk*

From *Publishers Weekly*

In this sturdy story collection, Yates (*Morkan's Quarry*) parades a cast of characters who, as diverse as they appear on the surface, have in common an underlying ignorance and mistrust of others. This trait manifests in a larger theme of historical prejudice in the "American Empire", the setting of these tales which range in time from 1833 to the present. [A] memorable ensemble… Instead of getting their comeuppance though, Yates's clueless characters get laid, get back together, or get a new SUV, which somehow rings true: good things happen to bad people, or more accurately in these cases, things happen to people.

From the *Greenwood Commonwealth*

Form always gives way to function, and Yates' elegant prose presents elegant characters, composed of grit, eccentricity and the respective landscapes that created them. Yates' characters are the products of the Missouri Ozarks, New Orleans and Mississippi, places that serve as the backdrop for stories about different kinds of love.

—Jeanie Riess

The Teeth
of the Souls

A Novel by Steve Yates

Springfield, Missouri
2015

mooncitypress.com

Text edited by Donald R. Holliday
Text layout by Elizabeth O'Gara
Cover design by Eric Pervukhin; cover photograph ©2015 by
Jeffrey Sweet, http://jeffreysweetphotography.zenfolio.com

ISBN 978-0-913785-52-2

This book is for my wife, Tammy Gebhart Yates, who has waited; and for my mother, Joy Evertz Yates, who has waited even longer.

Book 1

I Dream You

I

UPON THE DEATH OF THE OLD MORKAN IT WAS WIDELY supposed in Springfield that his son, Leighton Shea, would quickly meet with calamity. Silent save when bossing laborers at Morkan Quarry, the young man struggled without the easy gab and foxy acumen of his late father. Those wartime comrades who hunted and killed bushwhackers alongside him in the Federal Home Guards did not speak much of their service. Yet they alone brooked no ill word about him. And so it became the general lean that without a mate, without some truly Christian guidance, this one would fail, and his quarry fold, and maybe something quiet and respectable could succeed there, and that would be just as well, him being Irish and Catholic after all. What the Cross cannot abide, the rope will mend.

Whenever the town's intrigue and tumult bothered Leighton's household, neither servants nor master sought the source. All knew from long experience that the Negress Judith would bring the imagined disaster fully upon them, unbidden and soon.

Today it was a scandal and lynching in a nearby town much bandied among the Coloreds. Though Leighton was leery of talk about it, stopping her would take more effort than enduring her. Sitting in the mudroom of his farmhouse in Galway, Missouri, he dug two fingers through lime paste mixed in a spittoon. On a cedar bench knee-to-knee across from him sat his Negro hand Isaac, tense as a hound. Twice in the last two weeks Leighton's accountant was robbed at gunpoint riding from Morkan Quarry with new contracts and cash. It was time to set a trap. Horse thieves and bandits plagued the roads now that the Civil War was won. At least according to the Yankee Republican victors, it was won. Leighton drew the muck of lime across Isaac's stubbled face, painting the Negro ashen gray.

The bench creaked as Judith pressed her fleshy side to Leighton's arm. Though she longed to chatter at him, she shared little with Isaac, a field hand and beneath her. So she whispered in Leighton's ear as he worked to blanch Isaac's face.

"And they hanged that man and that woman at one rope from the bois d'arc right in the town square, can you believe? Together in death forever!"

The door to the mudroom was open, but no breeze lifted the hot July air. Isaac's eyes, black pupils in parchment yellow, ceased to follow Leighton's gray fingers and instead narrowed on Judith's bosom pressed to Leighton's shoulder. Leighton wore dungarees stiff and spotted with cement and an old white shirt thinning to show the ovals of his powerful chest and arms. On his feet were engineer's boots so hardened with lime they seemed hammered from iron. And on his head he wore, bill backwards, the Yankee campaign hat now mottled gray so that at a distance a person could not tell on which side he had served. With his trimmed, black beard and slanted, blue eyes, he was a White man to be reckoned with, full grown. Isaac shuddered at Judith's closeness to Leighton.

"All on account of them having babies. One Black and one White as milk from the butterfly weed." Her lips were so close to his ear, they left a wet circle as she spoke.

Leighton nudged her away with a hard shoulder. Judith snorted, and crossed her arms over her chest. Isaac smiled.

"Be still, Isaac," Leighton said, smearing lime at his lips and cheeks.

"I. Ain't. Moved…"

Leighton's father bought Isaac, a slave, eight years before in '57 with the Galway farm. Leighton's mother died of small pox the year after that. Losing his father to consumption at the war's end left him alone with three Negro hands, his former slaves. At nineteen years old, Leighton held a decaying farmhouse on one hundred acres of lime and chert amid brambly forest. And in nearby Springfield he owned the most mechanized quarry west of the Saint Francois Mountains. It surprised him even now that his freed slaves had stayed, but he felt no pride in it. The war was won leaving nothing but the charred fingers of chimneys where fine houses had been. Outside his circuit of farmhouse and quarry, greed married vengeance. Ancient catastrophes of the sword silvered the wood and bloodied the hills. To Judith, his sole confidante and friend, all this chaos seemed so new and dire, the world worsening to its end for sure. But from gory Irish legends of Maeve, Leighton knew this story was so very old, his own death and deeds might leave no more than a droplet in a wide and crimson fabric.

Beneath his fingers Isaac's whiskers crackled with the gritty lime. And Leighton slowed his hand, marveling at, fearing for this strange, familiar skin beneath his fingertips, skin he had owned. How he wished that through the lime and all its sorcery of cleansing, drying, purging, hardening, there were some surety of power he might alchemize painting Isaac with a skin insuperable. But this today was all sleight of hand, an evening's parlor trick.

Once she saw Isaac bristle, Judith crowded Leighton again. Though Leighton was unsure of Isaac's age, he knew Isaac was older than Judith. She was at most four years older than Leighton, but from the gloss of her cheeks, from her dark black, flawless complexion, she looked Leighton's junior. She wore her hair short as a burro's mane and kept her dresses altered with multicolored patches of curtain scrap, denim, yellow gingham, and poplin to accommodate her expanding girth. Isaac, a long, lean Negro, wore a battered pair of trousers and a purple shirt handed down from Leighton's dead father and brogans stitched together with bailing wire. In the crow's feet at the corners of Isaac's eyes, the lime dried from ashen gray to white.

"Get that part there." She pointed, her arm so thick now that the cuff of her dress creased her wrist making her seem swollen. For Leighton it was hard to reconcile her size to the scrawny slave girl who had been his companion ever since he was a babe. Her heavy body engulfed his back.

"Judith," Leighton said, his teeth clenching.

When she draped a hand over Leighton's shoulder, even Isaac scowled.

"Straighten out that frown," Leighton said. "I can't get under your chin when you grouse."

"What wrong with you?" Judith asked, swatting at Isaac.

9

Isaac ducked, then slapped both hands on the bench. "You two as bad as children," he said. "This here is a gag on a fellow, ain't it?" He stood and his knotty fists clenched at his sides. He looked like an enraged ghost.

Judith squawked with delight and Leighton's shoulders shook with laughter, brow pinched and eyes tearing. Recovering, he raised a hand to Isaac, but when he glanced up at the Negro, blue and furious before him, he lost composure again. He and Judith collapsed into one another's arms laughing.

They quieted when Isaac sat down on the bench, his face set and serious.

"Let loose of each other," Isaac said. It was a command that startled them both. "Look it," he said. "You two been cooped up here too long. Don't you carry on like that. Bolivar may not be the only place they got hangings."

They parted slowly, watching Isaac as they did. When Judith bowed her head, her round cheeks turned ruddy.

For a long while, Leighton sat glaring at Isaac until the room fell back into the order of employer and hands, of White and Negroes. "Isaac, look here," Leighton said, "this is no gag. I wish it was."

He turned to the corner of the room where he had set his Enfield. Leighton grunted as he lifted the rifle. He hesitated, then set the Enfield across Isaac's knees.

They both placed a hand on the rifle to hold it steady. "You step out in a public road and level this at a White man, you will have to be nearly White."

"Why? He a thief, ain't he?"

Leighton sighed. "Have you thought what may happen to you if he escapes? Have you thought what might happen to me, giving you the rifle?"

"Why not pick some fella from the quarry, then?

Leighton shook his head. "Tip the bandit off, it might."

Judith followed them both with a lowered brow and a frown. Faces grave, the men checked their guns, Leighton pushing paper cartridges into a Colt pistol. Isaac, sure just a bit ago, now glanced from the Enfield to Leighton and back to the Enfield. As they left for their horses, Judith carried the lime paste to the front parlor where she could watch Isaac and Leighton confer on the carriage drive. There in the parlor, the sun caught the gleam of Mrs. Charlotte's old mirror, an ancient silver bay surrounded by a purple archipelago of damage. Oh, how Judith filled that mirror as no woman in this house had ever done, and she felt mighty standing there, straining its walnut-framed oval, a mirror near as tall as her. Her black face, close cropped wiry hair. In the war, when thieves and killers commandeered the manse claiming to be billeting soldiers, she hid this mirror safe in her quarters, the slave cabins. Now anything in that mirror's reflection became her own, an argentic magic, so that the silver sea with its purple coves and islands was a shimmering curtain beyond which waited a world transformed. There all was hers, all within grasp.

In the silver of the mirror, a dark form crossed the entryway behind her, Isaac stooped and hustling with Leighton's Enfield rifle and going the wrong way.

"Coward! You!" she spun.

She heard the back door slam. Her Leighton's trap fell to naught. Suddenly the mirror was not magic, its silver as lethal as arsenic, its refractions and flaws a whirlpool in which all things were devoured—curtains, bureaus, settees, wardrobes, china, silver, sunlight, Leighton. Her Leighton. She dipped two fingers in the lime, then drew a gray, gritty stripe across the tar-black round of her cheek.

Odem rode his horse at a canter, his back rigid as a derrick's steel. Hidden in the trees ahead of him, Leighton watched his accountant approach on the road. Odem's shoulders bobbed and his stob of an arm jittered. With his Federal tunic open save for the top button at the collar, he looked like an invalid from the war hospital escaped and riding hard. Odem lost his arm to the elbow facing Rebel cannon in Mississippi, in a melee no one gave a name to or wrote a jot about. When Leighton asked him to come ahead that week with the till, he gave him the choice.

"It could mean your death, Odem," Leighton said. "I'll not lie to you."

Odem shrugged, the nub of his arm making his cuffed shirt rise and fall, a semaphore signaling battle. "This all needs fixing," he said. "If I go through with this, you are going to listen to me on some things." His eyes scoured the quarry as if parsing a stream for gar. "This place can be a go, but it needs all kind of squeezing." He was blond, Leighton's age exactly, thin and pale. Like so many Ozarkers now after the war, he spoke his mind bluntly but in a whisper.

After the war was won, Leighton and the Yankees he served under began rebuilding Springfield. Morkan Quarry was rejuvenated, chugging out a torrent of whitewash, mortar, and dimension stone for the new courthouse and for monuments to the dead. For medicine and for pickling and paint and the mordant to wool, the quarry billowed, its dust settling across the town. New amber framing and whitewashed clapboards rose along streets where the war had left scorched squares of soil in the place of homes. On the boardwalks women strolled carrying parasols to thwart the sun instead of nosegays to mask the dead. Mongers at muddy intersections cried the good news of iron nails, sorghum, brass, and laudanum, ivory teeth, cherries and whiskey. By night, in dirt floored saloons, discharged Federals and bitter Rebels honed their daggers at barrelhead tables. Leighton's money never lasted long. He paid the men cash and kept his pledge to his dead father—the quarry would be a place where a man could earn a living wage. With all the labor wandering around looking for work, Odem felt Leighton was a madman for not erecting a company store and paying men fortnightly in scrip like the big quarries in St. Louis.

Appearing on his horse, the accountant wore his Federal hat, and Leighton saw what he figured to be the glint of pistol handles at his belt. Though Leighton could not see him, he assumed Isaac sat on his horse across the road. He thought he heard the old nag—bartered from a Yankee wagon team—whinny just a minute ago. Along the road a green froth of oak, elm, and walnut created a humid canopy. Sweat trickled down Leighton's neck. In the oak leaves beneath a morass of hickory switches, honeysuckle, and goldenrod, he struck a path and let his horse take it as swiftly as the old gelding could. Now and again he stopped, though Odem threatened to overtake him. As Leighton rode, he thought he could detect another horse, not Isaac or Odem, but a third horse on Isaac's side of the road, maybe the thief. He halted, straining to spot Isaac.

Odem cleared the shacks and cabins of the outskirts and was nearing the home stretch. All around were overgrown lands owned by a German banker named Weitzer who retreated with the Federals to St. Louis at the start of the war and never returned. What should have been oak savannas and clear limestone ridges were now choked with poison ivy, sumac, wild grape, and scruffy cedar. When Leighton hesitated before a net of vegetation, the gelding stalled and shook its head, tack jingling so that Leighton tightened his rein.

Sunset turned the western sky silver and crimson, and gray clouds were veined with pink and orange along their bases. The evening star, a diamond's white, was still as a pinhole. If only he were holding a woman's hand on a night like this, when dew commenced to gather. Instead a familiar current bolted down his arms making them ache. In the war he had hunted and dodged bushwhackers, and he knew gunfights never proceeded as the grand accounts of battle cast them. Gunplay was clumsy, random; it could end as suddenly as it began. In a ritual, his fingers traveled his Colt, his pepper-box, his powder sac, and the bottom of a leather satchel in which he kept a bundle bound with telegraph wire—the penis bone of a wolf tied to two fingers, trigger and ring, off a bushwhacker he killed. Out of ammunition and running from Leighton, that one bushwhacker hooked a boot in a sinkhole and fell face down in a slough. Leighton fell on top of him, but managed to plant a knee in his spine. He blasted him in the back of the head. This one had come nearer to killing him than any man in the war. The back of his grimy neck was alive with squirming ticks. When Leighton turned him over, he recognized him, one of Bloody Bill Anderson's boys, Cody Robeson, a terror, downed by a clod like Leighton. In any gunfight, you were only as dangerous as your last blast. Around him now in the hickory and sycamore, tree frogs began their songs, a noise like an army of children clacking creek gravel in their fists. Suddenly near him they stopped and left a pool of quiet.

13

Odem slowed his horse. As he pulled parallel with Leighton, he drew one of the pistols from his belt, which caused him to waver in his saddle.

From the woods, a thief materialized wielding a shotgun.

Leighton drew the pistol and urged the gelding out of the trees and onto the road. The clatter of its hooves made the thief turn to Leighton. The thief wore a slouch hat so low on his head Leighton could only make out the tip of his nose above the bandana covering his chin. On his back was a greasy brown coat bristling with burdock and merry sprigs of blue-green cedar.

Odem raised the stob of his arm and steadied his pistol on it as one would steady a gun across a fence rail.

The thief pulled the trigger, but the hammer misfired with a greasy clack.

Leighton's gelding reared at the man anyway.

Odem fired and the thief backed away, letting the second barrel go wild at Odem and scrambling for the woods on Isaac's side of the road.

"Now, Isaac," Leighton hollered, wrenching the gelding's reins down.

Instead of Isaac stepping from the woods with the Enfield trained on the scoundrel, a bulky, gray form, stout as a hogshead rose in the thief's path. It was Judith. With lime smeared all about her face and arms, she appeared to glow in the twilight.

"Jesus!" the thief hollered.

Odem stopped firing as his horse lurched about. The thief stumbled, then swung his shotgun over his shoulder, ready to clobber Judith with the gunstock. She stood there and raised her arms above her head, baring her teeth.

With the gelding calmed, Leighton aimed the pistol at the thief's legs, but Judith was in his line of fire.

When the thief swept the gunstock toward Judith, she dove at him. Sidestepping her, the thief charged into the woods with Odem and Leighton firing after him. Leighton pushed the gelding into the trees and struggled to pursue, but the brown coat and weathered slouch hat vanished in the woods as completely as water into lime. Leighton sat for a long time, straining to pick a human sound out of the chattering forest. Just over the ridge the moon shone jaundiced among the green riot of the trees. Soon every stirring of a towhee, every hop of a toad in the leaves was the thief shifting his gunstock to his shoulder taking aim at Leighton again.

When Leighton returned to the road, Judith was walking alongside Odem's horse, stroking its neck with her ghostly hand. Along the horse's neck the glow of blood showed where shot raked it. Odem kept the pistol out, but rested it against his thigh. Judith started in again about the Bolivar lynching.

"And they took it on themselves to decide the wrong and right of that, can you believe?" she asked, her accent turning Irish.

Leighton panged with old memories. Judith learned most of her English from his dead mother, Charlotte Morkan, learned from listening to the plump Irish woman warble with friends and cousins in St. Louis and later in Springfield. Every so often, when addressing White folk, Judith wound out a phrase straight from Charlotte's tongue, and her voice made Leighton pine for the past. On this gravel road, after all that had happened, his feeling deepened to something altogether different. There walked Judith, gray with lime, even unto her hair. She could be a statue save that her round body beneath her dress quivered and sweat on her face was balling the lime in streaks dark gray as solder. And what was it in her eyes that looked on Leighton when she asked that question? "Took it on themselves to decide the wrong and the right?" It was keen intelligence, even playful mockery. Slow and gluttonous around the house, she proved smart and brave this evening. She might have foiled their killing the thief, but clearly she had known Isaac would not be there. Watching her chatter, Leighton felt a warmness he could not suppress come around his heart.

Odem was looking down at Judith with delight and awe. "Mmm. Aye, they did that, didn't they? Strung them up with little asking."

As Leighton reined beside them, the big Negress stuck her chest out. She had a wide nose, large nostrils, and these flared now with pride just as a horse's seem to after victory in a race.

"You reckon he'll be back?" Odem asked.

"Something like him," Leighton said.

15

At home, he and Judith found Leighton's Enfield in the mudroom, propped where it had been, but blued and oiled. They said nothing about it while Odem detailed the accounts between mouthfuls of cornmeal, fried ham, and milk. He was glum about the money, and was pressing hard for that company store, which he praised again as common business practice on railroads and quarries on the Ohio and Mississippi Rivers. Leighton endured it with a flat expression.

"Man to man, Leighton, I'd die for you. And you seen it, now. But this here is business, and if you don't make a go of it, I'm not sticking round to drop dirt on your casket."

Odem's face slackened when he spied Judith on the porch. By lantern light she was squatting over a bucket, splashing water down her arms and neck.

"They don't make them in White, do they?" Leighton asked, voice lowered.

Odem shook his head. "Not like that one." He shuddered, then sat up straight, eyes wide on his employer. "You'll be needing you a wife, Leighton Shea Morkan," the accountant said at a whisper. "Soon. And I'll say no more."

Leighton watched the milky water fall off her arms for a moment. He scrawled his name on each new contract and in his mind balanced each against a bill he owed.

When Odem left, Judith pulled a rocker scraping across the stone of the porch, placed the chair behind the steps where Leighton sat. Out in the woods beyond the house, crickets and locusts calibrated the evening, counting its passing with their ticks and hisses. He heard one katydid above all the rest, her noise like a chain straining in a hoist. The joints of the rocker creaked as they accepted Judith's weight.

She rocked a moment. Her sweat reached him, a rich smell like the meat of a nut mingled with the grease of dinner, sharp and salty.

"What you want with a store like that Odem talks about? What would your daddy think of that?"

"Judith," he said in a grunt he might give to keep a horse steady.

She shook her head and crossed her arms over her chest. The rattle of the night took over for a time. "Why you and Odem have to ride all that way?"

He ignored her—the question made no sense to him.

"Ain't there limestone right round here? Ain't that what this floor come from? These here stairs?"

The rocker crunched on the stone of the porch, flat lime slabs Leighton and his dead father quarried there on the farm. Judith remembered. She was sharp, steps ahead of him.

He turned to her. She was looking down her nose at him, her eyebrows raised, a challenge.

"Best lime's under that Dutchman's land. You need a deep run to quarry." A smear of grease on her apron caught the house's lamplight and for an instant a muted rainbow glimmered there.

"What do you care?" he asked.

"I swear," she said, stopping the rocker, jolting forward. "What do I care? I don't want you dead."

"Judith, every day at a quarry is a walk in the valley of the shadow."

"I don't worry about you there."

"How is it your place to worry about me anywhere?"

"Fine, then." She gripped the arms of the rocker tight. "Always that card with you, ain't there? What my place?" Along her right wrist was a band of scar tissue, dark blue imbedded in the black of her skin. His late mother clamped an iron band and ball at her wrist when Judith was a slave to break her of some habit—he could not remember what. She was a girl then. The blue skin was now a bracelet, a shining adornment in the dusk.

"Be still, Judith. Set a minute, will you?"

She settled, fussed with the hem of her dress. "And what you told Odem. Is that thief coming back?"

"Not him. We may not have killed him, but his type is cowardly. I figure we've scared him out of ambushing Odem again." He watched her. "You afraid?"

She glanced away as if indignant.

"No man's going to drive me off that quarry," he said. The katydid ratcheted. "Maybe round here the best bravery is just perseverance. You reckon?"

When she said nothing and would not look at him, he opened his palm and made to whack her knee in jest. Just as his hand came down with a smack, she caught it and held his fingers there. She looked straight at him, her round face softening, small wrinkles of scrutiny or maybe worry appearing at her eyes—so much about her was a cipher to him. Her brown eyes were very dark and edged by yellow, like a tobacco stain on cotton. They were inscrutable. Beneath his palm, her leg was as soft as the belly of a pup.

Slowly he pulled his hand from hers. The mellow blue nightfall draped across her shoulders.

"Leighton?" she asked. It was a whisper, the tenor of which was unmistakable. She touched her neck with her finger, touched her skin where there was just the slightest gloss of sweat.

He waited a minute, watching her there, letting temptation fill him. The better to purge it, he hoped. "Judith, there is some bravery you and I don't need. I need you here with me, not swinging from some bois d'arc."

Her face fell. With her fingers spread, she ran the palms of her hands along the rocker's arms as if pushing away a plate. "I don't know anything about being brave."

"Ha," he said. "Fair enough." He turned back toward the yard. Even in the gloom, he could feel her watching his back, the rocker creaking like a weather vane in the wind. When the rocker stopped, he tensed as if something on dark wings had fluttered up beside him. His mind ran the triune circuit—Colt, pepper-box, bone and fingers. She would surely persevere. Her smell swept around his collar, a smell like cracked black walnut hulls, wooden and tangy. And there was the hint of a new odor, bright and bitter. His lime. He rarely noticed it on himself. She hummed an old lullaby his late mother used to sing him. When her leg brushed his arm, she reached down for just a moment and gripped his shoulder as if to steady herself in the dark. Then her touch was gone. Her humming dwindled as she moved down the stairs and out into the chatter of evening.

II

EVEN AFTER THE NIGHT OF GUNFIRE AND CANNON, OF surging, drunken crowds on Market and Water Streets, all down the river front; after flares and rockets; even after the box-shaped gunboat finished thumping its bursts of fire and black mounds of smoke, men still staggered under the Weitzers' window and paused at the visage of the brown Mississippi River, the exhausted streets. One gentleman in glorious white trousers and a soiled but fine crimson coat with the collar pulled up to his cheeks swigged from a bottle then spat amber liquor in a glittering spray at the sun rising.

"Kerr! Bee! Smith!" He shouted each portion of the name with happy derision. The papers the evening before, dated June 5, 1865, proclaimed the Confederate general's surrender somewhere in Texas; so the last Confederate army in the West was no more.

The gentleman in the street drew a pistol and flung his bottle high into the air.

Pressing her cheek against the window frame, Patricia Weitzer cowered. In the mud beside the boardwalk, the bottle thumped, a surprise from Heaven. The gentleman slipped and fell to his knees, and blasted at the sky. When his pistol was empty he stared at it, then struggled up and weaved toward the river shouting the song about cock robin, just the chorus. She imagined he was Irish.

Any article or fixture the Weitzer hadn't already sold was stowed in steamer trunks. What the Weitzer kept, the few chairs and desks, her own Saxony spinning wheel he cowled in sheets so that the furniture squatted like the spirits of dead animals. Her mother groused at her father in German: "Is this not a city we can start in? After four years I lose two boys, and still we

19

leave?" Patricia's father, Claus Weitzer, had been a trustee of the National Mineral Bank in Springfield, had doled out most of his own currency to the bank's major depositors when the Federals liquidated it after Wilson's Creek. There were still dozens of individuals, several of them prominent citizens of Springfield whose entire accounts he would never be able to cover—the Martins, the Pearsons of Pearson's Tack, the Morkan Quarry, the Dixons.

Patricia turned but kept her head bowed. Claus Weitzer sat scowling at the window where the drunken man's song still floated above dazed St. Louis. Her father's eyes were black in the amber light; strands of gray wormed in his goatee where none had been before. Her mother, Marta, made sure Patricia understood the Weitzer had only a daughter left to barter with the world. Her brothers had died fighting for Franz Sigel, one at Second Manassas, the other in a Confederate prison after his capture at New Market. The family was just father, mother, and daughter now.

Marta drilled her questions again. Claus's face, resolute as the blade of a plow, fixed on the nothing at the center of the room.

"Step from the window, dear one," he said to Patricia in a terse whisper that kept both women silenced.

Patricia was a slim girl, taller than she wished to be. She had a long face and a prominent, rounded jaw that, if she raised her chin, assumed grave pride. Her eyes were a startling gray flecked with green, but because they were set in crescents, they appeared too full of scrutiny, or so a young cadet had told her at the Turnverein. With a daughter like her, the Weitzer was strapped indeed, she thought. She was thirteen. Marta often reminded her at meals that she was not growing as she should, and plied her with biscuits and cheap sweets. If she did not improve her attitude and figure, Marta said, she would end up a ward of the Lutheran Church or a nurse in some place seedy and hostile.

Mornings Patricia taught English to wounded German soldiers at the old Turnverein meeting hall, now a hospital. Today she wheeled her favorite patient into the stream of sunlight pouring from a high window. His name was Theodor, and he had lost both legs to the knee and both arms to the shoulder at Pea

Ridge on the second day of fighting during Franz Sigel's grand charge. He had sandy blond hair, brown eyes, the soft fuzz of a beard. She promised to shave him today, his first shave. Before that, though, she propped a primer beside him on an easel.

His feathery eyelashes flickered in the mote-filled light. Above his pale cheeks his eyes pinched with sleep, the skin around them rosy pink. She read a sentence in English, tracing the print with a wooden pointer. Theodor repeated the sentence, his accent thicker than hers.

"She adores the smart pony."

"Sie adures ze smart puhny."

Behind them in the hospital beds an old German begged for morphine, moaning about pain in his feet, which he no longer had. A nurse shushed him as she left the hall. Patricia scowled. With the nurse gone, she was the only healthy person in the building, no doctors, no nurses, not even an orderly. Tan with dust, the old pommel horses and parallel bars loomed among the wounded and limbless. In the yellow shafts of light, the gymnastic rings dangling from the high ceiling looked like implements of torture, one ring twirling lazily. She resumed with Theodor.

"I could buy it for her." The wooden pointer scooted on the page.

"I guhd buy it vor her."

His eyes watched her face rather than her lips. He was handsome, his jaw strong, skin ivory and perfect. Often, teaching him, desire so overwhelmed her, she wished to pick him up and carry him like a babe. When she imagined doing so now, her voice caught. "Maybe I will become an apprentice."

"May be I become *ein Apfelschimmel.*"

Patricia touched his nose with the pointer but could not suppress a giggle when he wagged his tongue and bobbed his eyebrows.

"Have you had enough of learning, my little soldier?" she asked him in German.

He nodded. "However, I have certainly not had enough of your company, Miss Weitzer."

They were in a quiet corner of the hall. Behind them, the supine patients snored and whimpered.

21

"You are leaving they say." His eyes implored her; he cocked his head.

"It is true. The Weitzer will have us return to Springfield."

"How is it there? Is it like it was here before, with dances and marches to attend?"

She shook her head. "Farms and fields. Hills." She smiled. "Hillbillies."

He laughed. She rose and fetched a basin of water from a pot warming on the hall's only stove. His eyes followed her as she slicked the straight razor against the strop.

"You are sure you know how?"

"I have shaved the Weitzer, and my brothers on occasion." She had shaved the Weitzer, but she had only shaved the backs of her brothers' necks. She could see them now, bending forward, their short bangs hanging and bobbing, their necks growing taut. Erich's hair was dark, wiry like Claus Weitzer's. Robart's hair was the same mousy brown as her own. "Ah, these little friends have come uninvited," she would say to her brothers, spotting the tendrils of hair at the backs of their necks. "We'll have to send them away." Only Robart laughed. Their necks were stiff in graves now, their lovely hair rotting against pine boards somewhere in Virginia, in Georgia.

"Close your eyes," she said to Theodor.

He did so and raised his chin. She wet her hands in the basin, ran her fingers along his neck, felt the knot of his Adam's apple, hard as a buckeye beneath the skin. On his cheeks the hair was so soft and plush it was like the fur of a new hat. She lingered on these hairs and on the solid line of his jaw so long she lost herself for a moment. She caught him trembling.

She swallowed. "Don't be afraid."

"I am not," he said, still trembling.

The hair on his head was fine and smelled of violets, and it was then that she realized he'd had an orderly wash and perfume it for her visit. She took the crucible from the Weitzer's shaving kit, dribbled the white powders in the porcelain. Theodor kept his eyes shut; his shoulders shook. At the ball of his shoulders, the long sleeves of his robe were rolled and pinned in wide cuffs. She admired the neatness of them, cuffs that used to startle and sadden her. Some nurse had done it. Theodor had come to America alone, had worked as a toolsmith in New York before coming to St. Louis and joining with Sigel. He had no mother or sisters or lovers that she knew of to cuff his robes or shave him.

Closed, his eyelids were pink with a tinge of gray; small veins ran in them. They were like the petals of a flower stretched over round stones. With the boar's-hair brush, she whipped the powders in water until a froth of gray-blue lather bubbled up. She was about to dab this on him with the brush but she hesitated, scooped the lather with her fingers, and began smoothing it across his jaw by hand.

"Your fingers are soft," he said.

"They are covered with lather. How could they not be soft?"

Though her fingers collapsed the lather a bit, soon his jaw and neck were coated with white foam. She stood behind his wheelchair, rested his head back against her chest. His eyes blinked open for a moment. "Just stay very still. Think of a wide meadow and a careful mower, reaping and reaping." Keeping rhythm with her voice, she drew the razor up his neck, along the soft skin beneath his chin, under the knot of jawbone near his ear. Against her breast, his head was warm and solid. His forehead slackened, the wrinkles of worry vanishing to leave a surface shining and smooth. She pressed her breasts against him to see over the tip of his chin, and for a moment she held him there, shaving nothing, her hands growing unsteady. His lips were blue and pink, thick and lined like a fine coil of embroidery.

She came around in front of him, knelt, and was brave enough to sink her elbows against his thighs before finishing the slip of skin beneath his nose. She paused, then ran a wet towel across his face. His eyes blinked at her, round and watery.

"Have I hurt you?" she asked.

"Oh no, Patricia."

She smiled and dribbled a chalky smelling talc over her hands. Without hesitation she placed her elbows again in his soft thighs and slowly massaged his face. His eyes and mouth were open, and he appeared dismayed, as if a terrible question waited on his lips.

23

"Patricia?" he said.

She held his face.

"I will never see you again."

She caught her breath.

"I will never see another woman again. I will be in a place like this all my life."

"Ssh." She continued to massage his face, though the talc had fully covered it. It was smooth, with hardly a fleck of red, the best shave she had ever given a man. She adored the way her elbows drew circles in his broad, soft thighs. They would stay soft; so much sitting he had to do.

"Patricia?" His voice had gone rough.

When she glanced up, his eyes were round and were looking down at her chest, she thought. But when she lowered her gaze, she saw that between his legs, his cock had filled and lifted his robe.

"I will never see another woman. Please."

She coughed, her face burning, but looking in his watery eyes she felt as if her heart had been crushed by a pestle. If a nurse returned, if a loved one came to visit one of the other poor soldiers, she would be dishonored, deemed unmarriageable, a harlot. Theodor's face was so lovely, and he was ruined. What were her prospects after all? What moral label could follow her to Springfield and make that place any worse? Poor Theodor. He would sit alone in dusty wards like this for the rest of his miserable life.

She glanced about the hall. With a shiver, she reached under his robe, followed his thigh past its rough hairs until her knuckle touched his cock. It was taut, slick, like the skin on the neck of a goose just plucked. She had done this for her brother Erich before, but he had no debilities, only powerful hands to force her still, a fierce jaw, angry eyes. She felt a betrayal in Theodor's wanting it. Was there no love without something like this? Erich forbade her ever to speak of it.

She rubbed Theodor's cock with her thumb and index finger and watched Theodor's face. His eyes began to jitter and swell. She kneaded it, then cupped it in her hand

and began to pull it—gently, though, more gently than she had Erich's. His chest arched and stiffened. His eyes closed. Such insistent things, cocks; they filled like the udders of a cow, needed milking, or so her Erich had partially explained. Dead now in Virginia sand, what would his spirit say to her fingers touching Theodor, to his ecstasy? She never envied men, considering this organ was such a governance.

Theodor whispered her name. She rested her cheek against his chest, still pulling; his cock grew thick as her wrist. It began to pulse like the heart of an animal, but she held to it, pulling and milking as her brother had taught her to render a full purge. Theodor was gasping, his chin digging hard into the top of her head in his throes.

When he stilled, she removed her hand.

"I did not mean to do this to you, to put you through this," he whispered. "You are noble." He was panting to catch his breath. "You are too kind."

She raised her head from his chest and stared into his eyes. If her heart were powdered in a crucible, his apology dashed it to the floor to scatter with the porcelain. "God be with you, Theodor," she said. "All your days." She lowered her head to his chest again, imagined that he was strong and swarthy, just in from plowing the fields, and that she had brought him a *Weißbier* and a block of cheese, and he had drawn her to him.

When no arms came around her, the shock was so great, she pressed her face tighter to his chest to stop the sobs that shook him. Outside the window, a drummer called in both German and English for passage west on a bonded wagon train.

In late July, the Weitzers left St. Louis. It took them a week to reach Rolla. The wagon, bought with almost the last of Weitzer's cash, was one the Federals had cast off, as were the two oxen. Camps of refugees cluttered the road. The Weitzers rode through them, muffling their mouths and noses with handkerchiefs dipped in rose water.

Scrubby trees south of Rolla gave way to fallow fields and every so often scorched chimneys. They joined a Federal supply train of oxen and mules driven by leering teamsters and rode with it under skies that each afternoon churned to gray and drenched them.

They rested one night in a town abandoned. Among the dozen houses and the courthouse with its gutted tower and burned cupolas, shutters slammed and chattered. An owl stuttered his question. In a bois d'arc under the moonlight the tatters of a hangman's rope waved. A cadre of militia galloped into the square. One of the officers strode to the Weitzers and stood at their fire staring at Claus then at Patricia. The Weitzer stood, hooked his thumbs at his belt.

The officer was a boy not much older than Patricia. Instead of a beard, he grew his hair long and it was curled and lovely at his shoulders. Stuffed into the tops of his boots, his trousers were tan with dust.

"*Deutsch?*" he asked.

He and Claus talked in German about a bushwhacker the officer was seeking. And Claus, to Patricia's wonder, gave no hint that English could be spoken. He made the young officer labor through every sentence. Claus stood as stiff and apprehensive as the big schnauzers at Hoerkstroetter's jewelry store.

The officer's German was halting, his grammar strange and hard to follow. As he spoke, Patricia watched his lips and fair face and chest. Though his manner was icy cold, he was terrifically handsome. Patricia squinted in the firelight at his spurs, which were fashioned from some sort of ivory.

"Have it to stand," the officer said in German. Claus nodded to Patricia.

As she rose her heart seized in her chest for a moment. The ivory spurs—she saw clearly in the firelight now—were not spurs at all. Fixed to the officer's boot and rowel, the bleached crescent at each of his heels was the arc of a human jawbone cloven in two.

Once she was risen, the officer stepped before her. His eyes were as dull and void of life as the eyes of a fish left on the bank. With a flash of his hand, he grabbed her neck and squeezed. Claus and Marta both cried out, but the officer drew and cocked his revolver, pressed the muzzle to Patricia's forehead.

"*Sitz sich,*" the officer hissed to her parents.

With his thumb and knuckle he kneaded at the middle of her neck as if feeling for something she had swallowed; then he released her. He lowered the hammer on the revolver.

As he strode to his companions he called out, "It is female after all."

When her father announced Springfield was near, she moved to the front of the wagon. They crested a hill, and Weitzer braked the oxen, which pulled for the water they could smell from Jordan Creek. The center of town was a patchwork of dingy shacks, new amber framing, and black shapes where buildings had been. A single Union soldier on horseback, a toy in a ravaged diorama, trotted across the square and vanished. She clung to the seat as the wheels yawed and pitched along what was left of the road.

The great pit mine at Summit and State Streets was broader and deeper than Patricia remembered. This was the Morkan Quarry, owned by the Irish her father owed money to as a trustee. Shouts and the lowings of oxen came from behind the rusted fence. A whole corps of spectral men were heaving alongside the beasts and at the wheels of the carts the animals drew. On each cart towered a gleaming iron rod with an immense gun-blue ball on top. Three of these were listing up the far hill to the cliffs. The rods reminded Patricia of the gallows poles outside Camp Jackson, where bushwhackers and deserters were hanged. A bearded young man on a draft horse was shouting and whistling at the dusty line. Trolls, she thought. Grubby Irish.

Her mother leaned to her father. With her handkerchief she patted her bun and the brown strands hanging behind her neck. "I see *that* survived," she muttered in German and nodded at the pit.

"And I had hoped it hadn't," Weitzer said.

On South Street, the windows of their former house gaped like empty mouths. Sparrows darted in and out of the eaves. A standard leaned against the back stoop. It was a red guidon bearing the marking 2D OHIO. A soldier lay on a cot reading a letter while another sat on a stump that had been a substantial elm tree. The soldier on the stump was spitting amber juice into a silver gravy boat so tarnished its edges were green. He blinked at the Weitzers.

"You can't park all that there." He stood and slapped his cap against his hip. He shook his head. "Get them oxen out of this yard."

Weitzer looped the reins on the brake and hopped down. He straightened his vest and put his hands on his belt. "This is my yard, with clear title."

The soldier turned and spat toward the gravy boat but showered the stump instead. He smiled at Weitzer. "Partner, just figure for me how many folks have pulled in here and said something near that."

Weitzer stepped directly before the soldier. "I am the only folk that matters here. You are speaking to a man who lost two sons to the great cause of the Union."

Patricia crawled over chairs and bedposts, tried to reach the desk where her father kept his papers. Behind her, Claus's voice rose. "Show me to the commander, now." Straining toward the drawer, she peered over her shoulder. Her mother had turned in the seat and was nodding to her. The tips of her fingers touched the scarred walnut of the drawer, then slipped. She could not reach beyond the chairs and luggage stacked. Shouting now outside, other soldiers rushing. Suddenly the wagon shook and in the canvas of the canopy, she saw the back of Claus's head bulge toward her as the Ohio soldier smashed him against the sideboards. The shadow of Claus's black hat fell away as if a piece of him had been amputated. The shouting ended, but she heard from her father a low growl of effort as he thrashed and struggled. It was fury like no sound she had ever heard escape him. Marta squalled and the wagon shifted as she came down to join the fight. The Ohio soldiers called for calm, everyone calm. Some officer had taken charge. The officer gave Claus the chance to explain again. Finally she heard a soldier laugh. "Even if it was yours, Dutchy, it's a headquarters till we muster out." The wagon tilted slightly as her father, very stiffly, resumed his seat. He undid the brake, and the oxen plodded through the backyard. The fencing was all gone; the yard had become mud. Two of the neighboring houses had been burned to the ground. The oxen clopped on the flagging of the Pearsons' garden, the wheels driving the mossy stones deep into the muck.

They proceeded southeast toward their summer cottage. Out in the overgrown meadows beyond the road, the rotting carcasses of horses, mules, and oxen steamed with squads of blowflies. Weitzer's jaw worked, made his goatee buckle and protrude. His cheeks were ashen. On his neck, terrible purple stripes from the soldier's vicious assault.

Off Rockbridge Road, the trail to the summer cottage was choked with cedar, lamb's quarter, and knee-high poke. The woods smelled wet and raw with soil. Relieved to have left behind the town's ash and garbage stench, Patricia leaned over the back of the seat, inhaled deeply. Weitzer was cursing under his breath, his shoulders jerking.

The summer cottage was merely a log cabin with a puncheon floor and a loft. Weitzer and Patricia's late brothers had cleared gardens behind the cabin and bordered the gardens with stones. This was the country life Patricia's mother had given up to come to America, or so Weitzer had said. Marta Grünhaagen Weitzer and her parents were the only Pomeranians to accompany a group of Saxon Lutherans to this country in 1839. Marta's mother was a von Below, the youngest daughter of a small estate in *Ostelbein*, but Grandfather Grünhaagen, America, and enterprise had brought Marta here, just as now the Weitzer and land and enterprise brought Marta and Patricia back to Springfield.

She turned the idea like a crystal doorknob in her mind. There was her mother, patting, fussing to save the bun that was deteriorating behind her head. Her broad lap, her muscular arms had dwindled in St. Louis. But Weitzer would have them back, chopping kindling, up to her elbows in cabbage, guiding the plow behind these oxen that knew their mothers and homeland no more than did Marta. The trail became so overgrown that the oxen halted and wagged their dumb heads. When Weitzer turned to Patricia, she clambered out, hooked a hand around the drool-slick riggings at the lead oxen's mouth. She yanked them toward the cabin she was sure was razed.

But there it was, a double-penned cabin with an upstairs loft, darkened by the overgrown forest, a thick coat of moss on the log walls. When the Weitzers entered, black beetles scurried from the opened door. The floor was warped at the corners, but only a few of the wooden pegs that held the puncheons had popped loose. Marta stood in the midst of this, wadding the fur muff against her waist. Her eyes shone like an animal's in the light of the lamp Weitzer held.

Weitzer grunted and returned to the wagon, began unpacking the kitchen gear in a noisy pile.

Patricia lowered the lamp and went to her mother's side. The von Belows had visions, but Patricia had far too much Weitzer in her to experience revelation, or so her mother said. Marta had told her of great revivals in Osterelbein, of the saints visiting, bestowing on the worshipful the sure knowledge that their church was the true reformed church while that of the rationalists of the King of Prussia was failed.

"*Was, Mutter?*" Patricia wanted to touch her quaking arm.

Marta closed her eyes. After a moment she caught her breath. "A wall with no endings," she said to Patricia in German. "A column of fire. Hail, so much white hail."

Patricia blinked, bowed her head, and they prayed together. "Lord, make your face to shine upon me. Lift up your countenance. Give me peace."

Marta took Patricia's chin in her hands and lifted her face. Marta's eyes appeared swollen in the dark. "It is the visage of the Lord," she said. She climbed the wooden stairs to the sleeping loft.

Weitzer dropped something hard against the bed of the wagon. He cursed. Patricia met him at the tailgate. He looked small wedged amid the furniture, balancing himself and wiping his forehead with the back of his hand. "Where is Mother?"

"Resting," Patricia said.

"A damn good way not to help with the wagon." He pointed to an end of the bureau. Though the wood bit her fingers and the weight strained her shoulders and arms, she and her father managed to get the bureau down.

They unloaded contents of the wagon onto the lawn. When they finished, Weitzer watched the sky to the south. Above the trees hung the gray puffs of a cooking fire, probably from the same house of the Irish that worked the pit mine—their lands neighbored the Weitzers' summer cabin. The sky was violet, the white first star out beside a devil's crescent moon.

Weitzer dug in his black vest and pulled out a slim sheaf of greenbacks. He peeled off five of the bills and handed them to Patricia. "Go see if Morkan has lard oil, and maybe milk and eggs. And fodder. The grass is bad."

Weitzer began shuffling their goods into the cabin. After a moment, Weitzer glared at Patricia. "I don't have your brothers to attend you. Go."

She took a lantern and drove the oxen around the house and onto the trail. Weitzer had watered the beasts, but they were weary and slow. With the trees closed around it, the trail was like a tunnel through a black mountain. Some insects had hatched, and their cries dominated the forest, a sound like a child's whistle shaken furiously. Nature is wanton and dissolute. For some reason, she thought of Theodor in the dark hospital and she clutched the reins.

Through the trees came the rank soil-and-fish odor of a cattle pond. That was what she would have here. Cesspools and drooling cows, bugs. None of the dances, gymnastics, speeches, or recitals; she might actually miss the German officers in St. Louis who drank and sang together, then closed the evenings with violent brawls.

The Irish house glowed white between the trees; its upper windows were black, but on the lower floor a yellow light wavered in the heart of the manse. Why hadn't the Weitzer bought goods in town? She braked the oxen and stepped down from the wagon. The wide stone steps of the Irish house were miraculous crescents. Though the glass was out of many of the lower windows, webs of intricate cast iron remained. Even the door frame was a baroque of lines and curlicues. From inside, she could smell meat roasting, a smell so thick it made her chest hurt.

She rapped on the door frame and held the lantern up. "This is Patricia Weitzer."

There was a shuffling, and a looming black shape moved for the door. A squat Negro woman stood kneading her work dress at the waist, drying her hands. The Negress smiled a devious, indolent smile.

Patricia had seen a dark wolf pup in a menagerie once, and that's how this Negress's smile struck her: too smart, three steps ahead to ruin you.

"Is Mister Morkan in?"

The Negress widened her eyes and pursed her lips. "You turn a wagon over on the road, Miss? You sure sound fraught."

"Please. I just want to see Mr. Morkan."

The Negress nodded twice to Patricia and then craned her neck and nodded to several other spots on the porch. Patricia looked around her, behind her. Just the trees, the maddening whistles.

The Negress blinked at her. "Elder or young Morkan? If it's elder, I can't get him. If it's younger, he ain't home yet. But soon."

"Is the elder Morkan indisposed?"

"Very. He dead."

"Younger, then. Please." Patricia backed away, her face hot.

"Come in. Please." The Negress mimicked her, then ushered her onto a cobblestone floor that glowed blue in the lantern light. She led her to a parlor where all the sofas and chairs were pushed against a wall away from the windows, which had shattered panes. The Negress struck a match and lit two lamps. Patricia sat in a red velvet chair done in American Empire. Rosewood, a mahogany end table, dusty but sturdy, little cornucopias everywhere, frills and idolators' angels. Such violent distractions. How could one ever get anything done in a house like this, and with this Negress hovering over one's every move? The chairs smelled of wood smoke. Several periodicals lay stacked—*Engineering News*, *Rock Forecast*, but none were from St. Louis save something called *Missouri Magnetoscope*. In *Engineering News*, she stared at a table and diagrams of a long ditch somewhere in California. A white crust crumbled from one of the pages. A clock ticked back in the house, its noise like a plunk of water in a cavern. The Negress stood still as a barrel. Such girth, with the sweat on her, her skin shone even without the lamplight. But Patricia did not know what to do with her. The Weitzers had never had servants and thought slavery abominable. Here in the room the Negress presented a dark question for which Patricia had no answer.

Lifting her legs, Patricia felt a clamminess on her calves: a stone floor, cobbles of big blue stone like chunks of the moon. The place stunk as if it were a cave. She held her spine rod straight, waiting, but still she felt like a peasant in her homespun work dress and cottage cloak, the hood pulled back. Beneath the dress she had on a little boy's pair of scuffed ankle jacks. She read and tucked her straight brown hair behind an ear on each side, shuddered as she replaced the periodical.

She remembered the elder Morkan, tall and handsome—or as handsome as the red and freckled Irish could be. The Weitzer had admired and despised him. Dead now, the traitor, good riddance. Rumor said the elder Morkan had given the Rebel army powder from his mine. The boy, she recalled, looked nothing like the father, was short, meaty, and loud, with jet-black hair. A brawler—she had seen him beat one of her cousins senseless at a harvest fair boxing match before the war.

The Negress stirred, and Patricia turned to her, then gaped. From the shadows behind her there rose a white-faced spirit in a pea jacket of ethereal gray. His hands were bloody, his mouth set in a snarl. He wore one of the blue Federal caps her brothers had worn to war. Her visions had finally begun, then, she thought. At last, the Lord's Countenance was come upon her, so various and full of the multitudes, as her mother said, It has everything in It.

The Negress glanced behind her where the spirit stood, its hands glistening. When she turned back to Patricia, her black face was unmoved. Patricia clasped her hands and muttered a prayer of praise and thanksgiving to her fingertips.

"Where the hell you been, Judith?" the spirit shouted.

Patricia dropped her hands from her lips. The Countenance of the Lord turned out to be only the loud Irish she'd seen supervising at the mine, the grubby troll.

"Mister Leighton," Judith said. "We have a guest."

"And my horse is stolen." He stomped down the hallway shouting for Judith to follow.

33

Patricia trailed the two into a sweltering kitchen where Leighton stood by a slops trough. Judith was plucking at his hands and dousing them with a gourd from a bucket. When the water hit, Leighton stood on tiptoes. Patricia could see his calves bulge inside his filthy jeans.

"I was riding asleep, I...." He reared his head back and Judith lost her grip on his hands. He talked to the Negress as if Patricia were not there.

Judith poked him in the middle of his chest with the gourd. "Be still."

From what she'd heard and read, Patricia expected the Negress would now be throttled. Instead, Judith resumed plucking bits of chatt from the young man's palms. Her round back bent, she set the gourd aside and held both his hands in hers and was gentle, winced when the Irish buckled, worried at the hands as if she were a mother or sister, whispering encouragements, "Now, now. There, look it there. Just a little one."

Leighton grumbled on about some rabble who'd swung down from a tree and whacked him across the back with a stick and off the horse, which the rabble then leapt on and rode away before Leighton could get a shot. And the Negress worked, her plump face so close to the white hands she could lay them on her cheeks. A slight smile turned the corners of her lips, and Patricia thought the smile came at the young man's pain. Leighton had stopped talking and was peering with an intent frown at something the Negress was plucking. And then Patricia saw the pained creases in his brow flatten and his whole aspect soften in anticipation of relief, the way that Theodor's eyes swelled with light when she touched him. She recognized the Negress's smile as an artisan's fascination with an intricate and difficult task. For a moment, Patricia could see the sliver of gravel emerge from the meat of Leighton's hand; then the Negress had it. Judith and Leighton exchanged a strange, quick grin, and a wave of heat crossed Patricia's forehead and chest. She touched her temple and found sweat beaded there. It was the kitchen; these Irish weren't bright enough to build a summer cookhouse and so forced one to stew in this heat.

34

Judith doused his hands several times, then lifted the empty bucket. "Mister Leighton," she said, pointing the dripping gourd at Patricia, "this is…."

Patricia cut her off. "I am Patricia Weitzer. Claus Weitzer sends his regards and wishes I ask if I may buy from you lard oil and milk and eggs, and fodder, if I may, for two oxen."

"Weitzer?" Leighton squinted at her. "How is your father?"

"Very fine, thank you."

Leighton nodded. "That's good." As he stepped forward in the lamplight, his face seemed leaner than she remembered. When she thought of the money her father owed him, her breath stopped. "And your brothers?" he asked.

She bowed her head. "They died fighting for General Sigel."

Leighton frowned. "I am sorry."

Leighton ordered Judith to bring any eggs and milk they had from the spring house, and to have Johnson Davis load Weitzer's wagon with fodder.

When the Negress had gone, Leighton stood over the trough, his hands dripping. He watched Patricia with eyes that appeared to her to be as slanted and devious as a Chinaman's. One pupil was lazy, and this disconcerted her. She could not tell if he was looking at her or at something behind her. His eyes were exceptionally bright, a blue that only human eyes could attain, and they shone from his face as if cast in polished silver. There would be no proper introduction here, and Patricia smiled inside at the thought of one. No brother or father to preside over bows and curtsies.

"Forgive me," Leighton said. "Have you been to dinner?"

Patricia wondered if she'd heard him right, then imagined he, too, might be disturbed by her presence—the German banker's daughter in the house when the place was dank as a rabbit's warren and the windows without glass.

"Yes, thank you. I have."

"You don't look it." Gingerly, he fetched a box lamp with a greasy wick from a cupboard. He handed it to her, then stood near her, flexing his bloody hands. What had been stockiness in youth was now a burliness, solid ovals of brute muscle at his arms and calves. The lime dust on him made him smell scoured clean. One eye ogled the top of her head and the other stared up to meet her eyes.

"You got real tall, didn't you?" he asked. "I remember you now. That quiet little Dutch girl with gray eyes and that long face." His skewed eyes ran the course of her body. His voice bounced; Irish it was, like his dead father's. "Are you still that sad, now? Tell me true."

Patricia's chin trembled and her skin felt afire. "You have been too long with that Negress, and so I might forgive your being so forward with me." She staved off calling him a Mick, but it was an immense effort. "Remember to whom you are speaking."

He smiled. "Trust me. I do."

Judith returned with six eggs and no milk.

Patricia pulled the bills from her cuff. Leighton took all five of them. Such a dusty face. If he would pay more attention to it than his hands, she thought.

"You will need an escort home."

"I will manage, thank you."

"You will not," said Leighton. He extended his hands to the Negress. "Judith?"

Judith rifled through the cupboard, found rags and stripped them, wrapped his hands. He watched her hands work, but also seemed at times to watch the Negress's face and tremendous bosom. Again, Patricia felt too warm.

Outside, another Negro helped her onto the wagon, an older man who appeared like a spirit from the dark. Leighton mounted a fresh horse and rode next to her. Very soon they crossed from Morkan holdings to the Weitzer's lands.

"Can you smell that?" he asked.

A panic raced through her—by now, after work and hard travel, she stunk like a refugee.

"You can't can you?" His chest swelled as he breathed in, smiling. "Limestone," he said. "Under your soil here, your father's soil, I mean. Hundreds of feet deep, I'll bet."

She straightened her spine. "It will be mine one day, you know."

The look he gave her was as cold and calculating as the face of a customs agent swindling on the riverfront. The lantern bobbed on its hook.

When they had turned onto Rockbridge, Leighton said. "You'd do better with that lantern out."

She stared at him.

36

"Let your eyes adjust, and you can see fine, even in heavy woods." He rode quite well, not stiffly or pompously, but shifting with the horse as she'd seen cavalry do. "You can't see a thing beyond this light." He motioned to the arc of yellow that swung as the lantern moved.

"Such sight certainly did not help you this evening," she said to him.

He blinked at her, then grinned. He fiddled for a moment with the white bindings on his hands, pushed the rags to his fingertips. Then he reached and lifted the globe on her lantern, puffed, and it was out.

"*Dummer Tropf!*" she said.

The trail vanished in absolute darkness. The oxen halted. The little whistles paused for an instant, then shrieked by the thousands. The sky eventually appeared, an emulsion of blue stars, but beneath the black trees, she could see nothing.

"Where are you?" she shouted. She set the brake and stood to look around the wagon's canvas. Damned Irish. She stamped the floorboards. Then her anger gave way to fear—his dead father was a Rebel traitor; what would Leighton think of the Dutch, his father's ruthless enemies?

"Be still," he said. His voice became a mesmerizing, warm whisper in the dark, suddenly full of concern. "Don't be afraid, darling. I only want you to learn from this. I tell you you have come home to a no-account world of thieves and ruffians lurking for vengeance."

When she turned, she spotted the blue-white of his cheeks. She blinked, and a fuzzy version of him emerged from the night as if from dusky water.

"See?" he asked.

In a few moments, even rocks and brambles under the trees became visible, casting vague shadows. She sat down.

"The leaves are out," he said. He lit a match, which threw an orange blotch on his bearded chin. He held the match to a cigar. The end glowed red. He wagged the match out and left her blinking at the orange swoops it had drawn on her eyes. "But still you should use a lantern only at a crossroads if you aren't sure where you're at. That light'll do nothing but draw a thief to you."

37

"You seem to have learned a great deal about thieves." She relaxed the brake and clucked at the oxen. They pulled; the wagon was light, easy to start—eggs and oil, not a bucket of milk, and she paid five dollars. But for the hay, she could have walked.

They moved on for what seemed to be many yards. "May I light the lantern?" she asked. He shrugged, sighed, and she lit it.

At the trail to the summer cottage, she braked. "I suppose there were no horse thieves left but your one."

He smirked. "I reckon they might not care for an empty wagon and two burnt oxen." With a lift of the reins, he stepped his horse so close she could see his eyes in the lantern's light. In their silver, there was the barter the Weitzer would make, there was revelation from God, more clear than any visitation Marta might foam about. He tipped the Federal cap and held the cigar in his teeth when he smiled. He turned the horse and sauntered from the light.

The Countenance of the Lord. Why should He set two such bright eyes so stupidly?

III

AN INCISION OF SILVER LIGHT STRUCK THE FEDERAL BLUE
of the eastern sky when Leighton stopped before the three
slumped Negroes. Beneath the willow at the quarry gates, shoulders hunched, hands clasped in their laps, the three seemed like
a charcoal drawing against the mica of dawn and ghostly blue of
the limestone archway. One rose and slapped a hand to his trousers, a big, rangy man who could look over the ass of Leighton's
gelding if he needed, flatfooted. This was their third morning
vulturing at the gate, ringing their hands. He had passed them
three dawns now, sliding his coat back to show the glint of his
Colt on his hip each morning.

"My accountant tells me it's work you're looking for," Leighton said, his voice low. "You're in the wrong spot." The dead
streets carried a voice for blocks this early.

"Knock and ye shall enter," the Negro said, removing a sagging felt hat.

"Bible verses won't help you any in a quarry. Men die in
there, able men with years at it. Tumble off the cliff. Blast rocks
clean through their necks. Put drills shaft deep in their thighs.
Smash hands to pulp under sledges." He watched them, their
yellow eyes up at him. "Know what I call a miner with one
hand smashed?"

"A man hurting?" asked the big Negro.

He leaned forward in the saddle. "Sacked."

Silence.

After a time, the big Negro stepped closer. "We may not
know stone. But we sure know sweat."

Leighton smiled. "Sure. I hire you three," Leighton started,
pulling a cigar from his coat, "and every hayseed in that quarry
walks. Gain three, lose seventy."

39

"There can be more of us. We do anything."

Leighton nudged the horse and rode through the gate.

Opening the office door, he smelled tallow in the air, and the musty, blood-like stink of iron rusting mingled with the slick metallic essence of gun oil. The stink came from the muskets his father bought before the war, one of which Odem held on his lap. In a child's cart beside him there mounded a tangle of prosthetics with complicated straps. A clipboard, a drafting pad, a hand level, a prism, a plumb bob with chalked string, all rigged to fit over his wooden prosthesis with its hexagonal end. Leighton reached in Odem's wagon for the clipboard and set this on his knee. He pulled the wooden prosthesis loose from its attachments, shaking it to get the leather straps untangled. In his hands, the wood was heavy as a bludgeon, its finish slick as glass, for Odem polished it nightly to fight the drying ravages of lime.

They traded no greetings. He took the nub of Odem's arm in his hand. The chapped skin, the knot of bone, touching Odem there was like gripping the head of a bull snake, stiff and asleep with cold. He recalled cutting the fingers off the bushwhacker, the cracking of bone, and the nubbins left at the task's grisly end. He forced the prosthesis against Odem's nub until that knot of bone and scar tissue popped into the notch carved for it. Such different wars they fought—Odem in meadows against columns of uniformed men, hailstorms of lead, and a score of gallant commanders like Sterling Price; Leighton over balds and down hollows against lice-ridden banshees with bulging eyes whose tack trailed scalps like dancing leaves of creeper, whose chests crackled with necklaces of bones and teeth. He and Odem never spoke of the difference. With his face buried in Odem's shoulder, he threaded a leather strap around the back of the nub, yanked the strap tight. Another set of bindings, arranged like the top of a sandal, fastened and supported the prosthesis along Odem's taut bicep and upper arm. Again Leighton worked with his face and chest close to Odem while the young accountant's eyes followed the wavering of the candle on the slat walls of the office. Their breathing fell in time. At war Leighton hunted men whose names he knew for they were townsmen, local hill boys gone wild. He tracked them through a wilderness where the tangle of grapevine and cedar and locust thorn was perfect scaffolding for the fear that canvassed the mind. And all that Death for the Negroes outside, now without labor, begging for work while Republicans strutted starry eyed over emancipation and victory. Struggling with the buckles, Leighton caught the hint of lye at Odem's collar, felt the warmth in the pit along his collar bone. Through the open windows behind them came the sound of miners' greetings, a rock tumbling to splash in the pool below the cliffs, a ringing, the hand drills opening the first holes for the big chucks and wedges. Odem's lips moved as if he were reciting. His brow wrinkled. Otherwise the young man with his feathery blonde hair, pale skin, and lanky frame sat rigidly while Leighton embraced him and made him whole. One last improvement: from a walnut case lined with crushed felt Leighton withdrew the cowhide band. Odem bowed as to a priest with the Host, and Leighton eased the band down Odem's scalp until the cowhide would not budge. Then to the sweat-darkened leather he snapped an armature from which a series of magnifying monocles spread in a glinting fan.

When finished, Leighton eased back from the cripple. After a few seconds, Odem's shoulders slouched a little. He swung the prosthetic up and down, then fitted the clipboard on it. The metal band on the clipboard moaned as it grew snug squirming onto the wooden prosthesis. Seated there with much of his body mechanized, what had been a handsome, fair-headed veteran was now an unholy contraption daily manufactured.

"I thank ye," Odem said.

In the silence that followed, in every fidget Odem made, in every knife stroke he bore on the quill's nib, Leighton perceived a condemnation. Without the company store, that modern fiscal miracle, Odem endured Leighton's assistance as a soldier will tolerate the orders of some gentlemanly local nabob turned general. To avoid wrangling at the subject, the two of them stepped out into the yard. What a pair they made! A burly, bearded proprietor in a Yankee campaign cap now spattered gray, one starlight blue eye lazy and crawling while the other steadied above deep, black rings of sleeplessness. And next to Leighton a mechanism of a man, a portrait of fair hill youth swarmed over by machines of leather, steel, and ground glass. Morning merriment died in an instant, and the miners drew up, an intent and chastened squadron.

Morkan Quarry was an anomaly at the edge of the encroaching town. From the two stone pillars that supported the iron gates at the northwest corner, a gravel trail disintegrated into an enormous sloping lot of red chert and pulverized limestone. In the midst of this, with one frazzled willow for shade, a tile-roofed shack perforated by slat windows overlooked a teal pool of water and cliffs of exposed lime thirty feet high on the pool's far side. The cliffs were moonlight blue and across their faces spread a system of rails and scaffolding, pulley-and-cable-drawn ore cars that hauled the stone down to the stone breaking yard upslope from a set of kilns and a stiff-legged derrick with a bull wheel and skip. Against the cliffs slouched the Mistress, old Morkan's makeshift steam derrick with its sixty foot boom, which creaked and squalled, lifting hunks of stone as if they weighed no more than soap. With the Mistress grunting, columns of dark smoke twisting up, black powder shots thumping, dust blooming in white clouds, the quarry made respectable Springfieldians curb their horses to the east side of National Avenue (the Yankee Republicans had renamed State Street) and pull the brims of their hats low.

Of late, with contracts from the Republican rebuilders beginning to flow his way, Leighton was eking by. But always in his memory was the war and its privations and sudden turns of fate. Before the war, the quarry would seasonally do well enough; but many transactions were barters. In winter and early spring, the Morkans had all their boots re-soled, the best pelts and tack from the tanneries, their larders replete with turkeys, hams, all manner of vegetables that came as payment in kind, but nothing for cash to start quarrying again. The war ended all barter systems—the contractors who bought from Leighton were carpetbaggers, builders from towns he'd never heard of, with accents that rang like coins in a tin cup. They wanted mortar and rip rap, ashlars and quoins, not the quick lime and occasional tombstones Springfieldians sought. Once these Republicans finished impressing everyone they had defeated and memorializing their fallen heroes, what then? No more contractors from Terre Haute, only Scots-Irish scowls and pockets empty of all but lint.

On the morning of a shootout in the public square, a long train of wagons wound down from the quarry gates and cluttered the lot. A young man in a chestnut suit hopped down from the lead wagon. Cocked back on his head was a crimson hat, the brim of which was curled. He wore smooth leather boots that took up most of his calf; his suede vest bore sunbursts and spirals of pearly mussel shells carved like tears and spearpoints.

Leighton had not seen such a riot of finery since Quantrill's men posed for portraits before the last secessionist photographer skedaddled. Leighton approached him with the hardest face he could muster.

The man removed his hat. He had fine-combed red hair that smelled of cologne. Beneath the cuff, his boots were stamped with the letter R. "This Morkan Quarry?"

"Must be," Leighton said.

The man extended his hand. "Mr. Morkan?"

Leighton took the man's hand. The palm was rough, and Leighton's callous snagged and bound with the newcomer's so much that they both smiled and glanced at their hands. "I'm Archer Newman, the City Engineer."

"You mean you're the only engineer in town."

Archer blinked. "Why, yes! I like that better." He slapped his hat against his palm. "To be honest with you, I just might have 'the city' change my title." His eyes were bright, a clear blue. They jumped from the mill, to the cliffs, to the mules, to a crew of stone breakers, regarding each in a flash of summation and judgment, then returning to Leighton with a steady assurance.

Archer explained that his first civic project was to Macadamize the main streets before winter, and after that he wanted to finish the stone courthouse with turrets, chimneys, cupolae, and gargoyles.

Leighton blinked at him. "Chat we've got on site. We do dimension stone to order. You want limestone or just creek gravel?"

Archer pursed his lips. "Going prices?"

"Limestone, seventy-five cents a perch. Chert, sixty cents. Both carry a twenty-five cent clearing fee."

Archer smiled. "One dollar gravel? Clearing fee on each perch?"

Easterner, clearly. Leighton removed his cap and smoothed his hair. He could take offense at this dandy, but maybe he was the city engineer. The world worked that way now, all things upended—slaves ran free, boats traveled underwater, actors shot presidents. Leighton replaced his cap. "Come see the stone."

With the sun already high in the sky, the lot, the cliffs, and the wood of the scaffolding shimmered in the heat. To Leighton's surprise, Archer braved each scaffold and railing. Twenty feet up, they crawled off the rails and onto a bench of stone. There, a laborer was on hands and knees inserting plugs into feather holes. The stone was gray-blue. Ten feet above them, the precipice loomed, all fine limestone, seamed in an intricate quilt of rectangles and squares. In the rough, where no stone had been split there were waves of fossils as manifold and various as stars in the night sky. Leighton pointed downward. Sunlight played off the pool onto the cliffs in wavering ribbons of yellow revealing the quality of the stone below them, tight grained and glowing like the surface of the moon. Archer ran his hand across the face of the stone the laborer was plugging.

Leighton crouched at one of the holes where there was a little white cone of dust. He scooped up the cone, let the dust dribble from his hand. "It hurts my soul to pound this into gravel."

Archer gazed again at the cliffs. "To nation with your soul. It's your wallet." He held Leighton's eyes. "Lucky man!" Archer smiled. "Go to, let us build us a city."

Leighton nodded. "Right now, why not?"

They climbed down the scaffolding, and when Archer's feet hit the ground, he gave Leighton's back three great whacks and left his arm draped over Leighton's shoulder as they descended the trail.

Once Archer produced a purchase order with the signature of the provost marshal, and the mayor, Leighton had him circle the wagons under the stiff-legged derrick. Inside of Archer's wagons shining sheets of iron were pounded into the beds. Metal axles and reinforced steel wheels, two huge Percherons, solid gray with rumps of rippling muscle hitched to each. Broken stone from Morkan Quarry weighed easily a long ton, or 2,500 pounds per cubic yard. Rigs such as Archer's, horses such as these, My God, Leighton thought. They might could haul two cubic yards per load.

Archer hooked his fingers in his mouth, whistled and directed the wagons under the chutes. He squinted up at Leighton. "Where's your skip scale?"

Leighton pointed up at the huge rectangular pan suspended from the derrick. "Skip's on the derrick. And a wagon's a perch. Twenty-five cubic feet."

Archer shielded his eyes, staring at Leighton for a moment. "Twenty-seven. I want twenty-seven in every one of these." Even without the sun, the pearly drops arrayed on his vest flashed like minnows rolling over a sandbar.

Leighton held out a fist. A tagman below the derrick's skip grabbed the drop chain. Leighton opened his hand as if casting seeds. In a dusty whoosh the limestone gravel pulsed down and rattled on the iron with such force that the Percherons hitched to the wagon rolled their eyes and stomped. When Leighton shut his fist, the skip raised its snout and the last of the stone trickled to a whisper, then dust, then no more.

Archer jumped on the sideboard and surveyed the load. He waved his open hand as Leighton had done. After a moment of waving with no result, he shot a glance behind him at the tagman by the chain.

Brow lowered, the tagman was rolling a cigarette, but watching Archer.

Archer hopped off the wagon. "What sort of perch is this?"

Another two wagons loaded, the teamsters waited for Archer's signal to haul.

Leighton leaned over the railing of one wagon. "Twenty-five cubic feet, unless you've got a bed size I don't know about."

"Get up here, Morkan."

Archer yanked the teamster off the wagon. Archer sat and took the reins. He patted the seat. "Take a ride with me here, chum."

Leighton hesitated, then climbed on the wagon and sat. He lit a cigar, offered one to Archer, who accepted the stogie but refused the light.

Archer popped the reins on the Percherons' hides, and they proceeded through the gates and on to Summit Street. Archer drove hunched down with his elbows digging into his legs just above the knees. He ground the unlit cigar between his teeth, but kept his eyes fixed on the road as if it might vanish. The wagon bounced hard on a rut, then another. Archer leaned on the reins steering for the next rut, and the wagon slammed and yawed. Leighton gripped the bottom of the seat with both hands.

After they'd gone past the center of town and into a clapboard district of new saloons and stores on McDaniel Street, Archer set the brake. "Okay, Morkan." He turned to look at the bed of the wagon. Leighton did likewise, though he knew what he would see. The load had shaken down so that inches of dusty sideboard and iron showed.

"Look it there!" Archer said. He removed the cigar from his mouth. "My twenty-five cubic feet is down about four or five."

Leighton scowled. "Newman, you're the first man since the war ended to figure this out." He extended his hand.

But Archer hesitated, looking Leighton over with a sudden coldness that raised all Leighton's hackles. The public street fell away. The booming summer sun darkened. If I can get my hand at his neck right quick, Leighton thought, watching Archer's chest and shoulders for the first hint of assault.

"I'm pretty certain," Archer said, carefully, "I get to be the one doing the cheating and bullying. At least," and he began to smile so that Leighton eased back bit by bit, "At least here for a little while."

In one last motion that tensed him up again, Archer raised his open hand from his knee and extended it slowly. They shook, and when they returned to the quarry, Leighton filled each wagon with two extra cubic feet.

He left work early and stood Archer Newman and a salesman from Horseley Powder to whiskeys at the Quarry Rand Saloon. Archer grinned while Leighton answered and eventually discouraged the salesman's questions and overt business solicitations. When the salesman rose to leave, Leighton asked Archer to stay. He and Leighton remained in the saloon well into the evening swapping engineering stories—Archer had worked canals in New York and on the Great Lakes. The R stood for Rutgers, where he'd taken his degree. Morkan Quarry was an anomalous fascination to him in that it was both a pit excavation and a naturally exposed face. Leighton explained how exposing the lime had bankrupted the original owners, how he would need a railroad spur eventually to exploit the stone to the fullest. Then their talk turned to falls from great heights, maimings, boiler explosions. Leighton told of a Moravian who would sleep off his drunks in the old kiln. When they had accidentally stoked the kiln with him in it, they knocked him out with a log to the head, ended up burning him with the stone. "He's glistening now in some wall holding bricks together. I reckon he's structurally liable for half the drafts in town," Leighton said. Archer slapped the table and laughed once.

Leighton grew quiet. In the wavering light of the candle, the mussel shells on Archer's vest shone like the eyes of insects in the dark. "You seen plenty of men die, then, haven't you?" Leighton asked.

"Why's that?"

"A man what's seen only a couple men die on the job, he gets pretty solemn. A man that's seen many, well, he can't help but laugh. It's that horrible."

Archer nodded, raised his eyebrows. "Two men shot it out today on your square over a watch fob. How's that strike you?"

Leighton put an open hand to his ear. "There will be wars and rumors of wars but somewhere someone is always making money."

Archer grinned. "Well, philosopher, what's a man see when those eyes go glassy and the soul escapes?"

"Damned if I know. And even in the war, I never did have a man die around me who asked after his commanders and enemies, and sent them his compliments." Leighton drank his whiskey. "How do you Easterners get to die them glorious deaths I read about, like ole Armistead?"

Archer tapped a match from a gleaming silver cylinder, its circumference turned and cross-turned at a precise lathe, roughened for striking. "You Missourians are cursed with practical memories like no other species of human." He gestured dramatically, striking the match. "Who cares what the fact is when we have made a constellation of it to hang in heaven an immortal sign?" With great satisfaction, he lit the cigar Leighton had given him hours ago. In the match's light, the lapels of Archer's chestnut suit glistened as if dusted with pyrite.

Leighton rode his best horse to Weitzer's summer place. It was a spread he admired, though not because of its sheltering hillock, or its spring that ran a rapid stream into Lone Pine Creek thence to the James River. He honed after the limestone he felt under the ground of it, solid sheets traveling down and down, exhaling a bitter, scouring wind. He could feel the stone passing under the horse, feel flashes of the blue and myriad fossils the way a fisherman can sense the school of fish below his skiff even in a moonless cove. The flavor of the air sharpened above a great deposit of limestone. Bouncing down Weitzer's path, he felt the base slick of caves, of eons of detritus from seas long receded dampening the cuffs of his shirt, cupping his bearded chin as if a washerwoman's dripping fingers caressed him.

He found Weitzer ripping long vines of creeper from a ring of limestone that defined an overgrown garden. The stone was dull blue. The Dutchman had unearthed some of these stones and plopped them in a garden border thinking nothing of their value.

The two Weitzer women glanced up; then the mother took the daughter by the shoulder, led her to the cabin. Weitzer stood with his hands on his hips. The cuffs of his battered gloves stuck out like funnels. He wore a white shirt and a black vest. His goatee was more gray than Leighton remembered.

Leighton dismounted. Finger by finger, Weitzer pulled the glove from his right hand and watched Leighton, who smiled.

"I thought we'd lost you, Mister Weitzer." He shook Weitzer's hand.

Weitzer nodded. "There were times I hoped I might lose all of you." His eyes were lean. They tightened at the corners.

Leighton removed his Federal cap. "Had the privilege of meeting your daughter t'other night. Since I've not had that privilege again, I trust all here is well now."

A bead of sweat crawled down Weitzer's neck and dissipated into his frayed collar. He held Leighton's eyes fiercely. "I do not have your money."

When the Battle of Wilson's Creek ended, Weitzer had stood outside the National Mineral Bank honoring currency receipts from only the largest accounts, cashing them from his personal savings. By the time Leighton and his father reached the bank that afternoon, Weitzer could only manage roughly one thousand dollars of the twenty-five hundred old Morkan had on deposit. Leighton both admired Weitzer and thought him a fool for cashing a dime of anyone's stash. Dutchman, Leighton thought, earnest to a fault. After a moment, Weitzer pulled the glove back on, stared at the glove as his fingers wriggled. "I do not imagine I will have it for some time." He held Leighton's eyes again. "But I promise you, I am still trustee. Your debt will be honored."

Leighton laughed. "You certainly sap the niceties out of it all, Weitzer."

Weitzer's goatee stretched in a frown. "No room for joking. There is no house of mirth even for the fool today." At this Weitzer grinned and his teeth were gray and sharp in angles Leighton had only seen in the mouths of certain Negroes.

Leighton smiled with him. He cleared his throat. "And I wonder what's left of the house of wisdom."

Weitzer snorted twice, and it took a moment for Leighton to realize this was a laugh. When Leighton reached into his coat and drew out his flask of whiskey, Weitzer smiled, his lips rising in the sharp oval of his goatee. They drank.

"Why not sell me this land?" Leighton asked.

Weitzer lowered the flask and stuck it back at him. "Thought we had finished with business talk."

"We may have." Leighton drank.

Weitzer's eyes thinned to slits.

"Would you consider selling?"

Weitzer shook his head. "This will be my daughter's dowry."

Leighton nodded. From his saddle bag, he took two tin cups and gave one to Weitzer. He emptied the flask into the cups. He raised his. "May it bring her a good husband."

Weitzer blinked. He did not raise his cup.

"You owe me fifteen hundred." He tipped his cup at Weitzer, then downed it.

For a long time as Leighton rode away, Weitzer remained staring at the amber rings that quivered down in the battered and dingy tin.

From racks on the wall Odem pulled the sheets of the old ledgers. He tucked each year's record into his armpit, clamping the papers to his ribs with his stob. Some of the ledgers bore the stamp of the provost marshal—they were evidence in holding Leighton's father prisoner during the war. Odem stacked them on Leighton's desk, then smoothed open the top one as if it were a royal robe. 1861 the sheet read. The handwriting belonged to Leighton's father. Each page turned revealed rows of orderly characters and numerals.

"He sure was a fine draftsman, Leighton," Odem said. "But that's altogether beside the point." Odem's fingers tracking over the ledgers made a sound like a fire devouring brush. "He kept square books considering so much was on the barter." Odem looked up at Leighton. "But there's a kind of moral calculus in these here. A mess of greens ain't worth the same in April as it is in September. These here pounds of flour and meal can't equal the time, labor, and stone gone to Greer's Mill."

"Greer was a good man. Lots of sons to feed."

Odem scowled. "Fine. Moral assets like them, though, are hard on accompts and harder to pay out to the laborer." He looked Leighton up and down. "Archer Newman has been plain with me on what he'll give per ton on these big contracts. You will run a deficit in labor cost meeting the deadlines. And until you have that kind of steady volume here with a railhead. Well, look."

Odem spread the current ledger before Leighton. Odem's lettering and numbering was rounded and so uniform it appeared to have come from a lead press. What he outlined very quickly made clear that the cash Leighton made just after the war was being swallowed. Margins on dimension stone were acceptable but shrinking; margins on gravel and cracked rock sometimes left an operation in the red paying all the stonebreakers.

"I don't suggest this because I'm a cruel man. I suggest it because it's common practice," Odem said, leaning hard on the ledger with his stob and pleading with his good hand. "Let me make you a company store, pay their monies to it. You'll see."

Leighton lifted his cap, pushed his fingers through his dry hair. "My Da was a wreck when he left me this, Odem. Ever seen a man die of consumption? I made my promise to a wraith spitting blood onto my dead mother's china."

"And you'll break that promise just as sure losing the quarry, won't you?" Odem's voice rose. His eyes narrowed. "You had to know even making that promise times was passed would let you run a quarry the old way."

Leighton paused, remembering that day, remembering how he did see his father's methods of quarrying as a cause as lost as the Confederate army of Missouri.

There came a knock on the door, and Archer Newman let himself in. Seeing Leighton and his cripple accountant squared against each other, Newman halted.

"Have I come at a bad time?"

"Not at all," Leighton said. He lifted a wooden chair and knocked the lime from it banging its legs against the puncheons.

But when Archer leaned against the back of the chair and reached into his coat for his pouch of tobacco and papers, there was silence again, Leighton and his accountant staring at one another in a standoff. Odem shuffled the ledgers so that only the old Morkan's accompts showed on top.

"You know, Leighton," Archer began, "you and I should travel to St. Louis. One good look at Whytlaw Stone and the company store it has, you'd drop all this nonsense." He pronounced store as "stah," and seemed disinterested, fiddling a cigarette together.

He scanned the ledger sheets, lit his cigarette, then bent and put his elbows to the desk and took a long look. He tucked his long auburn hair behind his ears. "Mr. Odem, you do have a grand touch with the pen." He traced a column with his fingers. "But, to be honest with you, Leighton, you're traveling down a culvert to a stinking French drain."

He straightened, tugged at his vest once to get it snug against his belt where the vest climbed. "The city, I should say, *I* will not pay any more than what this contract states." He pulled from his coat a long document folded secure in violet paper sealed with red wax. Carefully, he placed it on the open ledger. "To be quite honest, you stand not only to save your father's quarry, Leighton, but also to make a great deal of money over a long time. But only if you step out of this guildsman's past and into the present light of day." He took a long draw on his cigarette, which glowed bright red in the dim morning light of the office. "I leave you to your decision."

When Archer shut the door behind him, Leighton and Odem stared at the contract for a long while. Finally Odem stepped to it, clamped it flat with his stob and broke the seal with his thumb. His ink-darkened lips moved as he read.

He glanced up and Leighton, handed him the contract.

Leighton read over it. Such quantities. Such awful prices. "I sure wish Archer wouldn't say that, 'To be honest with you,'" he whispered to Odem, worried that Archer was again listening just outside the door. "It always makes me wonder if up to that point he hasn't bothered to be very honest."

Odem blinked at him.

"Go. Get the men started on this."

Later that same morning, Odem fetched Leighton from the office. Ten Negroes waited at the gate. They wore overalls, ratty brogans, long sleeve shirts or no shirt at all. The large Negro from the previous mornings stepped before Leighton. "These men is ever bit as good a workers as what you been hiring, I give my word."

Leighton lit a cigar, scowling at the big fellow, but the terrible numbers in Archer's contract still clawed at his mind, black nettles all along the fancy parchment. Negroes at the quarry. The tang of his smoke quickened his heart.

They might work for next to nothing. They could be trained if they were willing. All the Negro slaves from the Morkan farm had learned carpentry easily enough. Treated fairly, as his father had treated Judith and Johnson and Isaac, they would stay and work loyally. Much of the town would be shocked at seeing Negroes working there. But then this was the new world in which the slave was free. And if he brought in freedmen, he could pay them in kind at a company store. The tip of the cigar flared. There would be no promise broken. His father may have freed his slaves, but he never paid a Negro a man's wage.

Slowly Leighton pulled a cigar from his coat pocket, then handed it to the large Negro. The Negro took it, blinking at it as if the cigar were a live animal. Leighton tilted the wooden match, held it for the Negro, who arched his neck to receive the light. The Negro puffed, still staring at Leighton.

Leighton crossed his arms. He wagged his cigar in his teeth. "I won't get many men will work alongside a freedman."

The Negro lowered his head.

"You bring me one hundred sober men to this spot," Leighton said, poking the cigar at him, "and I'll hire them at fifty cents a day. Store goods."

"One hundred?"

Leighton nodded. "At the least."

"How 'bout us ten now?"

Leighton shook his head. "I need your ten and ninety more."

The Negro heaved a great sigh. He turned to the others, and they trudged across Summit Street in a clot. Leighton felt his chest tighten. They would change the quarry like nothing else he had done.

Odem tapped a pencil against his ledger. "Can he bring one hundred?"

Leighton shrugged.

"Will you take them if he does?"

"Said I would."

Odem's eyes glazed over—he was calculating. "You can run most of your labor force at just over fifty dollars a day. And paid in store goods" he said. "My God, Leighton. The money you'll make." He pulled at his bottom lip.

"Will the foremen stay?" Leighton asked. "Will the town still buy? Sure they are all for the Union in the daylight. They ready for commerce with freedmen?"

Odem rubbed his temple.

"Are you ready?"

Odem shrugged, his stob rising.

He followed Odem back into the office. "Does this break the promise or dodge it?"

"It solves a big problem. Brings a nation of them."

During the day, Leighton circulated around the quarry, and asked each foreman to have a drink with him at the Quarry Rand when work was done.

When Archer came by that afternoon, Leighton took him into the office and asked Odem to leave them.

Leighton paced the floor, and Archer whistled. "Need an extra gun?"

"Archer, what would you do if I worked freedmen in this quarry?"

Archer's eyes went wide. When he looked up at Leighton, his lips were drawn in a flat line. "I answer to a council of Republicans and carpetbaggers who freed those slaves. I see they will have only minor trouble about this from hypocrites and Rebel holdouts." He moved very close to Leighton, then put a hand on his shoulder. "Councils like the winds of war can change. If they turn against you and stop buying, there's nothing I can do."

Leighton nodded. "Nothing personal, but no drinks tonight."

"Tomorrow, then," Archer said.

Leighton took a pen from the desk and signed the city contract.

As he left for the saloon, Leighton noticed the same large Negro sitting beneath the willow at the quarry gate. The Negro frowned, tipped his felt hat and nodded as Leighton strode into the street.

Leighton hung his thumbs behind his belt. "Shouldn't you be out recruiting there?"

"Done been, sir." The Negro didn't smile.

Leighton swallowed. "Something you need?"

The Negro stood and came very near him. He had on the same long dress shirt with frayed cuffs. From the dust on it, Leighton reckoned the Negro had been in the streets all day. "Monday in the morning be a time to start?"

Leighton felt his shoulders rise. His heart thumped— Monday was so soon, the change so rapid, it was as if he were watching gravel swirl down the wrong chute. "If you've a hundred men, Monday will be fine."

"One hundred and ten," the Negro said.

Leighton was silent a moment. "Bring them," he finally said. "Recall what I said. Five dimes a day payable in scrip at the company store. Paid at the end of the week."

The Quarry Rand was dark as an old spring house. Its walls, cinder blocks reeking of lime, sweated. At the front, narrow windows let in sallow culverts of twilight made gray by the lime dust of Summit Street. Back where the foremen waited, the air dripped, dank and close as a cellar. Six of his foremen sat at three barrelheads littered with their truck—tobacco pouches, playing cards, pipe tools, cloves, a medal of the cult of Saint Louis IX. Odem had already bought them a round. They were smiling and joking, drinking thirstily.

Leighton took his stool and whistled at the barmaid, Danny Montbonne Beauchamp, ordering her to set out a round of whiskeys and stouts. The table grew so quiet that the ringing of the mugs and the gurgling of whiskey agitated and provoked the waiting drinkers. Odem paid her from his suede satchel, counting off the coins like pills between his thumb and index finger, holding the satchel open with his stob.

Leighton let out a long breath. "I'm going to hire freedmen at the quarry."

Some of the men shuddered. "Lordy," one said. Two of them finished their whiskeys at a single heave.

Jacob Ridinger put an elbow on the table, ran a finger around the rim of his mug. An old friend of the late Morkan, Ridinger had worked at the quarry longer than Leighton had. "I'm not showing any Nigger how to drill. I won't be teaching one of them a trade."

Billie Poole nodded at Ridinger. "That whole war was over them. I fought for 'em, done my part. Freedom means they're on their own." Poole wore a beard that grew more thickly under his chin than on his face.

"It's not charity I'm giving them," Leighton said. "They've agreed to work for a lot less than any man I ever hired. I'm going to open a company store and pay them in kind." Hard-jawed men, wrinkles at their eyes, all of them older than he—

they had always listened to him, but now he pushed a precarious line. Their eyes lowered. Their frowns tightened.

Ridinger's jaw muscles darkened his cheeks. "Where would the other men go?"

Leighton placed both hands on the table palms down. "They can stay."

"For what pay? Store coupons?" Ridinger said, leaning forward. His gums were purple and wet. A whore had pulled his front teeth so he could avoid conscription in the Union army. His black hair fell about his eyes so he appeared to be scowling under a hood.

"For the pay they have now." It was the foremen he couldn't lose; the others were negligible so long as the big Negro brought one hundred men. He could train Negroes to cut stone, he was sure of it, for he had seen Isaac do it under the old Morkan's direction. And even prisoners could grasp how to break stone.

Ridinger watched Leighton a moment, then fished in his shirt pocket and drew out a ball of wax paper. It crackled in his fingers as he squeezed until the boiled rabbit brain inside popped up gray and chalky. He scraped the brains on his slimy red gums, but he kept his eyes on Leighton as he soothed his aching.

Poole stood, his lips twisted in disgust. "A quarry's no place for a Nigra. I'll not have them smashing their hands and falling off the cut. I'd as soon work children in there."

"That's why I wanted you gathered to hear this," Leighton said. "If you can't take working with them, then I want you to go." He looked straight at Poole, then at Ridinger. "What say you, men?"

Ridinger's gray tongue wet his lips. With care, he stored the brains, wax paper crackling.

Poole gripped the back of his chair, his chapped knuckles standing out like blue lumps of lead shot. The others stared thoughtfully into their drinks, fidgeted in their chairs.

Leighton leaned back. He glanced at Odem, but found Odem's eyes focused tightly on a spot in the center of the table. "We've lived through this war," Leighton began, "and now we live in a chaos of thievery and vendetta. Surely we seen how quickly our lives can be turned on end. We could all be out in the street tomorrow, nothing over our heads!" He finished his own whiskey. His voice dropped. "I mined stone for the Federal army day and night for a whole season, more stone than I'd ever took from that quarry in a year, and what do I have to show for it? Not a shinplaster."

Ridinger hunched his shoulders. He kept his eyes lowered and his jaw wormed about as if he were conceiving words too ugly to utter. One of the foremen ground a clove with the butt of his knife.

Leighton's voice rose. "Damned Rebels took my livestock, took my father's powder and ruined him. Federals went off with half his stake in the world, sent him back from prison rotten with consumption." When spit escaped him in anger, he drew his hand across his lips; the grit of lime, still in his beard, fell to the table as if his words were made of it.

Danny came before them with a bottle of whiskey. Leighton circled his finger for drinks all around. They were silent while she poured. Poole returned to his seat. The angles of their expressions were softened in the booze's amber light.

"I don't mean to say all this for any sympathy," he continued. He held his mug of stout. "But I want you to understand. I fought for the Negro, too." He looked straight at Poole. He had not long considered what he wanted to say, but he felt the words welling in him. "I fought and killed men I didn't know and men I damn well did know, knew well. I watched folks starve here in town for the Negro. I don't do this out of any great kindness. But let me tell you something—I have owned slaves. I have seen them work and they will. They learn fast as hounds." He leaned both his elbows on the barrelhead, held his palms out to them. "And set me straight on this. If we freed them, and then keep them from making a living, think of the trouble we got ahead of us. Them in the streets. Us with the money."

They were quiet. Poole sipped from his whiskey.

Menzardo, a big olive skinned man, the foreman of Leighton's stonecutters, sat forward. His Louis ix medal showed the great king clutching a model of Sainte Chapelle. Menzardo fingered this as if deep in prayer. "This is a world of a narrow causeways." When he drank, his voice took on a lisp that made it liquid and pleasant. All the foremen turned to him. He was superbly skilled, could tool a bevel in dimension stone as if the lime were candle wax. "My men have one quarry to work for. And Morkan's done right by us. He never does nothing he won't tell us about first. So long as he treats skill right, I say bring up the freedmen. I can teach any kind of a man what to make of a stone."

"I'm in, too," another said. "I never had any problem with Niggers. Hell, out east they fought like any one of us. Probably harder, considering."

Odem sat forward, placed his stob against the table. "The savings to the quarry ... would be substantial."

"And that would come round to benefit all of us." Leighton drew a crusty finger around to indicate those gathered.

All but Poole and Ridinger nodded at this.

Poole rose. "I cannot do it. I'd say you're an honorable man for telling us what was coming, but you're only honest."

They were silent at this. Poole left.

"Ridinger?" Leighton asked.

In the sorry light, Ridinger's face appeared ugly as wet shale. "I'll stay. For now."

"I want your whole heart in it," Leighton said, "or I want you gone."

"I'm in, I said." He rose, reached in his pocket. Before Leighton could stop him, he flipped an Indian head dollar on the table, and strode for the door.

Leighton glanced around the table at the remaining foremen. Their lips were drawn and flat, their eyes stunned; they looked like troops that have been shelled. "No more long faces," he said. "We're gonna make a wad of money, chums." He called for Danny.

Danny served and they drank. One of them told a story about a bad fuse, but Leighton couldn't bring himself to pay attention. Sweat crawled down his sides; his tongue felt as if it had been smeared with paste. Across the bar, two of the stone breakers, already tipsy, began to play a snare and a set of bagpipes. The player aired the pipes and got the drone to rise. The reed screeched at first, but then the miner bullied it down. He was quite good. Notes swooped and tumbled.

The bagpipe's drone surrounded the hazy room. Several patrons scowled. Others stared, eyes glazed. They were small pipes, Irish or Galician, but they stuffed the bar with undulating notes. The snare snapped and patted and sounded for an instant like the approaching feet of many men. Monday, and Negroes would be working at his quarry. His heart stammered to think it. Hearing the rap of the drum, the trill of the pipes, he felt as if he were on an inevitable course now, the ancient war music weaving like an army through round hills. He was no crusader, no abolitionist zealot, yet here he was, ready to take advantage of freedmen, ready to give them the opportunity to be used. The song swelled. The entire bar stilled. Even the drill foreman mixing his cloves in oil paused and suffered his sour stomach, watching the players and holding his breath. For a moment there were no musicians, no instruments. The music was the distilled thought of every man in the room. The players—these were the men who would refuse to work for him come Monday, his people, Ozarkers. What a wretched pinch, lose the quarry or hire Negroes at a level he would pay no White! Over in a corner of the bar sat a long-legged old man in a black mackinaw, with his head bowed, and for just a moment in the gloom, Leighton saw his old, dead father, defeated and drunk and disapproving.

"Da," he whispered.

But only Odem, sitting by him now, listening with him to the beautiful piping, heard the sob in his voice. He stuck that solid stob of an arm against Leighton's shoulder, gave him three hard bumps. No other man in the world would he touch with his blasted limb. "Ain't they good," Odem said watching the band. "My God, but ain't they good."

IV

On MONDAY MORNING, LEIGHTON MET PATRICIA WEITZER as he was riding to the quarry. He slowed his horse. She was bent over picking wild dewberries that grew against a ledge of rock near the road. An inky mound of berries was heaped in her apron, the fringe of which she cradled to make a pouch. Rods of sunlight divided the oaks.

Seeing him, she straightened, then arched her back placing her free hand in the small of it. The dewberries made her apron bulge. She eased her way through the brambles toward him. She was picking on Morkan land.

"How is your horse this morning?" she asked. Her lips were drawn and smug. "Still fearful of shadows cast by lanterns?"

He bunched the animal's mane in his fist and pulled. It shook its head, sputtered. She shielded her face from its flying spittle, but stood her ground. He smiled. "Mornings he's tolerable brave," he said. "Your oxen?"

She frowned and cocked her head. "They are fat again."

Her expression was full of pride. Lovely pride, exactly what he wanted to see.

He dismounted, opened his saddle bag and took out his tin cup. He drew close enough to her that she tucked her chin toward her chest and scowled. She was at the least a foot taller than he. "May I?" he asked, nodding to the dewberries.

She glanced down where she held her apron closed. "They are yours." She opened her apron, the black mound resting against her flat stomach. "Morkan land, I know."

Moorken, she said. Like no other person in the world she changed his name speaking it. He was snagged with the desire that she speak it again. Moorken.

60

Before she could scoop berries out, he plunged the cup into the bulge her apron made, dug the cup around at her waist. He lifted the overflowing cup as if toasting her.

Her face flared red and her slight eyebrows formed a **v**. Tilting the cup back, he downed the berries, letting several thump on the road. He locked eyes with her and smiled until he chewed. In the flood of juice, his mouth ached as if someone were pulling his jawbone at the sockets. He buckled from the waist.

She laughed a lovely, ringing laugh of such volume that the horse backed off.

Bent, he held a hand to his mouth, great snorts of purple escaping. He turned from her, lost the reins in searching for his handkerchief, and the horse scooted to the other side of the road. When it stared at them with great rolling eyeballs, her laughter redoubled like a field of crystal bells. The horse turned for home and trotted away.

Leighton scrambled, still hunched, coughing and spitting berries, the hard seeds like filings in his throat. He caught the horse and managed to mount it. Straightening his shoulders and arching his chest, he passed her and tried to present some semblance of lordly dignity. The dumb horse stepped high as a Lipizzaner. She raised a hand to her mouth, but still the laugh rang and her thin shoulders shook. Her arm remained cupped about the apron. In her joy, she did not lose a single berry.

More than one hundred Negroes arrived at the quarry gates, some with picks and shovels; one old Negro brought a wheelbarrow. Six mounted deputies and two dozen Federal soldiers were arrayed in a skirmish line on Summit Street, rifles at their sides. They formed a barrier between the Negroes and the rest of the town. Before the war, Springfield was the only town in the Missouri Ozarks with a significant enslaved population of Blacks. Never before, during, or after the war had so many of the Negro race gathered for one occasion with one intent, not even outside the Freedmen's Bureau's ramshackle office. To see one hundred Black men congregated anywhere was a menace, frightening and rare to Leighton's townspeople.

The Negroes were scattered on stoops, seated on the board-walk, milling in the street. Despite the warm morning sun, Leighton wore his Federal pea coat, and he'd even tried to dust some of the gray lime out of his field cap. He unchained the gate. As each link fell and drooped, he thought of the tumblers in a lock falling and fastening this moment into place. There was no going back.

Odem moved next to him. "Son of a bitch," he whispered.

Leighton looked at him.

The large Negro, the original emissary, stepped to the front. He wore the same shirt, but puckers and lines in it made it look recently boiled.

Leighton stood before the Negro, and many others pressed and milled around him. "What's your name?" Leighton asked.

"Miasma Sullivan."

"In truth?"

The Negro flashed a smile showing just the edges of his teeth. "Marse Sullivan liked words with *sum* in it. This here's my brother, Prism." He pointed to a shorter Negro with arms stout as logs.

Shane Peale, an old Home Guard comrade of Leighton's and now a full deputy, edged his mount forward until the animal loomed over them. The deputy's face was red and sparkling with sweat. His hair stood up at wild angles, and Leighton wondered where Peale's hat was.

"Leighton, what the hell is this?" Peale asked.

"Hiring same as any morning. Shane Peale, let me introduce to you Miasma Sullivan and his brother, Prism." Leighton relished the names.

Peale glared at him and clenched his teeth. "If you *are* hiring these Niggers, you have them meet somewhere other than the public street."

Leighton reached in his coat and pulled out his battered cigar case. He handed a cigar first to Miasma, then to Prism. When he reached to hand one to Peale, the deputy leaned back in the saddle. "Get them off the streets," he hissed.

"How many are here?" Leighton asked Miasma.

"One hundred thirteen."

"They know the terms?"

Miasma pursed his lips and nodded.

"Miasma, Prism, get them in a line."

The Negroes were noisy, laughing. A knot of them in the back of the line had learned some sort of marching song and were singing it as they filed through the stone gates and into Morkan Quarry. They drew merchants and boarders to the windows across the street. Above the tobacconist's, the owner, hair frazzled, leaned far out of his window and hollered for quiet. Women stole glances then vanished behind their curtains. Men seated at the storefronts sat forward and scowled. Peale waited on his fitful horse, the blue skirmish line at astonished attention behind him.

The sun had not crested some eastern clouds, but the sky was a shocked, powdery blue. Odem held his revolver against his thigh. "Shouldn't we quiet them?"

Leighton snorted. "Hush starlings?"

"We're responsible for them."

"Sure are."

"Well, then …"

Leighton shrugged. "Sign 'em up, Odem."

Odem set his jaw, raised his eyebrows. "Miasma Sullivan," he called.

Miasma stepped before him.

Odem stuck his clipboard out, and the Negro's eyes gaped at the prosthetic and Odem's flashing monocles. "Make your mark." He handed the Negro a charcoal pencil. "You understand that Morkan Quarry hires you for five dimes a day, three dollars a week, made payable in scrip for store goods at the Morkan Store on Summit and Calhoun. Paid on Monday's. Hear?"

Miasma made his x, forcing Odem's stob to bow slightly with his imprint.

The foremen were waiting beside the office. Near the face of the cliff, three dozen or more stone breakers were gathered. A water boy was already swimming in the teal pool, and the laborers were chucking rocks at him. The laborers grew quiet as the Negroes began to enter the quarry lot.

"We lost a lot of men," Ridinger said, nodding to the laborers by the pool.

Leighton shrugged. "These will work better than any of you imagine. There are more hours of them to put to labor than we have ever had before at Morkan Quarry. Some will have skills."

Several of the foremen snorted and muttered.

"You *will* ask them," Leighton said.

The Negroes were all in the lot now, standing in a mass. The other laborers came up from the pool and waited behind their foremen. A few firemen, the carpenters, the blacksmith, and the coopers stewed there, too. Most of the Whites had their arms crossed over their chests.

"Any man who will not work with these freedmen around him," Leighton hollered, "I want you to feel free to go. Now!"

A carpenter stepped forward. "You'll be lucky to have a quarry by nightfall."

"Take your leave," Leighton said.

Four other laborers and a fireman followed him.

Leighton scanned the remainder. He kept twelve foremen, down a carpenter; the blacksmith stayed, thank God.

Odem stepped from the office bearing one of the old Belgian smoothbores, long and ugly, a new flint tapped in its cock. He handed this to Leighton, returned to the office to fetch more. The wood was so gritty and dry that the gunstock caught against the callous on his palm. Still, it had not begun to crack or warp. He hefted it, admired its weight and length. From the Negroes behind him, from the foremen before him, he could sense dismay, could feel them staring at him as if he had stepped from the cliffs above them and onto a trembling wire. He was about to change everything; the men would no longer work for him, but under him. And they all were about to become pariahs in town. The guns were more for what the town might level against them than for any trouble the Negroes might pose.

"All right, then," Leighton said. "Keep these men sledging, loading wagons, lugging buckets, tending chuck, breaking stone, whatever is in their power to do."

Foremen glanced at each other. Odem finished tamping down a musket.

"What are the muskets for?" Ridinger asked.

"Company." Leighton handed the musket to Ridinger, who held it for a moment.

Ridinger cocked the gun. He snarled at Leighton, his purple gums showing. "What would old Michael Morkan say to this?"

Odem scowled at the name. But Leighton gripped Ridinger's elbow. "He'd tell you that you've had ample time to consider. Now work or go."

Ridinger pulled his elbow away. "Give me four of you black-hearted devils."

Leighton followed a crew with Miasma up on the cliffs, and they leaned on the sledges they were handed and waited for drills.

Prism Sullivan came carrying a drill bit in front of the blacksmith and his ox cart full of more. Prism's carrying the heavy drill was an act of extravagant strength few men in the quarry would have attempted. Stooped but steady, the Negro bore the gleaming iron like a prize pig. Against the white lime the burdened Negro stood out. All across the quarry groups of them gathered with their foremen, dark faces, black hands. The traffic in the streets halted. Along the gate, the gawkers stood, called to others on the street. Leighton shuddered inside, reminded himself, this is but a day and the sun will set on it as well. Sweat dripped from Prism's cheeks to his union shirt. He smiled and extended the gleaming, sharpened iron to Leighton.

Leighton, Prism, and Miasma lowered the single chuck, which was slimy and cold with lime water.

The blacksmith set out a short chuck and a canvas roll of feather drills.

"You all have sledged?" Leighton asked.

Miasma nodded. "Drove post, sir."

"Split wood with a maul and wedge," one other answered.

Leighton bent to his knees, positioned the hand drill and a hammer to start the hole. The Negroes stood back. "Get around here," Leighton said. He pulled off his Federal cap and wiped his face with his forearm. Draped on the gates, the morning crowd of gawkers thronged larger than it had ever been before. Soldiers and townsmen pointed. The cliffs and quarry lot were speckled with Negroes, their black backs shining against the white and moon-gray of the limestone. The chuck rang in his fist, made his whole arm hum. "Turn it an eighth every stroke, see. Get that bucket a'water here." He spun the chuck. A Negro crouched close to him with a sloshing bucket. "Pour a dab in there with that gourd."

The Negro complied. Within three strokes, a tongue of gray slurry splashed from the hole and over Leighton's shins and the Negro's knees. After ringing a few more strokes, Leighton spun the chuck in the hole and lifted it. Once he fixed the leather washer against the hole, he and Miasma lowered the large drill chuck. "Sledges," Leighton called. The Negroes lifted their hammers and stood around Leighton, who knelt to hold the chuck. He fixed his eyes on the center of its head, the tiny shingles of gleaming iron where so many hammers had fallen. Everything around him was quiet. He looked up, and all the Negroes were standing, the heads of their sledges still resting on the ground. The Negroes glanced at one another, grinning.

Miasma cleared his throat. "You one brave man, Mr. Morkan."

Out at the gates, along the quarry's wrought iron boundaries, white, stunned faces looked on. "Come on," Leighton hollered.

When he felt the sledges rise, he braced himself, forced his fists down against the leather washer. One sledge fell. Two. Three. The Negroes were slow, but they held their intervals. One. Two. The water boy poured. Down came the sledges. Leighton turned the chuck, which was moving well. One. Two. Three. He turned the chuck. "Keep on," he hollered to them. His heart was pounding with delight. They learned quick as retrievers.

He looked up at Miasma, and the Negro's chest swelled. Miasma reared his head back, brought the hammer down, and from his pink mouth, he bellowed a sudden melody. "Ho-o-o-old on!"

Leighton flinched.

The water boy and two drillers shouted: "Hurrummmmm." Leighton whistled to the water boy, who dribbled water against the bit down near the washer.

Down came the sledges. Two. Three. Slurry squirted onto his shins.

"Ho-o-o-o-old on!"

Three. Then the first sledge rang.

"Hurrummm." The Negroes bellowed and hammered, their arms gleaming as they rose, their chests swelling, great cables of effort scoring their black necks. It was a song and a shout, rising an octave as the drill crept down. The falling hammers syncopated the song as it spread down the cliffs so that each drill crew sang a part of it to Leighton's alarm. Miasma introduced a new verse, and the original tune wove the background, the hammers ringing and syncopating Miasma's call and the crew's response.

O, Evangeline she keeps me (ring)	Ho-old on!
Workin on the road, hah! (ring)	Hurrum!
The captain's at her cabin, (ring)	Hurrum!
Driver waitin' in the fold. (ring)	Ho-old on!

At the gate, the onlookers stared, grim as wet goats.

The chuck reached mark. Leighton hooked two fingers in his mouth and whistled. The Negroes jolted, withdrew their sledges, blinked at him. All was quiet in their huddle.

He bent to the chuck, waved Miasma down to him. The Negro crouched with him. After hesitating, he clasped his hands over Leighton's. Miasma's hands were warm, the texture of his palms rasping like the chapped skin of a cow's udder. Leighton imagined for an instant how his hands must feel to Miasma, dried and hardened from years of lime. Together they spun the chuck, thrusting with their shoulders to lift it. His head was so close to Miasma's, he could smell the salt of the Negro's sweat and feel the needling of his whiskers. Together they heaved.

"Do you all have to sing?" Leighton asked him in a grunting whisper.

"Oh, yes sir."

"O, Sacred Heart of Jesus," Leighton said.

They raised the chuck, sloppy, wet, and heavy as a newborn calf.

Odem busied himself that week traveling to market. In the dust and dimness of a building the quarry bought for back taxes, Odem and his newly hired store boys arranged his goods— rows of third rate lumber, lanterns and boots and nails and bolts salvaged from wrecks on White River, onions and mel-

67

ons gone soft at monger barrows, army belts, powder that crackled, hardtack and wormy flour, whiskey that burned the throat, cider that smelled close to vinegar, and burlap sacks for curtains. After the first week's work, in the evening, gray as spirits, the Negroes entered bearing flimsy scrip coupons of sumac red blaring: TENDER OF MORKAN QUARRY. STORE MERCHANDISE ONLY. Leighton strode into the store expecting to feel exalted—he had fought in the war and now he had given the Negro opportunity as never before. But as he watched the Negroes' faces fall, watched them finger old army canvas and chewing tobacco dry as leather, a tumult grew in him. He stammered something to Odem about getting more light in the store, then he left. The new hires spent so long in the desultory choosing of goods for their pay, the slips left their fingers touched with rouge.

Patricia rode to the Irish house on a paint the Weitzer bought from a Union soldier returning to Arkansas. She named the horse Searcy. The soldier was from Searcy, but most appealing to her was that the name sounded inbred and British, like Chauncey or Cedric. The horse paused and shuddered, and she tensed in the saddle. If it had a real conniption, she intended to leap from it.

Today marked two weeks before her fourteenth birthday. To Germans of the Weitzer's caste, southern Germans, lapsed Catholics of Bohemia, it was the year of marriageable age. Sweat itched at her forehead and the humidity in the air made her head pound. She bore a note from the Weitzer to the young Morkan folded and sealed with wax. When Searcy stumbled toward the shade, she jerked him back to the sunlight. She held the note up. Along the road, a hot wind blew, waving the oak leaves to show their undersides tan with dust.

She could not make out all of Weitzer's writing, but the jist was what she expected—something about the arrival of cousins from Friestatt and of a concert and picnic in celebration of Patricia Weitzer's fourteenth birthday. The Weitzer cordially invited Leighton Shea Morkan.

She whacked the note against the horse's neck. Searcy ducked and bobbed his head as if in angry affirmation. At least today was Saturday, and the Irish would be grubbing in his pit.

She came across the Morkan Negress tromping from the spring house with two buckets. Patricia halted the horse, but the Negress only grunted and passed her.

"Girl!" Patricia shouted.

Judith stopped. Slowly she turned.

"I have a notice for the Morkan." Patricia extended the note. The Morkan. Before the war it would have been impossible to conceive of one so rough and young being the head of a household.

Judith shrugged the two buckets up. She turned back toward the house. A pump in the house made much sense, but here these Irish had no sense, and this poor creature had to slog around after their water.

Patricia wheeled the horse and forced the Negress to halt. She held the note before Judith. "You *will* take this to the Morkan."

Judith set the buckets down and snatched the note Patricia held to her.

"And please do spill all manner of water on it," Patricia said.

Judith lurched back from the horse, which began bobbing its head, mincing, and backing away. She watched the Dutch girl jerk and sway and finally turn the horse, then gallop in spurts down the hill. Judith rubbed the note between her thumb and fingers. It was fibrous, like a tobacco leaf, only thicker. The Dutch had stopped and was scolding the horse while the dumb animal circled.

Judith's father, Johnson Davis, lifted one of the buckets. Johnson was a tall Negro, only a ring of hair left above his ears. He peered over her shoulder at the folded note, then stuck his chin out at the Dutch girl battling her skittish horse. Judith nodded.

Johnson shook his head. "Mmph. Bad tribe a'coming."

The Dutch girl circled the horse again.

Leighton slapped the newspaper against the desk hard enough to make Odem jump. At the rickety easel across the office Odem was sorting invoices from the store, his prosthetic unstrapped beside him. It was late afternoon, and the heat and humidity were so tangible the air could be lapped.

"You read this?"

"It is *your* mail. I do not read your mail."

"Who does this son of a bitch think he is?" Leighton waved the newspaper, which was open to a column by Justinian Ziggler, the publisher of the *Daily Leader*. "Listen to this." Leighton held the paper up.

Two Negroes appeared at the slat window. They were arguing about an ox sled and jabbing each other. "Git," Odem said. They blinked and backed away. Negroes had been in Leighton's employ now for three full weeks. The crowd at the gates had dwindled to some former laborers, a few skulking locals, and bitter ex-Confederates. Unemployable by mandate of the new state constitution, they hooked their arms on the wrought iron gates and glowered at the Negroes all day.

"Listen," Leighton said. "Mister Ziggler says, 'It would be like an Irish to return our city's good favor by hiring Niggers at unlivable rates. A Nigger can eat lime, creosote, and sawdust and so can live off what this Mick pays; but Whites must eat human fair, or else eat humans. In my thirty-eight years of journalism ...' Why, that pecker gnat! He's not even forty year old! ' ... thirty years of ... I have had the good fortune to interview a cannibal chieftain from the Spice Islands name of Seth. Our Seth was a right fleshy, lusty fellow, and he claimed a fattened Irish made a fine six courses.'"

Leighton rolled the paper and flung it across the office. He stood and paced, struck a match against the desk but snapped the red phosphorous tip off. He threw the broken matchstick toward a window.

Odem turned slowly to him on the stool. "You expected what? Congratulations? A heart felt thank you?"

"If Mister Ziggler has a problem with my quarry, I'd like him to come here to me. I don't want him airing his piss in public."

Odem raised his eyebrows and smirked. "It has been a long time since we've had a regular one, but let's recall what newspapers are: the fount of knowledge for the rabble, composed for, of, and by our lowest common denominator."

"Well, I am longer a citizen of this place than he, longer than many here today I daresay. I got a right to speak my mind. I'm gonna write that man a letter for his paper."

"Write you one, then," Odem said, kneading his forehead, his eyebrows furrowing. He caressed the invoices as if they were suffering damage from all this fracas.

Scowling, Leighton sat behind his desk and took out a steel pen and ink well. The old pen was so battered it appeared to have been fired through a rifle. He penned a letter.

To Justinian Ziggler, the people of Springfield, and the Readers of The Daily Leader:

I trust that journalism is often brash and insolent and full of huggermugger and name calling in order to sell papers. What draws more dolts to the window than a whore in a tirade? Probably only honest pistol fire.

Not withstanding, I must answer Mr. Ziggler's column of this date. Mr. Ziggler claims my Irish-ness has caused me to hire freedmen and thus put Whites out of work. I have two difficulties with this. First, the war is won. The slave is now a freedman, and so is obligated to work, or lay about on your doorstep and discover trouble. I have given freedmen of this town an opportunity to tire themselves honestly and walk home with money in goods and wares. It's a simple idea, and simplicity, if I've read right, is rather American. Second, I have denied opportunity to no race. Any White, Negro, Red-man, Yellow skin, Turk, Spaniard, or Arkie that wishes may walk through the gates at Summit and National Sts. I will hire him for what these Negroes make, and keep him so long as he can work with other races and wield a hammer or crow bar. In addition, Whites hold

MY SKILLED POSITIONS OF BLASTER, BLACKSMITH, DERRICK MAN, CARPENTER, MECHANIC, MANY OTHERS TOO NUMEROUS TO NAME. THESE GOOD MEN MAY TAKE GRAVE OFFENSE AT MR. ZIGGLER'S LEAVING OUT THEIR NUMBERS AND ABILITIES WHILE INCLUDING THEM IN THE FOIBLES ZIGGLER SEES IN WHAT IS IN REALITY A CALM AND HARD WORKING RACE.

I APOLOGIZE IF LOGIC FAILS TO SPARK HUBBUB AND SALES. I IMAGINE THE CLARITY OF MY RHETORIC, THE PRECISION OF MY SPELLING, AND MY ABILITY TO FOCUS ON THE ISSUE AT HAND WILL KEEP THIS LETTER FROM APPEARING IN YOUR PAPER.

RESPECTFULLY YOUR SERVANT,
LEIGHTON SHEA MORKAN
PROPRIETOR, MORKAN QUARRY

Leighton folded the letter and handed it to Odem. "Get one of the boys to have this set at McCormack's and print up say four hundred of them. Then get them all over town, but save one for Mr. Ziggler's paper."

He followed Odem from the office and mounted his horse, rode the ox trail up the cliffs. A foreman stopped him. Two White blasters were waiting with their hands on their hips, kegs of powder at their feet. At the cliff's edge, three Negroes had their arms crossed over their chests, feather chucks and small hammers in their hands.

"Now, *you* tell the boss," the foreman rasped. His face was red and a purple vein stood out on his forehead.

One of the Negroes lowered his chin. "We don't want to feather no stone with them webbings on it." He had to yell over the singing of a drill team down the cliff. He pointed to the stone, which was webbed white in a geometric maze. Lovely stone, tight as quartz. "It's bad portent, sir," he said.

"Who are you?"

"Manfred."

"Manfred, youns want back on a stone breaking crew?" Leighton asked.

All three Negroes shook their heads quickly.

"Then quit or feather that."

Manfred's jaw buckled. He glanced at his fellows. The Negroes handed the foremen their feathering tools.

Leighton hopped down off the horse, gave the reins to a grinning White blaster. He took a drill and hammer from the foreman, grabbed Manfred's wrist, then jerked him to a spot lined between the large drill holes. With effort, he pulled Manfred to the ground. The Negro was trembling. The taut muscles of his black arms quivered.

Leighton forced the drill into Manfred's hand. Kneeling, he pressed the tip to the stone. Manfred lurched, but Leighton held him.

Leighton raised the hammer. "Manfred," he snapped. "I'll knock you right off this cliff, and no law will hang me for it."

Manfred let out a sob.

Leighton squeezed Manfred's fist around the drill and began to tap steel into the stone. Manfred shook, cast quick glances at Leighton, then at the edge of the cliff, then the sun. Every strike, Leighton yanked Manfred's wrist around to turn the drill.

When the drill reached mark, Leighton nodded to it, and released Manfred's hand. The black hand opened for an instant, the fingers stretching. Then Manfred plucked the drill from the powdery hole, where it left a blue cone.

Manfred stared, his head hanging down.

"See," Leighton said to Manfred and the other two. He stood. "See. He's still here. No lightning, no buzzards, no warlocks. It's just rock. God made it for you to pound on!"

The other two Negroes shook their heads, but took the feather drills back from the foreman. They helped Manfred to his feet. Manfred was weeping quietly. Leighton shook his head, and remounted his horse. These Negroes were a passing strange people. Yet he could recall laborers from the Ozarks hills who insisted that certain picks or shovels bore curses that made them inoperable. For all peoples life can be a daunting mystery.

After work, Leighton entered The Quarry Rand with Odem and Menzardo, the stonecutter. Leighton felt a keen sense of abandonment when he saw Archer was absent. Several of Leighton's printed tracts glowed in the muck of the floor. Some of the men at the counter were reading the tracts. Outside it was raining hard, so the bar was crowded, men hunched at tables or gathered around a cripple who was playing the accordion. The cripple had both legs amputated, one at the knee and one near his groin. He wobbled when he played. Every half minute or so, thunder clapped loudly, clinking the mugs on Shulty's wall and rattling the rafters above them, lightning revealing sodden faces. Near the door, a leak poured down loud as a cow pissing on canvas.

Leighton and his men leaned on the counter. Menzardo's height and shining, curly black hair and olive skin drew looks. Those who glanced at Menzardo stared at Leighton.

Shulty brought over three stouts. "Evening, author." He did not smile.

"How's the weather in here, Shulty?" Leighton asked.

Shulty shook his head. He moved down the counter to a customer who whispered to Shulty while glancing at Leighton. Shulty backed away from the customer but nodded.

Leighton complained to Odem and Menzardo that he was going to have to attend a Dutch girl's birthday picnic, Weitzer's daughter.

"Banker," said Odem, brightening.

"*Was* a banker," Leighton said. "Now a debtor in possession."

Not smiling, Menzardo nudged Leighton, who slowly turned to face the bar room.

A smith in dungarees and a soiled work shirt wobbled up. He wore a derby, too small for him, that sat high up on his greased red hair. His beard was neatly trimmed, and beneath it was soot-blackened skin. Above the yeast and urine stench of the bar, Leighton smelled charcoal on the smith's shirt. A dusting of metal filings made the backs of his hands and his cuffs sparkle like felt fresh rubbed with mercury. The crippled accordion player started a slow waltz.

The smith clenched Leighton's tract rolled in his fist and pointed the flyer at Leighton. "Folks says you're *this* writer fellow."

Leighton nodded.

"I think that man Zigguller was right."

"That's your prerogative."

The smith smiled at the men who watched from tables nearby. The cripple began to sing an un-rhyming gibberish of Spanish in a lovely baritone at the top of his lungs. The smith craned his neck. He had a hare lip and Leighton could not imagine the man appearing happy. The smith swallowed and raised his voice. "You ain't going to spend time convincing me otherwise?"

Leighton lifted his stout and drank, then shrugged. "I should try and convince a man who reads a newspaper and believes what's in it?"

The smith dropped the tract, which fluttered to the dirt floor.

"*Yo soy un hombre bueno, si alguien bueno en este lugar,*" the cripple sang. The accordion hummed and crackled.

Leighton eased off the counter and locked eyes with the smith.

The smith's eyes were clear, his pupils black and intent. His neck was rigid. "I'll feel real insulted if you don't convince me."

Thunder walloped the air above them, then rolled far away.

The cripple, watching them warily, charged into a rollicking version of "Camptown Races," his one good stump of a leg pumping at a set of brass cymbals.

With a lean forward, the smith touched one of his pockets and brought out a flash of silver. Menzardo grabbed the smith's shoulder, but the smith caught Leighton in the left arm just above his elbow. A spear of pain erupted and made Leighton's eyes bulge.

He snared the smith's knife hand and held it in his fist. The smith thrashed and glowered at Leighton, then Menzardo. Across the room, the accordion wheezed and quit like a stomped goose. The bar was silent save for the stools slopping in mud as men rose to back away from the disturbance.

The knife dangled from the sleeve of Leighton's coat. At his thumb a warm pulling began, and drops of blood hung and fell. He eased the knife free. It was a little pocket knife, just big enough to clean a man's nails. Folding it shut, he closed his fist around it.

"Let him go," Leighton said to Menzardo.

Menzardo complied. As the smith fell forward, Leighton caught him across the jaw with the knife vised in his fist. The smith reeled, struck out at Leighton, but cracked his chin against the counter. He slumped to the floor and lay breathing quickly, head twisted far to the side.

Odem stood wide eyed for an instant, then plucked the smith's derby off the floor. He placed the little hat in the middle of the smith's hunched ass.

Patrons around them laughed and applauded.

Leighton turned and propped the elbow of his wounded arm on the counter. He worked his fingers, then reached in his jacket, pulled out a tenspot eagle and let it spin to a rest on the sticky countertop.

"Get me a whiskey and set up the bar," he said to Shulty.

Danny Beauchamp scurried between tables, popping ales down before customers.

Later, once the rain quit, Leighton and Odem returned to the quarry for their horses. Rapidly the last blanket of clouds, hemmed in a line straight as a cut in fabric, pulled away to the northwest. The moon emerged searing white like an ancient seal.

Leighton's arm throbbed. "If that had been a real knife?"

Odem glanced at him, his blonde hair shining blue. "It was a real knife."

Leighton shook his head. "A man wanted to kill me so bad he tried a pocket knife. That scares the hell out of me."

"It ought to."

"And here you said this would solve every damn thing."

"We had an old Dutch cook in our regiment used to say, '*Immer etwas.*'"

"Meaning?"

"Ask that Dutch girl you're a'courting."

V

IN A WEEK, THE TOWN'S TAILOR CREATED A POPLIN COAT dyed indigo with high, thin lapels, and sharp creased pants from a gray material that shimmered. Johnson Davis groomed Leighton's horse until it gleamed and even braided its mane as if for a race. Leighton brought with him one of the new kerosene lamps from Providence, Rhode Island, a gift for the Weitzer girl's birthday soirée. Where the trail to Weitzer's began, laughter swirled in the woods; someone called out a number and a color in German, and children squealed.

In the clearing, there was a wide circle of kids and young adults with arms interlocked. As the circle turned, some children cavorted inside holding ribbons high while others tried to grab the ribbons from upheld hands. Off to the side was a party of a dozen adults. When Leighton cantered from the trees, even the children running in the circle fell silent and came to a stop. They blinked at him. Several of the women set down their drinks, and the men stood. Leighton readjusted the lamp cradled in the crook of his arm. He kept the lamp in its canvas sack. His hair was slicked with a grease carried at the Morkan store, his beard waxed. He felt as if he were wearing some strange helmet and chin strap.

A little girl asked in a high voice, "*Ist der Beamter oder Sodat?*"

Several of the older children laughed out loud. Claus Weitzer strode forward and offered to take Leighton's horse. Leighton handed Weitzer his gift, managed a nod as he dismounted.

"Gustave!" Weitzer called.

A young boy wandered forward, his hands crammed in his pockets. He stared at Leighton with wide eyes.

"Lead the Morkan's horse to the tie in the grove," Weitzer said. He pointed.

The boy did so, but stared at Leighton as long as he could.

Leighton cleared his throat. "Thank you, Mr. Weitzer, for your kind invitation." He put his hand to his chest and bowed slightly. In the corner of his eye, he caught a kid in knickers imitating him.

Weitzer led Leighton to the gathering of gentlemen. "May I present my brother Karl." A man in a long swallow-tailed coat bowed. Weitzer introduced several other men, whose grumpy, caustic names broke on Leighton then shattered away. He nodded to each. Those who wore coats chose drab blacks and browns; most of the men wore suspenders with fresh-boiled, white shirts and black trousers.

"Claus tells us you are a quarrymaster?" one asked.

Faces frowned, brows wrinkled. Leighton wondered if a quarrymaster were a good thing to be among these Dutchmen. "Yes, sir. And owner."

Karl, the brother, stared down at Leighton. He had a very thin face, and the top of his forehead shined. "I understand mines often have a short span of usefulness." He tapped his chin with his index finger as if impatient. His skin was exceptionally white, and his nails were crisp, rounded scallops. Leighton spotted him for a clerk, maybe another banker like Claus.

"Thankfully, ours falls the other side of *often*." Leighton expected a smile that did not come. All the Dutch wore faces as cold as bolts on an iron bridge truss.

"The Morkan Quarry," Claus began, "is a constant resource in our town." He nodded to each man. He blinked at Leighton and smiled, but his eyes wrinkled such that Leighton saw the effort. "I have seen quarries in bluffs and shelves. Yours, though, is a pit going down. Is this more practical?"

Leighton's collar itched and sweat crawled at his sides. More practical? The stone is under the earth; how else expose it? "We keep everything practical, sir."

All but Weitzer laughed.

The men chatted about fields and wheat, loans and interest, their English fading into long stints of German; a man with stiff cuffs and no collar talked about a complex irrigation system, and Leighton made the mistake of nodding when the man ended his sentences. Ditches and dikes, levers, sluices, percolation, Leighton nodded, but watched the young folks' circle, which had resumed its game. Many in the circle hooked fingers in their mouths and whistled shrilly. Patricia was among these. Her straight hair ended in thick, waxy curls, which bobbed as she whistled. Her neck colored and vertical cables of tendon stood out along it. Though she was taller than Leighton, he saw she was still a child with a merry heart, and belonged in the circle with the young.

The irrigation man was still speaking, gesticulating, his bulging hazel eyes imploring Leighton. Leighton nodded. From near the cabin a cowbell was ringing.

The man smiled. "I must talk with you more at dinner. I knew you would appreciate the difficulties I face."

All the guests gathered and lined up at a long table near the Weitzer cabin where a buffet had been set. There were potatoes and several kinds of bread, corn, beans, tart and glowing gooseberry preserves, and ham. The beer was exceptional, crisp and very dark. Leighton sat beneath an oak, and the irrigation man resumed his talk. Other men avoided the irrigation man when they chose their seats.

Leighton stood as Weitzer and his family stationed themselves very near him. Patricia nodded to him, but frowned as she sat. Leighton remembered Weitzer's wife as being stouter than the woman in black now at Weitzer's side.

Leighton lifted his mug to Weitzer. "This is very fine beer."

Weitzer nodded and thanked him.

Leighton resumed his seat. Only the irrigation man spoke, but often Mrs. Weitzer squinted at Leighton. She ate very little and watched Leighton as one might a hornet.

When the children grew restless, Karl began fetching gifts to Patricia from a small table. She opened these, and held each up to spatters of applause. There was a quilt, jars of colored liquid something—Patricia announced each gift in German—a turban-looking hat with silver braiding, which drew sighs of pleasure from the women.

Patricia grunted as she lifted Leighton's gift in its canvas bag. She read Leighton's full name from the card, then slowly undid the bindings. The irrigation man patted Leighton on the shoulder, then grinned at the Weitzers and company, pointing at Leighton. Leighton's back itched in pinpricks of sweat.

The canvas fell back, and Patricia stared at the kerosene lamp. There was silence. Several couples glanced at each other. An elderly woman raised a quizzing glass to her eye and glared, her head weaving.

Patricia raised the lamp higher, almost triumphantly, like a seated lady liberty. "*Ein guter Trick,*" Patricia announced.

There was laughter and clapping all around. Weitzer smiled his strained smile at Leighton. Somehow they all thought the present was a gag. Leighton nodded and let them do so. Patricia lit the lamp, and when it began to glow a searing white, everyone gathered around, murmuring in astonishment. Compared to the usual bear oil and whale oil lamps, this was penetrating starlight.

The elderly woman with the quizzing glass lowered her magnifier, then raised the square glass again. "Pah! *Zu rauchend.*" She shambled back to her spot beneath the trees.

Patricia stared intently at the lamp, her forehead wrinkling. She caught his eye, raised and bobbed her eyebrows, and this vexed him further.

Why had he come to the Weitzer's? Patricia was marriageable, and the land beneath him, her dowry, was perfect for a quarry, rife with lime, heavily wooded. Weitzer's silly sentence—the Morkan Quarry is an ever-present source of resources—whatever it was he said, confirmed that Weitzer entertained this marriage idea, too. In speaking well of Leighton, the man was defending a prospective son-in-law. He looked at Patricia. Such long thin arms, shoulders that stooped because she was ashamed of her height, her face, that chin with its horseshoe stiff jut, she reminded him of a painting he had seen in a Ruthenian immigrant's locket, some Habsburg princess, homely as a boot's heel. She stared at the lantern, a slight frown on her face. She was Claus and Marta's daughter. Like Leighton, no immigrant but the American child of immigrants.

"You must join the younger people," Weitzer said. "Take your beer and chat with them."

A dozen or more young adults gathered in a knot near Patricia, who was sitting on one of the stump benches. Leighton hesitated to join them, since they were examining her gifts. But when he saw two young gentlemen smoking he proceeded. All in the circle chattered in German, but this ceased when he approached. After a moment of silence, those who could resumed in English.

Leighton offered a cigar to a young man with mutton chop sideburns. The man had just opened his cigarette case, but closed the case and nodded at Leighton's cigar. Leighton pulled his cigar knife and pick from a coat pocket. The knife was on a golden Albert chain and bore a pearl handle engraved with his initials. Its flash of motion made several of the young men turn to him. He cut two cigars, burrowed a divot in one, then handed the prepared cigar to the man.

"An accomplished smoker." The man said bowing slightly.

"Accouterments are among the chief pleasures of any worthwhile vice."

Several laughed. Even the young women had turned to him now. Some glanced at Patricia, who was absorbed in reading a shoe box lid. Leighton offered cigars all around, and two other young men took him up on it. They introduced themselves— one with sideburns named Ferdinand; a tall boy with Karl's skin and face named Rodolphe; the last a jaundiced, thin boy named Ansel. The rest were young women.

"Tell me, Mr. Morkan, did you fight in the war?" Ferdinand asked.

Leighton nodded, puffed, his lips smacking around the cigar. "Yes."

"In the east, or did you remain here?" Rodolphe asked.

"Here. And don't sweat it, boys. Union Home Guards. Republican through and through."

"Of course," Ferdinand said. "How else would you still legally run such a great business that Claus speaks so highly of. And often."

Brows lowered, the three German men all flashed glances at one another. And Leighton felt himself tensing and assessing which of the Dutch would be best to take down first. That puny, jaundiced one? Or maybe the big and tipsy Ferdinand? Bloody him to the grass and the trouble would cease, yes.

"Still here must have been somewhat dull." Rodolphe said.

Leighton shook his head. "Sadly, it was all very exciting."

Rodolphe watched his own smoke curl up toward the trees. "I remember in the Cumberland in Virginia…"

"Please," said Patricia. "Could we not? I am trying to read."

Rodolphe scowled down into his beer.

Patricia held a shoe box lid from an outfit called DORING'S. A slogan on its top read, "Reliable Shoes, Slippers and Rubbers. EVERYBODY WEARS THEM."

"Ears, please," Patricia said. She smiled and held up a sheaf of paper gingerly between the nails of her thumb and middle finger. "This is the DORING'S WITCH. It will tell your future by revealing your true inner disposition. The witch, through me, will bare your soul."

The sheaf of paper was gray crepe, pointed at one end, dove-tailed at the other. It looked more like a minnow than a witch.

"Line up," Patricia said in a deep falsetto, "and I will uncover your past and mysteries to come." She tucked her chin, puffed her cheeks, and raised her shoulders, rocking from side to side. With the new Turkish turban pinned to her hair and her pretty dress spread like a fringed awning all across the stump she seemed comically mystical. Her polished black high-lows stuck up like two exclamation points at the dark gray hem of her dress. The dress was the soft gray and melon pink of a cloudy, humid dawn. And it was not homespun or cut loose as a sack, but tailored precisely to her long and narrow trunk and exceptionally long legs. The gray crescents of her eyes suddenly caught him watching her. She pursed her lips and cocked an eyebrow at him. Then she snapped her long arms out to draw all back to attention.

Rodolphe stood first in line, and all circled to watch.

"Make sure your left palm is moist." Patricia touched Rodolphe's palm, closed her eyes. She let her head roll back and gave her shoulders and long arms a subtle tremor. Some of the women giggled. She placed the witch in his palm.

Everyone pressed forward. The paper crackled and the pointed end of the witch rose. Patricia plucked the paper from

Rodolphe's hand. She consulted the box lid, keeping it close to her flat chest. Shutting her eyes, rubbing the bridge of her nose she intoned: "Rodolphe Weitzer, son of Karl and Yvonne," she spoke in the deep voice. "You have always been jealous and contentious. You will beat your poor wife with no mercy."

Squeals, laughter, and applause. Rodolphe grabbed for the box lid, but Patricia, who was holding the witch to dry in the sun, dodged side to side. "Grünhaagen trickery," Rodolphe said at last. He stomped off to the beer kegs amid more laughter. When he returned with his beer, he was still blushing.

Patricia read the fortunes of two other young ladies. They were both thin and tall like Patricia. The witch determined one girl coquettish, the other true and constant. Almost all participated, laughing; their chatter returned to German.

The best dressed among the young ladies was a squat woman whose figure was almost perfectly round. She wore a turban much fancier than the one given to Patricia, and under it her jowly, smiling face glowed with sweat. Above her astonishing bosom was a wad of black crepe. Sequins shone in stripes on her dress like brads stretched taut over a gas balloon. She swung herself forward in stages, and the young people parted and bowed. She extended her left hand, and, on a swollen finger, a large diamond sparkled.

Patricia held her hand for a moment. "Oh, Anna Julianna! What do you need to know of your fortune? It is already so well made."

Anna smiled and rolled her eyes at this.

Patricia placed the witch on Anna's palm. The witch crackled and curled in a perfect circle. Patricia removed it, and consulted the box. "Anna Julianna Weitzer Sonnenberg, daughter of Helmut and Gerta, widow of Colonel Sonnenberg of Silesia, you are in love and will soon remarry."

Anna grunted. "God forbid!"

The company and Anna laughed.

"Take my fortune, Anna?" Patricia asked. She held the witch to Anna, who plucked it with care.

Patricia extended her palm. Anna placed the witch there. After a moment, the paper made constant, rapid vibrations, so erratic that Anna cried out.

83

Patricia lifted the paper. "Not to worry." She handed Anna the box top.

Anna looked up at Patricia from the box top, astonished. Patricia's eyes implored her, a nervous smile suddenly flickering then vanishing once their eyes met. "This says. . ." Anna began.

Several called for her to read as Patricia had. Anna nodded, her chins trebling. Pausing, she consulted the box top more deeply. She managed a deep grumble, comically bad as it could not compare to Patricia's. "Patricia Grace Weitzer, daughter of Claus and Marta, you are very passionate and should leave this little place and come live with me and let us spoil ourselves in all our passion as women should."

"Bah!" Ferdinand said. "She's for women's suffrage, too." He elbowed Leighton. "Doring's wouldn't write that. Foul, I say!"

"Mr. Morkan's fortune is untold," Rodolphe said.

Leighton shook his head, held up a hand to silence the protests of the men and Anna. "It's a bloody story that ends in disaster."

"Come now, poet." Ferdinand weaved forward and gripped Leighton by the arm. Ferdinand's face was very red and his sweat smelled of beer. He led Leighton before Patricia.

She was staring down, fingering the witch. She looked up at him, and her frown made even Ferdinand fall quiet and release him.

"Really, I must abstain," Leighton said.

"Don't fear the fortune teller," Patricia said. She rolled her eyes back in her head so that only the trembling whites shone. She spoke in the deep, raspy voice. "Or have the Jesuits told you how we gypsies cavort with the dead?"

Leighton grinned at this, but he felt Ferdinand stiffen. Rodolphe, even Anna, blinked at her with earnest, pale looks.

Anna patted him on the shoulder, the flesh at her arm swinging like a sack. "Let me apologize. Our gypsy cousin is a little garrulous." Anna planted herself very near him; her sides gave, pressed against him, warm and oppressively sticky. "Extend your palm."

He did so; Patricia held the witch and stared at his hand. Anna gripped his arm. There was the gray callus that covered most of his palm, gnarled and rumpled, marbled with cracks of

84

white as a result of constant exposure to the alkali of the lime. It was thicker than any scab, and just as hard and ugly as the sole of a runaway Negro traveler's foot. The rest of the circle drew back. Leighton's arm wavered. With a detached almost scientific wonderment, Patricia drew her index finger slowly across the middle of his palm. Leighton felt her nail drag and bump over his callus as distantly as a drowsing creature at the bottom of a frozen pond might perceive a skate cutting along the ice above. All in the circle were quietened at this sudden intimacy and their cousin so boldly absorbed in this burly Mick's gross anatomy.

"Your palm is damp enough," she finally said. She placed the witch on his callus.

The paper remained perfectly flat. The men in the party edged forward. Several women withdrew and whispered. The gray crepe stayed absolutely still.

Patricia plucked it from him. She scanned the shoe box, blinked, scanned again. Then she tucked a curl behind her ear, turned to Leighton. "Leighton Shea Moorken, son of the late Michael Moorken, the earth has made a terrible impression on you, and has scoured away your soul entirely." She inserted the witch in the Doring's box and sealed the top.

Ferdinand patted Leighton on the back, his eyebrows rising as if there were a question he couldn't ask. "Well, fellow," he said, then stammered something. He left for the keg.

"This is good," Leighton said. He raised his beer to the air. "Praise Be! With no soul, I'm pleased to do as I see fit." He gave Anna a pinch, and she clopped him across the back of the head.

"I am sure you two are the most shocking set I have seen," Anna said, but she grinned.

Someone called that melons were ready, and the party gratefully left Patricia and Leighton alone.

"May I get you some melon?" he asked, once the others were gone.

Patricia shook her head and smoothed her dress over her gangly legs.

"May I see the top of the box?" he asked.

She removed the lid and stuck it at him. A label was glued to the underside of the lid. Leighton read past the testamentary for Doring's shoes to a description of how to use and interpret the witch. Each movement had only a brief surmise afterwards. "Witch rolls over—extremely modest." There was no mention of the witch remaining motionless.

Grinning, he handed the box top to her. She replaced it on the box, then stared at her lap. After a moment he asked if she wished him to leave.

She raised her eyes to him. "I feel I am expected to converse with you," she said. "I feel I am expected to enjoy your company."

"Has your father told you so?"

She shook her head.

"And my father is dead." He puffed from the nub of his cigar. "We aren't required to have this conversation. Our hearts are free."

She arched her neck and appeared to glance over his shoulder at the others who were gathered in the shade many yards away. "I have heard my mother and father speaking." She met his gaze squarely, and the skin beneath her crescent-shaped eyes wrinkled. "I will tell you a fortune. You will propose to the Weitzer, or the Weitzer will simply offer the land for his good name as trustee and for forgiveness of his debt, and require that I come with the land." She adjusted her dress across her shoulders. It was gray and pink with a velvety sheen that reminded Leighton of gray uniforms he had seen on a grand Louisiana regiment. "You own the great quarry. You are man enough and madman enough to hire Negroes at near indenture wages then write in favor of it in the papers." When Leighton reacted to this she raised her eyebrows. "Oh, yes. They've noticed, aghast and amazed. You are a Titan and a Devil among my people. Of course, we will be married. You are a rung up in society, even if it is bought with fists and usury. You pig! Mick! A step up on the ladder purchased with their least desirable daughter."

Leighton was shocked at her perceptiveness and her vile, proud anger. So young, and yet when the sunlight shone on her brown hair, she seemed older and wizened. What had she seen in St. Louis with its yellow fever, its shackled prisoners, its hospitals full of dying, its hanging gallows?

"What if we refuse?" he asked.

86

"Then, we risk our birthright."

"I have mine. No risk for me."

In the fortune teller's deep voice, she said, "You may be born to more destiny than you know."

Her eyes shone gray-green like new juniper berries in a chill rain. Fortune teller, he thought. And suddenly he had an urge to take her in his arms. "What does the gypsy wish to do?" he asked.

She blinked at him. Then a slight smile crept to her face. "It is pleasant to be asked that. But my wishes do not matter. My father will have me married. If not to you, then to the next profitable alliance. At least you seem extremely profitable."

He dropped the cigar on the ground and crushed it with his foot. "What sort of wife would you make?"

Her eyes widened. "Are you so forward?"

"If they're going to handle this as business, I see no reason why we shouldn't."

Her jaw knotted. "I will be faithful, loyal, caring for my family."

"Don't give me flim-flam."

She turned red. "What do you want?"

He slipped his thumb under his lapel, spread his hand across the frills of his shirt. "As a husband, I offer you a quarry capable of twenty barrels of cement every 24 hours, tons of dimension stone a month, with great diligence, $1,000 a year clear profit. For now. I offer you two hundred acres and one of the few substantial houses standing in this county." He breathed, and bit his lip thinking. "I will be in your way only late evenings and Sundays. I drink and smoke. I know nothing of romance and have no time to learn. I tend to get fat, especially in winter."

She laughed, and he stepped back a bit. She put the tips of her fingers to her lips and calmed. "This is certainly a singular method of courting."

He shrugged. "Courting? This is a negotiation."

She scowled. "Well, then. Let us be cold. As a wife I offer you almost six hundred acres of land, here and scattered around and about the city. I offer you this small cottage. I offer you myself as a teacher to any children. I have taught in the best schools of the Missouri Synod. I know German, Latin, French, English, and I am accomplished in Mathematics. I have read the philosophers. Possibly, later in life…" She blushed and spoke toward her lap. "Possibly later in life I will have a figure like my mother's or as Anna's was once, but I fear I will remain as this."

He reached, hesitated, then touched her cheek. It had a soft fuzz to it. He tucked her hair behind her ear, and touched her cheek again with only his fingertips. Her eyes were such a strange gray and green.

He dropped his hand to her waist and gave her a hard squeeze just below her ribs. Her back arched, and her face crimsoned. "You are damn thin," he said.

She punched him sharply in the gut, then grabbed the collar of his shirt and twisted it. They held each other in a taut grip, her jaw jutting as if she expected a slap. "And you are a cross-eyed mongoloid," she said.

She pulled him to her, gagging him; he pushed her away, thumb dug deeply in her abdomen, fingers scoring her back. He felt their centrifugal fury, felt the humid sky bump and spin a notch. Then like dancers concentrating in mid step caught in their fear by their audience, he grinned, and her face softened.

"I suppose we've terrified your folks," he said.

"No," she said. "To really terrify them, we'll have to go through with it." Her lips curved, showing the tips of her teeth in a smile like a hound's at play.

VI

LATE SEPTEMBER AND THE AIR TURNED CRISP ON THE ride home. Some mornings, arriving at the quarry, Leighton and Odem found steaming goat entrails arranged over the gate, or crossed hickory switches woven into the wrought iron. Otherwise the town and the papers were sullen and quiet. Work assumed a martial order. Archer's wagons came then left full of stone or cement. Gray as ghosts scrabbling at the rocks, the freedmen labored in the shadows of the rifle-toting foremen. Above them wisps of cloud froze in the turquoise sky. Monarchs stumbled across the yard and waited in applauding coveys by the teal pool, sipping its bitter water with the shepherd's crooks of their black tongues. By mid-morning the churn drills rang down, and the butterflies rose in a swirling column propelled by the heat off the rock, hundreds of them, orange and black. Exhausted, the Negroes watched their exodus as soldiers on campaign will follow sparks above a campfire.

Leighton invited Weitzer for dinner. They traded compliments and thank yous, then ate. After a time, Leighton explained that he wished to call on Patricia, but his work at the quarry made that difficult of a week. And he didn't want to disturb the family on Sundays.

"I have no parents to chaperone us. How can such a dinner be arranged?"

When Judith stepped forward to serve them, the corners of her mouth pulsed.

Weitzer stabbed at the beef tongue wilting on his plate. "You could rather snatch her from our window and ride down to Hot Springs."

The next evening, Judith met Leighton in the barn. She held a dish of bread pudding from which little curls of steam

89

rose. When his horse was stabled, his tack stowed, she assumed a stance at the barn door as if barring him from leaving. He eased up to her.

"I brung you this," she said.

She sounded pitiful, a tone he had never heard from her.

He took a spoonful. "It's got rum in it. Been a long time since we had rum." He chewed. "Oh, it's fine, Judith."

She didn't smile. "You gone marry that Dutch?"

"That why I'm eating bread pudding in the barn?"

Judith swallowed. "I don't know what I'm doing." Her gaze seemed trackless.

Suddenly then he remembered her as a little girl, hiding with him from his furious mother. Judith had cut his hair, which was long once, silken and jet black. He was four, maybe, five, delighted at her violent attentions, and she had sliced his hair painfully with a fabric shears and done it up in rag ribbons like a pickaninny's, and they were hiding because the hair was all over the house. And he had looked up at her from their cover— one of his earliest memories—and realized in her stunned gaze that the Negress knew she was going to be beaten viciously, and, knowing that peril well himself, recognizing it for the first time in another's face, made him reach his little hands out, flecked with his black hair like splinters of carbon, reach out to comfort His Judith. His mother whupped her to a crimson lather with an oak stick that morning. Years.

"Judith, you'll always have a place here. You said I needed a wife."

They were quiet. The smell of rum rose between them.

"I didn't mean her." Her voice was a whisper. Against the evening she was a shadow, hard to parse.

"Who did you have in mind?"

She touched the edge of the bowl, ran her finger along its rim, but did not take it from him.

Leighton stared intently at her. The dark, heavyset, mournful woman before him was no longer his companion in mischief, his co-conspirator in crimes of warfare, his caregiver, his shadow-skinned demisister. "Who is this?" Leighton asked. "This is not My Judith. Where are you from?"

He used the echoes of their old childhood game, My Leighton, My Leighton, Where are you from? White cliffs and green water and skies without sun. From her stone stillness and the blank devastation on her round face, he could see there was no retrieving that faerie-tale land where the two of them invented fabulous origins and rambled unfettered in sunny Crownlands of their own creation.

"What you going do, Leighton?"

Rather than annoyance or offense at her effrontery, he felt his heart overturned. His marrying Patricia and bringing the Dutch to become lady over the household was going to cut through Judith's placid existence like the prow of a Man-of-War from an alien empire. He shook his head. "I might just marry her, Judith. That land over there, near six hundred acres, all down Rockbridge to Marionville Road." The steam of the pudding warmed his chin and neck. "Why be concerned? She is not a bad person. She's not evil."

She snorted. "Do not defend her to me. I judge that my own self in time."

Across the barn lot, down the meadow to the white stone tongue of the mansion's stairs, there came a pall of silence, as if the night guard, the dozens of clacking frogs in the forest and sloughs all turned in their keys and sabers. What Judith said promised conflict but also a proving before final judgment, and he counted that a blessing.

"Any other Colored, any other employee in my way, Judith, you know I would stake to the ground about now."

With a deep intake of breath, she turned on him and her gaze became focused. She took a head-to-toe measure of him, an assessment he wished he did not understand. After a moment she said, "That smell good, don't it?"

He nodded. She scooped two fingers full of the bread pudding, and he felt the pressure and insistence of her fingertips pressing down on the bowl as he held it. She popped them in her mouth. "Get me some better sorghum, I do this up right."

He took a spoonful. "It's right, Judith. It's right just as it is."

They ate in silence from the same bowl, the horses stamping behind them. When they finished, she looked at him again, at his chest and arms, his groin, and last his face. "Judith, what are you thinking?"

Outside the barn, there rose just the fingernail of a moon glowing in a cobalt sky. The rest of the satellite was a dusky circle of astonishing clarity. With its puddles and ridges so crisply visible it seemed very near, hovering right above the oaks, as if from the treetops a body could step up and walk upon it, like any bald, and choose to travel a narrow shoreline of inextinguishable brightness or a vast waste of shadow and turmoil.

Her nostrils flared, her eyes narrowed as if she were calculating the cost of that one far step.

He hesitated, then touched her cheek. She held his hand there, stroked his wrist. Her voice was like a rustle of fabric. "I used to dream about you when you was at the war. I dream you through fires and bullets and mens that came running towards you. They part and turn like birds at a steeple in my dream." She lowered her head slightly.

For quite some time he said nothing, so humbled, his groin ached as if in a charley horse. "I dreamed of you in the war." He lied. In the war, he had never dreamed of anything or anyone but bushwhackers in the woods, and how cold a knife's blade might be slicing his throat, how fiery lead would feel slammed into his shoulder. "When it was cold. When we didn't have a thing to eat."

She smiled, and a sigh of such pleasure came from her that he shivered. It was the best lie he could tell.

"Whatever you are thinking, Judith, you must put it from your mind."

"You never can know what I'm thinking, My Leighton." Then they walked to the house, same as any autumn night, but to Judith the air was electric with change like a meadow in which a tree has just been razed by lightning.

Saturday evening, Leighton set a second lamp on the dining room table. Reflections of the front windows gleamed on the polished cherry wood. Beneath the sheen of its wax, scars ran like silver strands of silk. During the week, Leighton had replaced the wrought iron in each window with new panes of glass in simple wooden frames. They would have cost a fortune, but he was able to barter in a combination of brick, lime, and a promise to lay a chimney himself for the merchant's daughter. "She wants to raise her babes at a hearth that says MORKAN, like her mother did," the merchant said. The merchant was chewing hard on a fresh twist of tobacco, his mandibles smacking like boots in wet mud. Refusing to shake Leighton's hand, he left him with a grunt, swiping the back of a knuckle at his browned lips.

Leighton ran a finger along the table's edge. Through the open windows a breeze swept the room. Out in the yard, he heard Johnson's solicitations as the Negro welcomed the Germans and asked for Patricia's reins. He imagined hearing the same words outside for forty more years, the deep assurance of the Negro, Patricia's clipped German accent. He fussed with his string tie and starched collar, smoothed the tails of his coat, checked the polish on his shoes. A cicada grunted fiercely in the trees.

Leighton hollered at Judith to have well water and wine ready. Through the gauze of the curtains, he saw Patricia pinch her dress at the waist and adjust it. On her head was the crimson Turkish hat with gold braiding; her forehead was so wrinkled with worry that the hat was skewed slightly. Claus and her uncle Karl flanked her, dark pillars in their black suits and vests. She knocked.

He opened the door. She wore a yellow dress with wide, frilled collars. Lace circled her long neck. Her boots were tall, made of stiff, new leather. She extended a package wrapped and tied with a golden braid. Leighton bowed. Her lips remained curved in a frown, and her chin protruded. With her eyes holding him in incisive crescents, he was struck with how intelligent they were, set in a long face made even stranger and more maudlin because she was smart. Her conning her party-goers with the Doring's witch still astonished him. With a mind like that he could finagle anyone he couldn't bully or kill. She nodded. Her voice was tremulous. "I wish to thank you for this gracious invitation."

"Please, it's my pleasure. And thank you, Claus and Karl, for coming."

He ushered them to the parlor. Claus and Karl removed their hats. They frowned and, like twins, they began regarding Morkan's old books with their chins raised. "Quite a library," Claus said.

93

Leighton tugged at the cuffs of his coat. They all took seats. Judith brought each of them a glass of water and a glass of wine. Leighton stood and offered to mix Patricia's water with her wine, but she shook her head sharply. Her cheeks flushed with color.

All four sat stiffly for a moment. Never had Leighton seen men with pleats as crisp and cuffs as flat and square. Patricia drank her wine, swallowed, then drank more, her gulps as voluble in the quiet as a drop of water falling in a cistern. Karl and Claus looked away from him.

Leighton asked after Patricia's mother, and Patricia said she was well. Leighton noted what a treat it must be to have family guests still, nodding to Karl. Karl's brow furrowed, and he plucked at the crease in his trousers.

"Yes, sir," Patricia said. She drank.

Her eyes widened for an instant; then she finished her glass. Leighton called for Judith, who re-filled Patricia's drink. As she withdrew, backing toward the door, Judith's eyes kept to the floor.

"Yes," Karl said, "family is indeed a comfort. But for you, Master Morkan, where do you take comfort. Your father was... ?"

Leighton felt his face warm. He began slowly. "My father, in the war, was imprisoned. Price's Rebels forced him to give up black powder."

Seated across from him with a kerosene lamp beside her, Patricia turned white. Claus had one eyebrow raised. "Forced?"

"Half the powder we spirited home. The rest we gave to them." In a long pause, they could hear Judith clop the stove shut far back in the kitchen. "It was a choice between doing business and keeping the quarry running or certain destruction."

Claus's eyes narrowed. Leighton knew the powder his father had relinquished to the Rebels may as well have spit the lead that nailed Claus's boys. To the Dutch the South was all one camp of armed oppressors. "And what choice would you have made were it yours alone to make?"

The room shrank to just Leighton and Claus. In the twilight with lamps flickering, Claus and his goatee, his narrow chin and broad forehead, his dark wiry hair created a sinister, foreign visage to Leighton. Months ago at war's end, a face like Claus's, a challenge like Claus's would've caused Leighton to reach for the stubby pepper-box he kept even now in his coat pocket.

Leighton leaned forward in his chair, braced his palms against his knees. Patricia turned gray as a limed ditch, her back straight with alarm. "When my Pa made the choice, I would have given the Rebels everything we had—powder, money, my home, my life. I was very young and wildly romantic. I was fifteen."

Despite Leighton's caveat, Claus's nostrils flared and through his slightly parted lips his gray teeth clenched tightly. "Patricia was but eleven, and yet wise enough to be without such romantic sentiments. Even then."

"Understand, Mr. Weitzer, I stood beneath a tent with Price, McBride, Shelby, that whole lot when they coerced my father. He had no choice."

Claus gripped the arms of his chair and seemed ready to bolt from it.

"Looking back on it, had I murdered them all, shot them down in that tent like John Wilkes Booth shot our President, why our town, our state would have been spared years of waste and terror and destruction!"

The Dutch exchanged glances from which Leighton could read nothing.

He lowered his voice. "I wish now that I had. Had shot them. Every one."

After taking a long breath, Claus relaxed in his chair. "There is much bile in our hearts as well toward the men you name." With his long, perfect fingers he motioned to Karl and Patricia. Claus pressed the tips of his fingers together, and from his face, Leighton sensed that they found a common ground in hate, a garden they might till together. "What of your father? How did he fare once the decision was made?"

"In Gratiot Prison, my Pa contracted consumption. He died here on the farm in one of the old slave cabins. He'd slept so long lying on dirt and filth in Gratiot, when he could sleep, he preferred a dirt floor." Leighton's voice hung and he stopped.

Judith padded in and checked each glass clutching a water pitcher as if it were a prize hen. She was careful to turn her back on no one.

95

Patricia swallowed. "You have no relations, then?" she asked.

"Cousins in Ireland that I have nothing to do with. Business associates, good employees." Judith was backing from the room, as Charlotte had taught her to do when serving, a quirk Leighton had never seen in other slaves in service. He noted Claus and Karl watching her, and his heart clenched up worrying that she might thump into the door frame and embarrass herself. "And Judith," he said. Hearing her name made her gait catch before she disappeared. "She was once our slave. She has always been at my side."

All three Germans frowned.

After a gruelingly quiet dinner, they took coffee on the front porch. Claus and Karl leaned against the railings while Leighton smoked and stayed several steps down from them. He felt some relief that they had survived the meal and there was no talk of the quarry or the Negroes or the newspapers. But could he endure more "callings" like this? More profound and hostile silences?

Patricia fidgeted. She stammered through a story of a bridge in St. Charles that had collapsed, and held her coffee cup as if it were a delicate ornament. In her eyes, in the way she leaned forward, Leighton could see a great force of will. She was trying to be interesting to a young man she knew relatively little about, who did not speak her language. But he marveled that she had memorized so much about a bridge. Claus and Karl murmured in German, and Leighton could tell something had irked Patricia's uncle.

Watching them talk, he felt as if he were on a porch in some Dutch town, maybe Freistatt or Hermann up north, privy to an intimate conversation between people he did not know. Judith's form shifted behind a window. She must have been watching. On seeing him look her way, she withdrew into the shadows of the house.

The older men finished their coffees and Claus asked if he and Karl might further peruse the Morkan library. Patricia curtsied so deeply and slowly to her chaperones that Leighton expected her to fall. Claus and Karl stepped into the house.

Patricia followed them with her glance, then turned to Leighton. "Thank you for what you said to my father of the rebellion. However awkwardly." She braved a smile.

Had the night been as rough on her as it had been on him? After a moment, Leighton felt disappointed in himself. As he watched her stiff shoulders rise and fall, he began to dwell on troubling connections between points in his conversation—the powder, his romance with the rebellion, her father's lost sons. "After tonight, do you think he is still inclined to have us marry?"

Patricia's eyes grew blank. She shrugged.

Leighton drew on the cigar. Above the blue oaks, the hint of a constellation sparkled like a necklace of jewels emerging from a dark tide. "Your uncle. He's against it."

She raised her palms to him, and from the wrinkles in her forehead, he imagined the two old Germans were mysteries to her as well.

She stood very still, squinting at the dusky silver veil of evening. Then her hand reached inside his coat. She bowed and rested her forehead against his shoulder.

He gripped her arm and held her away. "Are you drunk?"

She looked up at him, her eyes softening. The last cicadas of evening thrummed and droned. She dropped her forehead to his shoulder again. "Everything is binding all around us. It sounds like a mill wheel, a grind stone."

He hesitated, then touched her cheek, lifted her face. "They're only bugs."

"Like a spinning wheel with a frayed band."

He grinned, then said in her low gypsy voice. "The awful music of the cosmos."

She retained her frown. "That is neither Classical nor reassuring."

She was tall wearing her boots and their heels, she looked down on him. In the evening light her cheeks were pristine, blue and unblemished as if they had touched nothing rougher than silk in her lifetime. To his surprise he felt a force welling in him as if he were stone sweating and dripping from a swollen wellspring in his heart.

"Don't be afraid," Leighton said. His voice fell to a whisper. "Because I'm too damned afraid most times to really know what to do." They both smiled, and she gripped his suspenders and hooked her thumb there for a second. "What do you want, dear?"

She pulled her hands away and clasped them in front of her as if in prayer. "I want quiet. I want security. I want the war to go away." For a moment she seemed maudlin with her big chin stuck at the ground. "Well, all but the glorious parts. I'll keep Franz Sigel and my Germans charging at Pea Ridge. All the rest is for nattering old farts."

He smiled, then touched her neck. The calluses at his fingertips were so hard, he sensed only a whisper of her skin moist with the evening's dew. "There will be no quiet with me. Nothing is assured. And the inglorious war will follow you everywhere. There just might be a great deal of money, though." He touched the back of her head beneath the turban and the callus on his palm caught strands of hair before he drew away.

"Do we need suffer anymore dinners like this? And suffer them to torture us?

"Oh, *groß Gott*, let's not, please."

"Will you marry me, then?" he asked.

Without hesitation or change of expression, she nodded. Then she burrowed her forehead to his chest, pressed so hard against him, the Turkish hat tilted, its pins pulling and crackling in her hair and against his beard. He paused, stared at the knobby arch of her spine. After a moment, he touched her shoulders, then her taut neck. Her skin was soft like felt after much crushing.

Judith cleared breakfast while Leighton sat on the cedar benches in the mud room stamping in and strapping on his brogans. In the grime and moss collected there under the opposite bench, he saw the impression of four, five crescents dug through the red clay and green filth all the way down to the hard blue bone of the limestone floor. His father's fingers had clawed there, seized in a night terror—the recognition stopped Leighton, and he covered his trembling bottom lip with his hand.

"Look see, the time not even right with her around," Judith said. "Don't even need a lamp, you so late this morning!"

When Leighton did not answer, Judith stared at him, her chins doubled, a pout on her face.

"What?" Leighton asked. "What are you standing around looking at me for?"

She snorted. "Cause I been looking at you a long time, coming up that hill there, in trouble, out of trouble. I can look if

I want to." She nestled her hands on her hips, then stuck her jaw east toward what had been Weitzers' property. "So you done gone marry that land over yonder?"

Despite a sting of anger, Leighton grinned to keep her guessing.

Judith stood for a long time, arms stiff at her sides, fists closing and opening. "What it'll be like round here with her?"

Leighton shrugged.

"She have mother fits, don't she? Hystericals. Gal I know says she one them Dutch sees the Lord's face in rump roast and barn doors. That true?"

"Judith, it's done. I asked her to marry me."

Judith took a step toward him, stood very close. Her eyes narrowed, but her face was soft, lips pursed. On her cheeks, there was a hint of sweat, and he could smell this in the mud room above the cedar paneling and benches, the lime and clay of the floor. He bowed his head at her scrutiny. Outside a long murmur of wind stirred oaks nearing their fall turn, and the sunlight in the kitchen shifted and sparkled. Every door and window stood wide, and from the chill in the air this might be the last day of the year the manse would remain open overnight. Leighton could just see the blue hint of his breath in the mudroom. Off Judith's round forearms the boil of the dishwater sent out gray tendrils.

"You don't love her a bit, do you?" she asked.

Leighton held her eyes a moment. "Such a question, Judith."

"Do you love anyone, Leighton?"

When the wind stilled, there was such a hush, it seemed the sparkling yellow air was made of spun glass.

He reddened, turned from her.

Her voice fell to the timbre he'd heard months ago on the front porch, but now it was a challenge. "Is they anybody you think about when you look on her?"

He set his jaw at her.

She only nodded.

After a long silence, she said, "I got a place I want to show you."

He stared at her. Maybe now came the question she'd hesitated to ask in the barn. What was it about this buxom Negress, stout as a barrel, that made his heart swell like a wet wedge in a stone wall? Long familiarity? It was not the affection he might feel for a kinsman, a cousin. When she was a slave, she was an animal companion to him, and looking at her now, he could not entirely dispel that notion. And yet this was My Judith. For all his childhood, My Judith. They were survivors. What was she now, standing there with this question at her lips? Her bottom lip was pink at its fullest round, but her upper lip was so dark there was hardly a distinction between it and her black skin. Why did he want to touch those lips now?

"Please?" Judith asked.

He expected her to lead him somewhere in the house, but when she did not, he followed with more curiosity. She led down the trail to Rockbridge Road, then across, still on Morkan land, heading toward a cave and stream where as children the two of them hunted crayfish, and in wartime, he and Johnson Davis had hidden many of the family's valuables. Clustered sycamores lined the stream, their trunks chalk-white and amber in the sun, their giant, velvet leaves turning yellow. She followed the bank upstream until they reached the source, the low-ceilinged cave from which clear water flowed so undisturbed it appeared not to move at all. The water, once past the cave mouth, was no more than three feet deep. But deep inside the cave, where the ribs and back of the cave vaulted two stories high, the water plunged blue-green in unreckonable depths.

Judith squatted where a wide ledge of cave floor bordered the water. With her rounded form and enormous hams, the strains of color in the patchwork fabric of her sides flowered and stretched. The air of the cave and the passing cool of the water chilled Leighton even beneath his coat. Judith cupped her hands and brought water to her face. From her knuckles, sparkling drops tumbled. When the water touched her lips, she did not drink. Her lips moved as if she spoke into the water.

Leighton stepped back, and the cave's ribs scraped the crown of his head. Her motions, the thick pout of her lips, her closed eyes, all told him this splashing was some sort of morning ritual as rote to her memory as the stations of the cross to his.

Her dress rustled as she rose. Her eyes, black pupils in ivory, held him. Her hands shone where they hung at her sides.

"Leighton." Her voice fell to the low register he dreaded. Yet he had followed her here. And he could have mounted his horse and left her pouting.

He glanced away at the wall of the cave. The stone was dark gray, a wider grained limestone than that at the quarry. On the outcropping above him fossils, the cogs and wheels, segments of worms bristled, and made a familiar and calming stubble on the rock. He touched the cool surface, condensation clinging to the limestone. As he felt her warmth close in behind him, he pressed his fingers tight against the cave wall.

"Them's the teeth of the souls come to rest," she said. In the muddy, chill air of the cave, her breath reached him, warm and loamy.

He turned slowly to her, but still held the wall. He was spellbound for a moment by what she said. She stood so close that if he stepped forward, her body would envelop him. He managed a smirk. "Dead creatures from an old sea."

She touched a conical fossil, and her warm, slick skin brushed his cheek. "Ain't no creatures save the hardest part of us." She opened her mouth and ran her index finger across her upper teeth. Her finger touched her eye tooth again. Then she brought her hand toward him.

Her finger, a warm wet circle at its tip, paused on his bottom lip and rested there as if she meant to shush him.

"Water says you going to love me. You think that's true?"

She ran the finger across his forehead where sweat beaded, then popped the finger in her mouth as if his sweat were a frosting.

"Judith, I will marry her," he said.

She frowned. "Not here you won't. Not here with me. Here it's just me and you like it always been. Before. When there was the war. When your Daddy was gone to prison. It was us. Just us. My Leighton."

She stepped backward into the dark of the cave. What she said struck chords of memory in him. He had hardly spent a day without her voice, her cooking, her help. His first memory was of standing in a pen by a stove where it had grown too warm, wanting out, and she had lifted him. He remembered pushing his hands against the bones of her chest, pushing hard, then giving up the struggle and burying his head against her.

In the dim light of the cave, she drew the bottom of her dress to her waist, exposing the brown of her thighs. Rolling her shoulders, she tugged and slipped each arm loose from its sleeve. Then she leaned forward and pulled the dress above her head. When she stood, her breasts wobbled.

He shivered. She opened her arms to him. He remembered those same arms beckoning in a frigid winter in St. Louis, when Judith was a slave and he her charge, long before Morkan bought the quarry at auction and moved the family to Springfield. She and he had crawled from a window onto the treacherous tile roof above Bodley Street where she guided him to a cascade of icicles covered in soot. Returning, they slipped and were too frightened to move. They shivered, and she held his head against her bony chest, sang a song about steamboats until someone saved them.

Now she took his coat, folded it neatly and placed it to the side. She drew his suspenders off his shoulders. Quick fingers plucked open his buttons, shirt and pants.

She spread her dress on the cave floor, smoothed it as if it were a picnic blanket, then lay on her back, her skin so dark it seemed a part of the cave wall. When she looked up at him, when she spread her palms out beside her, he saw a part of his life open, as if there were myriad secret freedoms ahead of him. The last few months of his life had been an inescapable path towards marriage with Patricia. He was about to sell his freedom for land he wanted. But here on her back, wanting him, was liberty.

He dropped to his knees, hands on her wide, soft thighs. She sat up, placed both hands on the back of his neck, and drew him forward. Her belly yielded as if it were full of water. Her breasts, which he groped for and gathered to him, were cushions of liquid. They swallowed his hands. The slave girl that had raised him, his companion at play. It was as if the world outside the cool hole of the cave had lurched apart, and, like the glass shards in a kaleidoscope had fallen into a new pattern. He was stone. She was water. Patricia, his bigoted townsfolk, and the yammering newspapers were nothing more than a trick of glass and light.

Her lips touched his ear. "When you with her, think of this. Only this, and you get by. I swear it."

He shuddered a moment, hesitated, but her hands gripped his rump and held him fast. He resumed, and when he did, her round face became placid, her eyes adoring.

She cupped her hands to his ears, murmured to him, My Leighton. And in her hands, there rose the shirring whisper of an ocean, the babble of a crowd bestirred and furious, and this swept over him, transfixed him. Beneath him, in the cave, a body his family had owned, gave herself of her own volition. And what new kind of bondage was this she ensnared him with? In her cupped hands the sound of the breeze shirred against the limestone hills, rising, rising, a tremendous clamor of souls.

Spent, he sat with his back against the cave, its serrated wall digging into his skin. She squatted by the stream and dipped handfuls of water against her, shivering as each trickled away. A rustle, and he opened his eyes to see Judith standing before him, the dress on again. At his feet, she laid his clothes folded in a stack as neat as her finished laundry at home. He dressed slowly, his chest tight and aching, his genitals sore.

Judith touched his chest. "I just wanted this once."

A dark wave of guilt crept over him, and he felt as if he had lain down with a member of his family, a sister.

"But I'll want it again."

She smiled. "Yes, I hoped you would."

"Why now? Why'd you wait?"

"Before I thought you would always be My Leighton without it. I dream you in the war, and you come home mine. I dream you on the stone, and you come home mine. But not any longer. Not if she get there first. Not if she give you what I just did first." She looked up from his chest, looked squarely in his eyes. "It's not a dream, is it, Leighton?"

He touched her hand. "No. Oh, My Judith, it's not a dream."

VII

IF THE DRILLING WENT PRECISELY, IF THE POWDER
monkeys managed the charges well, the benches in his lime
showed Leighton clefts and faults where the stone would split
to make the buyer a nearly perfect façade. He walked a contractor along a bench, asked him to kneel and touch the stone, its
fossils blue and white, its surface often cool and moist to the
hand even on hot days. To Leighton the stone was a gridwork of
obvious possibilities. To the buyer, the stone was an unyielding,
sparkling mass. With just two Negroes and a handful of feather
drills, Leighton popped stone free in blocks as sharp as soaps
from molds. The Mistress grunted, swung the stone into the air,
a gray proclamation of power over nature. Only the most jaded
buyers remained unimpressed.

Customers' faces revealed themselves in ways akin to the
seams of lime in the cliffs. There came to the quarry men with
placid faces, whose eyes had a light like the tip of a knife. They
were from Ohio, Illinois, Indiana, the rear guard of the Federal war machine. With brute indifference to the Negroes, they
watched stone fill their wagons. In their minds, Leighton figured, there were only archways and angles, amorts and actuaries.

Other men, the lifelong Ozarkers, arrived with twisted
expressions, lips pursed. Their faces were like a plane of stone in
which a red nodule of chert is squarely centered. Behind such
a face, there was likely more of the same material, flinty, hard.
These Ozarkers looked on the Negroes as one would a nest of
wasps, with loathing and a presentiment of trouble. In their
bearded faces and pug noses, Leighton saw himself, and experi-
enced a terrible pain in their condemnation. Even though Scots-
Irish and Scottish, they were his people, Ozarkers. When he fell
in with them outside the quarry, it took no sip of drink to make

him feel among kin. Like them, when he fell to sleep at night, the same green hills, the same bluffs of red chert and blue lime huddled round his mind to comfort him. And yet in daylight with whites glaring at him, with the Negroes busy around him he felt as alien and horrible as a captain in Beelzebub's vanguard.

Leighton spent his Sundays in awkward meals at the Weitzer's refurbished home on South Street. There he put on a pleasant smile and struggled to open his eyes a little wider as he listened to hours of Claus philosophizing about love and marriage while Marta looked glum. Afterwards he could not recall anything the Dutchman said. He and Weitzer conducted the wedding arrangements with no more emotion than a business contract—the wedding would take place November 16th in the Lutheran church. Afterwards, as dowry Claus would deed Leighton all the Weitzer acres bordering Morkan land, and Leighton would forgive Weitzer the money owed the Morkans from the National Mineral Bank where Weitzer was once trustee.

Patricia, who ate with ferocious appetite and never showed any sign of improvement, sat near Leighton and watched her father with heavy-lidded eyes. She grimaced as she forced down tea cakes and ginger cookies. On the way home, Leighton stopped at the Quarry Rand to drink shot after shot of bourbon and smoke cigars until he felt as if his skin and lips were afire. Some Sundays, Archer or Odem strapped him to the saddle and rode with him to home. Judith received him with a mournful expression.

Only the Negroes and the young children in the street were without façades. When Leighton rode to work, a pack of white urchins followed him each morning, snarling and kicking tin cans or blowing low notes from the tops of bottles, which they slapped against their palms. Dirty, ragged, clamorous, they taunted harmlessly, but their hate for Leighton was unmistakable. Their parents only muttered and squinted. This spectacle stopped traffic around Leighton at first. Surreys slowed, and men leaned from windows and rails to gawk. One morning a large Negro woman met Leighton and his yammering, hooting, hissing entourage. She held a big copper kettle and a rolling pin in her arms. Assuming the middle of the road, she curtsied to Leighton as he passed.

Leighton turned in the saddle.

The urchins hesitated.

With a flash of metal, she was in their midst, bashing the kettle and hollering, beige teeth bared. The urchins squealed and scattered. When the last was gone, she turned to Leighton, curtsied again, then resumed the boardwalk with bustling self-possession.

Due to the quarry's demands, Patricia and Leighton consulted with the minister only once after the second banns were posted. Leighton met her and Weitzer at the Lutheran church across the Jordan. Leighton rented a surrey, and Weitzer accepted his offer to drive Patricia home.

Before the minister, Leighton falsely promised to convert from Catholicism to Lutheranism and endure a year of catechism. After a prayer in which all were silent and the minister said nothing but Amen, they rose. When Leighton offered his arm to Patricia, she took it with a quick grin. Outside he helped her into the surrey and adjusted the canvas to keep the wind from her. November twilight bathed the city. Weitzer set out on horseback in front of the couple. There at Leighton's insistence for propriety's sake, Weitzer made clear he thought this chaperoning to be a waste of time. After lying with Judith, though, Leighton was consumed with the desire to make every motion of this marriage as proper and incontrovertible as the hard, red wax in a notary's seal.

With the sun nearly set, the sky silvered. Venus shone like a diamond shard, and the moon rose fat and harvest orange. "Would you enjoy a ride down the creek side?"

She said yes, and he tapped the reins. The Jordan was a creek only in the early spring and late fall. Now in November, the creek bed carried a black trickle amid stones webbed in brown algae. In the twilight, the bare sycamores twisted like sun-blanched driftwood. The horse's ass before them was so dusty Leighton joked that he could beat a cloud of locusts from it. She laughed the ringing laugh.

"How do you feel, Patricia?"

"I am hungry, but fine."

They inched along, the wheels crunching in the road. Far ahead of them, Claus—a violet shadow—slouched so low in the saddle he seemed to be asleep. The first lanterns rose against the darkness, and from the far side of the Jordan on a hillock they could see most of their little town.

Leighton slowed the horses. "Listen to me a minute. I mean how do you feel about all this?"

She stared at him, and the jutting chin he had seen as proud and dignified became a barrier to him now. The veins and rilled bones of her neck rose. She was reptilian and ugly, and looked a lot like her father.

"It is meant to be." She touched her temple with the tips of her long fingers. She had to bend her neck to keep her bonnet from catching in the surrey's canvas. "I saw my eyes in the eyes of a little boy on the street. I saw my skin on his arms and neck. He was a premonition of the son we are to have."

Leighton shivered. "Sometimes, Patricia, you say things that greatly alarm me."

"What is alarming?" She took her hand from her temple. "There is nothing in the world wrong with me or my people, is there?" She stared at him a moment, then asked at a higher pitch, "Is there?"

He lit a cigar, not knowing what to say.

As he sat smoking, as his brow creased beneath the gray-crusted campaign hat, she saw no love in him, only glum, cold, perpetual business. She began to weep, and Leighton halted them beneath the dark scrags of a bank of new sycamores. And she kept weeping partly out of immense embarrassment and frustration and partly because any chance for a miracle seemed gone. This would be a marriage without love—she had affection for him but no passion. And how could he have any passion for her? She had the physique of a gawky giant, the face of an old horse.

Once she composed herself, Leighton reached and took her hand. She blinked at him, her eyelashes shining an oily black. Her face resumed the proud frown, and she lowered her head. "There. That's it," he said. "You're strong. Tears are for children and fools, and we are not children." He squeezed her hand. "It is important for me to know," he said. "Once mother died ... you have to understand. I have no sisters. Women are a mystery to me. Why do you want to marry me?"

107

When she buried her forehead against his shoulder, he fell quiet. What could she say? Because, Leighton Morkan, if I do not marry you the prospect of my dying an old maid is assured. And what's more you have all the look of one about to attain great sums of money. And further my parents need me to do this. She wanted her heart to thrill with longing for him, but it could manage only a surprised tolerance.

What was love, then? A creamy delusion spilled on her hands and on the *Turnverein* floor. She was about to enter a forest of banalities—years of servitude, of slopping stone floors, of washing lime off under clothes. Why could not the Lord, whose countenance is fire and revelation, why could He not have granted her just a scintilla of passion to sustain her crossing this dull terrain? Even in the horse-tainted surrey, and with the syrupy smolder of the cigar burning, the Irish smelled so clean and lime-ridden his alkaline odor made her head pound. From her time with Theodor, folded on the easel in the hall closet were the silly English phrases and their German paramours traveling nowhere together, speaking to the water bugs. In the last two seasons, centuries had passed. "Does it matter beyond that I will say, 'yes,' and that I will say, 'I do?'"

"Let me just say that I'm having trouble parsing people of late," he said. "Folks *seem to be* around here. No one *is* anymore. And certainly no one is what they once were. I am not even what I once was."

She took a deep breath and sat for a long time silent— and Leighton could not tell whether she had listened and was absorbing what he said, honoring it with thought, or whether she was too young to understand. In the twilight, the jade cloak she wore shimmered like the surface of a lake. "The town looks almost like it is something." She nodded at the vista.

He sighed, defeated. Clearly she was too young to follow his line of reasoning. Small yellow and orange lights dotted the streets below. Some bobbed quickly on wagons. Others crawled in straight lines, miners lamps in the hands of foot travelers. Every now and again, one would wink out and a new one would flicker and rise.

"What sort of quest does that light have on such a cold night as this?" Patricia asked.

"Money," he said.

She kicked his calf. "How crass you can be!"

"Fine, then. What are they after?"

"I want you to tell me." She said this with clenched teeth, but there was a sort of glee in her voice, as if a delightful game had begun. She was so young, he thought, she could vacillate from dire subjects to pleasant fancies in an instant and with no remorse.

A single lantern angled between shacks close to the Jordan, paused, then whisked along again.

"What is that one light doing there by the creek?" she asked.

"Probably some scoundrel snaking along, looking for an old widow lady's open window, so's he can hive in there." He turned to her, and grabbed her waist. "And slit her throat."

She bellowed in disgust, popped her hand over his forehead and pushed him away. "That is not what I want to hear," she said. "Why does he have to be a thief?" She brushed and patted the lap of her dress.

"Look at him. There's no need to sneak around like that unless you took something or are about to."

"Have him do something else, please." She shifted her shoulders, straightened her cloak. She stuck her chin out, and when she caught his eyes, she sputtered with mirth.

"All right," he said. He watched the lamp, which was now slowly and steadily moving southwest away from them. "His wife has just gone to sleep, and so he's stacked the fire with so much green wood, it's cracking and popping, roasting warm, blowing and hissing like a boiler. He's snuck through the slat window in the back, and he's headed to see his lover."

She moved closer to him, her dress catching against the dowdy and tired upholstery. "And what is she like?"

"His lover's tall and thin, with long fingers, and ruddy, dark skin, and she's part Bulgarian. Her name is Ankarra D'mora Smith."

"Pssh! What do you know about Balkan peoples?"

"Settle down, now. We were both educated in St. Louis, you snit. Remember my scary Jesuits? Hmm?"

"Mmmph," she grunted. "Proceed." She was smiling. And it warmed his heart that she might be having fun and that he might be a source of pleasure for someone.

"Her hair is silky black, and her eyes are green. And she waits for him, and smokes little cubes of opium her father sends her from the Sandjak of Novi Pazar, where he is an ambassador that President Johnson has forgot about."

She pushed his shoulder. "Rich," she said.

"No, darling, an ambassador. For Johnson. The pay is abysmal."

"*Gross Gott.*" Patricia sighed and rested her back against his shoulder. He hesitated, then placed his arm around her. The bones of her shoulders were hard on his biceps and forearm. Long, thin bones arranged like the struts of an exotic kite.

"He has a gift in his pocket, and it's very annoying, for it's heavy, and the points of it scrape against his hip. He has to carry a large revolver, also, and this is troublesome—he hocked his holster and several other notions to get this gift to please Ankarra."

Her neck and scalp smelled of talc.

"He hocked his belt, a pair of boots, an anvil, two bridles and tack. He reaches Ankarra's house, there." He pointed to where the light had disappeared.

"And when he takes hold of the paw paw whip cords that are Ankarra's door lock, he looks up. There are stars. And he can't help but think how those stars are piercing through the night like the sparks in his fireplace, spitting in the dark of his cabin where his wife now sits up in bed and stares at that fire, knowing exactly where he is, knowing who he really loves. And he can't help but think, here these stars are burning like they have for a hundred thousand years, and they have blared on this same scene and listened to these same trivial thoughts between the same three souls for what is eons to us. But for the stars, the stink and sheen of him and his wife and Ankarra are relatively new, and, though reminiscent of several million other insects across the galaxy, he and his wife and Ankarra are novel and somewhat interesting. And so the stars listen."

Leighton paused. A slight breeze rustled the canvas.

Patricia frowned. "Our heroes are dawdling. Bring them together?"

"He unwinds the paw paw whip cords, once left, twice right, left, pull, then left again. He pushes open the door, and there stands Ankarra in her only night gown. Her eyes are dusky with opium and heavy-lidded. She is brushing her black hair in long, lovely strokes, and it's blue as coal oil her hair.

"He enters, and she flutters her eyes and says, 'Vat have you brung me?' He digs in his pocket. The gift is heavy and cold, like a warden's ring of keys. He holds it up to her, and it sparkles like his wife's eyes sparkle watching the fire, like the stars sparkle and turn, like. . ."

Patricia let out a sharp growl, pounding her fist on the seat. "What is the gift?"

"It's a Death Watch Beetle with legs of white gold, a giant ruby for its back, diamond white eyes, and emerald wings."

Patricia kept a sidelong glance on him. She was smiling, and with her eyes shifting, head bowed, she appeared devious, dubious, and yet greedily amused.

Is this what having a sister was like? Leighton marveled at the sentiment that swept over him—he longed to fulfill her intellect's desire, her endearing curiosity, and at the same time he wished to torment her. Extraordinary! He held her just a little closer, and she sank more deeply against his shoulder.

"It is the last extant of an Italian jewel-master whose name he cannot recall. He hands it to her, and she takes it, hefts it up and down, then pops that beetle over on a cabinet and holds her arms out to him.

" 'Don't you reckon you ought to look at that a little longer?' he asks.

"She shakes her head and does him on like this." Leighton held one arm out and waved the imaginary lover to him. And suddenly, in the twilight, he saw Judith in the murk of the cave, her arms open, beckoning. The vision stopped him cold.

Finally Patricia clasped his hand and squeezed. "Please?" she whispered, shaking his hand in hers as if finishing the story were an urgent necessity.

Leighton cleared his throat. "'She does him on. 'Vhy, darling?' she asks him.

" 'Because that fucker cost me a wad, I'll tell you!' "

"*Herr Gott!*" Patricia elbowed him in the ribs. "Must all your stories end in inanity?"

Laughing, he grabbed her elbow. "How do you think any story ends?" He pulled her to face him. "It all ends in dust. Is there anything more inane?"

Putting the cigar back in his mouth, he clucked to the horses, and they crept along.

She stared at him, then looked away to the road where her father halted, letting his horse drink from the creek. Her lips were curved in a sour expression. He felt for an instant that there was no one in the surrey with him, and out there were only the unfathomable lights of his town and the wind and the yawn of the surrey's springs.

She leveled her eyes on him as if some judgement locked into place in the cogs of her mind. "I do not understand you, Leighton Moorken," she said, very slowly. "You are not of my people. You speak the tongue of coarse commerce and hard living." She readjusted her posture, folded her long hands in her lap. "How shall I benefit you? Why do you want this match?"

When he didn't answer immediately, she looked away from him. In the set of her gray eyes, she appeared focused on some point hundreds of miles down the road, or hundreds of miles inside her.

He sat still for a moment. "Well, I tell you," he said. "I broke a deathbed promise to my old man, my Da. And I'm figuring in the life I got to lead, with Coloreds in a quarry owing their lives to a company store, it's going to take a ramrod bitch of an earnest woman, an unassailable Yankee Dutch priss to save my soul."

She sat still a moment. Then she reared back her fist and pounded him so hard in the arm he dropped the reins. As he sat rubbing his arm, she sneered at him and seemed poised to deliver another blow. Claus turned to face them for a moment.

"I had brothers, you know," she said, waving to Claus. "I'll whup you daily. You may ruin my life, you stupid Mick. But never have I felt so good about having proper posture and iron will, if that is what you are meaning." She touched his arm, smiling. "I hope that raises a knot, you bet."

"I be damned," he said. "Tell me a story, then. You saw the war, or some of it in St. Louis. Tell me about that."

"I was no warrior," she said.

"We were all in it, gal."

When the wind rattled the canvas, she looked up beyond the horses to the east as if St. Louis were shining right past the twilit sycamores. "That much is true," she said. She took a deep breath and let the air out slowly through her nose, closed her eyes and became suddenly very still.

"There was an advertisement entered in *Anzeiger des Westens* just after the Camp Jackson riots about a missing daughter of a German family, the Evertzs, owners of a butcher paper company and makers of the stoves you are familiar with. You own one. In *Anzeiger*, it was supposed that she had been kidnapped in revenge by Southern sympathizers, who singled her out as one who had aided the Federals in stopping a steamboat from being stolen. Her parents longed for her back, their cherished one."

She untied her bonnet, let it slip to her shoulders. Her hair was plain and brown, but so well combed and ordered, as if she had washed it just for this evening. In the November twilight it held a luster of red and copper.

"Edith Catherine Evertz was a beautiful girl, a true rarity among German girls, not plump like a muffin, but strung hard like an Osage girl, yet with unblemished skin, white, Baltic white like new meerschaum. And she could swim. I myself saw her swim across the Mississippi from the old quarry to Illinois. A gang of girls from the Lutheran school stood on our side of the water, and she plunged in swimming. Very soon she was gone. There was no seeing her, and we began to weep. We stood there for a long time crying among the stones.

"And then from across the water in Illinois, we saw Edith Catherine Evertz stand and walk from the river. She did not crawl. She did not struggle. She strode, and turned to us, naked and so lovely, with both arms raised. We were little girls then, but we could not swim in the nude without reprimand. After that day I remember being glad that I was made to cover my body whenever I swam. Considering her in her glory, we all were humbled and happy to be modest after that, I think."

113

Her accent thickened and grew more German as she became comfortable. The wind stretched the canvas again and stirred Patricia's hair, and for a moment, with her chin jutting east, her hair tussled, her gray-green eyes bright, she seemed very Bohemian to him, and, for the first time, beautiful. Claus had dismounted and stood staring across the creek as if dismayed by something in the eastern sky.

"Previous to the war," Patricia went on, "Edith Catherine fell in love with a Scots-Irish boy up from the Ozarks, a gambler and shootist. If this were not perilous enough, the boy was in league with Southern sympathizers in town, and was the first wounded when the Southerners stormed McDowell's School, which sadly became Gratiot, as you know.

"As a nurse, which I was then—I was so tall, Leighton, even then no one knew my real age—I treated the gambler from the Ozarks, McConnell was his name. McConnell was handsome in the extreme and told me stories of his people, who were kings in Ireland, chieftains who provided mercenaries called Gallowglasses, invincible terrors. And he told me of his love for Edith, and I was won over with the romance of it all. I shuttled messages between them. I was the one that kept their love afire, no easy task. You may not know, but after the riots, after Camp Jackson, St. Louis became a dangerous place for a German girl and Federal nurse. I was spit on in the streets, and once I was hit over the head by a peg lamp, and had to be carried home by one of Franz Sigel's men."

With her long fingers, she parted her brown hair, and there at the roots was a fat pink scar against her bluish scalp. Leighton clicked at the horses and without a sound they resumed a slow, easy plodding.

"McConnell's wound was grave, along the third and fourth rib, and it had gone putrid. In his fever he entrusted to me that on a boat at the landing there was a power-doctor from his home place. You know, a spirit doctor, a root conjurer, one whose specialty was the laying on of hands for wounds gone foul like his. If Edith could convince the power-doctor to steal into the hospital and visit him, McConnell would be saved. Delirious hillbilly palaver, I thought, but he persisted with an intelligence

114

and a faith. Eventually so convinced was I, and so convincing to Edith, that she determined to board the boat and entreat the power-doctor by whatever means, for she knew from McConnell that a power-doctor will take no money, but will demand instead a great gift for his intervention."

Her brow furrowed and she paused for a moment. "Here my story must rely on what came from the power-doctor himself in a last confession, which I received of him in the hospital where he died from his burns. Edith swam toward the boat, which that night would be taken under steam south by its pilot, who was a traitor and Confederate sympathizer, stolen to be fitted with armor in Memphis. On board she found the power-doctor drinking whiskey in his berth, and she told him of McConnell and his wound.

"The power-doctor was a grimy, bearded old *Hundswarze,* a fireman for the boilers. He told her he needn't go ashore, that by a phrase alone, a power phrase, an incantation known only in your hills, he could send her to McConnell with the spirit force to save him. But it would cost her dearly."

Slowing the horses, Leighton rested the reins in his hands and watched her. Her face was aglow as if she ran a fever.

"He took Edith Catherine Evertz's virginity there in the stink of his cabin."

With care, Patricia tied her bonnet back on her head. Far ahead of them, Claus's horse bobbed its head impatiently.

"Just then, when he had finished his business and sat in a stupor, the boat lurched and began huffing at full steam down the river. Edith struggled up. 'Quickly,' she said. 'You must tell me the power phrase.'

"The power-doctor motioned her close, closer. Then he took her cheek in his sooty hands, pressed his wiry beard to her ear.

"'You,' he said, 'are a goddamn Dutch fool.'"

Beneath the surrey wheels, the gravel sizzled.

"Edith was distraught, but she could not cry out—she was a stowaway. She wandered the deck and at last stood by the great paddlewheel, which purled and slammed the water. Watching the glow of her city recede, she knew the boat was steaming South, where no Federal boat had gone since Sumter. The boat, she realized, was being stolen.

"The power-doctor had followed her and held in his mind a word that when spoken in her ear would make her sink like a stone in the river. And at the back of the boat, he waited for his chance, watching the beautiful Edith, the swimmer, stare at the wheel and her city vanishing and her lover, McConnell, dying. Beneath him, the power-doctor could hear the boiler greatly overtaxed and thumping, and his confidence soared.

"When the power-doctor took his last step forward, Edith heard him move. She straightened her shoulders and said, 'I know your name. I know your name and the truth about you. And I will take your name to St. Peter's gate, and I will speak your name and your deeds even into the ear of the Almighty.'

"At this, the power-doctor froze with feet that were bolted to the deck. Edith Catherine turned to him, and her lips formed his name but the only sound from them was the gnashing of the paddles and of the pistons and the flames cracking round the boiler.

"Then she leapt from the rail and into the wheel, lodging herself to jam the mechanism to a halt. The boiler blew and the boat was kept from Rebel hands and the burned survivors were brought to the hospital, where I worked, and where I learned the truth about the lonely advertisement which the bereaved Evertz ran in *Anzeiger des Westens* every day for the remainder of the war."

She sat back and touched her lips as if telling the story had scalded them. Over a swale made icy blue by the risen moon, the wind pushed black snakes of motion through hissing winter wheat, rapid S shapes rushing up the bank then dissipating.

"You never told Evertz?"

She glanced sidelong at him, her lips pursed. "How could I? Their precious daughter, the beauty of German St. Louis, in love with a Rebel hillbilly gambler, defiled and humiliated by a rube from the hinterlands?" She snorted. "Better to let them believe in a miracle for the cost of an advert in *Anzeiger*."

Leighton removed the cigar from his mouth. He didn't believe the half of it—a slip of a girl jamming a sternwheeler; swimming the Mississippi!—but she told it damn well. "You," he said, "are quite a woman, Patricia Weitzer."

He raised the reins and was about to start the horses, but he stopped himself and scrutinized her very closely.

As never before she felt her heart pummeled, like a body in the blades of a paddlewheel that was whirling, unstoppable. "My God, Leighton," she said. She touched his shoulder, rested her head there again. "There are times you break my heart with your kindness. And there are many more times I want to knock you over the head."

His coat was slick against her hair, his shoulder warm and firm. It was a new coat, she realized, smooth along its shoulders, without the gray revenant of quarry dust. And yet that stink of lime, hardening and chilling the air around him. But rather than being repelled, leaning against him now, she felt steadied, as if some loose part of her had been stilled and slaked into solid soil that clutched it, drew it home. After a moment, he clucked to the horses, which nodded and pulled them on.

VIII

THE WEDDING COMMENCED AT THE LUTHERAN CHURCH, an A-frame whitewashed with Morkan lime on the inside and out, mortared tight with Leighton's stone at every joint. But even with such familiar materials around him, he felt he was in an alien shrine. An inornate iron cross lurked on the pulpit. No saint was visible. Not even Christ was embodied. Sweat dripped coldly down his sides, itched at his forehead and collar.

The crowd was larger than he expected. There were five of his foremen, two machinists, a number of drillers and blasters, Menzardo and all his masons, a derrickman, and Archer Newman. Odem, his best man, wore a porcelain prosthetic from Baltimore. Leighton recognized Patricia's other aunts and uncles, Ferdinand, the cousins, the scowling Karl.

For the last week at home Judith was oppressively present, asked incessant questions about what "notha woman" liked and disliked, days and nights she spent preparing the house for "notha woman." Buckets sloshed and brushes rasped, carpets trembled from poundings, and boiling hot waters crashed over the stone floors. When she was nearest Leighton, at the wash trough or on the porch or serving him a port in the den, there seemed to be a more forward question she wanted to ask—her brow always creased with phrasing it, her lips fumbling.

Among the wedding guests, the Germans all dressed in sober grays and blacks. Some of Leighton's foremen wore flamboyant vests, string ties of yellow and blue. His favorite contractors sat among the foremen, glaring as if they had been charged a terrible fee at the door, their noses red. The number of townspeople surprised him. Leighton saw in the congregation John S. Phelps; one of the Martin kids; the curly-headed bastard Ziggler from the papers; Wilson Shannon; Shane Peale; Captain Julian, two Campbells; even a Kimbrough.

Among the Germans Leighton recognized two from Schmook's mill and three of the Beiderlinder boys.

When the organist relaxed, his machine ceased its complex whistling and gagging for a moment. Then it heaved four notes into the crowd. The wax-skinned minister rose, lifted his arms to the rafters. Standing, the congregation turned to the sanctuary doors, which opened to reveal Claus and Patricia side-by-side in the November mist.

The organ grunted the march. Patricia stepped down the aisle, her head bowed. She wore a white, floor length dress, and a long white veil. Claus wore a black swallow-tail coat that shone even in the dim light.

The minister talked for long time in thick English then in German. He discussed what this marriage represented—"The merging of two peoples after a travail in the desert. A ray of hope and grace for a town so long wit'out none." He talked, to everyone's horror, about divisions in the town between German and Irish, Negro and White, Rebel and Federal, and the ways this marriage promised a redemption, how we all must repent. It was excruciating. The minister cocked his head, and his forehead wrinkled. "Yet we come together here. The wheel within a wheel that was the history of man that Ezekiel saw has turned. The face it shows us is not the lion or the eagle, but our own."

Finally he squinted, searched Leighton's eyes. He nodded as if Leighton passed some test. "Rejoice with the wife whom though lovest all the days of the life of thy vanity, which He hath given thee under the sun, *all* the days of thy vanity: for that is thy lot in life."

Such a prophecy! Leighton felt his heart would collapse around his ankles.

The minister looked at Patricia. "Whatsoever thy hand findeth to do, do *it* with thy might." Then the minister released their hands and turned to the congregation. "*Komm Heiliger Geist, Herr Gott*," he said.

The people stood, and after some coughing, the Germans sang a hymn. Next came a litany and many responses, a lengthy *mea culpa* in English, much more singing, and no Eucharist leading Leighton to wonder what—if anything—had transpired.

The minister led them through their vows, and the Lord's Prayer. "Then," he said, raising his arms as high above their heads as he could manage, "with the blessing of the Holy Bishop Walther, the Missouri Synod of the Lutheran Church and this entire congregation, I pronounce you man and wife. You may claim your bride."

Patricia turned to him, and her frown lifted. With the back of his hand he raised her vale, which was rough against his skin, the stiff lace grating. There were her lips, and they were pink and plain. Her eyes remained bright. He closed his eyes and kissed her quickly. Then, he lowered the vale, and they faced the congregation.

The crowd rose; the miners and contractors applauded. After a moment of dismay, some of the Germans joined them. Leighton held Patricia's hand, and they moved down the aisle and exited the church. A chill ran at the base of his neck and spread through his hair. With so many of Springfield's elite following him out of the church he thought for an instant he might could take the minister's words to heart. Maybe their marriage could bind the town together. The mist had cleared and in the new sun, he shielded his eyes, but remained on the steps.

There outside the church yard waited almost two dozen Negro miners and their wives, sons, and daughters. The shock of the sight made him hesitate. They were dressed as if for their own church—high starched collars throttling the men's necks, bonnets of lace and ribbon on the women's heads. Two Negroes wore the crisp blue of Yankee uniforms. They stood directly against the split rail fence of the church lot, dark fingers clasping its new wood. They did not applaud and they did not smile, only stared with solemn, flat lips. Their gazes appeared grave and concerned. The Whites halted, and Leighton and his new wife cautiously descended step by step.

At the rail fence, right at the gate, Miasma Sullivan stood close to the rented surrey. A short, thin Negress next to him held a wreath of wound vine swirled with dried clover and cock's comb. She extended this to Leighton, who released Patricia's hand.

Outside the churchyard in the cold morning, the faces of the Negroes—auburn and red, coffee and blue charcoal, tar black, and high yellow—held fast to the newlyweds where they stood, two in a gulf between the stunned Whites and the crowd of Coloreds. Behind him Leighton felt that empty gap as if he had turned his back unprotected on a malevolent bar room. There was the wreath of cock's comb and cat tail and ivy and straw flowers and rushes, extended by a hand with its black fingers and pink nails, skin darker than the shadow cast beneath it in the weak November sun. Miasma's companion raised the wreath higher as if Leighton had not seen it. Negro faces waited.

Leighton clasped the wreath. Dry rushes as sharp against his gnarled palm as the legs of angry wasps grasping. He willed his hand be careful so as not to crush this. "I thank you. It is lovely."

At the running bar of the surrey, one of Patricia's cousins played footman and helped Patricia up to her seat. The boy's face was red.

"If I should have had time, Mr. Morkan," Patricia's cousin whispered, "I would have called the constables."

Leighton glared at him and tucked the wreath under his arm.

He placed the wreath on the floorboard between him and Patricia. The Negroes were departing, walking away with their shoulders hunched, hands crammed in their pockets. On the feet of some of the Negroes were the sloppy, gray brogans sold at the Morkan company store, MQ branded on each. The brogans popped against the soles of their feet. The Whites waited for the Negroes to clear, neither people speaking. The Negroes had come in the cold mist in their Sunday best. He couldn't think of a marriage in his lifetime when any Negroes save servants attended, and them in the balcony.

He wobbled the reins, and the horse moved. The wreath crackled and shifted, fell against Patricia's dress. She pulled a hand from her muff, and he expected her to push the wreath away or even lift it and cast it from the surrey. But instead, with one shoulder stooped, she held the ornament standing. It left clover and a sprig of ivy hanging from the white frills of her dress. The sprig twirled merrily where it was caught, keeping time with the clopping of the horses.

At the reception at the Weitzer home on South Street, the miners enjoyed the beer, but not the company, and the Weitzers and friends, likewise, drank somberly apart from the miners. After several hours of drinking, Weitzer began to squint and waver. He sat with Leighton on the wooden back steps where there was a yeasty draft issuing from the kitchen.

Leighton swallowed a deep draw from his beer. It was cool and made his tongue ache with pleasure. Across the yard, Archer was talking with a trio of German girls including Patricia, and from what Leighton could hear, Archer was speaking German. Rutgers, he thought enviously. Patricia laughed too loudly, at something Archer said, then touched a hand to her chest.

"That is the City Engineer?" Weitzer stuck his goatee at Archer.

Leighton nodded. "Good friend of mine. Archer Newman."

Weitzer narrowed his eyes at Archer. "I bet his people are from Alsace. That red hair." He ran his knuckles under his chin. "I bet their name was Neimann and they changed it. Some Germans do that."

Leighton shrugged. "He does seem to speak German pretty passable."

Patricia brushed Archer's hand for just an instant, then blushed so deeply she had to walk away laughing and covering her face.

"Keep Patricia away from him," Weitzer said. "A man like that can turn a woman's soul from the world of necessities and into the faerie land of true love.

"Dat scene in the churchyard," Weitzer continued. It was the first time Leighton heard the German's accent thicken. Weitzer sat very still, but the top of his head swayed a little. He was in his cups and going deeper.

"Beg pardon? You mean with the Negroes?"

"Yes, with the Negroes."

Leighton brushed his palm very slowly down the leg of his crisp trousers. "Won't be the last one with them, I assure you."

They smoked, and Weitzer drank, held his mug so tightly, his hand shook. Then he grinned, but his goatee and the redness of his face made him appear ferocious. "Tell me about the children that are to come."

Leighton ran his thumb along the top of his mug.

"Level with me," Weitzer said. He leaned very close, and his shining forehead warmed Leighton's scalp. "We are men, here." He popped Leighton on the shoulder. "It has been studied and medical philosophers have determined that intensely deep penetration creates a stimulus for the male child in the female."

Leighton leaned away from him.

Weitzer nodded. "This I promise. It is a fact of glandular possibility." His grin was overpowering. His teeth, like Patricia's, were tiny and gray. "Are you prepared to achieve such?"

Leighton pulled on his beer. "You will have grandsons."

"Ah!" Weitzer slapped his hand against the top of the stair. Ashes scattered. "Ah!," he said again. He scooted very close to Leighton. "Now to ensure this, you must have Patricia recline at all times and keep a very hot object upon her abdomen, say a rock heated in the stove, or a brick, or an andiron."

Leighton finished his beer. "During the act?"

"No. *Gross Gott!* Afterwards." He shook his head at Leighton. "And also each evening you must get her to drink two pints of Dunkel, as dark and strong as you can find it. This ..." He brandished a finger. "This will ensure a boy."

"Did you do these sorts of things with Mrs. Weitzer?"

Weitzer frowned. "I had difficulty with all but the Dunkel. She enjoys beer, and so I was able to have two good boys by substituting quarts for the pints."

Leighton nodded. Patricia was across the yard, surrounded by older women who were pinching her dress, thumbing its fabric. She was frowning and nodding. Her eyes narrowed at his gaze. She looked as if she were about to accuse him of something. Some beer would do her well. What advice was she garnering from the Dutch women? More hot bricks and nonsense? "I will do all I can, Mr. Weitzer."

Weitzer grinned. "I knew you would. I know you will!"

123

"What I want to know is when do we sign the deed to that land?"

Weitzer's head jerked so rapidly to him that Leighton was startled.

"How does a German family go about issuing its dowries?"

Weitzer stood bolt upright. Behind them, the women in the kitchen fell silent.

"I will show you how we do so," Weitzer said. He stuck his head in the kitchen. "*Mutter*," he shouted. "*Meine Unterlagen.*"

Leighton stood as well.

Weitzer pulled at the bottom of his vest with such force Leighton thought the old German might tear the shoulder seams. "If this is what this is all about, if *dies ist der Markknochen von der Ehe,* then we will show the world how."

"Mr. Weitzer, we are men here, as you say. Forgive me. But we were being quite frank earlier." Leighton stepped closer to Weitzer, though the German's face was purpling and his gray goatee stuck forward like a block of iron. "For the sake of your daughter. Not here. I am only asking. For Patricia now, becalm yourself."

"I will not have you asking again. I knew your father. Always striving. The son is no better." Spit escaped him.

Leighton was used to Irish rage, which built like a thunderhead one could monitor. This was a squall he had not anticipated. "I ask you one last time. Be calm. For your daughter, for my wife's sake, not here."

"Wife? Transaction!"

A hush fell over the already quietened crowd. Leighton locked eyes with him. "Very well." He stuck two fingers in his mouth and whistled shrilly. "Captain Julian," Leighton called. "I beg you, come here, sir."

Julian was a chatterbox who had served in some Union division or other depending on whom he was burdening. Of late he was selling stock in a wool-carding plant he wished to start. He marched before them and saluted Leighton, bowed to Claus Weitzer, then hiccoughed.

"Captain," Leighton said, placing a hand on Julian's shoulder to steady him, "are you not a notary public?"

"No, but I *am* a notary public. I am not *not* a notary public!"

Leighton nodded. "Excellent!"

"Buffoon," Weitzer snapped.

Leighton cleared his throat. "This loyal servant of the Republic is my witness."

Weitzer glared at them both, cables of bone showing along his neck. With her head bowed, Marta stuck the papers at the three of them. When Weitzer took them he growled, "*Feder und Tinte.*" Marta handed him pen and ink.

"Well, then," Weitzer said. He breathed in like a bellows he was so enraged. The entire party was stilled, and only Patricia drew close. He cleared his throat. "Your attention, please. Mr. Morkan has asked how we Dutchmen dispose of dowries to our daughters." He swirled the pen in the air. "I hereby deed five hundred and sixty acres of meadow and brook and glen and hillock to Leighton Shea Morkan."

The crowd was still silent. Pressing the deed against the clapboard of the house Weitzer scrawled his name on the quit claim. Then he snapped the document at Leighton. "I am Claus Weitzer. Never let it be said that my word was anything but the truth."

Rather than hanging her head, Leighton saw Patricia jut her chin forward, even raise it a bit.

Captain Julian weaved and pulled from his coat an old brass notary stamp. He took the document from Weitzer and clamped it holding it before the crowd with ceremony as he squeezed. Looking up at them, still with the limp deed drooping from his stamp, he raised it high. "Five hundred and sixty acres. Hoo-raw for Morkan!"

Miners whooped and hollered, dancing jigs among sullen Germans.

Patricia changed into her traveling dress. In the parlor, she waited for the carriage and for her new husband to extricate himself from besotted well wishers. There was a thud, and the City Engineer, Archer Newman, stumbled into the parlor holding his hand to his eye.

"What have you done?" Patricia asked. The young nurse in her rose up. "*Komm!*" she ordered.

"*Ich kann Ihnen nie nicht gehorchen, Madamoiselle!*" he answered. His German was sometimes arch and dry, sometimes very colloquial, and often he spoke nonsense, as if he learned from a phrasebook written by a committee of half scholars, half tramps.

He was taller than Leighton but not taller than she. Standing close, she noticed the rare perfection of his skin, pale, red-freckled, but a clean complexion. His hair was a deep burgundy and the small hairs on the back of his hand were a brighter red. Even in distress, he was winsome, with a slightly Romanesque nose; very French it seemed to her. And she remembered with keen resentment the haughty and louche French in St. Louis.

She swiped her nails against the woolen sleeve of her dress. When she gripped the back of his neck, he quit squirming and dropped his hand. "Very good," she said. "Hands at your sides."

Still holding him, she spread the lids of the injured eye apart with the nails of her free hand. Wet and red, the eyeball danced and she could see an offending lash clinging to the sclera. "Blink," she said softly. "Hands at sides."

Archer complied. Such small lashes he had, auburn and short; they would make the next operation tedious in the extreme.

The lash troubling his eye vanished as he blinked.

"Patience," she said. "*Festhalten.*"

She moved her face so very close to his that she could smell the drink on his breath, something pleasant, one of the raspberry cordials mixed with a touch of tobacco, and women's rouge. Pinching the small reddish brown lashes of his upper eyelid, she pulled the lid down so that its pink and tender insides scraped against the lashes of the lower lid. Archer held very still. The black crescent hung in his lower lashes, and she plucked it, held it up. It was so dark it gleamed like metal.

Archer batted his eyes and moaned. "What an exquisite relief."

Fascinated with the lash and with Archer Newman, she did not retreat. Holding the crescent up, she placed a hand on her hip. "Why, how did you get this in your eye? It is not even your eye lash!"

Color rushed to Archer Newman's face. His lips—so wet and untroubled by weather he must have waxed them—broke into a lovely smile.

"Leighton said you are a married man," she whispered sharply.

Deeper color blossomed and with his eyes watering, he appeared sad and comical. Archer touched a fingertip to his lips.

And then Patricia did something she had only done to her brothers and to Leighton. She pushed him with both palms very hard against his shoulders.

He stumbled back but caught her wrist and righted himself smiling. "And now I witness the wonders my friend Leighton Shea Morkan sees in you, my dear. Thank you, Mademoiselle."

"Madame!" She wormed her wrist free, and pointed fiercely to the door.

No wedding party or newlyweds would risk the trek from the center of town to Galway in the dark. Replete with gifts, advertised by banns and in the papers, newlyweds riding home were a sure thief's target. The Leighton Shea Morkans would have to overnight in one of the new hotels, then ride to the Morkan land in daylight under armed escort.

The hotel was built with a prow that jutted into the board-walk. This was made to look like the bow of a paddle wheeler with two smokestacks setting off the entrance. In the hotel's saloon, a piano player banged away, a little German fellow with a small black mustache. The bartender, an old Federal, saluted Leighton. Leighton's cheeks and jaw were numb with cold and beer, so he lit a cigar. Despite the unseemly end of the reception—all the Germans accepted Claus's outburst as a matter of course and the miners drank on—he now felt giddy, full of life and adventure holding her thin hand. He had her land, all the lime. Hoo-raw, they had yelled. He stared at her long fingers, and in fits of delight, lifted them to his lips and said to the barkeep and the barroom, "My wife. My very own wife." Rather than blushing, Patricia curtsied, and once after one of his fits, she held up his hand and exclaimed, "*Mein Soldatchen!*" He wanted someone to stand him to a fight or a round of whiskey, but the bar had only two patrons in it, lead merchants, and they were both long in the face, hunched over their mugs. Leighton tipped the German piano player a dollar to lay into "It's a Grand Olde Flag."

The German grinned and thumped through it singing loudly in a thick accent. He knew only the chorus, but kept repeating it as if there were nothing more to the song.

Leighton ordered toddies, asked the bartender to fill up everyone's glasses. He tapped his mug against the counter in time to the song.

Patricia smiled at him and drank. She leaned toward him. "This makes me feel so grown up. Mrs. Morkan!"

He grabbed her waist. "I'll make you feel growed up here in a minute."

Patricia frowned at this. She finished her mug.

Leighton handed her his. "Drink thisun."

She finished half of it, had to pause. Then, she finished the remainder. She stared at him when she lowered the mug. Her lips were rounded and shining. She placed the mug on the bar.

"Is this the adventure?" She rested her long elbows on the bar, leaned her back against it. With her height and gray eyes, as curved as a surgeon's needles, she suddenly seemed to be a much older woman, jaded and world wise. "Is this a place where the great lovers go?"

He snatched her hand and they left the German singing and pumping his feet. He hustled her up the stairs and to their room, popped the door shut and tossed the key on the dresser.

"Take that shawl off," he said.

She leaned forward and pulled the shawl from her shoulders. It hissed across the dress. She paused and folded it neatly, tried to take in the room. In the weak light of a smoky candle, there was a dresser and a pewter wash basin, a tall mirror with many purple flaws at its edges.

"Undo the back of your dress."

She reached behind her and undid several of the dress's buttons. Even in the darkened room, her arms were very long. Watching her struggle with the buttons, he suddenly reckoned how little he truly felt for her, not pity, not even excitement. He had admired her in the carriage holding Miasma's wreath, was proud of her steadiness then. He admired her bearing, her stories, her mind, her ferocity. But that admiration carried no power in this hotel room. How empty the transaction was then! For this creature struggling to bare herself before him, his heart was suddenly as flat as a chalk line snapped on stone.

"Turn around."

She turned, bowed her head with her back to him. He undid the remaining ivory hasps. His knuckles brushed the skin of her back. He let them linger there, then pushed his fingertips inside the dress. The skin across her hatchet-like shoulder blades was taut and warm, riding and tightening across a network of bones.

The back of the young, scared girl who begged for eggs and fodder; the gypsy with juniper eyes, smart and savage.

He removed his hand. She touched his cheek, traced his jaw with her finger, her nail crackling through his beard. Her eyes held a watery light. Then she bent, gathered the hem of her dress and began to raise it from her ankles. Her stockings bound tight against her thin calves. Her knees were bare and ruddier than the skin of her thigh.

She held the dress, stared at him. "Why do you wait?"

He ran the back of his hand down her thigh to the cuff of the pantaloons she wore over her groin. He lifted the cuff; her skin beneath it was warm. The wiry hair of his knuckles tangled with the fine hair that covered her thighs. He pushed his hand far up the pants legs toward her crotch. There, in among her pubic hair, a warm wet gust caught his fingertips; he paused. He touched the lip of her quim, a vertical roll like a fat finger. She shuddered. So soft, blood-warm and slick. Her eyes were suddenly aglow.

"I'm sorry," he whispered. "Really, I have no experience. I've worked all my life."

He removed his hand and folded the dress back further. It piled at the sides of her hips. Her ribbed corset bunched loosely at her abdomen, jutted like the cowcatcher on a train. He reached under it, and beneath a chemise there was her stomach flat and hard. She bowed her head.

"Take all this off, maybe."

She reached across her waist, began unfastening the strings at her side. After several tugs at one knot, her arms dropped, and she slumped onto the corner of the bed. She shook her head, laughed and sputtered. "It is stuck." She laughed again, wiped her lips with the back of her knuckle. Very drunk. He wondered if she were too drunk.

He pulled the cigar knife from his coat. He tucked it under the draw strings of the corset and found they were only silk ribbons. He cut the first with a pop. She squeaked. He popped two more. She struck him hard in the shoulder with her closed fist. "This is costly in the extreme. It's from Bodenhauer's!"

He dropped the knife but grabbed both her elbows. "We can buy many others."

She let out a long sigh, pulled the corset aside, bent, and let the dress fall to the floor. Pushing herself backwards on the bed with the palms of her hands, she settled against the pillows, crossed her long arms at her waist, which was tiny, lined and taut as a young boy's. Her breasts were small as walnuts. In the flicker of the candlelight, her skin was porcelain white. She undid the pin at the back of her head and let her hair fall, leaned back on her elbows. Her eyes coddled him; they were as wet as her lips. All that carapace, all that struggle of escape from crinoline, ivory, whale bone, and silky shimmers to issue only this lean, paltry body... his own disappointment loomed and threatened to swallow him in a cistern of remorse.

She snorted, a laugh something like Weitzer's. "Don't think for a minute that *I* have any idea what we ought to do next." When his face grew perplexed she laughed the ringing laugh he remembered.

He sat down again on the bed. A chill like a frozen banner draped his chest and heart. Her long legs were there, salted with gooseflesh. What did he desire instead? He imagined her stouter, much stouter, her skin darkened.

She read the roving of his eyes as appetite and reached for his cheek. "We are married," she said with palpable joy and gratitude in her voice. "Claim your bride."

He looked into her eyes with the sudden thought that he might disappoint her and that he could, right now, refuse her. If he were truthful, in fact, he should refuse. "I promise I will try to love you. I mean, for the best. All I can. But...." It suddenly became too awful to say looking into her homely but warm and friendly face. Above that horseshoe of a chin was the tender smile and loving eyes of a woman who only wished to do her duty, to fulfill the role God and her people assigned her.

"Leighton Shea Moorken, shoosh. We are tired. No talking is necessary."

After a moment he rose and stood still. Five hundred and sixty acres. Lying in that bed, so young, she was fifteen, and yet wizened with losses like a war widow, a strange woman who suffered visions, from a family nothing like his. And his was gone, his mother, Charlotte, dead; his father, Michael, dead. Her eyes stared in drowsy crescents, and behind them, he realized, was not his language thinking, predicting, planning, but some other Barbar of which he knew hardly the first word.

"We did say we would have to go through with this to really scare them," she said. Her mouth smacked a bit as if she were parched.

"You've made a rich marriage," he said. He poured her a water, handed her the cool glass. Outside the wind moaned at one of the downspouts.

"You did not do so bad yourself."

"Well, then."

"Yes?" She frowned. "I may not know much, but I am quite sure you will need some of your clothes, at the least, to be off."

He disrobed. Lifting the covers, he scooted himself near her, but found her legs cold and abrasive. She kissed his arms, stroked his sides. "This is all that in the end matters, Leighton. Loving. You see people on the street—they all dwindle to this, are from it, live for it, die for lack of it. This is the keystone. This we must have."

He closed his eyes, saw Judith turning to him in the water before the cave, holding out her broad, dripping arms, gathering his head, burying it in the dark folds of her breasts. The cave surrounded them. Fossils flashed like stars.

Beneath him Patricia arched her back and neck. With his eyes shut, he imagined the give of Judith's thighs, the softness and breadth of her body. Patricia wrapped her long, thin arms around his neck, and eventually, with struggle, and some pain and much astonishment, he claimed his bride.

They lay there a moment on their backs, saying nothing, the candle bobbing its circle of flame and shadow. When Leighton touched her hand, she gripped his fiercely, and this grip did not relax until her breathing shallowed.

From the trunks the bellman left them, Leighton drew up a shimmering night gown. "This what you wear to bed?" She nodded sleepily, staring with those gray-green eyes, watching him while he found his nightshirt.

"Why did you ever marry me?" she asked once he was back in the bed.

He said nothing, squeezed her hand in his, and tried to feign sleep.

She gripped his hand sharply, rolled toward him. "I married you because you have the promise of wealth and great stability, very desirable traits. And," her voice fell to a whisper, "because I fear a life alone, unwed. Terribly fear it. And because I love my father and mother and could no longer see them shamed, owing you, owing many. They, too, have you. A defender. A brute. I have given them that. Now, you level with me."

"We need rest," Leighton said. "Everybody is going to expect us to be Mr. and Mrs. Morkan tomorrow."

She balled her fist and socked him in the chest.

"Damn!" he gasped. "All right, I wanted the land. Five hundred sixty acres. Your land. That lime under it."

She lay back with a thump that made the bed sway. "*Herr Gott. Mein Gott im Himmel,*" she whispered. "So on my wedding night, the only man to appreciate me is the City Engineer, and him I did not marry."

"Oh, Archer appreciates everybody when you first meet him."

She began to cry, and the bed shuddered for a long time. "Now where do we stand? Where do we go?"

"Home," he said. "Look, why are you crying? Here you wallop me and want the truth and next you're bawling when you get it? Mary, Mother of God!"

Her forehead pressed his shoulder, and the water of her tears beaded his nightshirt to his skin. After a minute, he stroked the back of her long neck, clutched her head to him and rocked her ever so slightly.

"I thought for a minute, when we were just now together, that you truly loved me," she said. She was icy calm, and the words did not seem hysterical or maudlin.

"I was trying to tell you that I thought eventually I could."

She snorted, but rested her chin on his shoulder. He could feel her eyes watching him in the dark. "You know," she said. "I think sometimes I will like to be lied to."

"Well, don't shoosh me, then. I'll get a good one out eventually."

"O, *Herr Gott*," she said shaking her head with her cheek crammed against his shoulder. He reached around her and kept her close.

Down in the lobby, the barkeep called time. Soon, her breathing, in and out, was quiet, like a tiny animal's in the dark.

In the late morning as they descended the stairs, the piano player saw them coming. He halted the ballade he was playing and romped into "It's a Grand Olde Flag."

Patricia stopped and after a few steps, Leighton turned to her. The bellman stumped on ahead with their luggage. Her face was so pale it appeared blue. "If I ever hear that song again, I will take your knife and hollow every one of my brains out like so much seed from a melon."

The bellman dropped the trunk he was carrying. He stood stammering and apologizing. Leighton fished an eagle from his pocket, asked him to run down and tell the piano player to cease, please, until Mrs. Morkan left the hotel.

Book 2

The Curtain of the Future World

Steve Yates

I

PATRICIA ENTERED THE KITCHEN AND FOUND JUDITH before the stove grumbling to herself. The floor, clammy, uneven rock, took most of Patricia's mind to negotiate. On the darkened window, frosty auroras seared the pane in a silver-blue haze.

Judith whirled. She clutched one of her immense teats. "Mercy, God!" she hollered, eyes wide, her shoulders rising. *Gross Gott*, she was a big thing. "You something from the grave, all white. Don't come up behind me like that," Judith said once she caught her breath.

Patricia frowned, and they both were silent. Patricia smoothed the white homespun against her thin body. In the skillet, grease smoked.

When she spoke, Patricia placed each syllable as carefully as she might a stitch in a shroud. "I shall come behind you in any manner I desire." She gripped a chair, the wood rough and in need of varnish. Wet, everything she touched!

Judith shook her head. "Ain't no need coming with that tone." She lifted the pot from the stove. "How you take your coffee, Miss Patricia?"

"It is Mrs. Patricia. And with whiskey, if I want."

"That'll sure start the day." Judith left the kitchen, then returned with a flask of whiskey. She poured the whiskey in a mug. "Like that?"

Patricia said nothing.

Judith doused the whiskey with coffee and set it before her.

Patricia lifted the mug and drank, returned Judith's stare without a flinch, though the whiskey scalded her throat and greatly soured the coffee.

Leighton strode through the kitchen to a mudroom lined with two cedar benches. Above the benches, lime crusted coats hung, and iron-colored brogans waited beneath in the shadows. He wore a faded shirt streaked with gray rivers. On his face was a frowzy look, his hair rising in plastered spikes, his eyes pinched.

Patricia rose, smiling at him, but he paid no mind. Judith hustled him some coffee. He gulped it, set it beside him, and began strapping crusty brogans on his stocking feet. Filth, the Negress let him wear it, things were so unclean. From the opened stove Judith began tossing sausage biscuits in a tow sack. One missed and rolled in a circle before it halted and came apart between the stones. Patricia gulped the coffee, felt the whiskey scour a tube of fire toward her middle. She had imagined him hoisting her in his arms, squeezing her, fawning for many minutes over her, finally tearing himself away for work. Surely what they had shared over these last nights changed everything. Instead all his attentions fell on the Negress and the task of getting him gone.

He stood and stomped his feet down in one of the brogans, debris ticking on the floor from the lime on his clothes. Judith held the tow sack before him. He planted a hand on her shoulder as he stood on one leg to hoist the other brogan on. Both of their expressions were level and unaffected by the touch. Patricia's eyebrows itched. Years of familiarity and need she witnessed in these parting gestures. Leighton had the boot on, and Judith handed him the sack of biscuits. With no change in expression, Leighton nodded and popped the Negress's meaty side twice as one would a champion milch cow.

Patricia cracked the mug against the tabletop, and the ceramic shattered, leaving her holding the handle, shards of the gray mug wobbling.

Leighton scowled at her. Then he turned to Judith. "Manage her."

Patricia tossed the handle, which shattered against the wall. He did not even pause exiting the back doorway.

She slumped into her seat at the kitchen table, buried her face in her arms. When she opened her eyes again, the wood grains, the deep gouges in the table made her wonder how many generations of filthy Irish had gorged at it, champing like swine.

Judith set another something beside her—a mug that scraped against the tabletop and warmed her forearm. A trail of steam wetted her nose. The whiskey in it smelled like autumn sunshine.

After drinks with Archer, it was almost nine p.m. when Leighton arrived home. Patricia gripped the kitchen table. Her eyes were bloodshot. Her shoulders weaved. She had a dishtowel wadded in her free hand.

Leighton sat on the mudroom bench and removed his brogans. The smell of vinegar, spices, and warm venison pervaded the air. "Where's Judith?"

Patricia's eyes narrowed. "Those are the first words you have spoken to me this day." She raised her eyebrows. "And they concern someone else."

"Judith?!" Leighton called.

"Your wife serves you tonight."

She wrapped the dishtowel around her hand, opened the stove. With the hook, she drew a Dutch oven from the coals. Her face was red and sweating as she held the Dutch oven up. When she lowered it to the table it clanged and the lid popped loose. Rising steam enveloped her arms, but she set the lid aside with slow conviction.

She fetched two oval masses onto a plate, then pulled a chair back for him. Her face grew even redder. She took a deep breath.

When he sat, she took a mug from the cupboard. From the mudroom, she drew a Dunkel from the keg Weitzer had given them. Then she set the mug carefully, ceremoniously at the edge of his plate.

The ovals were sliced potatoes beneath which was a thick layer of a dark meat. There was yellowed cabbage strung throughout this. The steam off the plate reeked of vinegar and black pepper. His fork sank into the potatoes and meat. Expecting to gag, he raised the morsel to his lips.

The potatoes were stewed but solid and tart around peppery venison and soft cabbage. It was like nothing he had ever eaten before. He drank the beer, and it quenched the tartness in the victuals, matched them like blood to flesh. "God Almighty," he said.

She glared at him, her head almost vibrating. Strands of her hair were pasted to her cheeks. Still creased with wrinkles from the packing trunk, the apron she wore was bordered with little blue fleur-de-les.

He ate again, took a draught. He touched his mouth with a napkin. Anytime he set his mug apart from the plate, she fetched it full again. She served him seconds when he cleared his plate. He ate. Standing at Judith's counter in the gloom, Patricia was a gauzy line of yellow and white, the rest of her in shadow, thin arms folded across her chest. Above her long jaw, the crescents of her eyes wavered, even softened. "What did you do with your day?" he asked. "Aside from fighting Judith."

She did not laugh and before she could speak he was talking again. "Ran Judith off, eh? Guess you won?" When she said nothing he paused in his eating and looked at her. He wiped his face clean again. "You made a fine meal, Patricia." He listened at the house, for Judith was large enough, one could hear her presence if she were moving. When he was certain the Negress was not in the manse he said, "Judith could never make any of this. And it really is a fine meal."

Patricia merely raised her eyebrows.

After that first morning, he saw Judith only in the early light, pre-dawn being the one time Patricia could not dislodge the Negress's presence. It was impossible to rise before Judith did. No matter what time you woke, you found her at the woodpile or coming from the dairy barn in the star light. When he saw Judith, the Negress hardly spoke. Patricia was always there in the kitchen, drinking her coffee at the table, the cooking already stacked for the eating—strange potato cakes with jellies, sausages unlike any he knew, berries, porridges. When a chore brought Judith into the kitchen both women hurried and frowned. The lick of Patricia's spatula against the pan was as loud and portentous as a razor against a strop. Patricia insisted on bending and giving him her shoulder to lean on, slight as a shelf made of cane rushes. Riding through the quarry gates, seeing Archer's wagons and Percherons waiting in a line beneath the derrick, holding Odem's crusty stump in his hand, he felt truly at home as if everything outside the quarry was part of a bad dream riven with conflict, a nightmare he was free of it the minute he snapped Odem's false forearm into place. But even that illusion of rectitude vanished when they emerged from the office to a Black quarry, freedmen clambering on every rock face, banging for a pittance. Leighton felt as low as the Devil in Hell, and the cascades of revenue only assured his fall.

In his dream a crystalline cathedral of bare forest glimmered in impossibly sharpened sun. Beneath rainbows of ice, a wooden core threaded its quilt of browns, blacks, parchment, and grays—bare hickories, oaks, sweet gum, beeches, sycamore. But then browns became hides of horses; the blacks soot on skin and cracked leather, the gray and parchment transformed into soiled and tattered butternut and smatters of campaign coats soldered to frames of men. Opal vapors rolled from their noses and from the lips of their mounts as off a pounding shoal. One thousand stepped forward, a single, scorched, and evil thought issued from the skeletal wood. There was no animal sound over this smoking field. The Battle of Springfield, but Leighton could not place himself with the line of patients. Where had his fellows gone? Where was the log wall, where the rifle pits? Dismounted figures scrabbled like gray lice among the stubble of blackened hearths on the wintered scalp of what once had been his town. How had it come to this—no one ready? None mustered but him? Rifles probing as they crept, cracking shots, nearer, nearer, no sound of men or horse over the ice, only armaments, every report ringing for miles. Maybe nothing could live in his dream. Then like winged angels, the white garbed patients gathered to him in a firing line that blasted flame and smoke. Faceless and still, one of the vermin woodsmen, his enemy, rested in his arms. The gore on his hands, warm and coagulated as clay off a spudding bit, clasped his palms. Across the shaggy, icy meadow, tree limbs cracked like gunfire in war everlasting. O Lord, let the winter sun go down.

Patricia learned never to waken him from the horror of a dream, never to startle him from sleeping. For what she wakened she

141

quickly knew was not her husband but something born else-where in creeping summer thickets, threatened, hunted, sleeping with eyes wide open in the dark. Not her husband. The first time she saw him seize and tremble, then cry out from night terrors, she reached tenderly for his back. One moment her long white fingers hovered in the moonlight; she petted his shoulder. In a flash he was on her, straddling her, heavy knees pinning her abdomen, fierce, rough hands expertly at her throat, squeezing. Not her husband, for in the moonlight the one lazy eye was centered and steadfast on a spot at her hairline joined in proper lockstep with its blue partner, eyes made whole and parallel and perfected in violence. One last desperate whack to the back of his head, all her strength do or die, she clocked him. The eyeball crawled diagonally like a blue beetle escaping behind a wall-board. Her husband returned with a gasp.

"Jesus. Patricia!" he released her, stared at his hands and her neck for an instant, then flailed his hands all around him on sheets and mattress, not to ascertain his surroundings, but as if, thump-ing them furiously, to rid himself of some frightful covering of blooded sin. "Jesus. Oh, God have I hurt you? Are you hurt?" He was gasping, and she grabbed his forearm to reassure and settle him, though she could not speak, her throat was so wrought. Through his sopping night shirt, her hands now stroking his chest, she could feel his monster of a heart hammering.

Riding home one night, Leighton noticed a hunched shadow shuffle through the woods. The moon blared across the hills in a kind of blue daylight, and rime the cold left made a field of sorghum stalks sparkle as if strewn with metal filings. Under him the horse raised its head and a tremor ran down its spine. Nudging, he got the animal to side step into the darkness where the shadows of the trees hung over the road. He stroked his ani-mal's hide and then eased the Colt from its holster, hid its metal along the horse's neck.

Gravel crunched as the figure stepped from the tree line, a squat shadow in a long coat. Then he caught the round face, the inky gloss of her cheeks.

"Judith," Leighton said. "You'll get shot poking around like this."

She stood beside the horse, which nuzzled at her bonnet. "Anymore I don't hardly get to tell you nothing," she said. "But I got something awful to tell you now."

Leighton dismounted and stood very close to her so that their voices would not carry. It was the first bitterly cold night of December. His toes were so brittle they hummed in his boots. One more freeze like this and he would shut the quarry down for the winter, give the men a millings bonus early—extra store coupons to make a Christmas and salve his conscience. The silence pervaded around them as completely as the moonlight above. Up on the hill before the road turned South, the white columns and jaundiced windows of the house stood out from the dark velvet tree line. Maybe it was the bulk of her clothes beneath the coat, but Judith seemed larger, more hulking.

"What's the matter?"

"I'm with child."

Back in the trees branches groaned as the wind rose.

"What do you expect me to do?" Leighton asked.

Judith grunted. "Ain't going to look very good in your household for the maid to drop a woodscolt and not have a beau in sight."

Leighton held his breath, running his mind over possibilities. He could send her away. But his heart shattered at the thought of it. He could ask her to marry a Negro in town. Or Isaac. "Name you a beau."

"And what do I get for it?"

"Whatever you call honor, I suppose."

"Child can't eat honor. And it's your honor gone to matter."

"Judith," he said. He ground his teeth so tightly the edges of them smarted. "I'm astonished. This is damned low." The cold crept round his arms.

"The hell it is. What you going to give me to say this here baby belongs to another man." She cocked her head, and her eyes, dull points of black in her moonlit face, seemed more fierce than ever.

143

"Did you plan it this way?" he asked. "Did you figure master would be damn partial if you had you a special problem? Was all that a lie in the cave?"

She stood in silence, her breath purling in silver.

"Name what you want then."

"I want me some of that Dutch gal's land. On the stream. Close enough to walk to from your house. I want Lawyer Daniels to come up and draw title."

"What's wrong with my land?"

Judith said nothing.

"I keep all mineral rights then."

She shrugged her shoulders. "Don't mean nothing to me."

"And you marry Isaac."

She paused. In the dark, he struggled to see her face.

"Fair enough," she said.

Her voice was so business-like he recalled the way he and Patricia had negotiated at her birthday picnic. He shuddered. "Judith, you didn't have to come to me this way. You didn't have to act ... you know I would never ..." He shook his head, unable to defend himself or explain. A child. God, what a condemnation. What a burden. What an inconvenience. But then, Judith was aiding him. Give her some acres away from the house. Marry her to Isaac. She'd have the baby off there, raise it in the Weitzer's woods. Patricia need know nothing but that the babe was Isaac's.

"Thank you for doing this. For coming to me," he said. He reached to touch her, but she lurched back. He stood still. "You are wise, Judith."

"I'll show you wise. Get Lawyer Daniels to the house and he can deed the land and marry us in one visit."

Leighton nodded.

"And don't you think I'm going to go asking Isaac about this. You going to do some serious courting for me starting right now." She backed away, then turned, her feet crackling on the frozen grass as she left him.

At the house, Patricia waited on the porch, her gray figure against one of the columns. When Johnson took his horse, Leighton strode up the steps. She wore a pair of white mittens, a heavy white coat with a hood trimmed in rabbit fur, something

Leighton had his tailor, Corvin Looney, make for her. With the hood pulled back, her hair bobbed, her eyes in their slick crescents, she appeared as if winter were her natural season. Down in the fur of the hood, where it parted at her neck, moonlight flashed on a single bead in the lace of her dress. Again, Leighton saw that his wife could be beautiful. Suddenly he wanted to tell her everything.

"*Schau mal, wie der Winter kommt, mein Soldatchen?*" To his surprise, she stuck her arms out to him, and they embraced warmly. He could smell the cordials she'd been drinking. He was growing used to wild vacillations, cold formality in the morning, histrionic passion at night, her eyes glazed with booze.

"What are you out here without a lantern for?" He gripped her waist where a silver belt held the coat close to her.

"*Die Augen für die langen Nächte, Herr Professor Morkan.*"

"Whatever the hell you're saying, don't stop."

They kissed, and between kisses, she issued a slurry of German. He lifted her, jerked the door aside, carried her across the threshold and across the stones to the couch in the library where they had first made love when they came home newly wed, where they made love roughly now, his knees sinking in the rabbit's fur lining of her coat.

He rested on the floor while she poured him a port and lit two cigars. She sat smoking on the couch, running her bare feet across his ribs. Naked she was still so thin and girl-like that she seemed too young for appetites of the flesh. Save for her height. God, her legs took up all kinds of space, they were so long.

"Judith wants to marry Isaac," he said.

The low smoky waver of the kerosene flame in her birthday lamp made the old books loom and recede. She stared at the end of her cigar, stuck her tongue out at its gray ash. "What do you see in these?" She drank her cordial. "I feel like spitting and spitting."

"Did you hear me?"

"Yes. Why should I care for them? *Pipi machen. Lächerlich.* They mean nothing to us." She crammed the cigar down in the cordial glass. "We should make ourselves sick with our own happiness."

145

"I'm going to give them some acres by the stream back on your land."

Her feet stilled. Then she shrugged. "What's a little out of hundreds?"

"It is your dowry." Were she Irish this would be no small matter.

"Don't speak of them." She gave his ribs a shove with her foot, long and boney.

He stared up at her, cigar clamped in his mouth. It was done then. Maybe all he had to worry about was the look of the child, the color of its skin. He set the cigar aside and clasped her legs.

Isaac kept four good hounds. Sunday evening, Leighton told the Negro to take him coon hunting. He and Isaac sat at a fire by the stream on what had been Weitzer's old acres. Isaac had been on Morkan land all his life, formerly a slave once of the broken farmer the old Morkan bought out. He made a fine hunting guide, but he was often worth little else in Leighton's esteem.

The dogs bayed trail very close by but returned to the fire time and again, stupid eyes bright, tongues hanging. Stiff as iron pokers, their tails pumped the air. They loped back to the forest. Disgusted, Leighton and Isaac rose.

The hounds bayed tree, and Leighton and Isaac followed their racket and soon found them circling and leaping toward a pine's branches. A raccoon tottered on a limb, glaring eyes red in the lantern light. The hounds were jumping at another raccoon higher in the tree. Dogs leapt, legs straight and stiff, teeth bared, black lips peeled back in grins.

Isaac held a lantern up. Red eyes appeared like embers in the boughs, eleven coons at least. Isaac handed Leighton the lantern and held up the ax. The ax rang against the pine. The dogs sidled back, their tails dancing, pink tongues rubbing their chops.

As the tree crackled and fell, several of the coons leapt to the ground. The tree crashed flat, then shivered. Coons went scuttling and the hounds rushed them. The ax flashed and Isaac caught a coon in the hindquarters—a hound barreled the coon over.

Leighton shot two coons with his rifle. Soon, the dogs milled before Leighton and Isaac, bloody snouts, tongues lapping. He and Isaac managed to keep six of eleven, losing two to the dogs, the rest to the woods.

Leighton lifted the branches of the pine, rubbed its needles in his fingertips. "Ripe, wonderful country, hey Isaac?"

Isaac nodded. He held up a dead raccoon, and the hounds cocked their heads and followed it.

Leighton picked up the lantern, then hoisted two coons over his shoulder. Instantly the bloody fur warmed his skin where the cuff of his coat joined his gloves.

Leighton patted Isaac on the shoulder, and the Negro blinked at him. "How would you like a piece of it?" His breath roiled white.

Isaac paused, his brow creased. Wrinkles rode the corners of his eyes. He nodded, but said, "Like Johnson have?" They resumed their walk.

"Much bigger. Right up here. And Judith comes with it."

Isaac frowned at him. "What you mean?"

"I'll give the two of you forty acres if you'll marry her." Leighton shifted the carcasses to his other shoulder. The blood there had dried, and now the cuffs of his gloves were pasty and his coat stiffened as if it were canvas.

"What's she say bout this?"

"She's all for it. It's time. At her age."

Isaac's eyes narrowed and his lips rose in a slight grin. "Why you need this?"

Leighton made no answer.

Isaac smirked. "She still going to work at the house?"

Leighton nodded.

Isaac shifted the coons higher on his shoulder, leaned into the uphill walk. "She gone wet nurse?"

Leighton stopped. He bent to catch Isaac's face, but found the Negro's gaze set placidly on the trail. "Why do you ask?"

The Negro shrugged, the coons rising with his shoulders, claws dangling. "Your daddy bought a farm run by slavery. Cooking, cleaning, cropping, nursing babies. Wasn't a thing done without there was a slave in it."

147

"That's not quite the house I'm running," Leighton said.

Isaac grinned, raised his eyebrows. "Sure," he said.

At the saw barn, Leighton watched him skin the coons. "So you accept."

"You need me to bad enough." He pulled at the carcass, at the skin around the face. "Just make sure that sixty acres come in both our names. And if it's a son, you treat him near your own as you can. Not like me or his mama." The raccoon's eyes glared from its mask of red gristle.

Leighton said nothing.

"You heard me, Mister Leighton?" Isaac's voice dropped so low, the words seemed a statement.

That next week Lawyer Daniels visited and wrote the deed, on which Leighton signed and Judith and Isaac made their marks. Then they were married on the Morkan porch with Leighton and Johnson Davis as witnesses. Johnson scowled the entire time, and no one raised an eye from the stone of the porch. It began to snow, tiny flakes whirling down like insects. Lawyer Daniels stamped in the cold, snuffled, but Leighton only paid him, did not ask him in for dinner. He rode on home since he would not eat with the newlyweds.

As Lawyer Daniels' sorrel disappeared, Judith and Isaac followed behind. The two newlyweds walked apart as if they were merely laborers who happened to be on the same trail to the same destination. Judith never once turned to look back. At the window, Patricia came up behind Leighton, wrapped her arms at his waist. She whispered something in German. Over a white chemise she wore one of his leather vests unbuttoned, a pair of his red wool stockings on her feet. The mug of Dunkel in her hand dribbled brown.

She took his hand, pressed it to her stomach, where he cupped his hand. He grinned, imagined all the liquor was finally going to put a belly on her. "I have missed my time a month and more now." She stroked his hair. "There will be another Morkan."

II

WINTER PASSED AND MARCH'S DAFFODILS AND SQUALLS brought the tease of spring. As Patricia began to show, her arms and fingers rounded, her face softened. In bed, she held his hand to her stomach and talked dreamily about souls entwined as one, her eyes glowing in the candlelight. "One from two, Leighton," she whispered, then repeated it in German.

The wind from the parted window pushed the smell of wet sheep across his nose. His side of the bed was now crammed against a squat spinning wheel of Patricia's, so polished it gleamed at night. Another piece of her truck he rued; it caused him to lurch up from sleep night upon night having dreamed that a wagon wheel was careening toward his head. Now seated on the bed with Patricia in one of her childbearing ecstasies, he thought of Judith running her knuckle across her sweaty forehead, his child growing in her also, hidden like a thief's cache. Suddenly he realized Patricia had been talking to him a very long time.

"I said, do you not know someone with a good flock of sheep?"

"Mmm?" He stared smilingly at her face.

She shook her head and frowned. "Where do you go when your eyes are so far away? You look right through me."

"Your body sets me in a reverie," he said. He nuzzled her ear. "You're stouter than a Christmas goose. And you've got months more."

She smiled up at the ceiling, closed her eyes. "Sometimes I feel I have inside me a famous soul from a thousand years ago." Sighing, she fell to stroking his hand where it rested on her. The baby moved, pushing against his palm.

149

† † †

Leighton expected Archer to become a homebody with a wife finally on hand. Instead his friend immersed himself in the formation of something awful—an anti-horse thief club. With its secret signs and covert membership, it smacked of Masons and Know Nothings.

In the cutting yard, five Negroes polished hundreds of new tombstones for Archer's National Cemetery, rubbing them with quartzite sanding blocks strapped to their palms. Leighton and Archer leaned on the gate to the yard. "I'm calling it the Gentlemen's Defense League," Archer said. "We *are* order moving against chaos."

Leighton snorted. "Let me show you something order gave me." He loosened his collar, and in the sunlight, bared the indicia along his neck, eight silvery crescents in two rows of four at the back of his spine, two deep pools of scarred silver in front where the fingernails of a St. Louis Mason bit young Leighton's neck when the Mason had shaken the wee Catholic Mick until his teeth cracked. "If I'd of had a gun and known soldiering then, I swear to God, Archer. I will not join your riders."

A bearded Armenian named Devie Hamra stooped to a row of stones and began chipping cross-hatches into their sides with an embossing tool, a chisel pointed like an ice pick. When Hamra had finished, each stone held a shadowed edge. Two Negroes stacked the stones for Menzardo to engrave.

"Archer, you have a wife. You have responsibilities to live peaceably," said Leighton. Even a façade of a marriage, like his own, could be made peaceable, functional, a better thing than vigilantes raging in the woods.

"To be honest with you, as with all your other damned obstinacies," Archer said, "you will lose out for holding back on to this one, too!"

Out in the yard, the stones scraped on one another, grinding and whispering.

Because Leighton made no motions to procure Patricia sheep or seek the wool she begged for, she took the cash she saved from what she squirreled from all his pocket dregs and her own frugality and buttoned this sum in a canvas sash, which fit beneath her maternity corset. She sat in the mudroom on the bench wearing a summer work dress, ankle jacks, and a broad straw milking hat. Thank God this was not St. Louis—no one she cared about would see her stout with child and on her own like a farmer's wife groaning in July fields.

"There will be wool in this house, Judit," she said, grunting at the laces, sweat riding her forehead. Her belly and its burden were terrible to contend with in summer.

Judith went about her duties with the same flat frown and glazed yellow eyes and no more engagement with the Universe than a milch cow standing in a scummy pond.

"There will be industry in this house." Patricia nodded, her eyes beads of steel coursing Judith's broad form. "I have a Saxony spinner with ivory finials, a rosewood wheel." She counted on her fingers, making each point glaring at Judith who was shoving sausage in a pan as if she meant to mash the pork into pudding. "In one season I can spin for him enough worsted for a coat and vest, trousers and scarf." When Judith shifted the big skillet, the sausage erupted in boisterous applause. "And yet he pisses off good money on coats sewn by Lunatic the Tailor from wool that hasn't even been mordanted properly. You can smell it stinking."

Leighton stumbled into the kitchen, one suspender drooping, his hair roused into a shaft of black bristles like a whisk-broom's. "Christ, the time," he muttered. Bleary eyed, he thumped to a seat in the mudroom across from Patricia. He gaped at her, then gazed at Judith as if for advice.

Judith turned from the stove and was watching them both with a grin.

Patricia pulled her riding gloves on finger by finger with the care of a cavalryman loading cartridges. Judith shrugged her broad shoulders, then without thinking ran a hand along the expanse of her belly, but pulled it away when she saw Leighton blanch.

"I am going," Patricia said.

Leighton kept his eyes on Judith. The Negress was showing, but like a cow, she only appeared heavier at first glance. You had to stare at her to discern the truth. "In your condition? Don't be foolish. Where? What do you mean?"

"You have shown yourself," Patricia said. When she folded her hands atop her stomach, the crescents of her eyes made her appear all knowing.

Leaning down, he pulled one of his boots from beneath the bench. The fog cleared from his mind and left a tumult. Did she know? Had Judith told her so?

"I should have known," she said, "that you would dally and leave me to wait until, 'in my condition,' there was no move I could make. Or so you think."

He sat holding the shoe, staring at her forlornly. Deep in the stove a log cracked. Judith's fingers strangled the handle of the spatula.

"But I tell you there is something to be done." Patricia's eyes sparkled.

Leighton's face clamped like a fist. He was posturing, she thought, looking ugly and angered so he could fend her off and refuse to buy the sheep. If there was one thing bearing a child loaned to the mind it was prescience. She could feel the air coruscate with the fire of truth even now. She could see like a searchlight sweeping dark water. He asked what she knew he would: "Well, what is to be done?"

She gripped the seat of the bench, and pulled herself forward. "Look at Judit." She popped the heel of her hand beside her on the bench. With a grunt she stood.

Leighton quailed as her tall, swollen form shadowed him. Were she a man, he would stand right now and prepare for to be pummeled.

"Look at Judit." She pointed. "Is that any way to leave a person? She wears rags, the sun on her everywhere. And, pardon me, Judit, but heaven knows she has eaten herself out of anything she might find comfortable."

Leighton stared hard at the stones of the floor.

"That's right," Patricia said. "It is plain to see from her the sort of man you are."

Leighton's face grew purple. He slammed the boot down on the bench. "She is pregnant by Isaac."

The searchlight vanished. All waters fell impenetrably black. The same air that had burned with truth now whirled with mystery and unforeseeable hazards. Patricia clenched her hands carefully into fists. "All the more reason, then" she said, but without a hint of that former confidence. How did he know this of Judith before Patricia could sense it? And how did this topic arise from a discussion of clothing and home industry?

For a long time they remained glaring at each other. Very slowly, Judith pulled the sausage from its griddle, the skillet grating on the burner.

"We will have wool in vis house."

"Wool?" His shoulders began to quiver he was so angry. "What the hell are you talking about?"

"*Hundswarze!*" Cables of tendon stood out along her neck as if steam had filled them. "Have you not listened to me these many nights and I have told you in so many ways? I want sheep on this land or wool in my house or I will lose my mind mit idleness."

"Sheep? Jesus." He stood, but a grin spread on his face, and she could only interpret his expression as malicious. He looked at Judith, who now kneaded the round of her belly with a genuine air of relief. "You two are out of your minds, the both of you." He tramped his feet down in his boots and buckled them swiftly. He exited the door without a glance behind him, leaving the two of them standing in the quiet, hot kitchen.

"Left us two crazy women with a mighty good breakfast," Judith said.

Breathing deeply, Patricia removed her gloves. "Set us a table, then, please, Judit. We shall eat heartily and together."

They sat down to a mound of biscuits and honey butter and greasy sausage, piles of eggs, and quivering gravy.

Patricia filled well before Judith, who ate with delight, spooning gravy over everything. "I am sorry at my comment on your stoutening of late," Patricia said. "I had no idea."

Judith grunted, but kept eating. With her mouth full, she said, "You a fine gal, Mrs. Patricia. You played him through every sound in the songbook."

Patricia watched her eat for so long that the Negress raised her eyes from her plate and held her head perfectly still as if her treachery was discovered. Patricia smiled—this world, the world of the grubby, cheap Mick stonebasher and his Negro wench were more alien than anything she could have envisioned. She was determined, though, to make a home of these stone floors where Judith had been a slave, where Rebels gat them the fire to kill Erich and Robart. "But I do not yet have my sheep Judit."

"Mmph. You will. You let that stomach settle, and I send Johnson to town for a surrey now. You get them sheep."

Patricia popped her fist on the table and grinned. "I will teach you to spin, Judit. Like the mothers of Saxony, I will."

The surrey took her southeast of town where a sheep farmer had kept his flock before the war. The jaunt was a gamble—she might find only acres of blackened stubble where the sheep farm had burned.

In the heat, the driver exuded a strange smell, as if his oily coat and grungy trousers had been boiled along with cabbage.

"Stop here," she said, sitting up.

In the summer sun that cooked the green fields, a dozen gray lumps crowded beneath the spread of a monstrous elm tree. Rambouillets, and among them a black ram circulating, testicles like big walnuts behind his haunches.

"Oh, *mein Gott*," she said, clutching her stomach and leaning forward.

The driver was so startled he dropped the reins and leapt down off the seat. But then he stood there staring in the direction her eyes took.

The sheep mobbed on the north side of the hill where the sun swarmed across their fleece and made them shiver with annoyance. Above them, clouds white as cotton crowded up. With the tree and its leaves shimmering, the sky pouring down sun, and the wind still, the sheep kept a fierce docility. When she touched her dress, her hands seemed waxy with lanolin. Her eyes watered. From the burly look of the animals, they had not been sheared and were suffering this late in the season.

"Get in the wagon, idiot," she whispered to the driver.

Climbing back in the surrey the driver cursed. One of the horses raised its tail, shat, and shivered. "Sheep, lady," the driver said. "Ain't you ever seen sheep before?"

"I have done more than see sheep, you clodhopper."

The surrey driver grinned—far back in his mouth several of his teeth were dark as spots of tar. "I thought you had to be a man to do much more to sheep." In the heat his cackle made her seethe. His throat bobbed and his eyes grew teary before he finished laughing.

"I am glad to amuse you," she said sullenly. "Now, take us up to that mess of stones there. There will be a shepherd."

The driver obeyed but remained hunched, shivering in fits of laughter. They approached a shelter of stones so jumbled and askew it appeared the structure had been dropped from a great height.

The driver stopped the surrey in the dirt lot that surrounded the hovel. From a hole in the thatch roof waves of smoke and heat warped the air.

"Shepherd?" she called.

The sheep rolled their eyes, the ram posing at the horses, stomping his back legs.

Patricia raised herself in the seat, held hard to the canvas so she could crane her head around it. "Shepherd?"

In the silence, a ewe bleated her staccato opinion—ma a a a a a d.

There came a greasy click behind them, and the surrey driver stiffened, his cheeks turning gray as talc. With a whisper on the grass, a gunman bearing a cocked revolver in his hand stepped into their view. It was a pistol she had never seen with a regular muzzle and below that one belled like a blunderbuss, but it sparkled with gun bluing and was cleaner than anything about the man. His face was so filthy it seemed green, and above the thicket of his beard he had but one blue eye. The other eye was capsized into a pit the bottom of which was as metallic and battered as the head of a nail. "The Hell do you want?" he asked, the one eye rolling as if it might reach out from the socket.

When Patricia began to speak the surrey driver gaped at her. "Tell me, shepherd, what of these sheep are for sale?"

The gunman said nothing, only stared with his one eye traveling between the driver and Patricia.

155

"You're Dutch," he said.

"I am Patricia Morkan, wife of Leighton Shea Morkan."

"That didn't help you one bit." The gunman pointed with the pistol, waving them back the way they had come.

The driver lifted the reins, but Patricia caught his wrists.

"I have come to buy your sheep. I carry cash."

"Jesus, Jesus, lady," the driver whined. Trembling he turned to the gunman. "I got no part in this, Mister. I'm just a working man from the transfer and drug her out here."

"Get her gone," the gunman said.

The driver yanked his arm from Patricia's and snapped the reins. The horses lurched forward, dropping her to her seat. When the rig was turned and headed back, the gunman fired in the air, and the horses shot off at a gallop.

Soon they were coursing through the woods, every shade of green zipping past, Patricia staring straight ahead, the driver hunching forward.

Finally, the driver slowed the horses. "Lady, I want my cash right now."

"You go to hell. We are not even home."

"And we'll be lucky to get her near home," the driver said. He was still so upset that his face held the strange blue and rosy red of a new corpse. "Lady, you told that fellow you has cash in hand."

Patricia scowled at him. "He will not be selling those sheep on credit."

The driver's eyes narrowed. "You pulling my leg or are you that stupid?"

Patricia crossed her arms above her stomach. "Yes, I know what you think. That he was an old bushwhacker who hates the Dutch and now he has turned to a ruthless horse thief who, rather than consider me a married woman with child would instead consider me fatter and easier prey."

The driver stared at her. "You knew all that and still you stood there an tole him you had cash and whose wife you was like they was no problem in that but a day's business?" Roving like two peas in white bowls, his eyes scanned the woods. "You're crazy, then. A Dutch lunatic."

156

She felt a wave of sympathy come over her. The driver had big pink ears, a scrawny neck, yellowed skin, a complexion like spoiled gravy, and such teeth. The genes of the British Isles must be a terrible burden. She hoped her child would turn out as German as possible.

"May I tell you something I have learned being of uncommon descent in these lands and having so far survived?"

With his neck rigid, he was fixated on something in the woods east of them—a deer maybe or some other animal that he could murder swiftly. She had seen teamsters of Scots-Irish descent chase down animals on foot and blast at them and not even bother to stay and dress the full carcass for use. Whispering, the driver sounded angry. "Lady, you may want to quieten down about now."

"I will ignore that," she said. She raised her chin and felt one of the surges of delight and energy carrying the child brought. The babe tumbled inside her, disturbed in its dreams of string and ladders and the mouths of tunnels. "What you do not realize, being of the predominant race in this region, is that people are often mirrors."

The driver crouched against the surrey hood, his wide eyes rolling on her.

"What you project they reflect. When you show cowardice, they too may show fear. You must learn to face your terrors unflinchingly with confidence and a smile. And the world will…" She paused, sensing the driver's whole spine had gone rigid and now it was humming taut as a violin string. All his attention was focused on something he probably could not kill.

Then through slats of yellow light scoring the leafy tapestry around them coursed a man on horse back, an evil thought in the green shade, two men, three, in shirtsleeves of butternut, with hair draping greasy, long as women's hair. They stepped dingy mounts parallel with the surrey and road as they weaved through trees, disappearing as into a mist, then reappearing, eyes dark as knots on a hackberry and fastened to the surrey and its contents. They neither called to one another, nor called to the wagon. With the sun and leaves flickering over them, they were spirits of the tangled wood, sylvan snarls of nightmare.

157

The driver slowed the horses to a halt. He took one long look at Patricia, his lips quivering, his eyes tearing. Then he dropped the reins in her hand, leapt from the seat, and dashed into wooded oblivion.

The horsemen halted, watched him go, faces flat. They neared the surrey, animals moving without guidance, without a touch of halter, without even a whisper.

Patricia secured the reins in her hands, pulled back hard enough to make the two horses champ their bits and roll their heads about. One of the horsemen stepped next to the team, hopped down from his saddle, and latched onto the lead horse's trace. The horses stamped. Patricia set the brake.

Another horseman halted beside her, the dusty hide of his animal bumping the surrey. He latched a hand to the canopy. His nails were green and gray from their tips to their quicks. Forcing the canopy back he peered at her with eyes as dull and inhuman as smears of clay. His nose had a divot hewn from it at the bridge, a square notch true as one the Weitzer might have cut for a tongue and groove joint.

She folded her hands in her lap. "You have driven my driver away," she said. "I wonder, did he know you?"

One of the rider's companions swung behind him. Pistol butts and knives jutted from their belts. Dappling their shoulders and waists were vests as gaudy as old upholstery. The man at the traces was now coaxing the riggings and harness off the shivering horses.

With her eyes narrowed, Patricia stared at the gunman. "I am going to step down off this seat before your man there pitches me in the dirt."

The gunman with the divot in his nose crossed his wrists on his saddle horn.

As she climbed down, her heel made the iron of the step creak, and in the forest, humid as a bottle in the sun, this moan of iron on wood was the only sound. Beneath the ankle jacks she felt the chert of the road hard and unrelenting as never before.

To her surprise, the men dismounted. The man with the divot in his nose drew a long pistol. Patricia glared at him.

158

One of the men grinned and his teeth were so black, it appeared he had dined on shoe polish. Through the trees, a hot wind came—she could feel it pressing her dress against her shins, a motion accompanied by the hiss of the air through the oaks. Now I see how the winter comes, she thought.

The baby moved inside her, pushed a foot or hand against her lower abdomen. She took a breath. It was a hand, she knew for the first time what appendage the child was pushing with. She felt, she was convinced, the thumb and four points of fingers tap, then push long and hard against the wall that bound them. The realization of that hand pushing out was like the vision of a star exploding over a blackened hillside.

She squatted slowly, drawing the hem of her dress up as she did. The brows of the men wrinkled, the knots of their eyes following her down.

"She gone drop that young'n right cheer."

The one with the mangled nose raised his hand to shush his partner.

Reaching beneath the corset, she caught the canvas belt in her fingers. She untied it, drew it out like a long, gray tapeworm from under her dress.

The men watched her very closely as did the two dull horses, now free of the fetters, the surrey nose down in the road. She straightened herself, smoothed her dress. Unzipping the canvas bag, she began taking the cash from it. Above them in the cauldron of the summer air, a flight of vultures circled so close to the treetops that the tips of their greasy wings spread like accusing fingers. She held the wad of cash in her hand, the bills clammy and limp.

She extended the bills to the man with the mangled nose. She cast her chin forward and bore herself with what she thought was pride.

Taking the cash, the man with the mangled nose turned his pistol so that he held the gun by the muzzle as if it were a heavy hammer. For a moment, Patricia thought he might hand her the pistol, that by some miracle of courage, this was over. Down in her she felt the babe cringe toward her spine.

The man with the mangled nose cocked his hand back and swept the pistol across her chin. Inside her jaw there was a crack as loud as a tree falling. A great white bolt of light descended on her, and the three men dwindled to animal tracks in a sky of white, new fallen snow.

She wrapped her arms around her belly, clutched it as she collapsed. Such a whirling of red and black. On the day of the feast of St. John the Baptist, the Catholic Germans in St. Louis set great wheels of scrap wood afire and rolled these downhill into the River, set the night ablaze with them. And she saw these fiery wheels in a black night.

A muttering near her, then laughter. A warm rain smelling of ammonia was falling. The babe tapped, then pushed against her abdomen. Her heart worked so hard she could feel it snapping and squirting down in her throat. Whole galaxies became clear in her mind as if an angel had shouted her name through a horn. But the world touching her tumbled fierily into a river of black. The babe rolled, all knees and noggin. The stinking rain pattered.

Shane Peale brought Leighton and Archer from the quarry to the house where the doctor met them. A telegraph lineman had found her pistol-whipped and defiled, curled off to the side of Brookline Road near an abandoned surrey from the Pickwick Transfer with all its horses stolen and the traces broken.

On the porch the doctor was pacing, pausing and gesturing as if he were explaining something troubling to a wide audience. When the doctor noticed them, his eyes narrowed. "First," he said, blinking rapidly. Then he paused for a long time. Finally he drew the silver tin of white snuff from his coat and snorted him some.

Leighton wadded his Federal cap against his chest. "Doctor. Please."

"The child is undisturbed." The doctor shrugged, then he raised his open palms.

"What of Patricia?" Leighton asked.

"I have her jaw wired shut. Set it as best I could." His voice dropped. "But Mr. Morkan, you're wife may never speak properly again, and she will certainly be permanently disfigured."

Leighton felt a piece of him crumble away as if a bench had been blasted in his chest. Poor Patricia. "May I see her?"

Patricia lay on a cot in the parlor. Around her head a canvas dressing was tied, and this was bulging and wet with ice. Even in the dressing's shadow, the blue and red of her demolished jaw showed through. Her open eyes followed the men with wide dread.

Leighton knelt at her bedside, touched her shoulder. Her eyes, no longer crescents, but frightened ovals of gray, held his for a moment then fell to the midst of his chest. Had he only rented a surrey and put two of his men on it; had he only taken seriously her desire for these damned sheep. His mind filled with self-accusations.

"–ayton." Then she closed her eyes and let out a moan, which rattled though it was baffled by the wires holding her jaw. The men shuddered.

Leighton lowered his lips to her shoulder and fell to stroking her forehead, holding his temple delicately away from the mask of her bandages. Touching her, feeling her shoulder steady a bit, he gulped once and fought back a flood. On her dear, delicate flesh the horrid black and purple damage. Above the arid plain that was his heart, a single searing light: who did this? She was obstinate, foreign, demanding, sometimes even crazy, but she had become to him, he realized, a dear possession. Now that possession was in agony and might be permanently marred—even through the swelling of her jaw and the dressing, her chin skewed hard to the right making the lips sour and twisted. She reeked of ammonia, clay, and blood.

On his palm, her hair was as dry as a horse's tail. He felt her trembling, and against his eyebrow, one of her warm tears spread. She was trembling hard, fraught with agony, her cries coming now in clipped gasps made even more intense by the restraints on her jaw. She would be weeping, he could tell, loudly, fully given over to sorrow, but she could not open her mouth, and so brief, high-pitched wails escaped her.

She clutched his arm. It was almost more than he could bear, and he felt his knees giving. The child, Thank God, the child was well, but this, his Patrica...

The three men who had pressed close when Patricia spoke now fidgeted. When her pale, weakened fingers ran through Leighton's lime-grayed hair, the men stiffened, solemn and embarrassed, for each saw the powerful sign of an unmistakable bond pass between this odd couple.

Archer gripped the doctor's and Peale's shoulders, and with a firm expression, spun them and bent them towards the door.

When the door was shut behind them, Archer whispered, "I cannot grasp what power she has over our friend. But to be honest, I deeply envy him. True love!"

"Oh, their hearts! My God!" Peale said. Archer and the doctor grunted.

When Leighton at last emerged, Archer put a hand on his shoulder. The doctor stammered apologies about Patricia's future countenance.

Leighton raised a hand to halt him. "Peale," he said, his mouth dry, his lips smacking. "Please, I want you to find who did this. Start with the telegraph lineman. Then at Pickwick Transfer. Work your way back."

Peale rubbed the bridge of his nose. "I'll tell you, they's a lot in the way. And even if I catch someone, they's no way I can seat a jury that'll have the brass to convict. Gentlemen, this cuts it, a pregnant woman? Someone's wife? We have about lost this here county."

Leighton stared at him, a wind howling through his chest. "Whatever you do is appreciated."

Peale pulled on his hat and glanced at Archer, then headed for the door.

The doctor apologized until Leighton squeezed his arm. "Will you excuse my partner and me for a moment, sir?"

When he was gone, Archer said, "Leighton, I'm sorry, but ... her face."

"She was looking for a shepherd," Leighton mumbled, pulling on the whiskers at his chin as if he meant to pluck them in dozens. "And for sheep."

"Can you blame her for longing after simplicity?"

Leighton gripped his suspenders, the leather crackling.

"You know him, don't you?" Archer asked.

Leighton squinted at him. "Know him? He's some hillbilly shepherd." He rubbed his temples. "She just wanted me to buy

162

her some sheep. A Saxony wheel she has by our bed. She only wanted to use it."

They were both silent some time. A hot wind blew against the windows kicking up dust, which ticked against the glass like sleet falling.

"What do you intend to do?" Archer finally asked.

"Kill the shepherd, and work my way back."

Archer nodded slowly. "I know just the men for the game." His voice fell to a whisper. "You should have joined us from the start." Reaching into his coatpocket, he drew out a closed fist, held it to Leighton.

Leighton frowned but opened his hand. Archer had dropped something in his palm, a small crucifix carved of yellow bois d'arc to which a bundle of seeds were tied. Leighton raised it to his burning eyes and smelled mustard. "What is this?"

"Close to the vest," Archer whispered. "It is your revenge."

Patricia could sense the prominence, the new twist of her chin by the rose-colored, scaly lump of it that hovered at the base of her vision. Drawing on the cup—a mug for children, ceramic topped with a funnel—she winced. She was propped on a bank of pillows trying to sip the last of a mixture of heavy cream, sorghum, and beef broth, a chilled concoction Marta had devised to keep Patricia's strength up and to keep her weight from plummeting. The mixture tasted like smoke and whenever she tilted the cup to her, she was gripped with such vertigo she felt the bed lurch from under her. If she became sick to her stomach, how could she even open her mouth to vomit properly? All around her threats and danger.

Marta sat at her bedside, the newspaper in her hands popping and crinkling—her hands were shaking as she read very slowly, badly translating the English into German, so that the result, though shocking in its report, made Patricia buckle with laughter. Her jaw sang in pain where the diabolical wires clamped it. Whenever she was tickled the wires seemed like a live lampreys gnashing at her gums.

"The body was found on the courthouse steps suffering from what the conductor of the mayor's inquest will describe as a violent slander to the skull," Marta translated. "Mr. Archer Newman, city construction, and Mr. Leighton Shea Morkan, proprietor of Morkan Quarry, were questioned by Undersheriff Shane Peale and both confirm the coroner's pop. Undersheriff Peale will resign from the Concession of the sheriff once a chuckle is forward. The Undersheriff who has served Springfield with decoration through the war and now, claimed he has been well fed with this horse's outcasts. Neither the quarrymaster nor the engineer had anything to add for this columnist at creation."

Marta waited a long time. Then she folded the paper with care. "Patricia, he killed that shepherd. The City Engineer. And Leighton. The town's quarrymaster. Your husband! They had that shepherd broken out of the jail for them. And they killed that shepherd on the courthouse steps by throwing him down them. As if he were the one escaping! Claus said so himself." She held the paper up. "This is full of lies, Patricia. Lies your husband and that Archer Newman told the newspaper."

Patricia stared at a gap along the wall where it met the ceiling, a hollow, moaning, drafty space. If she could but open her jaw once and deliver the frantic rapping of her baby's heart inside her during the assault, like a bird's heart pulsing maniacally against a fist that would crush it. And those boot tips and blows coming at her, piss spattering on her shoulders and cheek. To hell with you, Mother. To hell with justice.

"And the law will do nothing to them, that is why the Undersheriff is abandoning his post," Marta whispered.

A door opened in the house, the front door, Patricia imagined, for the air pressure fluctuated in her ears, which still felt as if they were filled with gravel. A pair of boots came down the hall and then there came a knock. Marta tucked the paper beneath her lap.

The door opened a crack and Leighton stuck his head in.

"–ayton," Patricia said, holding her arms out.

Without a glance at Marta, Leighton strode into the room, sat gently on the bed. He stroked her hair, his fingers rough and hard as carding blocks.

164

Marta twisted in the chair, turning her gaze away.

"–ayton," Patricia said again, a cry like a babe's or a deaf and idiot child's squawk to be loved and held.

He strained his neck to be gentle and kissed her lightly on the forehead. "I have something for you."

Her gray-green eyes sparkled like stones on a creek bottom in sunlight. From his coat pocket, he pulled out a hunk of the ram's black wool.

Patricia grasped it, long, crackling fibers from the sheep's shoulders, the best wool. It stunk of lanolin and tar and rotted post oak and clay and burlap.

"The bastard hadn't sheared the poor souls," Leighton said. "We have."

"Mmmnnh," Patricia moaned and pressed the wool to her swollen cheek.

Leighton nodded to the old woman and pronounced her name as one might identify a weed. He shut the door carefully behind him.

Marta glowered at the doorknob. When she finally turned to Patricia, her daughter combed the black wool with her fingers.

Patricia watched her mother for a moment. Then she shook the wool at her mother. "Pawr," she said.

"What?"

"Pawr," she said again, snarling.

"I do not understand," Marta said, flipping the paper open. Far off, they could hear the sheep bleating happily, clear of their wool. Ugh, how these awful Irish manage to turn even catastrophe to advantage, Marta thought, staring at the newsprint and the dead, smashed face of the shepherd of the hills in a suit someone loaned his carcass and a pine box coffin charity had made. She knew very well her daughter had said, "Power. Power."

III

HER DEVASTATED FACE AND THE PAIN THAT CREASED HER brow, the hint of blood that darkened the corners of her lips set him chanting a curse in his mind. When she was lying in and near delivery Archer slipped him one of the bois d'arc crosses in a handshake. Leighton left Patricia resting, stolid as a boulder beneath the sheets, her marred face tranquil.

The new amber wood of a barn yellowed the twilight as Leighton led his horse over the dusty ground. The land belonged to Wilson Shannon, who had bought it at auction from one of the old Southern-sympathizing families. Leighton stopped at the broad double doors and knocked. About head high, a small cross perforated the pine door, and an eye appeared there blinking.

Leighton reached in his pocket for the crucifix Archer had given him. He held it up to the door. The eye swiveled, then vanished.

Shannon emerged and held his hand out to Leighton. In Shannon's open hand, there was a small, yellow crucifix. Shannon nodded at it. They exchanged. Shannon sniffed Leighton's, then turned it over and over. At last, Shannon nodded.

Taking Leighton's horse, Shannon pointed at the ladder to the loft. Leighton climbed. Eleven men were upstairs seated around a rough-hewn table. Rising, Archer nodded to an empty chair. Leighton settled himself at the table and eyed the men.

"Welcome, Leighton," Archer said. "We know this is yet a trying time for you and your family, so we deeply appreciate your joining us."

They were a mix of men: one of the foremen from the quarry; the new bank president; a printer named Cox; a young surgeon; the saloon owner from the Galena Road Saloon; the undertaker's son. Archer had chosen well. Other than Archer himself, every member was a Missourian who had seen Union war service, who had ridden, and had killed. And they were all former Federals. Still this pomp and huggermugger! In the heat of the loft, the stink of hay, mud, and horse sweat was stifling.

Archer rose to his feet, held his ale high. "I would like to begin tonight with a toast." All the men raised their glasses. "To the man who has caused all of our fair state's troubles by refusing us that status of even the most defeated, when clearly, gentlemen." His eyes worked the table. "Clearly, regardless of your former allegiance, we were all defeated in Missouri." The men were silent; the low settings of the lamps left dark shadows on their cheeks. Leighton scowled, thinking of what an outworlder Archer was, from Rhode Island, and how little he really knew of defeat in Missouri. That his fellow Ozarkers were listening to this and following astonished him. Maybe it was the desperate longing to be citified, and here was Archer, sophisticated, polished.

"Here's to Andrew Johnson," Archer said, holding the cup higher. "May him and his cabinet and its many-headed generals of the retreat-construction be all crammed into the rankest honey hole of hell; may thunderbolts brast them; may their wives all be made flatulent widows of the straw-like, contentious sort; may they be cast into some desert place, say for example Texas, and be compromised so much as to be forced to plead for the right to beg for a living."

There were grunts and nods all around; all drank.

"Finely put," the banker said.

"Real fine," said the undertaker's son.

"Thank you." Archer ran his tongue over his teeth and nodded. "Here again this week has nearly passed, and are we any closer to achieving order and justice?" When Archer spoke, he hooked his thumbs behind the auburn lapels of his coat and strode about like an orator. Behind him the hay reeked. "And has our sheriff and his intrepid deputies proved effective in eliminating the menace of the burglar, the random and violent horse thief?" Archer glanced all around the table.

Cox, the printer, popped his mug on the tabletop. "They sat them a jury Wednesday that acquitted Absalom Grimes, known killer, and a mail carrier and spy for the Rebels. Acquitted and loose again."

Archer nodded. "The man of honor has no recourse. Until this evening." He lowered his eyes. "To be honest with you, we are about to take a step, my townsmen, from which there is no return. If any man's heart should hesitate now, he should flee and know no more of this." Leaning forward, he scoured them to see that none wavered.

The men nodded at each other, and as Leighton watched them, and followed Archer's lean face, his lips wet with ale, there came a spell creeping around these men in the heat. When some of them glanced at Leighton and nodded, he felt to his alarm that he was a key ingredient in Archer's incantation.

Finally Archer nodded. "Good, then. We have been meeting as the Gentlemen's Defense League, but tonight, thanks to our secret partners, we have..." He pulled a crate from under the table. "The ability to make ourselves as anonymous as the wind."

He thumped a stack of what appeared to be cloth napkins onto the tabletop. He handed them around. Potato sacks cut to be hoods with two ovals sliced for the eyes, a small, horizontal slit for the nose. On the back of each, a cross embroidered in blood red.

Archer turned, stooped so that all the men saw was his backside. When he straightened, the hood covered his head, the crimson cross centered in the back. His eyes watched them from inside dark ovals. The potato sack peaked at the top of his head, a seam running from nose to chin. His visage appeared stiff, reptilian, jutted and seamed like the heads of the skinks that darted on the quarry cliffs.

"We are as invisible now as we are fearless," Archer said, his voice slightly muffled in the hood.

Leighton dug his nails into his palms to keep from laughing out loud.

To his surprise, the men bent their heads to the table, slipped the potato sacks on, began tucking the hoods beneath their shirts. Leighton hesitated a moment. Archer's eyes, magnified by the mask, stared at him, then narrowed. Leighton bent his head to the table; he pulled, and the cotton slid over his ears, clung to the back of his neck. He ran his fingers along the hood's fringe. The humid line of it sunk to touch his collarbone, his vertebrae. He pulled the holes before his eyes, the fabric catching in his beard, then buttoned his shirt. When he raised his head, the frayed edges of the slits in the sack hampered his vision. But the ragged cloth, the damp heat of the mask gripped his mind and matched the boiling world he cursed when crouched at Patricia's bedside.

Shannon handed out more ale.

"Tonight, brothers," Archer resumed. "I have brought a man wronged. Yea, more than wronged. A man whose own wife, great with child, was attacked, beaten, and disfigured by these brigands."

Leighton scanned the table. His vision was narrowed and troubled by the slits in the hood. The hooded faces blended, gray upon gray. He considered what Archer had said so far. A moment ago, when Archer pulled on the potato sack, all this sounded like a dissipation of energy and time. But his townsmen were serious now—they had uniforms again, if only hoods, and were as stern as he had seen them in battle lines during the war. With the ale warming his gut, the anger he had felt toward Patricia's attackers rose.

"I will now ask him to stand," Archer said, gesturing to Leighton.

When he stood, he felt rising with him the strands of that incantation Archer was weaving. And it mingled with the curse he had recited at Patricia's bedside.

"Gentlemen," Leighton began. "I have lost a father, horses, the wealth of my family and now nearly my beloved to the disorder of our war." He paused. "Who here has also lost?"

The hoods nodded.

"Tell us, then. There's no shame. We are all of the Ozarks. We are Springfield's best." Leighton jerked his chin at one of the men seated.

"Two walking horses."

"My sister."

"One hundred dollars and a real good hound."

Leighton nodded, the hood scratching and binding at his beard. As he looked at them, the slits of their eyes tracked him.

"Shall we wait until we have all lost fathers, sons, homes, our livelihoods?"

A chorus of nos.

He had lead men most of his young life, but only on the stone. This was beyond the dust and sweat of everyday life. He smacked a fist against his palm.

"We have fought a crusade against rabble with all a crusade's pain and poverties, where the enemy's line was: 'Black flag' and 'Total war.' That war has not yet passed. But *we* will be the ones to end it." He pointed around the table.

Gray sacks, black slits, they stared and waited. His ribs and arms ached, and from the men he could sense a focused hate that he had gathered and built around him, that paused in the way a dust devil at the quarry pauses, sinks and hovers between dissipating or reforming into a tower of gravel and wind and dust whirling in fury. That will was here now, the possibility for raw, swirling violence. He could smell it in their sweat.

He glanced at Archer.

Archer rose. "His name is Millard Carragher. Cousin of our departed shepherd. And he led the men who assaulted Mrs. Patricia Morkan."

Archer outlined the horse thief's habits, described a plan of attack. The printer Cox held up a scrolled banner that read "A DAMNED HORSE THIEF" to drape upon a carcass. Archer told each of them to remove their coats, turn them inside out, then put them back on. They complied and some became ragged scarecrows while the coat linings of those well off made them shine like the costumes of charlatans.

The men shouted and whooped. In the manger, they armed themselves with pistols and rifles. Anyone without a swift mount received one from Wilson Shannon. When one of the men reared his horse and whooped, Archer managed to catch his reins, bear the horse steady. The men paused, huddled their antsy mounts.

Archer's eyeballs worked in the gray fabric as if in a new, unfamiliar skull. He snapped his head around at each gaze he could catch. "We ride in silence. From this moment forth, no man speaks, save behind a door bearing our cross, and no man enters a crossed door unmasked." His eyes bulged at them. After a moment, they all nodded.

In the warm air, the hood made Leighton's scalp and forehead itch. He worried this was a fool's errand and would end in spent horses, drunkenness, and a sore ass. The trees were stone gray in the starlight. The moon hung waxing and blue. The riders bore together down Ozark Road, past the smooth black fields and blue hillsides, out of Shannon's land into Morkan holdings. They clung in a tight, swift knot, tack ringing. When moonlight cut between the trees, the horses' hides gleamed, and the riders bore low against the horses' manes. Led on hand rides, knowing the paths, they coursed like gar in a river, nosed and parted only to close at the turns.

Archer raised his hand near a crossroads. To the south, in a valley between two black hills they could see the far off lights of Ozark. Here Archer moved beside each rider. With quick jabs at the forest, he directed each horseman to a niche in the woods until the band surrounded the clearing, the road bare and open for at least thirty yards.

Leighton patted the neck of his horse, a gray roan, dumb but unflappable and fast. Its muscles twitched and fluttered. He whispered the horse's name and it grunted, nodding its head with pleasure. All around the road, riders stilled their horses.

Far away, he heard a horse's hooves scraping and clicking at the gravel, a pace so slow, it indicated the rider was either asleep or extremely wary. The horse halted before it entered the clearing's oval of moonlight. A glimmer of the horse's neck and legs hovered in the darkness. Leighton heard a saddle creak.

The horse took two steps forward. On its back, a man hunkered close to its neck and held a revolver up. When the horse took two more steps, the man straightened in the saddle, looked around, leather groaning.

"They's quite a lot of you cowards," the man said. He scanned the darkness, his nose stuck high in the air. He wore a slouch hat. His trousers and the ends of his sleeves were ragged. He was a small man in the saddle, not much taller than Leighton,

171

but much thinner. The man let the horse walk forward step by step. "Are ye Federals?" Hooves crunched in the gravel. "I smell your stinking horses." He stopped. "They's ten of ye." He crossed his arms over his chest. "What ye about, boys, hidin' in the trees?"

Archer moved into the clearing. In the blue moonlight, his hood was bright, his body shimmering. Leighton drew his pistol, closed behind the thief. In the trees, the other hooded men appeared deformed, faces twisted and bald like those of burn victims.

The thief gaped for an instant, then swung the revolver up, and cocked it. Archer halted, sat straight in the saddle. Jesus, Leighton thought. The bravery of Archer sitting there was exalting. The horse thief glanced to his left. All around him, hooded riders nudged their horses into the circle of moonlight.

"Well, shit." The thief still held the gun out. Then he grinned with his head cocked, his teeth gray specks in a blue face. "I got six shots. They's a dozen of you. Half of you willing to die? Ready to die, Your Honor?" He wagged his pistol at Archer.

The men sat rigidly, and Leighton realized there might be no bravery in them. Archer's stance could be the stiffness of terror. But with the hoods on, there was no way of telling. Seeing the hollow black slits of their eyes, the dusty gray of their trousers turned dull blue in the starlight, seeing the strange coats turned inside out so that the seams shown like weird insignia, the thief could as well be witnessing a pack of the dead stepped from the forest for a jaunt among the living.

After a moment, the thief propped his elbow on the saddle horn, the gun lolling as he spoke. "So it takes a hood and masked escort to make a man come settle a score in the Ozarks."

One by one, men were removing pistols from their holsters. The thief glanced about, watching each man draw.

Archer rode closer and spoke: "You Millard Carragher?"

"Who's asking?"

Down in the horse's mane Archer cocked his pistol.

"Death," Archer said.

The thief snorted.

Archer fired. A spray of debris smacked against Leighton's chest and hood. Archer fought his horse, which reared. The thief slumped in the saddle as if he were dozing. From the trees a single bird clattered up and flew, crying frantically. The thief's pistol dropped, and he fell forward against his horse's neck. The horse lunged, but stopped hard facing the riders' mounts.

Leaning out, Leighton took the animal's reins and steadied it. Its eyes rolled. Archer struck a match against his tack. A few riders unwrapped torches from their saddlebags and lit the torches. The thief's hat was blown off, and the hair on the back of his head shone and moved. The riders huddled forward. One hooded rider reached and pinched the fabric at the thief's shoulder. Another hesitated, then touched the thief's arm, steadied the corpse.

"Grimy, ain't he?"

"Weren't we gone hang him?" one asked.

"They's still time," another offered.

"What the hell would we hang him for?"

"Well," the rider shrugged.

The body slid as its horse fidgeted, but a rider grabbed the corpse by the collar, its arms flopping as it righted.

"How else we gone show folks we mean bidness?"

"Shouldn't we first ought to draw and quarter him? I thought that was the priority. Then we hang him."

"What you think draw and quarter means besides hang?"

They were silent for a time holding the body up, horses weaving as the riders closed ranks. Only two held back from the circle, one with his back hunched and shivering, the other Archer, his horse still jittery. Judging from his coat, even turned inside out, Leighton spotted the one shivering as the banker.

"Morkan, is this here the man?"

"He'll do," Leighton said.

Leighton remembered the thief now; he was riff-raff and had worked a few days indentured at the quarry to pay off a jail sentence, but Odem threatened to shoot him if he came back—he fought too often—and so he was relieved of his duty and sent back to gaol. The bridge of his nose collapsed in a divot as if someone had hewn a notch there. "You know," Leighton said, "I

173

seen a fellow hit in nearly the same place at the Battle of Springfield. Lived for about forty minutes, chattering like they'll do.
Told me bout his ma and kin and some kind of worms in China
that shit fabric. Damndest thing."

"That so?" Several nodded. They too had held such dead in
their arms and attended last ramblings. When the dead man's
head lolled toward Leighton for a moment, the corpse appeared
to listen very closely.

"He's right, boys. I read bout them worms in Chiney."

One man hooked a finger in his mouth at the hood, lifted it,
and stuck in a chaw. "Shit fabric?" he asked, the gob of tobacco
marring his words. "Now how can a worm, which is round, crap
cloth, which is flat?"

Leighton pinched the back of the corpse's blood-wet coat
so that its shoulders seemed to shrug, its arms flicking its hands
in mock exasperation. There was laughter. With a splatter, the
banker retched.

Archer danced his horse in an agitated circle. "God damn it!"
They all turned to him.

"You rubes. Don't you grasp the magnitude of this moment?" The circle parted as he pressed forward. He raised a hand
to them. From the blue, he recited:

> For man endowed with mortal life,
> Whose shroud of sentient clay can still
> Feel feverish pang and fainting chill,
> Whose eye can stare in stony trance,
> Whose hair can rouse like warrior's lance,—
> 'T is hard for such to view, unfurled,
> The curtain of the future world.

He pointed at the ass of the thief's mount. The brand on the
rump of the thief's horse was clearly the barred p from the Pickwick Transfer Company. This was very likely one of the horses
stolen from Patricia's rented carriage. "You've killed a notorious
horse thief, a menace to society. You've taken the first step toward achieving higher civilization."

They all glanced at one another.

"Hey," one said. "Hey, maybe we have done something here."

"Yeah. We're all right, boys. We done justice."

"Hoo-raw for Sir Walter Scott."

They began to whoop and slap each other on the back.

"Jesus. Shut up! Get him roped," Archer said. "I want his ass swinging."

Archer reached behind him and produced a long rope tied in a noose. He held the head of it up, the noose flopping, the amber coil of it draped like a snake across his arm. Bowing in the saddle, he handed it to Leighton. The grooved hemp caught Leighton's hand, itched like a cable made of splinters. The hoods watched him, slits for eyes, blue shadowed faces, hands gripping saddle horns, horses bowing and weaving their dark necks, the flames of the torches dappling them. The men became serious. For all Archer's showmanship, the Sir Walter Scott he recited, he was a sincere murderer, and his posse had succeeded.

Leighton touched the back of the thief's neck. The skin was soft, the muscle and backbone taut. His fingertips discovered a space in the vertebrae, and he could imagine the deep groove about to come there. A wind shook the highest branches.

With a shudder, the corpse trembled and gulped air, its back rising. Leighton had seen the dead take agonal gasps before on the battlefield and after falls at the quarry, so he waited for the corpse to go still. The thief's back rose again. The riders had not seen this or did not care, for they circled in the torchlight and murmured happily to each other. When Leighton yanked the head up by its greasy hair, he could feel parts of the skull bumping and moving like rocks in a bag.

The riders shouted victory. After one sang out a line of "Run, Johnny, Run," they all took up the old war song as if they had beaten the rabble back down to Arkansas again. The corpse's eyes were wide. At the corner of its lips was a swath of blood that bubbled as the thief gasped. He was still alive then.

The riders saw this, for they slowed and wound their horses in a silenced circle. Breathing and alive despite the grizzled back of his head, the red aster of a wound above his temple—this tremor of crimson was the last scrabbling for life, and the men fell suddenly reverent.

Leighton loosened the knot on the rope, slipped it over the dying man's head as if the loop were a medal. "Give me that sign," he said to Cox.

The parchment rattled as Cox unrolled it. Leighton took the sign in his teeth, widened the twine strung along the top of parchment. The two hoods holding the thief allowed his head to droop forward, and Leighton pulled the twine down over his head. The parchment banner, with its words—"A DAMNED HORSE THIEF"—spread across the dying man's chest.

Leighton coiled the rope, and in a slow procession, he and the two hoods led the victim on his horse to a spot under a tree. They tied the rope to the thief's saddle horn, thence from the saddle horn over the tree limb to the thief's neck. Leighton pulled on the rope hitched to the saddle and tightened the knot. Two riders dismounted and freed the thief's feet from the stirrups.

Archer raised his arm. "The new justice is here, and it is we who have made it." He dug his heels into his horse's flank, made the animal rise and spin.

When he brought his hand down, Leighton popped the thief's horse on the rump. It moved forward, hesitating and rolling its eyes. The victim rose off the saddle into the torchlight. The thief twirled. The rope creaked. Against the fabric at the crotch of his pants, the cadaver's pecker stuck out, hard, bulging. The two hoods unfastened the knot from the saddle horn and secured it to the tree. The wind blew, and there was a gagging man wobbling above the road, a banner scraping the bark and the inside of his coat: "A DAMNED HORSE THIEF."

The men raised their guns, whooped and shouted. Archer spun his horse once more. Every hair on Leighton's neck bristled.

Riding in a tight pack, they slapped each other on the back, hollering and whooping, their vows of silence long forgotten.

The posse left Leighton at the trail to the Morkan house. The eyes the house's big windows created blazed yellow. Leighton urged the horse up the drive, dismounted at the steps, hobbled the horse at the porch railing. Johnson rounded the corner of the house, then froze when he saw Leighton standing, hooded and bloody.

Leighton pointed at the barn.

Johnson grabbed the reins of the horse and led it off at a jog.

Without removing the hood, Leighton slammed open the door. Judith screamed.

He shook her by the arm. "Hush. Why are you still here?"

She blinked, her lips quivering. "Mrs. Patricia having the baby, and we all been waiting." She was rotund with child; her skin had darkened until on her face there was a mask so black she seemed to have been scorched.

Leighton pushed her aside and headed for the library and parlor where Patricia had been lying in so as to be on the first floor. From behind the door came a shout of pain so intensely desperate, it made Leighton cringe and hesitate. He heard a man's voice encouraging Patricia, heard Marta's German.

With some struggle he removed the hood. He tried to shove it in his coat pocket, but with his coat turned inside out, his hand flailed down that familiar course three times obstinately before he recognized, yes, everything was changed. He folded the sack and tucked it in his belt. At his waist, the bloody, brain-spattered tongue of it hung forward, and he pulled his transformed coat close around him.

He opened the door. Patricia's legs were bare and thrust apart. Patricia's knees wavered near the doctor's head. Marta sat at the head of the bed, wiping Patricia's brow. Patricia glared at Leighton, her face reddish purple, her eyebrows pinched, her hair shining and soaked, hanging like sopping string. Marta's eyes went wide, then narrowed. The doctor swallowed. "Well," he said, breathing deeply. "Here is the culprit, by God."

"I am here," Leighton said.

Patricia threw her head back, her forehead buckling. She bared her teeth and screeched.

The doctor nodded at Marta, who leaned and whispered, her German soft, like the cooing nonsense of a dove. Patricia's body buckled and her heavy face transformed into a red contortion of teeth and muscle and sweat. There was a touch of blood at her lips and her teeth were red—her agony was causing the wires holding her jaw in place to bind and bite. The doctor's shoulders twisted, his arms scrambling. He lifted a purple creature free of her. Strands of crimson and brown muck dripped from its legs and wriggling arms. The creature was born in the same wet squirt of any calf or piglet, yet when Patricia flung herself back against the pillows and sheet, the agony of relief on her face, her cracked lips, the words she spoke through teeth still clamped by wire, "*Herr Gott, Herr Gott, Mein Gott,*" the dismay of it made the birth human. The doctor set the babe on his knee, fished something from its nostrils and mouth. Patricia leaned on her elbows and, wobbling, strained to see. Her cheeks were drenched with tears and sweat, and she breathed in sobs. The doctor lifted the long black cord that emanated from between her legs. For a moment, Leighton recalled his mother's horror stories of how the babes of indecent women were always born strangling on that awful gray-black rope, two souls entwined if ever they would be, and here the babe squirmed in the doctor's hands with the cord draped across its neck. In a rush, Leighton's palms tingled where the hemp had grooved them. Born tethered, squalling. In Leighton's mind the horse thief rose off the saddle into the torchlight. Thank God the doctor nipped the cord between his thumb and the silver blade of a knife. The cord lay amid a yellow puddle on the bedding.

The doctor cradled the babe in his arms and stood. He glanced at Leighton, hesitated, then nodded to the child.

The room was powerfully hot, the stove roaring as wind sucked at its pipes. He reached between the babe's wet skin and the doctor's rigid arm. He took the babe, held it under its arms. The white flap of a penis hung down between its red, vigorous legs. It kicked the air once, face screwed and pinched at him. Leighton lifted the babe.

Red fingers like tiny worms latched onto Leighton's cheek and mixed family blood there with the gore of the man who had nearly killed Patricia and this child. Little arms, slick and warm, cartilage, the beautiful blood, red and pulsing in the three thousand rivers coursing under its skin. He lowered it and brought it close in to his belly, felt the heft of it as it hung there in his hands, its little legs dangling, arms trembling, its skin like a sack around quivering hot suet. The shaking arms and tiny fingers briefly brushed the hood and caught upon it. Shifting, he held his son up to the new world he had made tonight, held the boy high to the dusty books of his father, held him up to the ashen face of Judith, the pale, round faces of its mother, of Marta, of the doctor shuffling for the door. It bawled, and Leighton laughed a laugh of joy so deep and profound, the women and the doctor were sure he had shouted in pain.

IV

PATRICIA RAN A RAGING FEVER FOR A WEEK AFTER THE birth. Leighton sat with her in her tossing and turning delirium. Often she woke and gripped his arm, growled something like German, her voice stifled into an awful slur by the wires. In a fit of sweat and hallucinations, she wrote on a pad: "Gustasson Robart Erich Morkan." Fearing it was her last wish, Leighton acquiesced and named the boy that. On the edge of the bed he sat chewing the stub of a cigar watching her sleep. Her face glistened. Her injured chin jutted. He fingered the fabric of the hood waiting in his coat pocket until it frayed.

In the kitchen, he found Judith, her big pap exposed, nursing the plump, White baby, while her own boy lay in a bread pan by the stove, dazzling itself with its pink palms in the air. Leighton touched the Negro babe's arm, dark as the heartwood of a cedar, not as dark as Judith or Isaac, but dark enough.

"Ain't he a lucky man, Gussy," she whispered to the babe at her breast.

Leighton shot a glance at her, then returned to his examination of Judith's babe, curly black hair, almost blue like ink in the light, a thin face. Judith named it Holofernes, Holy for short, knowing only that her name and that name were somewhere connected in Leighton's Bible. Leighton wanted to warn her away from this, but kept himself clear of such a deep association. Already he could sense growing in that cramped kitchen the two polarities of his future—love and vigor in Gus at Judith's breast; betrayal and remorse in Holofernes in his forlorn crib.

Next to Judith in a crock was a loam of black charcoal and gray mortar. Leighton grimaced as she ran two wet fingers through the mix and swiped this into her mouth. She had been eating a spittoon of it every day since returning to the house.

"Judith, when was this child born?" he asked as the babe in the bread pan gave his finger a mighty squeeze.

"What you care?" She was still enormous.

From the way her veins cracked thick, blue, and pitted black at her breasts and cheek and arms, he worried she had suffered. "You didn't have to go off like an animal and birth it all on your own," he whispered. "Were you at least under a roof?"

She glowered at him. "I went down to our cave. Started drinking the stream like I couldn't get enough. Then I swelled up twice, three times my size, till I was broad as I am tall. I clawed and chewed on what the teeth of the souls give me. Without I would have done that, that child there would have brast me like a pig's bladder full of water. I saw my heart beat on every inch of my flesh. I was thumping like a drumskin."

"You could have died."

"I should have."

He stood beside her and touched her shoulder. Her skin was as dry as plaster and gave beneath his fingers as if it had been stretched. He shook has head. "No," he said. "You call on me from here on. Let me know what is happening."

She looked up at him fiercely, but her eyes began to shine with tears. "This would be a great deal easier if you didn't care."

Gustasson stopped nursing and looked up at her.

When she looked down, she chuckled. "Mmm. I hate that look. You know that. Them's you mamma's eyes. Crying make my milk sour. Get away, Leighton Morkan."

The babe blinked up at the immense black face above him. Beaded at his lips were the blue pearl's of the Negress's milk. Judith smiled at Leighton, a smile of propriety and triumph so broad it made him want to snatch the child from her.

A day later, Patricia's fever broke, and Leighton returned to the quarry, which Odem had been running. That same day, Archer dismounted in front of the office. When he shook Leighton's hand, Leighton felt the wood of a crucifix pressed against his palm. He cupped his hand around the cross and pocketed it.

"I'm glad to see you back. Odem told me of your troubles." Archer said this with a lilt of sarcasm.

"The mother has lived," Leighton said. "And thanks be to God."

181

Archer nodded with a smug frown. He handed Leighton a folder full of newspaper clippings. Leighton held the folder open. The Gentlemen's Defense League had created a week of headlines: "Local Vigilence Commitee Commits Grisly Shooting and Lenching!" "Church-Based Killers Said to have Founded Justice on Biblical Principals." "Radical Republicans Join Band of Hooded Justice Seekers." "A Horse Thief and Local Leathercraftsmen is First Victim."

The stories often ended with a reporter's lament that justice had come to such barbarism, and one column, by an intelligent but drearily verbose local lawyer, called the Defense League, "criminal in its usurpation of a defendant's rights to due process."

Leighton closed the folder. "Why save this? You shouldn't have this around." He watched his friend with renewed caution. "You're the city engineer. I own the biggest quarry in the city. We should not be in this for notoriety."

Archer's face fell as if he had hoped something more of Leighton. Leighton let him into the office, and over brandy and a flagstone contract, Leighton passed Archer the cross he carried and so sealed their fellowship.

That evening Leighton approached Shannon's woods. Before he reached the cleared barn lot, he walked his horse into a dense clump of trees. From his saddle bag, he retrieved the rumpled gray hood and pulled it over his head. Through the woods, he could see other men doing the same, shuffling in the twilight. Above in the verdant green of the trees, cicadas were chittering, a sound like a steam valve venting pressure. The air was hot and the wet smell of soil pervaded. Leighton removed his coat, turned it inside out with slow and deliberate tugs. More than loading any weapon, tying any noose, whetting any blade, this action saddened him. Here the peaceable, acceptable uniform of a businessman was inverted and abused so that beneath the poplin skin a horrifying, glistening gristle and meat was exposed to the world. Pulling at the sleeves and seams, he recalled goresoaked stories of Maeve, and now he was easily one of her skull crushing henchmen at Cuailnge. He tucked the bottom of the hood into his shirt and led the horse to the barn.

† † †

When the doctor removed the wires, Leighton clasped her hand. The last crimson sliver rose in the doctor's snips. Unaccustomed to holding its own weight her jaw dropped and she had to swallow and struggle mightily to make it close. It fell open again and she could smell immediately how rank her breath had become. With her jaw hanging down, her breath stinking, she felt like a battered dragon, and here Leighton knelt beside her clutching her hand and looking anxiously, even lovingly in her eyes.

"What have you done?" she asked, trying to joke with him, her tongue clicking in her pasty mouth.

He was such a dense one, for instead of a smile, his face tensed and colored as if he were really in dire trouble. Times like these his devotion awed her, but his dull mind cheapened the moment.

"Beg pardon?"

She gave up and let her face slump. Even her breathing did not sound right, liquid and rough. The butt of the thief's pistol came to her mind, a metal crescent she had tried to scrub from memory's slate. A rusty, awful screw at the butt of it, like Hell's star.

Leighton was paying the doctor. For what, she wondered? Leaving her mangled of face and scalded between her legs? The fever—she knew more than a fever had happened. It was an infection of all her feminine parts and she could sense from her dryness much was lost. She felt hideous, ravaged, spent, a black locust bean, furry gray, all the seed gone.

Leighton brought a tin basin, a hand towel and a glass of water. Setting the basin down, he fetched a kit from his coat. Inside were mint leaves and a phial of blue-white powder. He poured the powder into the water glass. Then, over the milky water, he tore mint leaf after mint leaf into tiny strips. Their fragrance, leaves and rain and crushed moss, stilled her. She watched him work and began to take intense pleasure in the meticulous actions of those big thumbs and meat hook fingers working so carefully with miniature knives and phials, a tiny whisk to stir.

"Wash your mouth with this, dear. It's a wonder."

The milky water fizzed, and it was icy cold.

"What is it?" she asked. Oh, and her voice freed. She wished to shout and sing.

"Lime and water and mint and just a touch of vinegar."

His beard made a sharp goatee and the whiskers, though normally very black in the out of doors, seemed red to her in candlelight. As he bent attentively to her, waiting for her to rinse and spit, holding the basin near her chest, she realized for the first time that she trusted him absolutely, even knowing he was a murderer, a maker of mayhem. And sadly that knowledge made the trust of this moment even grander as it required so much faith that with her he would not be the Wilde Heruli, ecstatic huntsman of Odin, presage of death storming in the wode. The same hands that held the glass now of a night held hemp and lead and blood and the necks of thieves or, God forbid, the innocent. The overage of love she felt welling in her and the sure knowledge of his ability even proclivity to murder grated and moiled her heart until she felt like weeping and clinging to his neck. Worse—his murdering, she knew her mishap had unleashed it.

She drank the fizzing mixture. It crackled around her teeth, snapped her tongue clean with its bite of vinegar and miraculous grit. As she drooled into the basin, the mixture lay a cold stream of mint across her gums. He dabbed her mouth as she looked up into his eyes with adoration and a little terror.

"There, there," he said. "That's better. There, there, my love."

Patricia sat in a rocker with the child, the white light of morning pouring onto her through the front window. Her face was lowered to the baby's, and she was singing to it. Leighton paused at the bottom of the stairs. Patricia's voice was high and clear, no longer hindered by the wires, though her L's seemed to catch as if her tongue had atrophied. She sang German in rhythm with her rocking, sang to the babe though her face buckled with pain in doing so.

The babe's head jerked about, a sheen of drool on its protruding tongue and lips. Leighton stepped toward them, and Patricia smiled at him. She clutched the babe to her chest proudly and rocked in the chair. Blaring Missouri sunlight in its face, the milk of a Negro on its breath, German in its ears, and already the tiny curls of his late grandfather's red hair swirled on its head. This child would be the first Morkan that was an actual American, a remarkable mutt.

"How is mother?" Leighton asked. He stepped into the room and stood beside her.

She nodded, still smiling, and continued rocking the babe. The jut and skew of her chin made her dry, chafed lips when smiling seem tiny, and so the act became to Leighton magnified and dear to him—she had every excuse not to smile. The child slept, its head on her shoulder, its gooey eyes closed.

"And how is Gus?" Leighton asked.

"We are fine," she said.

"You gave us a good deal of fright, dear."

Her eyes, cupped in pink swollen crescents of worry and fatigue, held him for a moment, then returned to the babe. "Why do you still go at night vis Archer?" she asked. The child in her arms, the porcelain shine of her skin, the arch of her neck as she turned from him, and her words, all were unassailable blows of condemnation. How could you lie to and despise a woman holding your only son? "There were but three thieves and one shepherd. How many nights must you ride?"

He closed a fist. "Oh, it's too much for mother. You can't possibly understand."

Her impressive jaw tightened and her eyes narrowed. "Leighton, I understand. Perfectly. You kill men at night vis a potato sack on your head. All my attackers are gone or have died. Leighton. It is barbarity. Why ride?"

"This is not something easily walked away from. These men aided us as neighbors. Now I am their neighbor, brother, and keeper." He spoke so sternly the babe looked up at him and whimpered. "Patricia, it is nothing you need worry about."

When she lowered the baby to her lap, Leighton felt the babe falling away from him already, permanently to stay in the clutches of its mother. Its mouth twisted in a pout of red-faced consternation. Leighton lowered his face to it, and it took hold of his beard for an instant. Its tiny eyes were Patricia's green and gray.

She smoothed the babe's hair, shifted the child in her arms so that Leighton could see its round face and frightened eyes. "Will he need to worry, Leighton?"

Anna Julianna, Patricia's rotund cousin, visited from St. Louis and the Weitzer women arranged to go to the market together. Patricia wore a dress she hadn't sewn a stitch of, a luxurious novelty to her, one Looney had tailored at Easter, a gift from Leighton. Her jaw had healed and though her chin listed and jutted she could still think of herself as stately, even in Anna's Dearborn coach and seated across from Anna's stout form. Adjusting the lace at her neck under Anna's frown of approval, Patricia felt that she had accomplished some heroic feat in bearing a child, marrying an established man, and surviving both trials. The new devotion Leighton showed had not waned. In fact the more he rode and killed and terrorized, the more he doted on her. When Johnson helped Marta into the Dearborn, Marta's eyes grew radiant and wet as they gazed on Patricia in her yellow shirtwaist, her ivory gigot sleeves, and long creme skirts.

"*Mutter*," she said lowering her chin and extending her gloved hand, which Marta gripped delicately.

"Johnson," Patricia called, "*zum Markt!*"

Marta beamed as they thumped along. "You've taught his Negroes the Mother Tongue, Patricia?" she asked in German. "How admirable of you! What a service to them!"

Anna snorted, dabbed the sweat at her upper lip. "Pooh!" she said. She leaned back and rapped on the roof behind Johnson, her plump arm quaking. "Johnson, Johnson, *Frau Morkan hat ein paar Löcher in den Wagenkasten gelocht!*"

"Oh yes, ma'am," Johnson hollered over the rattle of the wheels. "We be thar right away."

Anna screeched with laughter—Johnson, Johnson, Mrs. Morkan has punched a great big hole in the side of the coach! She slapped her fat thighs. When neither Patricia nor Marta were amused, Anna settled, humming and holding the handkerchief to her lips.

"Johnson is a good man," Patricia said in English. "Do not degrade him."

"Ugh," Anna said. "I swear, Marta Weitzer, the pride. I almost forgot how a rough polling or two each week and a fat line of credit will make a grand bitch of a girl."

Patricia blushed, sweat pricking her scalp. She gritted her teeth.

"Good Lord, Anna," Marta said. "Shocking as ever."

"And as fat," Patricia said. "You nearly exploded this morning at the breakfast table. Do you realize what you cost per meal stuffing yourself like that?"

Anna gripped the sides of her stomach, which bulged like a ripe watermelon in her lap. "I know. My God, Marta, I have to tell you that Negro wench of theirs can cook. She'll kill me, Patricia, in all sincerity." Her brow creased as if she were suffering a terrible cramp.

Patricia put her hand on Anna's knee, smiled cautiously, and Anna gradually began to grin back. They giggled and in an instant it was as if they were girls together again after a long stint of earnest play-acting in the roles of adults. As Patricia and Anna chattered, Marta looked out the window at the passing buildings. To Patricia, her mother appeared very lonely without a friend like Anna or a grand husband like Leighton.

At the market, they circled the stalls where the smell of ripe fruit and onions and the reek of fresh fish mingled with the clay and lime dust of the roads. Both Marta and Anna complained about the selection and freshness of the goods, how they were hardly comparable to the markets in St. Louis, so much so that Patricia became angry and led them back to the Dearborn. They circled the square and stopped the coach at the gleaming fortress of the courthouse. Johnson helped them out and they stood in the hot sun before its steps and arches, the traffic clattering behind them.

"There is Leighton's stone," Patricia said. "The work of my husband. He cut the angles himself, even those little loaves topping the turrets."

Anna and Marta shielded their eyes. "In St. Louis," Anna said, "he would make a fortune. He's better than those godawful Italians."

Patricia frowned but nodded. "It is a structure to be proud of."

187

Marta pinched them both at the shoulder and drew them close. She whispered. "Patricia, Claus tells me there still has been no inquest for that shepherd. He died on those steps." Marta pulled at Patricia's shoulder. "Patricia? Isn't that so?"

Anger welled in her. Was her mother's life so hollow that the old woman had to sully everything Patricia could take pride in? Patricia was so taken aback, she nodded at first, but then shook her head. "It is nothing I know about."

Anna's face darkened. "Where was our Leighton last night when I arrived? He came in very late, didn't he?" Anna exchanged a glance with Marta that made Patricia wonder how much her mother had corresponded with Cousin Anna about the sheep and Gustasson's birth and events at the Morkan home.

"He has business to attend to," Patricia said.

"In the dead of night?" Anna asked.

Marta paled, and Patricia remembered the look of horror on her mother's face when Leighton stormed in, the hood at his waist, the blood on his coat.

"Mother is getting overheated," Patricia said quickly. "There is a café at the corner there with a nice awning."

Patricia was comforted when the proprietor served them and called her Mrs. Morkan and bowed slightly at her every request as if he were some café waiter in Vienna. He brought them all chilled cordials and ice water, putting the whole on Leighton's bill. Anna drank her liqueur at a jolt, then fingered the beads of water on her glass.

"Is it illicit, what he does?" she asked. Her voice fell. "Is he one of the Partisans?" When Patricia said nothing, Anna reached and touched Patricia's hands. "In St. Louis there have been articles. Even *Anzeiger des Westens* has been critical and is recommending Germans not settle here."

On the boardwalk, two young wheelwrights slowed their steps. Both their shoulders were draped with the iron hoops soon to bind wagon wheels, and wherever they moved they rang like eerie, walking bells. Quickly the women realized the wheelwrights had not slowed out of deference to ladies but out of horror and fascination at Patricia's mangled chin. They stared. Finally one nudged the other, and they jangled away.

Patricia felt her face boil. "You don't understand, Anna. This place went through a war nothing like St. Louis, where we were all safe and sheltered. And nothing like order has yet been restored." She moved her glass across the rough table top. "I was left for dead on the roadside by the ruffians who attacked me." Her voice fell to a whisper. "Some of the fiercest guerillas remain in the bush, lurking, and were it not for Leighton and some of the better men in town, there would be mayhem. We will not stand for any more of these vagabonds, these brush apes." There it was; she had as much as revealed the nature of Leighton's night riding. It was only her anger and wounded pride, though, that allowed her to advocate it.

Marta looked at her coldly. "I hope it wasn't you who stitched that hood for him." She said this at a low growl.

Patricia glared at her.

"So he *is* a Partisan," Anna said, touching the infernal handkerchief to her lips. "Oh, my God."

They sat in silence for a long time.

Anna ordered another cordial and two ices, paid for them herself. "It is the same terror and wanton destruction they practiced on one another in wartime." She sighed. "Oh, Patricia."

"You're just spouting what you read in the papers."

Anna was about to protest, when Patricia cut her off. "And remember, he fought for the Union, the same as Erich and Robart."

Marta popped her open hand on the table. "Not the same. Not hardly the same. Your brothers fought under Franz Sigel, fought like lions. In the open. With pride. They did not hunt men like wolves in the woods." She was shaking when she finished.

A stone wagon rattled past returning to the quarry. The foreman stood in the seat, doffed his cap and called to Mrs. Morkan. "One cannot help the war in which one serves." Patricia watched the foreman pass with her chin raised. "I can trust that it will all come to good someday," she said, lying again.

Anna shook her head, gripped Patricia's hand in both of hers. "Let me please tell you something in the way only family can. Please. If there was one thing that old bag Colonel Sonnenberg understood it was that his actions in the world bore my name and honor as well."

Patricia sat fiercely still.

"My dear, you must take control of your family," Anna went on. "You are its nobility, its chastity, its conscience. And above all, you are its true protector." She squeezed Patricia's hand. "He is not the only ruffian who can shoot and kill. You may bury him beside his father, the old Rebel, one day. And what do you know of running a quarry? Of sharpening stones?"

With a last mournful contraction of her round face, she released Patricia. Then she withdrew her hands slowly across the table.

After a long moment when all three women were silent, Patricia asked Anna to go and fetch Johnson and the carriage. "I must get back to my baby."

In the coach ride back, Anna told Marta of gay parties and dances in St. Louis, of the old Turnverein cleared of invalids opening up to recitals and gymnastics, and the lovely times she was having with another war widow.

Patricia felt suddenly very alone. She gazed out the window where buildings flashed by glazed in her husband's stark white-wash and bound in his mortar.

Leighton tried to come straight home from the quarry for dinner. He wished to be at least sociable with Anna Julianna. But a threatening note wrapped round a hunk of flint crashed through the window onto Bright's telegraph desk. With Wilson Shannon he spent a night at the Bright's farm hidden in the cedars waiting for trouble that never came.

Taking a candle, he walked the stairs. He could hear Anna Julianna snoring like a lazy saw on the bed fixed in the library. On the sleeping porch, Patricia's form beneath the sheets glowed gray in the starlight. Crossing the bedroom, his feet tangled in some inexplicable fiber. He stopped, watched her sleeping. He moved with a stealth unconscious to him, born of the woods and night and war and now vigilantism. Carefully he felt at the floor—the fiber was everywhere; it left a wax on his hands—wool.

There were wooden parts on the floor, a block with bristles harder than a horse brush, dowels, a cog with ivory spokes jutting from it. He rolled this in his hands, marveling at its workmanship, questioning its function. Eventually exhaustion dazed him, and he removed his clothes, extinguished the candle, and slipped beneath the sheet.

As he moved behind her, she whimpered something in German, and he froze but soon realized she was asleep and mumbling at some shrift prowling her dreams. He touched her back, then wrapped his arm around her. She lay there breathing, her small frame rising and pressing against his arm then shrinking. Then she whimpered three times, the last a cry carried mournfully across porch and bedroom. A wraith in his own home. And worse, he was the haunt darkening her dreams.

V

To Isaac's mind the course of the farm had flowed without a ripple for fifteen summers before the Morkans and all their building and tumult, then the war, and then it was all over-turned once more by this Dutch woman. After the assault on her and her birthing a child, she kept to herself and entertained few visitors. Even her gloomy mother was a rarity. But Leighton insisted Isaac keep watch on the Mrs. Morkan.

Every day brought a new madness. Into town they went, Isaac driving the buggy with Patricia sitting at his side. Often a White man rode horseback along with them—Mr. Cox, Mr. Bright, Mr. Cooper, members of Morkan's gang—always with a rifle at ready.

"Mrs. Morkan, I own a rifle and I ride every bit as good as that gentleman there," he whispered to her. A lunatic, she encouraged Negroes to speak regardless of whether or not they had been spoken to, but he kept his voice low in public.

"Isaac, I would like nothing better," she said. Since the accident she had a mule's chin, and she could make faces like a damned old burro, too. "You may ride our woods and hunt, but I will not in my time see a Negro on the road to town with a loaded rifle at his hip." Then her voice dropped very low and she raised her eyebrows at him. "These clodhoppers will not abide it." She swung her big chin at Wilson Shannon, who doffed his hat.

She was Dutchy and said things that would get a Negro hung.

At the chemists, out she came with phials, crocks, and bags. She chattered in the carriage and showed Isaac the stuff—copperas and chrome, alum, indigo, and lime. Married to the quarrymaster and yet she paid merchants for his makings when he could bring it home in barrels if she asked. Then out in the woods

192

she took him and they scrabbled for such useless truck as walnut hulls and sumac, madder root, dogwood bark, goldenrod and poke. A year this went on through all seasons and she overran one of the old slave cabins and made her a shack hanging crud she gat and afternoons she would burn a fire in that shack all the hours of sun, then come out in the twilight with her hands purple or brown and yellow, smiling and talking to herself in Dutch and this warmed him. On humid days, she sat outside the shack stroking the wool through two blocks bristled like horse brushes. Then she rolled the yellow-white stuff into what she called a rolag, like an oversized twist of tobacco.

He lounged in the afternoon with the sheep gathered to him on a hillock, the ewes and ram what Morkan had taken from the shepherd he killed. Isaac watched Mrs. Morkan scurry around that shack, listened to pots banging, and wondered what it was like to hump on someone so tall. He knew too well what it was like to hump on Judith. Facing her sour expression, her eyes screwed tight, her ever swelling body, he felt like a weevil sticking its beak into a poke berry. He sought her only when his hand wouldn't do. When Mrs. Morkan bent for something, Isaac could envision the sharp lines of her legs and hips through her work dress. Everything about Mrs. Morkan had an edge to it. Her long fingers seemed to come to points. Her chin struck solid and scaly as an andiron. Her mind produced notions that hewed like an ax. It was no wonder to him that a band of crackers dragged her off a coach, beat her, and pissed on her, for she was in no way of their kind. Lord knows what she said to provoke them.

"Mrs. Morkan?" Isaac asked. They were in the woods on a February day when the temperature seemed to drop to freezing if a cloud took the sun. She sat with her legs spraddled digging furiously at the base of a locust tree, its black thorns lancing for her.

Holy tottered to her with a handful of pine needles, and taking them, she said something in Dutch that made him laugh and dance.

"Mrs. Morkan? What we after this for?"

"Dice," she said, resuming her trowel work.

193

He dropped to one knee and scooped Holy to his chest. He whispered, "Lord God, Mrs. Morkan, Judith'd kill me if she knew you was planning that with Holy around."

"What problem would Judit have with dying for wool except that it may mean more work for her? Dice, Isaac, dice! What on earth?"

He let Holy loose, and the babe wobbled to her side. About work she was a hard captain. Stabbing at the ground with her trowel, she caught her forearm on one of the shining black thorns and it plunged deep, even lifted her skin. To his surprise she didn't cuss or scream, didn't even jump. She stilled herself, then backed her arm free of the thorn. Isaac knew not to run for cobweb. She would only belittle this. She pinched her wound, and once she thought she had it stopped, she watched him.

"Does Judith not take to working?" Isaac asked. Any sparks between the two women fascinated him.

Her brow bunched in annoyance. Blood seeped around her fingernails. The wound was more than a pinch could handle, but he wanted an answer before he aided her.

"Do either of you take to working?" she asked.

They were quiet for a time—his anger kept him sitting. He would let her bleed to death right now for no more than a dip of snuff.

Holy tottered to her. "Ooo," he said. "Ow."

Holy touched her wrist, and after a moment her squared shoulders softened. She patted his leg.

"I worry about her, Isaac. I fear she suffered edema in birthing Holofernes. May I ask you something?"

She did not wait for his answer. "When she gave birth did her fingers, arms, and legs swell massively? Did she pass out or tremble?"

He shrugged. "I don't know what all she done."

She stared at him as a mule will, walloped and looking who to kick.

"What you worried about?" he asked pulling the babe to him. Stroking the boy's head, he looked over the babe's cedar-colored skin. Had the kid been harmed, is that what the Dutch meant?

She lost interest in her own wound and scooted forward.

She touched the toddler's cheek and left on it a trace of blood, which seemed to disappear into Holy's reddish skin. When her eyes met Isaac's stare, he thought surely this woman, crazy-smart as she was, could see the kid weren't sired by any Isaac. Her eyes were narrow as the tip of an augur.

"Isaac?" She still held the toddler's face, tipping his head with her fingertips on the boy's chin as if she were examining a torn lampshade. "Do you imagine Judit will help me in spinning wool?"

Isaac was still for some time watching her examine the boy. "She a smart gal." She understood full well who Holy's father was, but God-damn if she wasn't going to keep quiet on it, like any wise, old Negro would.

"Yes, she is that," Mrs. Morkan said. She released Holy's chin, patted his head. She looked away toward the columns of the farm house. Seeing her mule's chin cast stubbornly toward that stone, Isaac was filled with admiration and dread.

"I have been working at this without a woman's help too long," she said.

That same month, a member of the Gentlemen's Defense League, the surgeon Charley Weaver, was waylaid, and his horse was stolen along with forty dollars, his boots and coat. Wandering dazed, he lost the tips of all his toes and fingers to frostbite. The same thief killed the sheriff in a chase through the woods.

The league gathered at Shannon's and all expressed their sympathies to Weaver, who sat with his head bowed, bandaged hands folded in his lap. A surgeon with no fingertips weren't no surgeon at all, he said.

From the stables below came a long, high whistle of alarm. Shannon grabbed the ladder, stashed it in the hay. Men scrambled in the loft, stanched the flew, doused lanterns, scattered themselves to the corners.

Leighton tried to worm himself into the tightly packed hay, but gave up and lay flat on the floor. At the barn door a banging commenced. Leighton scooted to the edge of the loft and peered over.

Shannon stepped to the door. When he held up a lantern, his curly, brown hair glowed in its light. "Who needs me?" he asked.

Leighton could not hear the answer. Shannon opened the door, and there was Shane Peale, his hair swirled from riding. He wore a thick, shining overcoat with flared shoulders and riding chaps. He placed one hand at his belt so that his revolver and its shining grip glinted in the lantern light. His face glistened, pink and wet, eyes pinched as if he had burrowed through snow. His fist, thrusting up the lamp, seemed hammered of stone, and a huge chaw of tobacco bulged in his bottom lip. Two men accompanied him, big, burley deputies with waxy goatees. Between them, they dragged a prisoner by his arms. The prisoner's head drooped, and the back of the prisoner's neck shone sallow in the lantern light .

"What's the meaning of this?" Shannon asked.

Peale held the lantern well above his head, and with his height and reach, the light shone over most of the stables. Leighton pressed his face low against the wooden floor of the loft. Across the front of Peale's coat, blood was spattered and a streak of it mingled with mud on his cheek. He gazed up toward the loft, then noted each stall down the length of the barn. He leaned forward and spat a gout of brown. The lantern bobbed. "Would that horse there be Morkan's Walker?"

Shannon planted his hand on his hips. "Ain't Morkan's Walker. Wouldn't let that Irish shit on my land." Shannon snarled. "Papist! Idolator!" The gray wad of his hood poked up from his back pocket, innocent as a handkerchief. "These horses are from a big coon hunting party. From Neosho. Cousins. Vis'ting."

Peale scratched his long nose. "I hear them Morkans don't make too good a hunting partners."

He turned to the deputies, and they dragged the prisoner forward.

"What's all this about?" Shannon asked, wiping his hands on the front of his overalls. "That fellow hurt? Youns need help?"

Peale stared at the young farmer with the inscrutable coins of his eyes glowing in the lamplight. Hunting guerrillas with Peale, Leighton had seen those eyes become blind and glazed to violence and bloodshed over the course of the war. For an instant, Leighton saw Peale stare up at him. Peale's lips lifted in the glimmer of a smile. Peale looked down at

Shannon again. He nodded to the deputies, and they dropped the prisoner face down in the dirt. The deputies hesitated glancing up at the loft, then around at the dark stalls. Peale motioned them out. Once they were gone, he spat squarely between the prisoner's shoulders. "I jess watched this Spawn of Hell kill our sherff earlier this evening. Tell Morkan that for tonight I leave him the keys to the city. And tell him come tomorrow, I'm the new sheriff. The time for hunting men in the dark, that's over."

Peale eased the door shut behind him. Shannon drew the bolt home, then stood on tip-toe, his face pressed to the crucifix cut in the door. After quite some time, he replaced the ladder, and the men scrambled down from the loft.

Shannon lit two miner's lamps, and the hooded men huddled around the prisoner who had not budged. Short black hair salted with sparks of gray, muddy dungarees, a suede vest that smelled new. His face was thin and clean-shaven. Leighton drew his revolver, grabbed the prisoner by the shoulder and rolled him over.

Charley Weaver, the surgeon, lurched forward, took the limp prisoner by the vest, shook him. "This here's the man."

Finger by stubbed, blackened finger, Leighton loosened Weaver's fierce grip.

"And what do we do with the keys to the city, Mr. Morkan?" Archer asked with a sneer in his voice, not hiding his resentment at going unrecognized by Peale.

"It is February," Leighton said, ignoring Archer's sense of this slight.

The prisoner did not wake up, and they took him in a wagon to the crossroads of Rockbridge and Wire. The prisoner did not awaken even when the men stripped off his vest, shirt, and pants, and thumped him on his back along the freezing roadside. For good measure, Weaver took out a blast augur for sheep, and poked two holes in the thief's left side, one to air him like a can, and one aortally deep from which the prisoner's life drained away sure as bilge from a spigot. A ledge of limestone bordered Rockbridge Road there draped with creeper. They lifted the leaking man and wove his arms and shoulders between the vines. Early in the morning, when the last lonely stars burned and fell, Cox the printer returned to hang on the dead a sign: I KILT YOUR SHERFF.

Judith bolted awake from a dream, and shivered at the morning, her breath sending blue coils into the cold of the cabin. She left Isaac sleeping with his pasty mouth ajar. Snatching up Holofernes, she tramped through the thin blue light and up the hill where the house jutted like a butte of lime from the woods. A long snake of silver smoke crawled from the stovepipe at the kitchen ell. Previous to this moment nothing at the house had preceded her arrival. Rising there, the smoke was as disturbing as a battleflag cresting the hill.

In the back lot near the ell of the house another fire burned and Johnson stood by this sleeping with his chin on his wrists draped over the handle of a pitchfork carved of wood. The cauldron simmering there reeked of alum and lime. Beneath it the fire, a mild one, flexed its brassy claws. In a line leading to the cauldron were tubs of shining water. Wool rolags waited in a pile beside one of the tubs. The backdoor was open and through the mudroom came a waft of sassafras in the air thick as gravy.

"Good, Judit." Patricia stepped through the door holding a boiling pot of water. "Now we begin." She wore an apron Judith had never seen and a ratty blouse, both colored with deep forest green, with splashes of black, indigo, yellow, and peach, a muddled rainbow.

Judith, Johnson, even Isaac learned mordanting, moving the rolags of wool from cool to tepid and last to the warm, biting water of the cauldron. In each tub they kept the wool swirling in a slow circle never raising it above the surface of the water.

Patricia laced her fingers and extended her arms in front of her. The Negroes stared. "In ever activity from here forward, think that you are binding, working toward the moment when the wool will twist into a single thread," she said. "If you drag it from the water, it will pull itself apart. If you move it into water with much greater heat, you weaken it. Never boil it. Care in ever step, for ever step is toward the binding."

Each rolag they dipped from the tubs with deep copper colanders. Seeing the flash of these, spying the rolags on the ground and those that had hung drying by her shed in the woods, Judith newly comprehended the witchy things about this woman. There was a practical wizardry in each strange curio, the horse brushes she called cards, the pitch forks made of wood, the bottles and phials and roots and weeds. After the lime bath, they hung the wool to dry, then dipped a first wool roll from her shed into water sassafras had turned brown as coffee. With all of them huddled round watching, the wool lolled in the liquid, then began to sink. Patricia recited a poem in Dutch, and it was so like an incantation that Isaac and Johnson backed away.

"Help me lift, Judit, my brave one." She winked at Judith and whispered. "The poem lets you know how long to wait." They pushed the colander beneath the rusty surface. The wool that emerged in it was blood crimson. Patricia let the rolag drape across her chest and arm and bleed onto her apron and blouse. Judith touched it in amazement, as if the Dutch woman held against her chest a massive skinned fish. Judith's pink palm immediately colored as dark as Holy's skin. Patricia clasped her hand in Judith's. "Any color under the sun, Judit. Any color you can imagine."

After the night Shane Peale appeared at Shannon's barn, Leighton avoided him. Peale was elected sheriff officially on the first of March. Then Leighton sent Miasma to the courthouse with a note asking the new sheriff to meet him at Jack Reardon's Barber Shop so Leighton could "return his keys." A foot of snow had fallen and the air hung cool and thick.

Jack the barber snapped the white cloth out above the gleaming chair. His Colored hand, Darnit, began sweeping the last patron's clippings toward the stove where he scooped it in a pile against his broom, opened the stove and sent the hairs into the coals. As Leighton sat in the chair, Darnit took the shaving basin to a brass slat fixed in the wall. When he poured the basin out, frigid outside air forced steam from its edge. Jack wrapped the white cape around Leighton and tucked it down along his sides.

The door shuddered open, and Peale stepped in, ducking to miss the top of the doorjamb. Blue crystals of snow shimmered on the rim of his black slouch hat. He removed the hat, nodded at the barber. He wore a dingy cutaway coat and an amazing teal string tie. His boots were silvered with snow. Jack's mongoloid son rose and flipped the cape out.

Peale waved the cape away as the mongoloid extended it. "Leighton, I don't need no haircut." Peale paused and glared at himself in one of the mirrors across the room. He was tall, lanky, and now he was growing his hair in long brown curls.

Frowning, Leighton shook his head, the cape swishing across his shirt front. "Jack the Barber's deaf, Peale. The boy's a idiot, and you know Darnit can't speak anything but that real bad French."

Darnit grinned, motioned Peale to a chair.

Peale's chin stiffened. "Oh, I don't mind being public. Just don't need a cutting."

A leach wagged its tail and rose to the top of one of the hundreds of jars Jack the Barber kept on shelves against the clapboard wall. Many of the jars were full of alcohol in which there floated massive locusts, a centipede more than eighteen inches long, a sparrow with five legs. One jar held thousands of dead wasps of every color and size, and next to them in a smaller jar their thousands of stingers had been removed and collected, shining like the thistles of some foreign spice. Jack the Barber always maintained that Darnit had been a slave in Haiti and knew the black arts, and with such arts could reduce goiters, eradicate lice, even mollify flatulence.

Peale crossed the puncheon floor, stood before the mongoloid, who held out the cape as if he were a plump matador. The mongoloid had pale skin, a round face, pinched, dismayed eyes, like a Chinaman after too much sun. With the yellowed eyes and brown teeth of the Negro, the mongoloid's wet stare, the twisted puncheons, the stinking black stove—it would give Leighton no pause at all to see a Devonian dragonfly push itself up from the jars on the opposite wall and rattle about the shop. Sitting in Jack's always gave him the eerie sensation of listing in a musty, humid river-boat's hold amid some menagerie's truck. "You ever been to a barber, sheriff?" he asked.

Peale sat, and the mongoloid swept the cape across his chest, strapped it at his collar. "My gal cuts hair pretty fair."

Jack and the mongoloid sharpened their razors against the strops that hung like the braids of Chinamen in back of each chair. Each stroke of the strop jerked the patron a notch, a drumbeat to ready him for the blade's onslaught.

"Well, I'm buying," Leighton said. "And hush. There's men at work."

Darnit held out an array of five brightly colored bottles to Leighton. Leighton swirled his finger free of the cape and touched a purple bottle. Darnit nodded, and poured a little liquid in Jack's open hand. The smell of violets crept across the frigid shop.

"You ought to have your neck shaved." He watched Peale in the mirror as he spoke. "And a trim all around, about an eighth of an inch." The mirror, a gleaming oval tall as a man and supported in a stout walnut frame, was ringed with purple flaws where the mica and silver had separated from the glass. In it, he and Peale seemed small in their capes, like boys again. They had posed for a picture once in the war in their new Home Guard uniforms. They were drunk. The wave of that memory swept over Leighton. He had no idea where the old tintype was, but here he and Peale were framed in the purpling mirror, adults, wearing pistols and badges, blaster's vests and money belts. And Peale was a sheriff. And Leighton was a vigilante.

With his tiny scissors, Jack the Barber began nipping Leighton's beard. The mongoloid took a steel marble from his apron; he opened his scissors and began squeezing them against the marble, making a grating sound that had Peale cringing in his chair. Leighton held his hand up, and Jack paused at his beard. "The mongoloid only gives one kind of haircut." Leighton nodded at Jack's son, who was squinting at the marble, grinding down on it. The little pink tip of his tongue poked between his lips. "It just looks different because everybody's head's different."

Peale raised up in the chair. "Just a shave, then. Will you tell him that?"

Leighton stretched and caught the mongoloid's sleeve. He winked at him. "Shave." He winked again, pointed at his beard.

The mongoloid pouted, but nodded. Peale leaned his head back baring his prominent Adam's apple with whiskers on it like pepper in red gravy.

They sat in silence, Jack's scissors clicking and snipping, the mongoloid drawing the razor crackling along Peale's neck. Under the cape, Peale's back was as a bow.

Peale began, "I will…" He paused, and let the mongoloid finish his Adam's apple. "I want some rules set down."

Leighton stared at the tumbling hair that fell like shards of magnetized iron from his shoulders and lap. In a week, ten days, Peale could have the state militia in town and martial law return. Peale's eyes were closed and his cheeks and chest had relaxed.

"The deputies I have are no account," he said. "They got family to worry about, and seems like ever no good thief's got him a whole pile of brothers and cousins willing to revenge any little ole thing. And there ain't a jury any braver than these deputies. Chicken shit county full of peckerwoods."

"Juries of your peers!" Leighton said. "Profoundly ill-conceived!"

Jack began kneading dabs of the violet perfume into Leighton's hair. Jack's fingers numbed and warmed his scalp, so he had to squint to hear Peale

"I'm saying, much as I hate it, they's times when what you do works."

Leighton waved Jack aside. Over at Peale's chair, the mongoloid frowned in deep concentration, his big bottom lip pouting as he drew the razor along Peale's cheek. Peale grabbed the mongoloid's wrist. Everything in the barbershop halted, and even the leech waggling in its jar seemed stilled in the cold.

"At least for now, you let me gather the evidence. Then if there's a fellow that needs taken care of …" He let go of the mongoloid's wrist and eased himself back in the chair. "Just for now. Not for always."

A warm splash of water ran from the basin in the mongoloid's hands. Peale jolted upright. The mongoloid paused and

202

blinked. After glaring at the mongoloid, Peale resumed. "But you get one innocent man that I know of, or one man I ain't told you to get." Peale turned to him. "Then I put my hood on."

"Well, this is a surprise. I heard tell you were mighty upset with hunting at night. Wanted no more of it."

Jack banged a tin comb against its jar. The comb shimmered with oil.

"They's public policy. And then there is truth. We been through enough together to know the both." Peale paused, watched Darnit and the two barbers, his breath steaming at his nostrils. In the cold of the shop, the bite of hair burning in the stove sent both men's pulses racing, and they separately relived in their minds the two of them tromping together the scorched foundations on burial detail after the Battle of Springfield or searching the blackened homesteads where Father, Mother, Daughter had all fried.

"This'll end in peace, I swear to God," Peale continued. He leaned toward Leighton's reflection. "Because I know that after a time, you won't last with these fellows. And they can't stay together without you or something like you. Know why?"

Jack the Barber hesitated, then flicked a brush at Leighton's neck as if he were shooing hornets. The mongoloid kicked the lock on the bottom of the barber chair, and Peale swung toward Leighton. Leighton's eyes narrowed. In the mirror, he and Peale made an intense portrait, listing in the dimly lit shop, the window blasting the white of the snowscape outside, stingers and tongues floating above them.

Peale's voice fell to a whisper. "Leighton, how could ye forget? The killers get killed, the hunters get hunted. No God but death. Black flag. That's how you're a'riding." One of the curls of Peale's hair brushed Leighton's cheek. "We come so close to putting all that behind us." Beneath the cape Peale's hand made a lump at his hip and Leighton's hand made a lump at his coat pocket where his pepperbox waited. The barbers eased back. Rattling the silence hot water pipes knocked and hissed as the steam came up.

"You can't outlast what you are—you hire Niggers and run a mean old company store. You gave freedmen a living. How long till you face hoods?"

Peale showed Leighton his palms. Then he slowly took his chaw and knife from his coat and began scraping.

He continued, his eyes roving Leighton's shining black hair. "You'll get yourself killed or that wife of yours." Slowly he stood, looking down at Leighton holding the chaw on the blade of his knife. "Or that poor baby boy."

"I make this pact with you instead of Mr. Newman," he continued. His eyebrows bobbed as if the significance of what he said escalated whenever he paused. "I believe that Archer Newman's got all kind of ambition. But he's got nothing to ground him." His eyebrows bobbed again. "You, Leighton, got you something to live for. I seen it when Mrs. Patricia was down. You love that Dutch. Take aholt of her. Let all this terrible wastage go." He affixed the chaw in his mouth.

Jack unfastened the cape, and the mongoloid removed Peale's. Leighton rose, brushed off his pants. The meeting had given him more than he bargained for—the town, the law was on his side for now, but Peale's warnings made a terrible sense. In the jars the barbs of the wasp stingers shone like iron nails.

Peale glared at the mongoloid who clutched the basin and backed away. He fixed his hat on his head, wished them all a good day. His leaving sent a cold burst of air and white light and blowing shards of brilliant snow whirling across the slat floor.

The mongoloid handed Darnit the basin full of Peale's whiskers. Darnit offered them up to Leighton. "Mr. Leighton, if you mixed these here whiskers with your spit and rubs it under your nose, you have power over that man all your days."

Leighton paid Darnit extra for a spell. "Remember," Leighton said. "You speak French around him." Leighton spit on the Negro's proffered thumb, and Darnit pulled his wetted digit through the sheriff's plentiful whiskers.

Darnit bared his teeth and said something awful in French, then stubbed his thumb beneath Leighton's nose in two stinging streaks that smelled like ashes.

Riding in the cold, shivering, he pulled his scarf up to cover his nose. The strong smell of oil and roses caught him by surprise. Patricia had worn the scarf lately, had taken it from the mud room to run across the yard maybe for wood, or milk, or yarn. The smell was from a jar of lotion she used, for he had seen her rub it about her long fingers of a morning as she watched him pull on his boots and slip his pistol in his coat.

When Leighton told the Gentlemen's Defense League what Peale said, he felt exultant and powerful.

After he finished, there was a cheer and most of the hooded men pounded one another's shoulders and applauded. But three hoods held back; one of them was Archer.

The hood seated next to Archer rose. "Why wasn't the White Knight consulted before this meeting?" He meant Archer Newman, elected to be Exalted White Knight in a lull when pomp filled in for violence. The table fell silent.

Another hood rose. "Ask yourselves why we all weren't consulted so that rather than one brother's voice, the good brother could have spoken with our unified voice."

Heads bowed around the table, as if suddenly ashamed of their cheering. Archer, the White Knight, rose, crossed his arms over his chest. "Now, gentlemen, we have here a sterling example of why we must commune at one table under one White Knight. With good intentions and no ill will, our brother has engaged the new sheriff without tapping the strength and counsel of his fellow riders. To be honest, I am not sure what about our band has made our brother feel so cocksure as to speak for all of us on such short notice."

Now he stared directly at Leighton, who still had not resumed his seat.

"But know this, gentlemen. Ours is a deadly business—live by the rope, die by the rope. If you speak before consulting your brethren, you may bear the results of your conversation alone." He spread his hands on the table, looming over it. "We shall work with the new sheriff, but if we see anything lacking in his law enforcement, in all candor, you may be assured we will ride!"

The meeting adjourned, but when Leighton did not file down the ladder with his hooded compadres, Archer stopped and waited for the brothers to leave. Soon only Wilson Shannon remained, whirling his grindstone on some blade beneath them.

Leighton rose. "That was low, Archer Newman."

"Listen," Archer said, his voice icy. "You were asked into this. And you can be asked to leave." Down below the loft, sparks off the grindstone made the walls flicker.

"This that's yours has its uses," Leighton said. "But it will pass,"

Archer stared at him a long while. "Rely on your brothers while you have them."

By post, with a woman's script on the address and return, Archer Newman sent a note to Patricia requesting a visit without Leighton's knowledge. At first she thought she might take the note to Leighton as if appalled and so alarm him into severing all association with Archer. But she knew, with two men so volatile, such a course could backfire and redound in disasters of all kinds. Besides no evil was beyond reforming, her Lutheran ministers told her, and about Archer she bore a strange desire she felt sure was *Herr Gott's* own drive for Reformation Universal.

She replied telling him to come on a Thursday morning. He rode up the hill on his black colt and she received him from the porch. He did not dismount, though Johnson Davis came round the corner of the house to take his reins. Archer stared down at her with a pained expression.

"Johnson," Patricia said, "go on about business."

The Negro looked puzzled, but eventually pulled his slouch hat off and gave Archer and Patricia a little bow before ambling away.

"Thank you for meeting me," Archer said. "Leighton does not know?"

"Correct," Patricia said. "This is quite forward. But not entirely inappropriate. You are still a friend of the family from all I know."

Archer grimaced. He began in his awkward German. "These have been difficult times. And I am sure that some of my actions have caused you pain." *Seelenqualen,* he spoke for pain, meaning precisely mental pain, madness, rather than anguish, *Seelenqualen,* which was not far off the truth.

"And pain of the heart," she said in German. If Judith or Johnson were listening it was a comfort to speak her tongue, something she could not do with Leighton.

"I have come to ask forgiveness." He bowed his head, and she looked him over, the slim muscular legs well clad with cotton breeches, a tan suit coat to match them not able to hide his powerful shoulders. She remembered the feel of those shoulders and his grip when she shoved him on her wedding day.

"Why is it men are ever asking me for forgiveness? Why? Did you two not really think of me when you set off rampaging to avenge me?"

Archer raised his glance to her and his eyes appeared shrewd and aged. "Men rarely think in any thorough way until consequences fall upon them. Again forgive me. There is a slight breach now between Leighton and me, but it is a business matter. Please let there be no such divide between us." There was sorrow in his voice, and she wondered if the sentiment were real. And if it were real, wasn't it a little preposterous? What did this peculiar man want?

"You need ask nothing of me. Leighton makes his own choices. He is wise enough, or fool enough, to follow his own counsel."

He dismounted, and holding the reins in one hand, he extended a hand to her. She hesitated then stepped forward. Nonplussed, she took his hand, and was surprised to feel there the same callous Leighton bore.

He looked on her a long time and his shrewdness faded to a gaze that unnerved her. "I feel relieved then," he said, and he gave her hand a squeeze before releasing it.

She felt flush, a radiance at her cheeks, and could hardly believe that one now as ugly and awkward as she deserved this chivalrous posturing. She both despised and cherished the sentiment flooding her.

He mounted again, and circled the horse quickly to settle it.

"You have certainly ridden a long way and employed some subterfuge to accomplish this," she said. "Whatever *this* is!"

He watched her for a moment. "What a proud and sharp woman you are! Let's say that I can stomach having your husband against me. But to be honest, I will not have you set against me. There will be no need for subterfuge next time I see you."

"Forward, as always, Archer Newman."

He gave a bow in the saddle and turned his horse for town.

† † †

With a crochet hook Patricia reached through the orifice and drew the yarn forward, old yarn—she showed Judith—from before the war. Twilight was rushing on outside, the setting sun making an orange and gray swirl of the sky. Patricia sat at the wheel, foot curled and tensed near the treadle.

"This wool is from '61. You probably do not remember that spring's wool, do you, Judit?"

Behind them the two toddlers were patting the floor with their hands and pushing the waiting rolls of wool against each other's faces. They played as naturally as brothers, and often fell asleep in each others arms as Patricia had seen twins do.

Judith knelt to see the wheel in the lantern light, balanced herself by touching Patricia's shoulder, which startled Patricia at first. But she braced her spine, let the massive Negress put her full weight there. Over the last weeks, Patricia's industry and determination never waned and Judith's sullenness and surliness had vanished, replaced by an abiding curiosity.

"This is from a Shropshire, but you would think better. What a year, '61! So much promise, so much abundance then before so much wasted. Do you remember?"

"No 'm. Mrs. Charlotte was long dead by then and the dead Morkan sold her wheel pretty soon after, and course she didn't let me near it."

Patricia shook her head. "She had a wheel, then? Of what sort?"

"Lot bigger'n this un. An she walked beside it miles a night."

"Never dyed the wool?"

"I never seen her. But she kept me out of it. Said I wasn't sharp enough to spin."

"I tell you, Judit, the Irish retain such awful notions about the other races." Patricia patted the wheel as if it were a small horse. "This is a Saxony wheel. My great grandmother's. Rosewood. The ivory here on the maidens and at the finials carved from the tusks of a mastodon dug from the icy depths of a snow bank in far Eastern Prussia."

She took one of the rolags from the black rambouillet, gray-black as an umbilical cord. "Give me your hands, Judit."

Judith stuck her hands out. Green and crimson dye still streaked the creases in her fleshy pink palms. Patricia placed the end of the rolag in Judith's left palm, then began rubbing her hands gently across Judith's hand. Greasy and soft, the wool soon made a wispy fan. Patricia commented on the good mix of color the mordant had achieved.

"Look like the wall of a cave," Judith said. Then the Negress's brow creased with sudden concern. She mystified Patricia. Any one of a conglomerate of things set the Negress to sweating. Poor thing, getting so fat now. How did she ever carry it all?

Patricia pulled the old yarn from the wheel until it met the fan of fibers in Judith's hand. "Pinch the ends against the old yarn."

Judith's fingers worked at the new wool and its fibers bound with the old, softened by the new lanolin and the sweaty oil of Judith's plump fingers.

"Good! See! You have the ideal fingers for this." She patted Judith on the shoulder. "The very oil of your skin, Judit, off your body is making that bond occur, old wool, from past, to now, to future. See? Beautiful. My hands never could do it so fast."

"For true?"

"With apologies, but I have nothing but truth for you, Judit," she said. "Now, I want you to stand back and watch." She took the wool from her. "We will talk about what you see after. Watch carefully."

Judith frowned and crossed her arms over her big chest.

Patricia bounced her eyebrows at Judith, and the Negress was startled at the look of mirth on Patricia's face. Then Patricia gave the wheel a pull with her right hand. In a flash her foot went thumping at the treadle and both her hands molded at the rolag, her body swaying, fingers moving quick as a spider's legs. At the bobbin the yarn grew, appearing as if by sorcery from the moment her long fingers joined. Judith held her breath—the teeth of the mastodon sparkled as the spokes whirled and became things other than ivory and rosewood in the wheel's motion: lions leaping, birds up from ashes, the blades of knives. Alongside it were cogs and whirlpools, wheels and shafts and bobbins humming above the solid mother-of-all that bore them up. The fibers that wound off her fingers from the dwindling umbilical rolag spun toward the bobbin, the yarn taut in a rope snaking out, whirling diamonds and suns in the orange twilight and amber lantern glow.

The wool was rapidly going. Patricia puckered her lips together and let loose a whistle that could have ripped from a herdsman. "Haul up another rolag, Judit. It's only a wheel." But she was smiling. They were both smiling.

Judith feathered the rolag, stroking it into the fan Patricia had shown her, loving the waxen feel of the wool on her palms, the biting hint of lime. Patricia stood from the wheel, motioned for Judith to sit. She pulled the yarn from the bobbin, new yarn they had just made, nestled its end in the fan of wool Judith held.

Judith pinched the wool onto the yarn. Hesitating, she glanced up at Patricia, but her arm rose to touch the wheel.

Patricia nodded, her chin stern in its skewed and crusted state. "You know where you are. You know what to do, Judit."

Judith gave the wheel a pull, and the rolag jerked from her hand. She grunted and retrieved it.

Patricia stood by the wheel. "Here. Let me start you. Get those hands ready. Foot on the treadle. There."

Patricia pulled, and Judith's foot began pumping the treadle. Her hands scrambled to knead the wool forward to that magical point hanging in air where the urge of the wheel swept the fibers together, twisted them, and from chaos they became yarn. Soon, with Patricia nodding, the wheel began to make a kind of music, steady and quick.

Patricia smiled and blushed. Judith felt a warmth flood all across her face, felt a smile curve her lips and a laugh ache at her jaw.

Nodding to the treadle's clacking, Patricia breathed deeply and began to sing in her high reedy voice:

> *Ein Backfisch ging,*
> *'Nen Todten Fink,*
> *Der ausgestopft,*
> *Auf 'nen Hut gepropft*
> *Den Weg entlang,*
> *Da plötzlich drang*
> *Das Wort zu ihr:*

"Ei, Sieh doch hier
Den Balg, wie nett!"
Sie schielt kokett,
Nach dem der's sprach
Der aber, ach,
Rief aüsserst slink
"Ich meint den Fink!"

The two toddlers clapped and yammered imitating her. Laughing, Judith wound the wheel down until she held just the frayed wisps of the spent rolag in her hands. The last of the sun flowed in orange as the meat of a melon. Outside water spattered off the roof onto the balcony as the big snow melted.

Judith looked up at her. "I never thought I'd learn a thing from you."

Patricia looked down frowning. But then she raised her eyes to Judith. "We have worked apart too long for no good reason."

Patricia quickly stooped to the next rolag.

So Dutchy, Judith thought. Right back to work when the sun is good and people get to talking.

Patricia held the wool fan in her hand, and Judith brought the yarn to it, pinched the yarn in while Patricia still held the new rolag. Amazing the feel of her white, hard hand—Mrs. Charlotte never let Judith touch her once save when she was dying. This Dutch let her knead her palm like bread dough. "Pride is mortal sin, Judit," Patricia whispered to her.

Judith shuddered as an unfamiliar feeling of closeness and care for the Dutch crept over her.

"But if there is one thing I can do consistently that is to teach." With her free hand, the Dutch squeezed Judith's arm. "I thank you so much for letting me teach again."

Shocked at this sudden tenderness, Judith nodded as she worked. Behind them the toddlers wrestled, grunting and squealing. "Mrs. Patricia, you got such long fingers," Judith said, stroking her white hand now in wonder.

Patricia stiffened, and Judith thought she had misstepped again. But when she looked up at Patricia, the Dutch's eyes were wide on the window.

The shadow of a man cut across the twilight. The toddlers stilled. Holy stroked Gustasson's head as if comforting him already from coming disaster.

The shadow was tall, wore a coat that didn't fit him for his sleeve hung low where it met his wrist. In his hand: the round chamber of a revolver and the stub of its muzzle. The room, which had been singing with music, fell silent and the women and children held still.

"Is Isaac out there?" Patricia whispered, placing her lips very close to Judith's ear and gripping the Negress's shoulder and pushing her down to the floor. Holy said something to Gus, and both women groped for their children. Gus ran to Judith along with Holy. Judith pressed the babes to the floor, and they squawked.

The shadow froze. The curtains billowed inward in a wind, revealing a frayed gray coat, white, hairy hands, no one who belonged on the balcony. Judith pressed both toddlers faces to her breasts, tucked her chin over their heads.

Outside, a musket cracked. The lead hit the house and went humming off into the trees. The shadow dove beneath the window. From the yard came the clatter of melting snow. Another musket shot, and shingles off the eaves spattered and rained down in the room. The squirming babes screamed into Judith's bosom, and the force of their mighty voices shook her heart against her spine.

After a long time, the intruder scuttled across the balcony. The trellis creaked, then there was a splash and a thud, the thump of feet running across the sodden yard.

Trembling, Judith raised herself from covering the two boys. Gus gasped and rushed for the window, but Patricia caught his arm.

"*Setz sich,*" she hissed.

He cowered, then sat Indian style, his big eyes staring at her. "Who was that, Mrs. Patricia?"

Patricia stared at the open window as if she meant to leap two stories down on the assailant. "Some rabble Leighton has brought on vis family." She stood clenching and unclenching her fists. Then she jolted and paled. "Good, Lord, Judit, where is Isaac? Do you think he is harmed?" Crossing the room on hands and knees, she knelt at the curtains.

There was a silence, and when she turned to Judith, the big Negress's face was wrinkled in puzzlement. "Judit?"

"If Isaac had shot that man, would you gone out there and take the blame for it? Would you taken that gun and said you done it? Sherff might of hung Isaac for shootin at a White man. Even if he were rabble."

She remained kneeling at the window. "I care for Isaac, Judit. Very much."

Judith's face softened.

Patricia shook her head. "But until such a test, I do not know what I would do."

Judith stared at her. Then she stretched her arm out to Gus, waggled her fingers. Gus darted to her, buried his face in her chest. "There, sweetie, there." Judith looked up at Patricia again. She smiled. "Mamma all right. Pa be home, and I reckon Mamma gone give him Hell."

Patricia snorted a laugh. "That she will, Judit."

For a long time, the women listened hard at the spatter of the snow melting.

VI

ALL THE TOWN'S LANDED LUMINARIES PACKED THE
public school house—the Pearsons, the Martins, the Campbells. Weitzer wedged himself in among several other German
merchants and farmers, and most of the Gentlemen's Defense
League was there: Cox, Daniels, Bright, Shannon. Peale sat
on a window sill, kicking his long legs and scowling at all his
fellow rubes. Leighton stood just outside the door. They were
waiting for the railroad negotiator from the South Pacific line
to arrive. Earlier at the quarry, Weitzer told Leighton that a
lawyer named Robertson, a doctor, and a Republican congress-
man had rigged a survey so that the railroad would build the
spur almost a mile north of town where Robertson and the
two other conspirators owned land. Archer had negotiated a
charter that drove the railroad straight through town, but Robertson and company, Weitzer said, had put this in jeopardy by
promising the railroad a deplorably low cost per acre and offering to build the railroad a depot, shops and two hotels, sharing
profits there with South Pacific.

Speculation of the railroad's arrival consumed the town,
which had become sizeable in the time since Leighton and Peale
had taken a shave together. The Gentlemen's Defense League
rarely rode, and usually the culprit was a newcomer, someone
who had never heard how the town was policed. Hangings were
rare. Now the League settled with a good horse-whipping, or
just riding a man down and thumping him off his mount. Of
course, a couple fellows had their necks broke this way, but Archer made it clear that such was the price of civilization.

The Springfield Wagon Company was revived and joined
by a sawmill, an iron foundry, three tobacco processors, two
woolen mills, warehouses empty and waiting, smelling of new

pine lumber. The cliffs at the quarry were wider and steeper, and now Leighton had driven several shafts into the best lime. The longest extended one hundred feet, cut deep below the new flagstone of National Avenue. The depths of the tunnel comprised a square of unparalleled darkness. In the last year, his life had become too much like that tunnel. Gus and Holy had grown and he had lost himself in the quarry and profits. While Patricia was awake, the dark presence of the half-breed child in his home kept Leighton ensconced in the lime, in the books, in the carving of deals in a city he and Archer were building.

After the gunman appeared at the house, Patricia shunned Leighton. They slept apart and moved through the house at a tense distance like two magnets pushing away from one another. Late at night, though when he returned, Judith held his meals for him, and with the half-breed child watching them, he and Judith ate in the near dark as they had done in the war that had for a time seemed so far behind them. In the way Judith set table, brought his ale, sat and listened to him, he found the axle that steadied him. And sometimes, despite many hesitations, he asked Judith downstairs to the root cellar where they fucked among barrels of cider and the stink of onions and beer. She held his face fiercely, chanted his name. Afterwards when he was spent, when he rested against her broad, soft body, they sometimes could hear Holy upstairs singing a little song in a babble none of them understood, a tune he made up as he went along. When they snuck to the top of the stairs, he was still singing it, crouched under the table, his eyes deviously awaiting their ascension.

Leighton stood outside the schoolhouse in the warm March air, one hand hooked in his collar. Filthy with lime and blinking at the sun, he felt like a cave fish up from a blackened pool. With his other hand, he checked the two revolvers hidden beneath his coat. Men tipped their hats to him as they entered. He was too dusty to sit inside with them. They were a lovely pack, all suited up in wool and the first linens of spring, their hats sparkling with mercury, necks reeking of chamomile and rose, all for the railroad fellow from Chicago. They chattered and brandished land abstracts at each other. Robertson, the lawyer in a dark European cut suit, glanced up and caught Leighton's eye. He winked and nodded, held out his hand for Leighton to take a seat among them. At the door, the crowd was still pouring in. Placing a hand on Leighton's shoulder, Archer Newman gave him a shake. He pulled the sliver of a cigarette from his lips and flicked the smoking ember of it at the corner of the school. "Look at Robertson."

Leighton grunted.

"Bastard. He's screwed us on this one."

Archer leaned to Leighton, lips almost touching Leighton's ear. "We ought to ride against him. Scare the piss from him. Get this straightened out."

Leighton grunted again.

With a last deft shake, Archer released a bois d'arc cross into Leighton's hand. "Tomorrow evening."

A carriage and four lovely horses lurched to a stop behind them. A dust cloud swept over the carriage and the school windows. Archer squeezed Leighton's shoulder then hustled into the schoolhouse. A short man with mutton chop sideburns and a red nose and cheeks stepped down from the cab. His red face stared blankly at Leighton, then he passed into the building. The few men still left on the sidewalk scuttled in behind the newcomer. Someone shut the double doors, and Leighton was left to watch through an open window along with some Negroes who scooted aside for him.

The red-faced man took the teacher's lectern on a raised stage at the front of the schoolroom. Archer rose from his seat on the stage, hooked two fingers in his mouth and whistled. The hall grew quiet, all the white faces blinking at the man behind the lectern.

"Gentlemen," Archer said. "I give you Andrew Pierce, negotiator for South Pacific Railway."

One fool in the front applauded twice and then squirmed in the glare of all those around him.

Pierce nodded at the fellow who had clapped. Pierce wore a brown coat, a frilled white shirt, and a yellow vest. He gripped the lectern, and for a full minute stood there silent, his face as buckled and pink as a fist in an ice storm. The Negro next to Leighton glanced at Leighton and clucked.

The Negro was right. Pierce was a brave fool.

Finally, Pierce's eyes flashed wide and his shoulders rose. He gripped the lectern as if he were about to heave it into the audience. "Well!" He glared at them, leaning far over the lectern. "What the hell do you want?!"

The front rows erupted in exclamations of surprise, men twisting about in their seats, wide eyes, open mouths. Several shook their abstracts and bellowed at Pierce, who crossed his arms over his chest, shoved his chin forward.

Archer held a hand above his head. "Citizens, citizens," he shouted.

Pierce blinked at him.

The crowd settled. Behind Leighton, Pierce's coach wheeled around then came to a stop in front of an open window parallel with the lectern.

Archer tugged a folded document from his coat pocket. "I have here, Mr. Pierce, a charter dated January 15th, 18 and 69 stating clearly that South Pacific agrees to drive its spur, according to the original survey accompanying this charter, squarely through Springfield." Archer frowned and waited, his back rigid. "And this is signed by all four of your company's principals."

Pierce was busy spit-scrubbing some dirt at the hem of his coat.

Archer cleared his throat, but continued even though Pierce did not look up. "Your current survey provided by Misters Robertson, Boyd, and Harbaugh, places the proposed spur two miles north of any existing building in Springfield. How can this be?"

Pierce scratched one of his sideburns. "How much would you people give for using that first survey of yours?"

"Come again?" Archer asked.

Brows all across the room furrowed.

"How much you got?" Pierce cocked his head, pushed back from the lectern. "Would you have $25,000?"

Robertson's eyes widened. He glanced quickly around the room; then his smug expression returned. Peale's scowl changed to a grin.

"If any of you all have $25,000 right now to give me, cash money, I'll use that first survey." Pierce nodded at Archer.

The Germans were astir. "That is bribery," Weitzer shouted.

Pierce shrugged, looked back at Archer. Leighton glanced behind him, saw the coach driver smoking a cigarette and watching traffic pass on the far side of the street.

Archer moved closer to Pierce and smacked the charter against his open palm. "By this document and by your company's signatures and word, the railroad must drive the spur as agreed."

"You got $25,000?"

"Of course not."

Pierce whacked the lectern with an open palm. "Then I'll damned soon show you where I'll build!"

There were bellows of protest. The Negroes around Leighton roared with laughter and slapped their thighs. A banker in front stood and started a blustery diatribe.

Leighton backed away from the window. The coachman's eyes caught him as he approached. The coachman reached in his coat, but Leighton drew his revolver first. The coachman froze. "Throw it on the ground, Bub," Leighton hollered, cocking his revolver. The coachman tossed his piece into the dusty street and sat looking glum. Leighton drew his other revolver. He stuck it through the coach window. In the cab sat an old woman wearing a hat exploding with black feathers. Her eyes were wide, and she raised both her hands in the air.

"Open the door," Leighton said. The coachman was twisting around in his seat, but froze when Leighton jabbed a revolver at him again. The old woman opened the door and Leighton scrambled in, reached over the woman's head and slapped the driver's slat open. He held a revolver again on the driver. The woman cried out and shifted herself to the bench opposite Leighton.

Leighton sat on the edge of the seat where he could see the driver. He held one pistol on him, the other on the old woman. "Driver, I'll kill her if you make a move," he said. "Set there like it's all right."

"My God, my God! They warned us of this," she cried, fists at her eyes. "Backwater heathen!"

Leighton glanced from the cab to see Pierce clamber through the window of the school house and shove the Negroes

218

aside. Leighton leaned back in the shadows of the coach. The crowd was shouting. Pierce unlatched the cab door, hauled himself part way in. When he met Leighton's muzzle he hesitated.

"Come into the house," Leighton said.

With the crowd surging from the schoolhouse, Pierce heaved himself into the cab, plopped down next to the old woman, and the carriage lunged to a run.

They banged down the road. After gripping the seat and watching Leighton for awhile, Pierce snorted and pulled a slim black cigar from his coat pocket. He struck a match, and his head bounced around following the flame until he managed to light the cigar.

"Quite a speech, Mr. Pierce," Leighton said.

Pierce swirled the cigar around in the air as if dismissing the statement. He removed his hat and his bald shiny head was entirely red and sparkling with diamonds of sweat.

Leighton rattled a muzzle on the edges of the driver's window. "Left," he hollered, "You'll see smokestacks. Go to them."

The driver took a left turn and the carriage tilted, then righted itself.

The old woman lifted a varnished wooden case from the floor. She set it on her lap. Leighton cocked a revolver. She spun the box to face him and sprung it open. Leighton lurched back, then peered at the box. Set in crimson felt cubbies, dozens of flasks and phials gleamed.

Pierce snatched a flask and uncorked it. He drank, nodded to Leighton, who shook his head. "Laudanum," Pierce said. "Good for what ails you." He drank from other bottles, then sat back and belched a liquid belch. "So you're the brashest rube in this pisspot?" Pierce asked.

Leighton holstered one of the revolvers. "And you're about to drive a spur a mile north of where anyone in this piss pot resides. I imagine Robertson and Boyd and Harbaugh promised you a sweet run of this and that, eh?"

Pierce smoked and stared out the window. The old woman arranged the bottles, tapped two white pills from one into her palm. She curled her hand, shook it. The pills clicked like dice. Pierce waved them away.

219

"Through the gates," Leighton hollered at the driver.

The stone arch and wrought iron gates of the quarry flickered past the carriage window. Pierce sat forward, wiped his forehead with his sleeve, and blinked. The carriage slowed.

"Down to the pool," Leighton said to the driver. They rolled forward, then stopped. The fracas of the quarry rose all around them, iron singing against stone, the chug and grunt of the steam derricks, the rail cars sliding and banging to the stone-breakers' yard.

"What Robertson and his folks didn't give you," Leighton said, his voice rising, his words slowing, "is bedding for the rails. And in this clay and trash, you're going to have to build it."

Pierce poked his head out the window.

"Come on out," Leighton said to him.

Pierce opened the door, and he and Leighton stepped down from the carriage. The pool shimmered at their feet. Beside it were mountainous piles of white gravel. All across the face of the cliffs intricate webs of scaffolding stretched. Behind them, the mules turned their circle, the rollers of the mill popping and crumbling the stone. An ore car shot down the rails. Negroes emerged from the black square of the deepest shaft into the sunlight. They were head-to-toe as gray as ash.

Pierce pulled the cigar from his mouth. "Well, well. A limestone quarry."

Leighton smiled. "And if you drive a spur to right there," Leighton pointed behind the office. "I'll give you gravel, give it, to bed every track between the county line and this spot and any further rail work in town for the next five years. You transport it. But it will be here."

Pierce blinked. "Lime like that?" He jabbed his cigar at the pile.

Leighton nodded. "I'll let you come stare at it yourself any hour."

Pierce grinned. He watched the quarry for a moment, the Negroes rushing about. A derrick growled like an old man snoring, then raised its load. "Let's write this up."

Leighton shook his hand and they took the carriage to the office where they spent the afternoon wrangling over words and measures, sampling moonshine from the fourteen states represented in Pierce's box, tapping sticky slivers of opium into the ends of their cigars. Leighton had out his father's old handbooks. To Pierce's frustration, he could figure base quantities in a blink. There was no way of rooking this rube. On a silver mirror, Pierce's nurse spread out some white tooth powder that numbed Leighton's mouth but made his heart sing with joy.

Riding home, Leighton felt as if his head, eyes, and ears were wrapped in a warm, woolen blanket. The trees conjoined in the depths of the forest to make boiling green alcoves where elfin choruses of insects bounced and whirled, singing and fanning their brilliant new wings. At times, late evening fog congealed the air into oak-framed quadrilaterals, which quivered, then gave their shapes away into the next sylvan green mosaic forming and shimmering. Leighton paused on his porch. The western sky was a gaudy pink with violet blossoms of cloud. To the east were the winking town lamps beginning to burn against the dark. From somewhere deep in his head, one of Holy's songs sprang up and suddenly made sense, as if all Holy's ditties had been overtures to grander songs that belonged up in the evening leaves.

Leighton glanced at his watch. Six p.m. He was home two hours early. When he stepped through the door, the mulatto child was on tiptoes reaching for something beside the stove, his little calves straining beneath the frayed bottom of his gunny sack gown. Seeing Leighton, he dropped his hands at his sides and stared down at his feet.

Judith turned from the stove. Leighton reached in his coat pocket and slowly, bobbing his eyebrows, he drew out a shining coil of copper tubing a mechanic had forged into the shape of a snake for him.

Holy reached for it, then popped the head of the snake in his mouth. Immediately, his round face furrowed and he pulled the tubing from his mouth, stood drooling and wrinkling his nose at the copper. Infantile things like these made Leighton wonder at him. "Da?" the boy asked, irking Leighton again. At least the boy refrained from the habit when anyone else was around. Da, like an Irish child might say to its father, what Leighton called his own father when times were dire.

Upstairs Patricia's footsteps creaked across the floor. In each pop of wood he heard intense carefulness. A door sloughed shut.

Leighton placed a hand on top of Holy's head and the boy raised his arms, dandled his fingers on top of Leighton's, tiny fingers, the color of seal skin with pink tips.

"Ain't he a good lookin' chile?" Judith whispered.

Leighton pulled his hand away as if he'd been stung.

They hunched over their stews while Holy munched milk toast in the low lamplight. Clearing her place and serving Leighton a second helping, Judith sniffed his hair. "You smell good, like flowers and spice. What you been rollin' in?" Leighton shrugged, absorbed in the stew, which was transformed and incredible.

When he was done, Judith said, "Go upstairs quiet." She grinned. "You catch Mama and the boy reading and praying fire and damnation."

Upstairs, Leighton paused at the door to the nursery, once his boyhood room, and peered in. His head was still frowzy and humming. Patricia sat on Gustasson's bed with her legs crossed. She wore a white chemise that revealed the shadows of her small breasts. She held the massive Lutheran Bible in her lap. In the corner of the room the spinning wheel waited surrounded by pyramids of wool rolags, piles of carded wool and skeined yarn.

Gus was now five. A thin, already long little fellow with curly reddish hair, he knelt in prayer at the foot of the bed, his tiny nose crammed against his fingertips. With his curly hair and slim face, he sometimes struck Leighton as a miniature of the late Morkan, Gus's grandfather. His gray eyes skated devilishly just above the footboard's trim. They widened when they caught Leighton at the door, but Leighton put his finger to his lips to keep the boy quiet. Gus grinned, and said something to himself, which made him snicker and touch a hand to his mouth. He rolled his eyes at Leighton, then glanced at Patricia whose eyes were closed as she fingered the pages, reciting from rote:

And they brought up an evil report of the land which they had searched unto the children of Israel, saying,

The land, through which we have gone to search it, IS a
land that eateth up the inhabitants thereof; and all the
people we saw in it ARE men of great stature.

The Israelites proceeded to weep and rend their clothes and
eat ashes and eventually they decided to stone the bearers of the
bad news. Patricia related all of this with her shoulders hunched,
her head rocking to and fro. Gus's eyes widened at the giants and
the ash eating and clothes rending; otherwise, he watched Leighton, and his shoulders shivered with delight. He tried to keep his
hands in prayer, but often had to cover his mouth to stifle laughter.

Finally, the Lord spoke to Moses and passed judgment on
the Israelites. Patricia raised her fist, her long white arm waving
with an air of triumph. She read, "I will smite them with pesti-
lence, and disinherit them."

Patricia clapped the bible shut. When she noticed the direction of Gustasson's gaze, she turned, and her eyes narrowed when
she saw Leighton. She stuck her chin forward and scowled. She
swung her gaze to Gustasson, who ducked his nose to his fingertips. His grin vanished.

"Let us say our prayers, young man," she said.

Gustasson took a deep breath, his back rising. He prayed:

> Much wickedness a child must see
> And evil is learned easily.
> Protect, Dear Lord, this little lad
> So that he will learn nothing bad.

"Good," Patricia said. "And?"

Gus craned his neck, and in a high voice said: "God gives
grace to those who fear Him. Therefore I pray:

> O, My Dear Rod,
> Teach Me to Fear God.
> Make Me Good, I Beg,
> Or the Hangman Will Have My Neck. Amen

"Amen," Patricia said, nodding.

"Good Lord!" Leighton stepped into the room.

Gus blinked at him, and Patricia glared.

"What the Hell kind of prayer is that?"

"Language, Mr. Morkan," Patricia squawked. "It is the prayer I was raised on. Papist!" She moved off the bed and smoothed the sheets then ordered the boy to bed. He crawled into the sheets, and she folded the top of the sheet across his chest and pulled it taut. Kissing him on the forehead, she then raised the wooden railings that prevented Gus from rolling out in his sleep. The metal springs whined as they tightened. With a grunt, she fitted the railings into place, and a perfect wooden cage of headboards and railings surrounded the boy. Such protection—Leighton remembered sleeping on the cold smooth stones of the floor with the struts of the house framing starlight, sleeping in stone wagons where the lime dust would crust his eyes shut by morning. When Patricia backed away, Gus's eyes were on Leighton, and his lips turned in a smile. Leighton stepped to the bedside and rubbed a hard knuckle against Gus's cheek.

"I tell you a secret, Papá!" Gus whispered. *Papá!*, as if the lad were Dutch.

Leighton leaned over the railings and bent his ear to the boy's lips.

"Mamá says I cannot ride with you at night. But I do in my dreams."

Leighton hesitated as he backed away. Gus was grinning broadly. "No one rides at night, son." Leighton said. "The woods are far too dark."

Leighton waited in the hall while Patricia kissed the boy once more. Mother and son whispered to each other in German for a long time, the boy fussing for something, the mother denying him. Listening to them, he felt such a gulf between him and the child and its mother, it was as if he were a boarding laborer from a foreign land. Eventually she rose, shut the door, and scowled at Leighton.

"God gives grace to those who fear him?" Leighton asked her. "What are you doing having him pray like that?"

"If you'd ever taken your catechism, you wouldn't need to

ask." Patricia pushed past him and walked to the stairs.

"Wait," Leighton said. She stopped on the stairs but did not look up. The staircase and landing felt close and warm to Leighton. The trim of the walls, the lines of the ceiling vaulted in odd angles. "Please, sit with me on the porch."

She stood for a moment, head bent as if listening to another voice and its advice. Then she turned toward him.

On the sleeping porch, they sat in the silver dusk. He dropped his coat around her shoulders. It fell stiffly and remained rigid like the brim of a bonnet. She pulled it close, the grit of the lime itching at her fingertips.

Leighton hollered for Judith and sent her for port. Frowning, Judith brought glasses and two bottles. Leighton poured and Patricia drank. In the growing dark, he could see the knots of her eyes watching him.

"Is there a reason for our sitting here?" she asked. "Have you hanged all your drinking partners?"

"Something wonderful has happened today."

She drank, her eyes averted from him.

"Today the negotiator from the railroad stopped at the quarry, and I will have a spur into the line for St. Louis and Joplin." He drank. "You and I should go to St. Louis when it is finished. As celebration."

She snorted. "Celebration?"

Leighton leaned forward and took her hand. The porch rails shone outside in the blue-white glare of the moon. "A toast?" he asked.

She struggled to pull her hand away, but he pinned it to the cold, slick arm of her chair. Her eyes sprang in alarm, and he saw for the first time in her damaged chin, in the frail bones of her jaw and face what a brute he had become to her. He released her, murmured, "I'm sorry. Patricia, I'm so sorry."

Slowly a change came over her face, a softening, he had not seen in many months. After a bit she raised her glass.

"To the surprises we call blessings," he said.

She touched her glass to his but watched him closely.

"Tonight," he said, "is a beautiful night."

She frowned.

"What keeps us apart?" he asked. "We have a lovely, healthy

boy, more money than a dozen people deserve." He still felt elated and invincible and rather wished he had more of Pierce's white tooth powders.

"There are times of late," she said, "when I do not desire your company."

"Why?"

Her chin jutted. "You're a killer. You ride masked like a bandit. You work Negroes at your quarry and let them wallow in indebtedness." She stopped, stared at him. "But worst of all you have put this house, where innocents love you, in mortal danger."

He sat still for a moment. "Look, I nearly lost my life to a highwayman. And I almost lost you." Deep down in the house Judith snapped a cupboard shut.

"I cherish you," he whispered. He held his palms out to her. "Have you ever held dust in your hands? I fear what our lives would be without vigilance. If we don't create and keep some kind of law and order, it would be nothing but uproar down here."

A smug smile came over her face. "Leighton Moorken, I lost two brothers. My family's fortunes were vanquished. I have seen all the dust I need in one lifetime. Yet I had no desire to ride hooded on your father or any other Rebel, or treat Negroes like chattel once more." She stared out at the purple of falling night, and her chin slackened, the pride vanished. A look of profound resignation came over her. "You shame me. You shame your son."

He scowled at her. But at last he said quietly, "I never imagined."

"Of course, you didn't. There is nothing like pain to make us myopic."

"What if I could change that?" Again he was pleased with the leap and bound of his voice. From his heart there flowed a river of energy, bright as a new snowfall, quick as electricity. It was as if his words could bring about change, as if he could speak and there would be light.

She stared at him, her eyes in black crescents.

"We are building right upon the ruins of the war. Ashes and rubble will make our cinder blocks."

She drank, rubbed her thumb along the edge of her glass, then glanced up at him with her eyes narrowed as if inspecting, re-evaluating.

"A man asked me this afternoon how I imagined myself in this city. Can you guess how I answered?"

"You said you imagined yourself the mayor."

He laughed and she winced. He shook his head, smiling. He lit a candle, placed it on the table beside her. He took her hand again, and turned it, examining its pale skin and knobby ligaments. Her brown hair was pulled into a knot at the back of her head. Her eyes were cold, drawn in their scrupulous crescents. Behind those eyes ran German, sentences of condemnation, but, he hoped, also of the possibility of redemption. She was as alien to him as Judith should have been. He and Patricia had been raised hardly an acre from one another, but looking at her chalky skin, thin pale lips, the fine brown hairs along her forearm, she seemed to him a being from any continent but his own.

"You don't really know who I am? Who I've become?" Leighton asked.

She raised her shoulders and at once appeared haughty. "You run a quarry," she said. "You are a thug, a murderer. Vigilante. What more need I know?"

"It's never a need to know that matters. It's what I can make you want to know of me. After everything that's happened."

She blinked at him. The note of apology in his voice startled him. He rose and held her hand to his chest. After a moment, she rose and he led her toward the bedroom. She hesitated before crossing from the porch.

He smiled at her. "I will win your trust again, Miss Weitzer."

He nodded to the bed, and after a moment of watching him, she climbed in but kept the sheets folded down at her waist.

He slipped in beside her. Her spine was rigid and her arms were folded tightly across her chest. "Someone to sleep by is all I'm asking, and I can't think of a better someone than my wife."

She turned to him, her chin shifting. "Do let me know if you should happen to think of someone better! I'll have her fetched."

He waited for a moment, tense, watching her. But she turned and blew out the candle. Then she sat rigidly, back to the headboard, arms bolted like the clasps of a locket across her chest. As he fell asleep, he imagined he could hear her eyes sizzling and open in their sockets, watching the darkness.

When he woke in the morning, he was startled to find her still sleeping beside him. Her mouth gaped in a mournful oval. One long arm was flung above her head and her hand and fingers formed a delicate cup near his forehead. Small red and blue vessels made river systems under her white skin, making her knuckles and shoulders pink in places. There was a thin line of curled black hair in her armpit, so much more contained than any hair on him. He listened to her breathe, watched her lips and strange gray teeth. As her breathing echoed off the walls, he pulled the sheet closer to comfort her. The ends of his fingers grew warm where they rested beside her.

The door creaked. Gus held the knob and eased his head into the room. His eyes grew wide, and he looked from Leighton to Patricia, then narrowed his eyes at Leighton. "What is mother doing?" He whispered.

Leighton waved him toward the bed. "Sleeping."

Gus approached the bed, and Leighton grasped him by the back of the head, ruffled his hair. "With you?" Gus asked.

"It ain't that bad," he whispered. He took Gus by the arm, marveled at his own monstrous hand wrapped about such a tiny stalk of flesh. And yet he could recall Gus much smaller. It seemed just days ago. "Come on up here. Quiet, now."

Gus hoisted a leg up, hesitated, then Leighton lifted him. Gus rested his head against Leighton's chest. They both lay watching Patricia.

After a moment her eyes blinked, grew wide. She watched them both for an instant as if they were strangers; then she licked her lips. "I fell asleep."

Gus squirmed toward her, his arms extended, fingers groping. She gave him her cheek to kiss. Gus curled against Leighton's chest again and fingered his beard. "Is daddy good to sleep with?" Gus asked. "You don't sleep with him always, do you, Mamá?"

Patricia rubbed her eyes, then stroked the child's shoulder. The boy rose and fell slightly with Leighton's breathing. He was leaned back against the headboard to allow Gus a resting space. One hand held the boy, and with the other, Leighton pushed a strand of hair from her eyes. The dry tips of his fingers raked her forehead.

Gus mimicked his father moving Patricia's hair around absent-mindedly, his fingers playing on her cheeks. "Is he like sleeping with a bear?" Gus asked.

Her throat and neck ached as if she were about to sob even after hours of weeping. Joy flowed through her again, gone so long.

Gus burrowed his head deeper in Leighton's chest. "We can all sleep this way," he announced as if it were a remarkable discovery. They dozed together for a time.

Gus's eyes popped open. "If we all fall back asleep, will Judith throw a fit?"

Leighton laughed and Gus braced his palms against Leighton's chest, which rolled with laughter

"Stop, please," Gus said. "Stop."

Gus settled again, resumed fiddling with Patricia's hair. Mother and son closed their eyes. Patricia waited, for something surely had to shatter this, and she would awake alone on the nursery floor, the frigid hardwood reeking like a bucket of lime water. After a while, the boy's hand fell from her face to the coverlet and she fell asleep listening to his soft breathing. The three lay in a peace and silence Leighton wished he could have bottled.

When he left that evening for the Defense League, Patricia scowled at him. "I thought we were finished with this. I thought there was to be 'change.'"

He took her hand. "It's over tonight, but I tell them face to face."

Gus and Holy shouted something at one another and ran from the top of the stairs, their feet clomping like horses' hooves. Each had on an old pair of Leighton's boots that swallowed their little legs up to the knees.

She gripped his arm tightly at the elbow. "You and Archer think you are building some great city, some oasis of order. I don't care how many railroads you secure if it's with blood." She glanced upstairs where the boots of the boys made a joyous cavalcade. "There is all the order a city needs. Gustasson's safety and happiness. No more riding."

"Just this last night. Time," he said. "Please. I have to pull
loose from this. But face-to-face."

Panting, the two boys peered over the staircase, just their
mischievous eyes and the tops of their heads.

She shook his arm and her face was creased with exasperation. "Look at them, Leighton. They are innocents. Do
not lose sight of that."

She turned to the boys, then lifted her skirts and stomped
up the stairs shouting. "*Das Pferd im Hänger ist frei herumzu-
laufen! Ruft den Sattler!*"

The boys screamed and ran in delight.

The Gentlemen's Defense League had graduated to a cavern northeast of Springfield, hardly half-an-hour's ride from
Robertson's and Harbaugh's, the offenders who had wooed
the railroad. Inside the massive cavern sparkled crystal gal-
leries of blue and yellow-green, stalactites and stalagmites
hanging and vaulting like the some repository of failed pipe
organs, pools still as mirrors in which pink and white creatures floated. Meetings had become elaborate ceremonies
and even the dullest hood among them could now recite long
passages of Sir Walter Scott's flapdoodle, though Leighton
had been spared. Often no ride was planned as the pack of
them was sated in paying homage to their Anglo-Scots-Irish
heritage and to the Grand White Knight, Archer Newman.
Ceremonies were long and elaborate and Gothic with the
backdrop of the cavern, and at times, in the orange revelry
of flames against the gray stone walls, Leighton could bring
himself to feel he was participating in one of the primal
rituals of man. Archer had grown to crave his role, and the
adulation and reverence it entailed. With dissenters, he was
severe. Only the banker had quit their ranks, and after a hail
of harassment and burning carcasses staked in his yard, he
left for California.

Shannon traded crosses with Leighton at the entrance, and
Leighton wended his way back through passages lit by a series
of tall yellow candles crammed in nooks of the cave wall. The

passage rose, then leveled into the enormous gallery they called the Cathedral, decked with massive floor to ceiling columns and stunted blue translucent lumps of stone they called the icons. Far back in the Cathedral, the Defense League hunched around a long, moist table, the smoky flames of candles licking the walls.

Archer stood, unmistakably Archer for his hood bore a spatter of brown. The others thought the stain was blood, but Leighton had been with the Grand White Knight, and had seen the Grand White Knight smack his noggin against a muddy overhang in the cave's dark and gain his stripes. Legend accreted to Archer faster than crystal to a crag.

"Robertson has got to be stopped. He's taken the railroad clean out of the town, hornswaggled us," Archer said.

"The deal's done," Leighton said loudly. It echoed in the cave. "We'd be pissing in the wind."

The hoods turned to him, stared. There was a long silence.

"You tell me what the hell we all could do would matter to them when they have everything they want," Leighton said.

Archer stood stiff as a post.

Leighton continued, "This league was founded for order, to keep vagabonds and horse thieves in check. And it worked."

Two of the men bowed their heads, their hoods riding up on their necks.

"Robertson can build him half a town, but what's between us and that town but distance. A road's what we ought to lay. Not hickory switches at their doors." Leighton popped his fist on the table, a dull thump; the old wood of the table was rotting from sitting in the damp.

Archer leaned forward, resting both hands on the tabletop. "You'd let them thwart Springfield? Strangers? One's a New York Jew? One's a carpetbagger from Chicago?"

"Let?" Leighton asked. "Ride against them and you may as well pull these hoods off and throw them in a fire. No railroad will tolerate that. Railroads have agents, their own little militias. You might as well ride, swords drawn on Washington."

They were quiet. Finally Shannon leaned his elbows on the table, gripped his hood at the ears and rumpled it. "Brother's right. He grew up with them railroad people. His old man was one of them before they came here."

Some of the others nodded. Back in the shadows, the icons seemed to cower and peer around the columns.

"All right, then," Archer said. "Let's take us a vote. All those who says we let Robertson and his stooges bugger Springfield into half a town, take your hoods off and throw 'em right there in the middle of the table."

"Hey, now," Shannon said. There were curses. "This is a secret society!"

Gripping the top of his hood, Leighton pulled it upward, folded it. He tossed it to the middle of the tabletop.

They stared at him. When no one moved, Archer crossed his arms over his chest. With a smirk, he was about to speak. But then Shannon eased his hood off, chucked it on top of Leighton's. Slowly, as they all eyed one another, five more men removed their masks, their potato sacks. Their faces appeared pale and glum in the candle light. They fidgeted, and Leighton was sure he was not alone in feeling exposed and mean, seated as he was with his coat and shirt turned inside out, pants frayed and ragged at the cuffs, a greasy bandana hanging at his neck, the nightly uniform of Archer's hooded riders, the Gentlemen's Defense League. All around the room, he felt a spell had been broken—the incantation of pomp and the mystery of Gothic intrigue and secrecy, hoods and handshakes and symbols were at an end. When Shannon took a long look at him, then nodded, Leighton was sure of it.

"Seven to five," Leighton said. "I think it's clear. They'll be no riding."

Retrieving their hoods, they sullenly disbanded without prayer or ceremony.

Archer caught up with Leighton as Leighton walked his horse down the trail. Archer rode alongside him in a burning silence. On his black horse, with his hood still on, the mud spattered across it, the evening sky loaned him a wicked cast. "They won't soon forget this," he said. The cloth rustling as he spoke. "I won't ever forget it."

"Remember it as long as you like," Leighton said. He extended his hand, and in the tips of his fingers, he held the wooden cross Shannon had given him. "I'm done."

Archer snorted, spurred his horse down the trail.

When Leighton mounted his horse where the trail met the road, he let the cross drop amidst the dust.

Archer avoided Morkan Quarry for months, placing his orders through foremen and teamsters. But when it was reported—to the town's surprise—that Chinese workmen had started laying tracks from the quarry toward Robertson's new railways, Archer rode out to see. The two sets of tracks were under way. A straight spur of limestone gravel mounded from north of town to this stretch of turnabout track. An engine and rail straightener inched forward, its hostler staring grimly at the steel screeching beneath him. Framing and walls were going up and the ties and platform set for a roundhouse and freight dock.

Leighton and a crew of Negroes were shucking gravel from a wagon into a pile, and Negroes scurried behind the straightener tossing shovels full of gravel in gaps the straightener's work created. In the frame of the roundhouse, the steam plants hissed, gathering power for their first test turns. The air smelled of wood smoke and grease packed around the massive turntable, a stink so thick and oily, it seemed the autumn air had to be waded through.

Archer stepped from his horse, which was rolling its eyes and stamping at the jets of steam coursing from the rail straightener.

Leighton kept his hands in his vest pockets.

Archer's gaze followed the gray gravel north, piled and shaped like a long, miniature levee. His lips pursed as if he were examining arid scar tissue risen along a wound. His eyes fell on Leighton. "What's the cost?"

"We'll see. They're railroad people."

Archer snorted. "You're railroad people."

Leighton gave no answer. Blaring up from the white gravel, the sun was so brightly reflected that the gravel and rails appeared blue and electrified.

"The world, our world, our justice, will go on without you," Archer said. He leaned very close to Leighton, and Leighton could smell the hint of cologne at his collar. "But if you betray us, I will have no choice."

233

"Oh, even the Lord gets His vengeance someday, Archer."

Archer's jaw buckled so tightly, a dark shadow flickered across his chin. "When we voted, did you know they were going to build this here for you?"

"What do you think?"

The rail straightener gasped. When the clamps along the engine's front lifted, releasing the steel, they left a high ringing in the air like a knife singing across a whetstone. Archer blinked at the steam. "For now, I think you win."

VII

Through Claus, now on the board of the Bank of Freistatt, Patricia obtained several sheets of bank letterhead as souvenir of her father's steady recovery to prominence. On this she wrote a note in German to Archer Newman, City Engineer. She posed as Herr Lieberman wishing to assess certain properties in Springfield for mortgage purposes.

"I will be arriving by train at North Springfield Station, so if you will meet me on the 3:00 Tuesday October 5, I will be pleased." She gave a postal box in Freistatt as the return. And, through a cousin, she received Archer's affirmative.

On the appointed day Isaac drove her to the station, and she swore him to secrecy. As they approached the station, she saw everywhere bags of cement, wagon rails, stone rollers behind oxen all bearing the MQ mark for MORKAN QUARRY. Even on the Negroes' brogans MQ stared after her like third eyes—the M lazy; the Q vigilant. She was safe, though, she assured herself as she waited at the depot where carpenters pounded and stonemasons scraped. As disguise she wore a broad brimmed black straw hat hung with a black gauze veil. Added to her long black dress were coal-blue gloves. No person leaving from or returning to North Springfield would recognize her. In these times no one imagined that the Morkans need mourn anything. And those at the station were railroad workmen and travelers, White men and women who did not know Isaac and certainly would not know a veiled Mrs. Morkan unless Leighton were with her.

A tremendous gray Percheron bearing MQ on his rear halted as his driver jawed with a hostler. The letters loomed over her, quivering and growing upon the immense muscles of the creature's lead-colored behind. Archer arrived on his black horse. With Isaac's help she stepped down from the wagon. She walked

235

the new amber pine of the platforms until she stood beneath his mount. Archer fidgeted and checked his watch. The 3:00 train was unloading—Germans, academy students, a party of wide-eyed Czechs. None to see Archer, though here hovered a tall, veiled woman with an oblong face.

After a moment he glanced down at her, then paused and a smile bent his lips. "*Du hießt* Herr Lieberman."

Though impressed at his deduction, she settled herself to say, yes, of the Bank of Freistatt.

Archer lifted his hat. "You pick a difficult location for private consultation," he said, his German arch. "We must repair to a spot where the king's huntsman are not traveling."

She curtsied.

He tied his horse, then turned to her and offered his arm.

Down the platforms and boardwalks they walked stiffly, Archer holding back her stride so that they marched with the delicate cadence of mourners. How quickly he took to any artifice! Each building, the rails, the piles of ties and bolts and bands were all sparkling new. North Springfield. Moon City. The Railroad's Town.

At a cantina they stopped and Archer went in to scout who was inside. He left her a long time standing at the door, which was new and so chalky with whitewash it glowed. As she ran her fingers down its wood, a blue powder of Leighton's lime dried and dusted her fingertips. Travelers passed in and out, many with sooty faces, their coats and trousers spattered with tobacco. At the approach of each she stiffened and they took in a breath, some bowing or removing their caps on seeing such a tall, thin figure in mourning. What an awful omen she was to any man beginning a journey!

Finally Archer emerged. He drew her into the cantina and held her hand tightly, tapping her knuckles with the tips of his fingers. The floor was hard-packed dirt, and narrow slats high along the tops of cinderblock walls gave the cantina dim light. In a corner two iron benches squeezed a table that was not much broader than a piano stool. Clawed iron feet dug into the dirt floor.

"*Sitz sich, sitz sich.* May we continue in German?" he asked.

Patricia nodded as he helped her to the bench. She smoothed her dress down. "Maybe it will be better. But you must stop me if you do not understand something, Herr Newman." As he sat down she leaned to him and gripped his coat sleeve. "This is critical."

He paused. "*Ja,*" he said, glancing around. The wall sheltered his back, and he faced the exit, scanning all comers with a fox's caution. "To what do I owe pleasures?"

She squinted trying to parse his meaning and worried his German couldn't bear the freight. "Archer, ever since we met I have felt a special bond between us, an understanding, a connection."

"Indeed," he said.

Typical of him. An affirmation that confirmed nothing. "Very good, then." She felt so sure of herself standing beneath his horse, but now she sat across from a lyncher, a murderer of murderers. With his auburn hair and fair complexion, high cheekbones and strong chin, he bore the sort of Austrian look her mother thought was a sure sign of noble birth. When he plucked his trousers at the knee to set his cuffs, she noted how powerful the muscle of his thigh appeared, as if an animal hunched beneath the fabric, a cat bowing its back. She struggled to start. "Archer, I am not Leighton…."

"You have left him?"

She paused. Then her voice fell to a whisper as she resumed in English. "No, I mean I am separate from him. His business— while it may be sustenance for a family—is not…." Here she struggled for the first time since childhood to find the right English phrase. All around the cantina travelers sat in quiet clusters drinking, and it seemed they were all listening to her, all awaiting some vulnerability, some quarter to pass her lips.

He raised a hand. "You need money."

"*Nein, Gott sei dank.*"

Archer's brow furrowed and for once he lost his air of confidence. "Herr Lieberman, I have lost the service." *Bedienung,* he said in German, and she thought for a moment that he meant the waiter had yet to serve them. From his pinched face, though, she could see he meant that he was confused.

She took both his hands in hers and spoke softly in English. "Archer, Leighton has broken with you and your riders. But I beg you… for my sake… for Gustasson's sake, please do not retaliate against my family."

Instantly his face darkened. He released her hands casting them down to the cheap, shiny tabletop as if flicking swamp water from his fingers. "What sort of man do you think I am?"

With care she leaned her elbows on the table, rolled and raised her veil. When the crackling lace cleared the shiny purple mass of her chin, then rose above her jaw scaly as a sow's breast, Archer's eyes lost their look of indignation and grew in wonder at her unalloyed ugliness, earned in battle with evil and like a veteran's crusty stump.

In German she said, "Archer, do not toy with me. I know well you have hanged and killed men." His arms were rigid at his sides. She put her hands once more across the table, palms up to him in supplication, all defenses down. "I know exactly the sort of man you are." He paused a long while staring at her hands. Even when a patron rose and lurched toward the door, Archer kept his eyes on her.

Finally he put one hand in hers. "I will show you a different sort of man." She felt the same callous that marred her husband's palms now tugging at her gloves. "But there will be a price."

She breathed in, steeled herself. "*Nennen Sie Ihren Preis.*"

Still holding her hand, he reached across the table. With his free hand he rolled her veil back at her collar and hat to reveal fully all of her very long, deformed face in the weak light. Then he took both her hands, squeezed them and kept hold of them. His voice fell to a whisper, and he said in precise German, as if he had thought long in phrasing it, "Wait with me in this place a while. As if you are my own."

A warm wave of shame washed over her neck, and chest. But she kept her hands still. Staring intently at her, never speaking, he clung to her hands until they grew slick with the sweat of her discomfort. Her gloves seemed to be cooking her fingers and forearms. Patrons came and went. His face, though very handsome, became ominous, devilish, devouring. And his eyes roved her chin, her battered jaw, her thin, blue lips. She recalled

238

the lash she plucked from beneath his exquisite silvery eye. The lash, a sickle. A surgeon's curved needle. Satan's crescent moon. When at last he released her hands, she tried to—but could not—suppress a gasp.

He bowed his head, rested his hands before him, palms up as if they were anointed. "The man you defend has no notion of his good fortune."

In the wagon she hunched her shoulders and could not sit comfortably. She felt like a woman returning in disgrace from a violent, impassioned, unholy liaison.

"Mrs. Morkan?" Isaac said. He repeated it until she looked at him. "He's a terrible man. I take a bet it was him on the balcony in the first place."

Judith lifted Gus's arm, holding him by his small wrist. Holy sat beside him moaning and shivering despite the warmth of the kitchen. Tears glossed both of their faces and they snuffled. One of them had poked a stick into a nest of red paper wasps and found them still at home. The two kept their secret as to who courted the trouble.

Gus's arm was pale, a color like cream around the pulp of berries. He hadn't touched the stone yet—his daddy's arms were dry and leathern, almost blue like stones from the moon sometimes, or a white like the dust of lime on his boots. The stone aged these Morkans and tore their skin down to the gray she saw on the dead Morkan's body when they slung his spent carcass across this table to wash it for the casket, the same table the boys sat on now. She rubbed a paste of baking soda and lime water into the welts at Gus's ribs and the child stilled, narrowed his eyes at her.

His eyes were the same gray crescents as Patricia's and they could level a meanness like no other set, fixed as they were in a lean child's face with red curls of hair, a blend of the dead Morkan's face and the Dutch girl's that made Judith shudder.

Isaac's hounds barked out in the yard, then stopped abruptly. The back door opened and Leighton entered. Both boys cried out in surprise and began rattling separate accounts of the wasps. Leighton frowned and his face hardened. The two boys snapped to attention, hands at their sides.

"Where's Mother?" Leighton asked.

239

"Across town visiting them Dutch," Judith said.

Leighton nodded. He wore his thicker winter beard and at his brow were wet droplets of sweat. It was election day, but the air had a strange heat to it. The sun was roaring off the brown and red oaks, the orange maples. Confused wasps were swarming and trying to nest at the eaves on the upper story. Judith felt the juices of spring moving in her, though it was the wrong end of the year.

"Come down in the cellar a minute and dig out that whiskey with me."

Judith grunted to bend and grab Holy by the arms. "Quiet'n down." She shook him. His eyes widened. "You set there. You'll get Gussy killed one day."

She thumped down the stairs, holding an arm under her breasts, her chest warming like a little girl's again. Leighton's shadow loomed behind her until he lit the lamp. Her heart delighted to hear the cellar door crunch shut. As the boys grew, Patricia had thinned and waned while Judith waxed fuller than a pumpkin. Even after the boys were weaned, hunger gnawed her, and while Patricia went off to mope or be pious with her Dutch folk or dye wools and chase sheep, the house and boys were Judith's. She left them mostly to their own pursuits and grew sedate and now was heavier than she had ever been. Reaching the dirt floor of the cellar, she panted and could not speak.

When Leighton embraced her, he gathered as much of her behind as he could in his hands. His pecker burrowed in her stomach. The more civil he got with Patricia, the more he wanted to paw Judith in the dark, and of late the Mr. and Mrs. had been civil in the extreme. Best, there were no hesitations from him now, no stammered requests, no furrowed brows or dire questions about his soul in jeopardy, just good, quick screwing.

She laughed. "What you doing home?" Without a pause, without even caring what his answer was, she wrapped her arms around him, mashed his face against her shoulder.

He rared his head up. "What's it feel like I'm doing?" he asked, thrusting himself against her.

She struggled to lift her work dress while he kneaded the fat on her backside. "Come on like lightning. I got them young'uns to mind." When he dropped his dungarees, she lifted her belly and parted her thighs. He was in her and squirming. She hummed, couldn't help herself, though she was smashed back against casks of potatoes that stunk like dirt. Over the whole cellar hung a warm boozy reek that made her dizzy and ill. She held his face in her hands. "Hurry, darlin'. Hurry now," she whispered.

"I'm taking Johnson Davis and Isaac to vote," he said, his voice thinning.

"That so?" she asked. "Mmmm. Do that a'way again."

His shoulders began to twitch.

The door to the cellar slammed open.

"Jesus!" Leighton hissed. He stumbled back, fell on his ass, but managed to dim the lamp to nothing.

"Mama, come quick! Gus got them things flying in his pants now!"

Judith shifted her weight, popped the side of her foot against his bare leg. "Get up there. He be stung to death before I make the first stair."

Leighton hitched his pants. His boots pounded the wooden stairs. Somewhere above them, Gus was howling.

She flattened her dress, brushed her hands across its front. From the cask she lifted a big potato, rubbed it against her side. When she bit into it, the taste of dirt and water made her sigh. Holy held the door open at the top of the stairs, pointing an insistent little finger Gus's direction.

"I'm a'coming," she said. She pulled a bottle of Bourbon from the racks. Walking the steps, she felt as heavy as the elephants Gus read to her about in his primers. What was the Dutch word he said meant elephant—*Mammut, Mampfen, Mahnen?*

Gus was perched on the kitchen table with his pants at his ankles. In his fingers he held the carcass of a red wasp. He wasn't crying, but sitting very still, watching Leighton mount his horse outside the kitchen window. Red dots were rising along his right thigh. "*Handsworst,*" he mumbled.

Holy blinked at Judith as she munched the potato. "Mr. Leighton took that wasp out'n Gus's trouser leg and mashed it alive in his own two fingers. Like it was nothing."

"Take this bottle to Mr. Leighton and go with them." Judith nodded at Holy. The boy took the bottle carefully, held it as if it

241

were a babe. He and Gus exchanged a glance with raised eye-brows, and she could only wonder at what passed between them, though watching the two she flushed. Suddenly the weight of her body bore her down like a millstone. In her dizziness, she clutched her round belly to her like a melon. So fat and wicked. These tusslings had to cease—the boys would soon be too wise.

Holy walked off on tip toes, staring at the amber bottle, call-ing for Isaac.

After rubbing Gus's thigh with the poultice of baking soda, witch hazel, and lime, she dressed him in fresh clothes, and fetched one of the Dutch primers and a blanket. The men were long gone; the house was hers. The primer had a cover on it imprinted with a troop of gnomes in hats, vests, and short pants wrestling a cow. She set Gus in her lap, covered his legs with the blanket. He wormed back against her as if fluffing a cushion, then rested the back of his head on her bosom. She munched another potato. As the boy read, she plucked at the blanket. The wool was Patricia's and hers woven together by Patricia in an astonishing effect, a rambling pattern of greens and yellows and grays like looking at the sun through the tops of trees. A pang of guilt shot for a moment like scalding water down her legs—she was frolicking with the husband of a woman who had taken the time to teach her, the first White to say she could learn and cre-ate and was better than a White at anything. She stilled while the boy read on in Dutch.

But what to do? She held the picture of Leighton's face in her mind as she would a crystal goblet, so lovely, so not hers. His face threw light into parts of her that little else could touch. And she imagined these parts as the inside of a fruit she had seen long ago in St. Louis. The fruit inside was made of beaded red gal-leries, and the mistress of the house had long coveted it. When she held Leighton's face in her mind, that light shone on the red beads of her heartwood and swelled her until she trembled and panted with the terrible pressure of her own indulgence.

She remembered being small, sleek, starved, so clearly that her billowing skin seemed a dream to her. And she recalled that first crazy pleasure: Leighton's mother Mrs. Charlotte gone to market, leaving stale cake, fish, corn puppies, biscuits, potatoes, and a heap of crispings. All of it Judith's. Stretched, her stomach sang to her. With each subsequent gorge she felt power come to her as her arms grew stout; her hips rounded. Isaac, Johnson, even Mrs. Charlotte gave her new room. Her thighs plumped; her chest enlarged painfully. Leighton touched her with tenderness rather than his former brotherly smacking and elbowing.

Then power stopped coming. Without a full stomach she felt agitated and hollow, and satisfaction took more and more eating. When Charlotte died there were no limits, save the war's privations, now long past. And after it she ate and ate as if to regain a lost country. Her fingers swelled like float bladders; her cheeks bulged. Her belly lapped upon her widening thighs. True Love she couldn't have. So many afternoons she put the boys to rest, then binged. With her stomach strained to splitting she lay hardly able to breathe on the sofa, and for a fleeting moment the wings of an angel swept round her and the down of his feathers warmed her and his sweet, yeasty lips whispered: "Peace."

With a start she noticed that Gus, still prattling from the book, was absent-mindedly kneading his little fingers deep in her fat as if she were no more than soft furniture. He stopped, glanced up at her, his brow furrowed. Then he resumed reading and massaging her. Those lips, not so long ago they had suckled at her nipple, when she had felt a mighty wellspring of life-giving power like none she would feel again. She sighed, then budged so that his small hand found all the purchase it could want along her abundant body.

He read her the Dutch nonsense until his voice trailed, his eyes closed, and, finally, the book fell from his hand. She kissed the top of his warm, red head and let him sleep cushioned deep within her.

Isaac came home late that night very merry and stinking of whiskey.

"I voted, I voted," he sang. His boots collapsed on the dirt floor with a jingle. "Vaken sie oop, Frau Judit, I hatte made a vote." Mocking the Dutch, his voice bounced as if he rode a barrel down a flight of stairs.

"Quiet'n down, now," Judith said pressing her face hard against the pillow. Only a blanket drenched yellow with wood smoke and strung across the cabin on bailing wire separated the straw tick Judith and Isaac slept on from the cot where Holy dozed. The cabin Isaac built her was no account and not nearly as solid as the slave cabin she left behind. Even as early as November the walls crackled and popped from shrinking, and drafts striped her with gooseflesh.

"Judit, dat Morkan. He let all dem Nigras loose from dat qvarry."

Judith elbowed Isaac hard. "Don't you let Holy hear you mocking her. He say anything he hear. Leave that be."

Isaac laughed then recovered. "Morkan had him this big buck name My Asthma. That man was a story tall. Had teeth what could crack a chinkypin."

Grunting, Judith rolled herself over and faced Isaac. "Didn't."

"I'm saying. That big son walked them Nigras side by side with Leighton Morkan all the way to the square. And, Judith, you had to step you in front of a little window and shout who you was a'going to vote for even if that man you was voting against was setting at the window taking down the names. You could vote right against him to his face, and me a Colored man and him a White." His voice fell. "Judith, it was like whamming master in the mouth with your fist hard as you can it felt that good. Son of a bitch, if I could, I'd vote every day for the rest of my life. County Clerk, well kiss my balls. I voted right against that White bastard taking them names."

"Didn't," Judith said stroking his shoulder with not a little wonderment.

"I'm saying," he said with more pride and strength than Judith ever remembered in his voice. Isaac's face and body were lost in the semi-dark of the cabin. In the midst of the room was the persimmon orange of the fire and above it the star-blue smoke hole. Isaac's voice was a warm, wet circle of whiskey.

"And every vote them Nigras cast was just for exactly the man Leighton Shea Morkan picked. Except for what Johnson Davis done."

Judith touched his face. "What?"

Isaac's voice fell to a whisper and he moved his slick lips close to her forehead. "Voted McClurg for Governor, and Shane Peale for sherff, can you believe?"

"Didn't."

"I'm saying."

"What Leighton Morkan do?"

"Why laugh, my God! That White man's got dirt in his hinges. Mmm."

Drunkenly Isaac hummed a happy ditty, then suddenly punched a fist straight up in the air. "Wham in the mouth!" With a last chortle, he turned over.

She listened at him breathe awhile, then poked him in the back. "Look here," she said. "What you doing wake me up this late and not give me none?"

He feigned sleep and she jabbed him again.

"Play hell, woman. I done walked the soles of my feet off voting."

"Well damn you and the Republic anyhow!"

Between spinning and weaving and sewing Patricia and Judith made Leighton a coat from stone gray wool. Hurrying about the kitchen, they readied his dinner. Judith paused and lifted her apron to catch the sweat at her chins. She was panting.

He came home and sat in the mud room with his shoulders slumped and eyes closed. Resting that way with his shoulders bowed, the skin around his eyes dark and bruised, Leighton seemed old to Patricia for the first time, always staring at a spot among those stones as if there were a private altar there. Catholic, idolater, she cherished him suddenly in his reverent exhaustion. She and Judith waited at the table, where their package lay wrapped in crepe.

Rubbing his beard Leighton paled as if he feared something. Patricia laughed. "Well, open it."

He rose, placed a hand on the package. Carefully he pulled back the crepe as if there might be knives waiting for him inside. He stared a moment, then lifted the coat.

"Judith," he said. He held the coat up as if it were gold mail. Stooping he slipped it over his shoulders, then grasped its lapels and beamed at the Negress. "Judith."

"You like it?" Judith asked, unbidden.

"Why, it's a fine coat."

Holy stepped in through the mud room with a towel over his arm.

"Look a'here, Holy. Your momma's made me a coat. I'm gonna go for a mirror," he said, brushing Patricia's arm as he strode deeper into the house.

When he was out of earshot, Patricia stared at Judith, her stiff chin before her. Judith smoothed her apron against her stomach.

"I will not tell him any different." Her voice bit like she'd been drinking mordant. "You have learned much, Judit."

Patricia and Leighton sat with a German grammar *Wörterbuch* between them. March, and the library windows were open to the cool breeze of late evening.

"You see," Patricia said, "it's a rather simple language. Brutally practical, an engineer's tongue really."

She tucked a bit of her brown hair behind her ear. Her chin and eyes were set so seriously, it took little for Leighton to imagine her as a stern young teacher drilling German *Kinder*. He grabbed her thigh, and dug his thumb into it.

"*Acht!*" she blurted. She swatted his wrist, but smiled. When he lifted his hand from her thigh, she kept her fingertips on his knuckles.

"Now, see how the verb is always at the end of the declarative sentence."

On the stone steps outside, he heard the click and scrape of a boot that belonged to no one on the farm. Whoever was approaching hesitated, listening.

Leighton lifted a hand up to Patricia, flashed his eyes at the window. "Keep talking," he whispered. "Slip down." He pointed to the floor.

She paled. "And the nouns are all capitalized." Pulling her dress close to her legs, she slid to the floor. "There is no subjunctive," she said loudly to hide her rustling.

Leighton took the pepperbox from his coat, hooked his finger in the ring trigger. The boots clicked forward again, and Leighton reckoned the man outside had reached the front door. Leighton crouched by the window, placed his cheek against the wall. In the sliver of evening between the curtain and the window frame, he made out a man in a long duster, a slouch hat. In the man's hand, a bit of metal glinted in the twilight.

"One must take care," Patricia's voice never wavered, "for the verb changes to indicate person." "*Ich hatte.*" She lay flat on her stomach, her gray-green eyes watchful and wide, holding fearfully and wetly on him. She taught aloud, from memory, as if nothing in the world were the matter. In that moment, watching his wife's frightened face and hearing her fearless voice, seeing the shine of despair at the rims of those eyes, his heart cracked like a hedge apple dashed against a wall. I have brought this here. God, let not one hair on her head be harmed. "*Du hattest,*" she said firmly. "*Sie hatte.*"

The gunman outside knocked. Then came a long pause. Leighton waited to hear the greasy click of a hammer cocked. Finally a nasal voice rang out. "Leighton? It's Sherff Peale."

Breathing heavily, Patricia covered her eyes with the Wörterbuch, and he could not tell if she laughed or wept. Head bowed, he dropped the pepperbox in his coat. Pulling a trembling hand through his hair, he asked Peale to pardon him for a moment.

Patricia rose, gathered and composed herself on the sofa. Leighton touched her shaking shoulder, and with that touch they both exhaled deeply, volubly, then steadied.

Leaning against the porch railing, Peale tipped his hat back with his thumb. The pocket knife in his hand shone as he scraped it on his block of chaw. "Sorry to drop in all sudden."

Leighton was silent.

Peale scooped the chaw into his mouth. "You know, Leighton, it was a hard campaign. But I won fair and square."

"Fine. Chalk one up for the Radical Republicans of Greene County."

"Well." He tapped the heel of his boot against the stones. "I think I'm doing a fair job, and I'd appreciate it if you told Archer and all them to leave me to my work."

"I think you best tell Archer yourself. And tell all them yourself."

Peale was quiet. Behind him in the dusk, a pearly mist shrouded the jade hills, and the moon was rising, orange and impossibly large. "So, it's true, then."

Leighton did not move, did not shake his head or nod. "You'll have to sheriff without me."

After a bit, Peale stepped off the rail. "You learning Dutch in there?"

247

"German."

"Figured you'd have to." Peale leaned over the rail and spit. "It's been a long, raw time." He glanced at the enormous moon clearing the hilltops.

"Shane Peale," Leighton said. He stood very close to him. "I am trying very hard to put everything back in right order with my life. With her above all. With the town."

Peale grinned in a brown and gooey leer. "I scared Hell out of you coming up?"

Leighton said nothing.

Peale set his hat straight. "We was in the woods a long time, weren't we?" He descended a stair. "We about let it all get away from us again here, Leighton. Almost let it all slide back into that ole wode. Riding, avenge, revenge. No God but Death."

Leighton watched his old comrade as violet talons of shadow claimed his brow and face. "Good luck," Leighton said. "Please next time, ride up to the house and let Johnson tend your horse and announce you like a friend of the family."

Peale spit again then gave Leighton a quick salute.

In the library, Patricia still sat on the sofa, but the workbook was closed. Leighton sat next to her, opened the book, the pages whispering.

"Forgive me," he said.

She nodded. Then, her chin stern once more, she began, "Many call German harsh, gnashing. But sung, or spoken properly, calmly, or in endearment, it is one of the most elegant languages mankind has ever conceived." Expressionless, the teacher, she watched him carefully for a while. "Of German spoken in endearment you should have some firm memory." Her tone was not altogether cold.

"Yes," he said. "I have a sure recollection."

Book 3

How Merry Are We

I

OVER TEN YEARS IT SEEMED TO LEIGHTON THAT HE AND Archer forged the peace that tremendous exchanges of money and mutual profit create. In a seasonal cycle, rumors erupted that hooded men rode the outskirts again, but Leighton paid whispers no heed. No vengeance came to his doorstep; no terrors in the night visited his family. And his rival Archer found it just as convenient to manipulate justice politically within the city in the spaces when he could get no one to ride. For you see, back then, the town grew bitterly divided between Leighton's Republicans, who had freed the Negro and won the war and sometimes expressed a high and sunny ideal that America might yet be God's beacon unto the world and Archer's Democrats, who, on the whole, felt themselves to be dispossessed southerners who had "lost" the war, and who now wished the Negro (and everyone else who worked for a living) back into a near-cost-free labor pool, and also believed that America could yet be God's white shining city upon the hills, beacon of freedom to the world, if we could but crank back the hands of time. The city got along fine, thank you, without the encumbrance of taxing anyone to pay for professional policemen. Whenever an election swept Democrats from city office, their appointed police force of thugs, boot lickers, and snuff suckers was sacked as well and replaced by brutes, factotums, and chuckleheads, stalwart Republicans all! Archer might ride with recently unemployed "lawmen," and Leighton, rumor had it, might ride with him or against him. But a stable fairness pervaded—Justice for anyone without money or power was as inconsistent and terrifying as it was swift and merciless.

For the town, the Negroes Leighton employed and the way he used them confirmed any ill-wind. Back then Leighton's Republicans still needed the Negro vote and a few even cared, in a misty, charitable sense, how Negroes were treated. So Leighton's usury of so many Blacks made him irredeemable yet kin to the Democrat and valuable but socially offensive to the Republican. Both sides kept a welcome distance. He took to riding one of the great Percherons he bought from Archer. On this stout French warhorse, he led a work crew of Negroes as if under a black flag, cigar stuck like a relief valve from his scowling face. Along his cheekbones, lime hardened twin scars as gray and crusty as the callous on his palm. When he stared back at a stranger, his winnowed mug appeared as if his skull were baring itself. The Negroes, sweating in the blocky, poor fitting overalls and dungarees from the Morkan store, were his banners of pariahdom flowing behind him, dozens of them, singing, pounding with sledges, faces and arms gray and ghastly.

Springfield was becoming a city. All around Morkan Quarry, shops and warehouses lined National Avenue. Mule-drawn trolleys crawled the streets. Pausing, drivers allowed visitors decked in traveling dresses, bonnets, top hats, and vests a chance to gawk at the modern fracas of the quarry's rails and mills, at its brick yards and smithies, at the gleaming stillness of its teal pool, at its roundhouse hissing and turning, and at the bone white kilns rising one after the next, squat as siege mortars and flanked by huge piles of felled trees cut long.

On the old Weitzer land in Galway, laborers cleared and grubbed the hills and bared stone of such quality it made Leighton's breath catch. Mornings, Patricia stood with Gustasson watching the Galway crew of Coloreds and Whites as they destroyed the woods. With their derricks and steam skids webbed with cables, scoops gaping, booms swinging, they opened the earth. Red clay bled, and gray and white limestone jutted from the ruptured ground. A long ridge of lime striped a favorite hillside—Patricia and her brothers used to dangle theirs legs at its edge, watching the sunsets. There Erich and Robart whispered grand dreams, gone now, never to know that Leighton's scalding dream of America had always breathed beneath them.

As the new quarry in Galway progressed Leighton changed the name of the original quarry to what the many newcomers had always called it—Sunken Quarry.

After seeing an old daguerreotype of Leighton and the late Morkan at Sunken Quarry before the war, Gustasson insisted on wearing a battered slouch hat like the late Morkan's. Standing obediently, wiry arms crossed on his chest, he was a spectacle in his spotless blue knickers and white-trimmed vest. He spat when other men spat. Often he knelt and picked at outcroppings of the gray lime, breaking the fossils into white powder.

"Why do you bring him?" Leighton asked Patricia. They were in bed. Moonlight through bare trees painted a blue web across her face.

"It is for the boy to see how his father is working. Why don't you ask him to join and work with you?"

Leighton grunted. "What do you tell him?"

Her brow furrowed. "What is there to tell anyone? It is his father working. You don't have to tell a boy that. It is a girl I would have to worry about." She said this with a flat tone of voice that made Leighton feel hollow.

They copulated frequently and when they did, Patricia lay rail stiff, her eyes and face placid. For both of them intercourse was a job of work without much tenderness, and they labored quickly and resolutely, like farmers who have lost a crop to a late spring frost. He finished, and she rested with her hands folded on her waist, her frown somber, as if she were in mourning. The grit and residue of the lime puckered Leighton's hands and face. He wondered if it sucked away his virility as it must have his father's. One day she would be too old for child-bearing. Patricia's face was as blue as stone in the January moon. Together, they had reached a truce of coming and going, of eating and sleeping and coupling. Their life was a gray prairie they could both comprehend with a single glance. It neither excited nor perturbed them. It simply continued in all directions and it was beyond their imaginations that something so solid and placid might change or end.

The next morning, Gus came alone to the Galway Quarry. Leighton found himself shifting in the saddle. At age eleven, Leighton had started work at Sunken Quarry. Gus was fourteen now, free to join the work at any time. And Leighton wanted it to happen that way, wanted a fascination to grow in Gus, wanted Gus to negotiate the stobs and felled logs in the same way Leighton had wandered from the farm house and slipped through the gates to see Morkan and his lime-covered men sledging the stone.

Gus wore the tiresome slouch hat. He cupped his hands together and blew in them, mimicking miners beneath the ridge.

A new blaster was thawing dynamite outside the warming oven, holding it in his hands over a campfire, grouping the sticks on a flat rock near the flames. Leighton dismounted but stood warily away from him. The man tilted a single stick of dynamite over the fire, as if the explosive were some sort of sausage.

He looked up and grinned at Leighton. The sticks on the rocks were sweating so hard they shone. "I'm a old hand at this," the blaster said. "Been warming sticks this way since before the war. Way before them fancy ovens."

Men around him were beginning to move back. Leighton felt someone step beside him and brush his leg. Leighton edged forward. "Set that down. Real easy," he said.

In an instant, a tiny ball of glycerin swelled and hung at one end of the stick the blaster held. The glycerin dropped, hit the hot rock with a loud bap. In a blast of orange and yellow, Leighton was thrown backwards. He fell hard on his ass. The blaster disappeared entirely.

Gus stood in the fog of yellow and black smoke, his arms stiff at his sides as if he were enraged. All around, splinters of logs from the campfire smoldered. There was a hollow bowl in the earth where the man and fire had been.

"Gus," Leighton called to him, choking and reaching though his mind after the concussion couldn't yet make his body rise.

In a moment, the boy turned. He met Leighton's gaze with eyes as sure and undeviating as Patricia's. "Papá," he said. He walked to Leighton.

When the boy's expression changed to a concerned frown, Leighton held out a hand to him.

Gus took his father's hand, and immediately strained to pull him upward. "Everything is fine," the boy said firmly. "I saw where he went. God is to be feared."

"As are fools," Leighton added.

From then on he rode with his father to the quarries. Following Leighton about the stone, he learned how to spot fractures where the lime broke with the least amount of labor. Leighton taught him how to gauge the balance of fire to stone in cooking cement, how to determine when to use black powder, when to use dynamite, when to feather and wedge, and when to abandon a whole strata.

One morning, he taught Gus how to test aging black powder. "Hold still now."

Leighton felt an eerie bow of emotion tense within him—he was about to pass deep knowledge from his long dead father to his son, Old Morkan's grandson, standing before him, red curls sprouting out from under a black slouch hat, spectacles shining like coins. Only the gray crescent eyes of his mother watching, eagerly waiting, separated the child from being the Old Morkan in miniature.

Leighton took a pinch of powder from the cask, then cupped one hand over Gus's left ear. Slowly he brought the pinch of black powder to his son's right ear.

The boy did not flinch but stood calmly still. Already he knew the principles.

Leighton rolled the black powder between his fingers, then stopped. "What did you hear?"

"Crackling. Like wool against sandstone."

Leighton nodded, held the powder to his ear and rolled it. "Water's got in it when you hear that. Shouldn't be any sound at all. You'll have an exciting time using it now."

Gus took a pinch for himself, listening at it, memorizing. "They say grandfather gave black powder to the Rebel army. In the war."

"Yes. He did that. He had to do that."

"And that powder could have killed Mamá's brothers.

Mamá, he said. Bruzhers, he said. Since his birth, he and his mother spoke German in the house. English was the language for when Leighton came home.

"There was a lot of powder banging around back then."

"And yet she loves you. And the both of you have made me."

"Lucky you."

Gus smiled and brushed the powder from his delicate fingers. "But Papá, why do some people think always that we are traitors, that I am a traitor?" Gus touched Leighton's Federal campaign cap. "You fought against traitors. Mamá's people who died, all fought against traitors." As he continued to finger and examine Leighton's cap, his lips curled and his nose wrinkled. "This hat is a mess, Papá!"

Overcome Leighton embraced him quickly, something he had vowed not to do on the job. "And you, Gustasson Morkan, are a very fast study."

Gus took to Odem and the ledgers and numbers as quickly as a hound takes to the trail. He soon had a command of the finances that even Odem relied on when setting prices, and Leighton asked the boy to sit beside him when negotiating any major contract. Wherever there was building, or in the quarry office, the two were together, the squat quarrymaster in his gray-streaked coat and engineer's boots, Gus in the white shirt and black suspenders like old Morkan had worn. When he fixed spectacles on his nose and began to speak in the meticulous English his mother used, men thought he was much older, possibly even a beardless youth in his early twenties. Arriving at a worksite in North Town, Gus even overheard an old Springfield contractor joke with one of his foremen, "Look'a there. It's Mick and Echo."

Feigning a boy's curiosity in the construction, Gus grilled the contractor about costs and materials until the man broke a sweat and stammered. At the bargaining table under an old canvas army tent, the prices Gus suggested were ambitious, but Leighton wanted to humor him and let his son's declarations stand. The contractor, flustered and red in the face, signed the agreement, sure that the boy had told Leighton of his disparaging comment.

Riding back from the jobsite, Gus kept his spectacles on, and his whole aspect, though precocious, made Leighton shiver with memories.

Gus leaned toward him. "How much did Mr. Newman let on the bid to that man?"

Leighton quoted the figure he'd read in the *Daily Leader*.

"He'll lose a dollar a square foot."

Leighton halted his horse. "For certain?"

"Unless he lied about his costs." Gus pushed his spectacles up on his nose. "Is it possible to make him pay a percentage up front?"

Leighton grinned, took a cigar from his coat, hesitated, then offered one to Gus. Leaning forward with the match he lit his son's first cigar. "Now, you're a Morkan."

Judith was setting beans in a pot to stew when Patricia stepped in the back door and sat down at the kitchen table. She had been to the doctor's, and she looked wan. Instead of the busy smile she kept around Judith, Patricia's jaw slackened and her eyes held a glaze like grease shines on the top of barrel water.

With Gus gone to the quarries and Holy off with Johnson or Isaac, the house echoed and creaked, hollow sounding. Though Judith felt lonesome, the Dutch never changed—her soul was made for work and solitude.

"Where is Holofernes?" Patricia asked.

"I reckon fishing with Isaac or in the gardens with Johnson."

Patricia untied her hat, her fingers working with a dreadful slowness. She set it on the table. "Will you make me one of those whiskey coffees you used to make, please?"

Judith set the pot on the stove. Turning slightly as she stoked the fire, she saw Patricia was still staring at a spot of nothing in the middle of the table.

"You with child again, Mrs. Patricia?"

Patricia raised her eyebrows, but made no answer for a time. "Tell me, Judit. You and Isaac have but one child. Does that bother Isaac? Does he wish to have more?"

Judith took the coffee grinder down and set it on the counter with such care that not even one bean rattled. "Beg pardon. You banging at a door I might not want open."

"My apologies," Patricia said, looking down at her lap.

Judith churned the grinder, and the smashing of beans filled the kitchen.

When she finished, she turned and found Patricia smiling at her.

Judith filled the percolator.

"I would like you to send for Holy when you are finished there."

"I think he's pretty happy where he is now."

"That is the bliss of ignorance," Patricia said.

Judith turned very slowly, the little measuring spoon still in her hand. "Pardon, Mrs. Patricia, but what's he ignorant of?"

"Judit, I swear," Patricia said, "no matter what the proposal, I can without question predict where you will stand." She rose and stood before Judith. Her long face, angry when she stood from the table, soon softened. Her fingers, cold and hard as thimbles at their tips, touched Judith's arm. "So often you react with distrust and you proceed to hide and protect."

Normally, Judith would straighten her spine and arch her shoulders and face Patricia squarely, despite the Dutch woman's height. But now, with the Dutch standing thin and sleek before her and looking kindly down into her face, Judith felt sluggish and fagged and helpless, like a tom overly fattened.

"Oh, Judit, look at us" Patricia exclaimed. She held both Judith's arms, gave them a gentle squeeze, which made Judith's whole body become rigid. "Here we are two women growing old, alone in a house where we used to matter." Her smashed face was just beginning to catch age. She bowed her head. "Judit, whatever happened to love? To possibility? To passion?" Outside a robin raised a feverish alarm.

Patricia backed away, sensing Judith's discomfort. "Judit." She shook her head, crossed her long arms beneath her chest. "Do you understand what I am saying?" With her gray eyes, she scoured Judith's body from bare feet to the top of her shoulders. "Do you still love Isaac? Have you come to love Isaac?" Water sizzled against the iron. Judith was silent.

"I feel so hollow, Judit. So spent." Her eyes narrowed. "How could you understand, though? You, so stout and happy! So fulfilled!"

Though her voice came out like ashes from a pit, Judith whispered, "I be glad to get Holy for you now, Mrs."

Patricia brightened. "Yes, do. I have decided to teach our Holofernes to read."

When Leighton arrived home, Judith had a meal set for him and Gus. Now the dinner table of Leighton and Judith and Holy included Gus, and often Holy was absent, eating out in the field with Johnson or at a hunter's fire with Isaac. Once Gus began eating with Leighton, Judith no longer ate at table but instead stood apart and served them as was her custom before the war as if in Gus the dead Morkan again ruled the house and she were his slave once more. Tonight, Holy was gone, and Judith stood in the shadows at their beck and call. But Leighton paid this no mind. Here was his Gus, with gray lime dusting his sweaty neck, sun coloring his cheeks rose, lime water from the curing tanks wrinkling his hands, and ink from the ledgers darkening his fingers. Thin, growing tall like his grandfather, he ate hungrily. Leighton gripped his forearm and squeezed it hard, nodded at him, hardly knowing what to say for his heart felt swollen, and his collarbone ached with a mighty surge of affection.

"Ale, Judith. Two ales."

Judith fetched them a pitcher and mugs.

"Have you ever wanted to see a lead mine, Father?" Gus asked after he'd finished most of his food.

Leighton shook his head. "Seen the old ones. Reverberators even." He spoke with his mouth full, but stopped, remembering how this bothered Gus. He swallowed a drink of ale. "You'll get more money in a lifetime out of a sand or gravel pit or what we've got than any ditch in Granby."

Gus stared at the top of his ale. "I have been reading about them."

"Well, we can go see one."

"Do you know what I want?" Judith asked, stepping from the shadows.

Both men jolted at the table—it was a singular instance. She never spoke, save to Holy, and spoke to Gus and Leighton only when asking if they wanted for anything.

She talked slowly, her hands tensed at her sides. "I would like very much for you to take Holy to the mine and learn him something other to do than what Johnson and Isaac are about."

Leighton and Gus sat in silence for a moment. Staring at his son, trying to divine his thoughts from his flat expression, Leighton felt a great encroachment on the affection that had warmed him, as if Judith had threatened Gus somehow. He stared at Gus so intensely, the boy felt leave to speak.

"That will not bother me," he said. He took a draw on his ale, then made a face.

Leighton turned his mug on the tabletop. "Gus, I'll see you in the library."

Lowering his head, Gus took his ale to the library.

Leighton stared at Judith, then spoke once the library door shut. "What are you thinking?"

"Leighton, please, I …" She reached for his fist balled on the table.

He pinned her hand to the tabletop. "Had we asked for anything or for you to speak?"

Her eyes narrowed on him. "Leighton Morkan."

"Don't Leighton Morkan me," he said.

She trembled, and slowly he released her hand. He rose and stood beside her, touched her shoulder. Her eyes followed him but she did not move her head. He placed an arm around her waist. "Judith, I will do anything for Holy. You know that." With his other hand he fell to stroking and kneading the side of her breast. "But don't ask me with my son sitting here at table." He gave her breast two pats with his cupped hand.

Her frown was intense in her round face. She did not look at him. "They's times when you make my heart soar," she said. "And times when you grind me into dust."

Leighton took the pitcher from the table and poured himself another ale.

In the old nursery, now Gus's bedroom by night and Patricia's work room by day, Patricia set the drawing of a hat on the shaky easel. It was the easel from the Turnverein, still solid, though the white pearls of spider eggs and the carapaces of dead beetles clung to its struts. Holy's plump face gawked at the drawing and the writing below it. She worried that the German below the English might confuse him, but he seemed satisfied that the topmost letters were English, and beneath them were letters from the language she and Gus spoke when Leighton was not around. Holy had learned the alphabet that afternoon, and did not seem at all fatigued, though they'd been drilling for hours.

"H-A-T, Mrs. Mo'kan," Holy said. "And H-U-T." He was squat like Judith, but through constant activity he had kept from going to fat. His eyes had a slight slant to them that made him appear oriental at times. Patricia had long watched Judith's eyes and Isaac's and Johnson's to see if any Negroes' eyes bore a resemblance to Holy's. He was lighter of skin than they, and there were times she could not help but think that this was no child of Isaac's. It brought over her a burning resentment, and she wanted to see Holy sent away, but then she convinced herself that his skin was not too light. His eyes certainly bore the dull animal-black irises and yellow sclera, even bulged slightly like Johnson's. She smiled to think of the Colored boy losing all his kinky hair like Johnson had—Holy would look like a well-fed Nubian merchant.

"H-E-D-G-E," Holy read. "And H-E-C-K-E. You're telling me both them means brush?" His forehead bunched and he cocked his head at her. "Hey, now. How come when you and Gus gets going in that Dutch it don't sound like it would look nothing near what we all speak? Sounds like you two been eating grasshoppers."

She frowned. "German, Holy. Not Dutch. German. A mighty language of poets, philosophers, devout men, and warriors."

At the door the puncheons creaked. Leighton stood with a mug of ale in his hand. He took the room in with raised eyebrows and dazed eyes, his mouth slightly open.

Holy stood like a bolt and stared at Leighton with a gaze that struck Patricia as both fearful and somehow joyful.

"What are we busy doing?" Leighton asked.

Patricia did not answer but placed another yellowed portrait on the easel.

Holy glanced at her and fidgeted. Eyes wide, he looked at Leighton. "We learning our letters. And a little Dutch, Mister Leighton."

"Did Judith ask you to do this, Patricia?"

Patricia blinked at him. "No. In fact, I think she's against it."

"Well then." Leighton stared down in his mug.

Seeing Holy's stiff back, his big hands at his sides, skin no darker than suede leather, Patricia was overwhelmed for a moment by that feeling of resentment. She stared at Leighton, and

261

the skew of his eyes matched Holy's in a way that made her seethe, and then made her question her own judgement. It had been such a long day with the doctor's terrible news—there was for certain no way, the doctor had said, that she could conceive a child again. And she knew her own pathology well enough to surmise that's why she labored here with the old reading cards and the keen comfort of teaching Holofernes, who was somehow, for Hell or Heaven's purposes, the child of all of them.

Leighton smiled at Holy. "Holy, how about tomorrow you come to the quarries with Gus and me?"

Holy's shoulders rose. He nodded.

"Is this her request?" Patricia asked Leighton in German.

"Yes," Leighton said, in English, "and let's not talk over his head."

Patricia scowled. "My desires negate hers." In German again. "You may have him at the quarries once I have taught him to read."

Leighton rubbed his beard and his eyes narrowed. "I'm not paying him to sit around the house."

They were silent. Outside in the woods, one of Isaac's hounds bayed with great energy.

Hands clasped in front of him, Holy leaned his head toward Leighton, hoping for permission to speak.

Patricia stamped her foot. "Holy! Just speak out. In my presence you will zay your mind." She was so angry, her accent slipped, and she took a breath.

Holy ducked from her, even took a step in Leighton's direction. When he spoke his voice was so subdued, both Leighton and Patricia cocked their heads toward him. "Mister Leighton, I do this learning at no charge."

After a moment, Leighton muttered, "Son of a bitch." Then he stepped aside, and Holy hustled through the door and down the hall to the stairs.

Patricia stood for some time staring at a void in the puncheons where a peg had rotted until it left a black and green hole. Her face felt scorched, pinched as if she had been in the sun for hours. At the door, Leighton's shadow loomed.

"Thank you, Leighton," she said. "This means a great deal to me."

"What can it possibly mean to you?"

"I might ask you the same." She glared. "Why not let me have this pleasure?"

He bored a divot in a cigar with infuriating care. She remembered his shining tools impressing her male cousins so long ago. Now his eyes, their oriental slant, matched Holy's when he parsed the alphabet. "You don't teach a Negro to read and write," he said. "No need." His lazy eye roved as if searching for its object.

"What if he is not a Negro?"

His chin stiffened, and the light fell from his eyes as if a bright lamp had been extinguished. Maybe this was a question he had long been expecting. "Look at his skin. What else would he be?"

She turned to the easel, began stacking the drawings, her arms trembling. "He is a smart young man. This afternoon he was irrepressible. He learned more in a few hours than any student I have ever taught."

"I didn't say he couldn't. Negroes learn plenty fast. I said there was no need."

She collapsed the easel and set it against the wall. "If he comes here tomorrow, I will teach him."

He lit the cigar, waved the match out. "You and Judith decide, then. I'll hear no more of this."

She smiled at him. "Actually, Holy will decide."

The next morning, Leighton and Gus waited on their horses at the trail to Judith's cabin until well after the sun was up and the fog of the creek began to burn away.

"He's not coming," Gus said. "I know him. He will sulk. Intending no disrespect, but you and mother have him confused. And scared."

Leighton shifted on his Percheron. Gus went on about how well he knew Holy, all the years they'd spent as playmates together, how Holy's mind was nearly as predictable as Judith's but hardly as dull as Isaac's, more of the ilk of Johnson's. With his back straight and Patricia's elocution streaming from him like calligraphy, Gus amazed and even sometimes annoyed Leighton. Gus stopped in mid-sentence and his brow clenched.

Back in the woods, the door to a cabin thumped shut. There came through the verdant maze of the oaks a complex whistling, as if the whistler had heard nothing but the drone of bagpipes all his life. Holy's stout form trundled towards them, quick and determined. Leighton saw his own narrow eyes in the boy's head, some of the burliness of his own stature melded with Judith's round redundancies and softness. In his heart Leighton felt a mix of gladness and deep dread turning and oscillating.

Passing them, Holy raised his eyebrows but didn't pause a beat in his whistling or his pace. He headed up Rockbridge for the house.

"You're so right, Gustasson," Leighton said. He set his horse for town. "Out of his mind with fear."

Patricia paced in Gus's room while Holy read to her. He sat with his round shoulders hunched over the Bible. Outside the oaks were still green and waving. Monarchs struggled up in the sun, whirling in lazy spirals against the east face of the house to light on the balcony and warm themselves. With their wings opening and closing languidly the insects looked like tarnished lockets of bronze on display.

Holy read ponderously, added or deleted words whenever he came across trouble, and his revisions always made a maddening kind of sense. "'Go now to the flock, and fetch me from the fence two good kid goats; and I will make them some way a meat for thy father, such as he. . . loves.'" He looked up at her. "That ain't going to work. You ever eat a goat, Mrs. Mo'kan?"

The change in his voice, from methodical diction to muddled and rapid Negro speech, made her fingernails ache. "That does not matter, Holy. Keep reading. You are doing wonderfully." And he was. This was September, a summer gone and he could read and copy out sentences onto paper. Even Gustasson had not learned so quickly, and he had teachers at the Lutheran school to aid Patricia. Holy's intelligence, the build of his face, the set of his eyes, even the brutish way he gawked when he listened, as if at any moment he might stomp off—when she turned these notions in her mind, they rankled her. Often, rather than being pleased at his progress, she found herself embittered, sweat crawling along her hairline.

Holy read on. "'And Jacob said to Rebekah his mother, Hold on, Esau my brother...' Why he has to tell her that? Ain't no news to her. 'Esau my brother is a hairy man, and I am a smooth man: My father. . . the vulture, will feel me, and I shall seem to him as a. . . dog; and I shall bring a curse upon me, and not a blessing.'" Holy narrowed his eyes at the book as if the letters were not to be trusted. "He got that right. She setting that boy for a fall. Would a mother get so full of desire, she'd sacrifice her only boy?"

"Holy, keep reading. See what happens."

Holy read on. "'And she put the skins of the kid goats upon his hands and upon the smooth of his neck.' That's mighty hairy. He's a dead man for sure." He continued, his eyes widening. "'And Isaac said unto his son, How is it that thou has found it so quickly, my son?' Old man's got a pernt there! 'And he said, Because the Lord thy God brought it to me.' You dead, boy."

"Holy, you are missing the point. Something wonderful is about to happen to Jacob, and God is teaching us that the inheritors of the earth will come from the most unexpected places."

"Shoot," Holy said. "He ain't teaching no such thing. All's he teaching is watch what your momma says, cause she tricky, and keep them goats handy."

"Holy!"

"Why you know that's right, Mrs. Morkan. What saved Isaac not a chapter or two ago but a goat in a bush? If it wasn't for that goat." He ran a finger across his plump neck and made a gagging sound. Catching her eyes and maybe even her agitation, he bent to the book again, drawing his finger across it. "Mmm! It don't come to no good. Look it here at the top the page, says, 'Jacob Flees to Pay Them Rams.' See! Goats again!"

The mirth in his voice fired her hairline to itching. So smart he was, this could all be shines and games. She scowled. "What does it say about fathers and sons? About who a person really is?"

265

Carefully stretching the ribbon from the top of the Bible down across its pages, Holy squinted at the sun on the floor. "It says whoever Esau was and whoever Jacob was, to old Isaac it wasn't nothing but skin. Which of you'ns is hairy and which of you'ns ain't. It says for some folks it don't take a lot to fool them, and for some it don't take much to make them want to fool."

She stared at him until his eyes, which had been on her, fell to the closed book in his lap. "Whom do you want to fool, Holy?" she asked.

He kneaded the spine of the book. "I don't understand."

Though she felt as if she were shouting at one of her sheep for no reason but her own selfish cruelty, she pressed him. "Who are you, Holy?"

His face buckled and darkened. Though he kept his head down, when his eyes caught hers, they were dark fangs full of venom. "You making a pernt, Mrs. Patricia? You writing you a Bible?"

A flush of heat rose across her arms and chest. He continued speaking, and her mind fell benumbed as if she were dreaming. The words coming from his mouth were impossible. It was as though in her dream, one of the cattle, drooling cud, commenced to recite a poem of Heine's. "I tell you who I am. I am the fisherman," Holy said. "I run down a ten-point buck, killed it in two shots and dressed it, and you put it on your table. You sunk your teeth in it, fed it to Gus, fed it to Mr. Leighton. It was savoury meat unto your bodies, just like Mr. Leighton prays for if he has grace to say. Now I can read. Soon I can write everything. Then you better watch. I'll write me a Bible and tell who you are."

"Holofernes," she roared, wanting to scold him. But then when no words came to her, they both sat stunned for a long while. Quieted she whispered, "Enough."

Exhausted, she crossed the room to her sewing chest which sat on the work table Holy and Johnson had built for her. From it, she pulled a package wrapped in green crepe. "I have something for you." She spoke drily and quietly, and, she thought, there seemed to be a note of defeat in her voice.

Holy's eyes widened. He took the package, hesitating as if something evil might erupt from it.

"Open it now. This is a reward for the wonderful work you have done."

Slowly he parted the folds in the paper. The shining morocco cover and gold-leaf inlays caught the sunlight. Holy began to tremble as he lifted the bound journal from its wrapping, and Patricia felt a strange surge in her heart. A dizzying confusion—she knew teaching him to read, giving him the journal, was good and right. But at times she detested him, detested ministering to him, his smell, the strong lye stink of his clothes, the odor off of him, like yeast and salt. All these months she had persevered, at first to spite Leighton, but then as one soul perseveres against the lure of a Mortal sin. Her own wont to hate made her wish to deny this boy all learning. But thinking such, she was shot through with pains in her wrists and across her knuckles, and she swore she heard the whoop of the old Lutheran school ruler coming down for her. From the worktable's drawer, she drew out a steel pen and inkwell and set them beside Holy.

Holy opened the journal, and its interior pages were so white, they cast a creamy light on his skin. Running his finger across the page, he paused, bent closer. He looked up at Patricia. "You want me to write in a book."

She smiled. "Exactly."

He bowed his head a long time, his hands shaking. She could not tell if this was from glee or shock. "Thank you, Mrs. Morkan." After a moment fingering the journal, he looked up at her. "This mean I can go to the quarry now?"

She felt her face flush and her arms stiffen. "Soon. As soon as I can get you to quit reading words that are not on the page. But you can start writing in the journal right away. It is yours." She paused. "Write your story in it. Talk with others. your mother and father. Write what they say. I don't want you copying what you read for handwriting practice. I want you to write the story of Holofernes Lovell."

After a moment, he nodded. She left him in the dusty sun, dipping the nib of the steel pen into the black ink. Outside the monarchs were flying in their wavering caravan. Minutes ago, he had longed to leave. Isaac kept a hammock hung in a clearing where over you in a silver oval of evening monarchs lofted like rose petals set loose in a river of lazy currents. Watching a white cloud scoot across the sky, he thought of Gus and all the fine times he was having at the quarry. Isaac told him stories of the place, of its rocks that slithered up from the ground and foamed the air with clouds that never brought rain, but sparkled like the shards of stars were in them and held impressions of the thoughts of the dead. Holy could picture Gus astride the rocks with a flag, like a man on a mountain, or a Templar on a pile of dead Moors in the books Gus read at him. I will read them now, he thought, and we see if he read the truth about the little man who sleeps for a thousand years and wants to hear his name, or the beast under the bridge who eats goats.

Painstakingly, he scrawled: "Holofernes Lovell. I was born yellow as the sun. With the cowl, but stid of on my face, it rolt roun my neck, which mean i can never lie, less I want to die by the rope, least that's what my ma Judit, says. We see.

"Better than me, I will write all this here bout Leighton Shea Morkan. I will tell the whole world who he is."

On a February morning, Holy stepped from the trees into the blue fog and met Leighton and Gus riding to the quarries. It was early to go learning. Maybe Holy wanted to work awhile with Johnson before his lessons with Patricia.

Gus crossed his arms over his chest, watched Holy coming through the orange miracle of first light struck on mottled sycamores. Gus didn't wait to be asked to speak. "I have found myself among Coloreds who would be better workers if they could read the Blasting Handbook or the manual from Bessemer."

"Bullshit," Leighton snorted.

Holy stood beneath Gus's horse, watched Gus smoke the cigar as if Gus were putting a revolver's muzzle between his teeth. "Don't breathe a word," Gus said.

Holy nodded. "Who'm I to tell?"

Gus reached down a hand, and much to the chagrin of Gus's horse, the Negro clambered up and on. Gus was still slim enough for the husky Negro to ride behind him in the saddle. Raising the reins Gus circled the horse to set its mind straight.

Its lips squirmed. "Don't go *knallen rum* in the saddle, there," Gus warned Holy. "*Meine Kastanien* are flat against the horn, *Fettsack.*"

"That so? Well, *Laterne Blatt Schreiben Blitz.*"

Gus twisted in the saddle trying to look over his shoulder at Holy. His brow wrinkled. "Lantern leaf letter lightning?"

"Damn right. Ain't nobody talkin' no Dutch over my head no more."

Leighton turned his Percheron. "No more learning, Holy?"

Holy was long silent, head bowed. "Only from you two, now, if that's all right, Mr. Leighton."

At the quarry gates, Leighton halted. "Get down off there, Holy."

Holy grunted and slid down from the saddle. Odem and Miasma were pitching nickels against the battens of the office. Throwing with his one good arm, Odem astonished Holy, whose eyes were wide on the flailing accountant. Gus watched only the spot where the nickel puffed in the dust.

"Miasma," Leighton said, "I want you to take this young'un and teach him everything you know. Everything."

Miasma nodded and popped one of his enormous palms over the entire top of Holy's head.

Gus's face grew taut, and Leighton could see the realization come over the boy—Holy was not here to be his chum. They would be separate, Negro laborer and White employer. "Odem," Leighton said, "you write this boy down as Holofernes Lovell at a water boy's wage. Store goods." Leighton watched Gus's face. "Till he learns."

Through the day Holy was on the cliffs with a drill crew and a bucket. Resting in the office, Leighton noticed Gus now and again looking away from the accounts he was aging, gazing out the slat window to the stone where the miners worked, anonymous as ghosts roaming Potter's Field.

"You had to know this was how it would be," Leighton said. Leighton was filthy, his face caked in a sludge of gray, his hands and hair sticky with tar and full of splinters from the timbers they'd been placing in a shaft.

"Of course," Gus said, his pen still poised above the ledger. He was clean other than the purple ink at his fingertips and at his lips.

Odem stole a glance at both of them, then bent to reckoning his bills of lading.

Holy kept a morocco notebook and inkpot strapped to his back in one of the leather packs Miasma used to walk blasting wire from batteries to drill holes. The Negro miners smacked him for reading the Horseley Powder Catalog out loud. Often he laughed to himself when he, Leighton, and Gus rode to Sunken Quarry. When Leighton asked him what he laughed for, the Negro recited whatever he had been reading—recipes for soap, advice for nursing mothers, methods for furrowing with Deere tools.

One March morning, shivering with cold and laughter, Holy stopped his roan. Leighton and Gus eventually slowed and turned to him. Around them the oaks and sycamores had yet to show their leaves. They were near Galway Quarry and the trees were coated with lime so that their bare limbs glowed in the dawn as if the trees were spirits of some forest lost long ago to the kilns.

In a staccato voice, the Negro blurted to the hills: "Horse's Brain is Different. This idea so many people have, about a horse's ability to reason, does not benefit the horse, but does him more harm than good. This harm is often caused by people punishing the horse for not obeying certain commands or signals. . . " Steam curled from his lips; his eyes shone like dark marbles. Seated on the roan in his lime-caked coatee, ragged flannel shirts and stiff leather vest, he enunciated perfectly, but slowly as if he were in a trance. "Signals, which he has never been taught and which, because of his in-a-bil-i-ty to reason, he cannot understand." Beneath him the ribbon of road glowed slick and red and the blue sky and clouds above shimmered in the still mirrors of puddles as if sketched expertly in graphite. "A horse may stand while three feet are shod but blaze away when the fourth is touched." His chin was up, his shoulders thrust forward so proudly, Leighton could imagine him bursting into song like Miasma and his drill crew, and a great part of him wished the boy would sing, for if he did, Leighton would join him. It was a spring morn made for betting on horses, riding down bushwhackers, and stringing up thieves.

Gus smiled at his father. "I have to say, I have noticed the Negro race takes spring rather personally."

Leighton's brow creased.

When Gus looked at him, the crescents of his eyes narrowed. His voice dropped, so that only Leighton could hear. "For all your strictures around him, you care for him a great deal." When Leighton rode silently for a distance, Gus pulled alongside him and continued, "Almost as much as for Judith."

Leighton looked at him sharply. "Gus, you have a lot of your mother in you."

In the fall, on Gus's insistence, Leighton experimented by trundling a small boiler and compressor deep down into the tunnels and running one of the railroad's complex steam drills off the pressure. He hired a Dutch mechanic named Düer on Pierce's recommendation. Leighton and Düer set up the boiler, waiting on Gus to bring them more asbestos tubing and ring clamps. Holy had hauled down buckets of water, and now that the boiler was filled, he was sitting on an upended bucket, rattling an anarchy of Dutch verbiage at Düer. The German's soot-blacked face was a knot of consternation listening to Holy, and with his agitated yellow mustache and rail hostler's cap, Düer's expression made Leighton laugh out loud.

Düer glared at Leighton. "He's possessed, isn't he?" he asked Leighton in German. He stuck his greasy chin at Holy. "He's mad. He's going to kill us any minute."

"He's saner than I am," Leighton answered him in German.

"God damn tunnels," Düer muttered.

"Well," Holy said, standing off the bucket. Even in the dingy light, Leighton could see where tar from the bottom of the bucket ringed Holy's butt. "I know me a song Johnson taught me that the Texans used to sing to entertain Germans in the war."

He launched into it before Leighton recognized the song. The close acoustics of the tunnel made his high voice sound as if it emanated from inside a person's ear.

> Ven first I comes from Lauterbach,
> I try my hands at bakin'
> Und next I runs my beer saloon
> Und den I tries shoemakin'

271

"Jesus, don't you sing that!" Leighton took him by the arms, which were slick and shining with the damp slurry of the tunnel. Holy's eyes leapt wide and he squeaked. Leighton crouched to look him square in the eyes. He dropped his voice. "*You* can't sing that around Germans. Where the hell'd you pick that up?" He gave him a quick shake. "Are you mad?"

The boy's bottom lip trembled. "Sometimes I don't know what I am."

When the boy began to sob, Leighton held him stiffly for a moment, then gathered his head to his shoulder and embraced the Negro as a loved one might. The Negro's hair was brittle as a wire brush against his fingers. Holy's shoulders began to roll and heave.

For a long time, the only sound was the thumping and gasping of the compressor. Leighton cut a glance at Düer and found him staring dumbfounded at him and Holy.

"*Zum Arbeiten, Hundswarze!*" Leighton snapped.

Düer disappeared behind the black cowling of the compressor.

Gus entered the tunnel bearing a set of Allan wrenches and tubes of asbestos and copper tucked in his armpit. Stopping to wipe his specs with a handkerchief, he heard his father bark something in German, and he stole forward, eager to see if the Dutch mechanic Düer would lose his temper as Odem claimed he might. Gus had yet to see his father whup someone, but Odem and Menzardo told him wonderful tales that made his father out to be a colossus in a fight.

When he emerged from the dark into the light near the compressor, he found his father and Holy locked in embrace, Leighton crouching, patting the Negro on his shoulders, the sobbing Negro boy clutching Leighton's blasting vest. Steam folded and hissed around them. The German mechanic glanced over the cowling, then curled his lip at Gus.

"Turns my stomach," he growled in German.

At once, Holy and Leighton moved apart, and looked Gus's way. When their eyes met Gus's, the echoed slant he marked between them for the first time stunned him, and he felt his heart drop from its youthful zenith to the darkest nadir of old age.

II

Archer Newman arranged for telephone lines to be run between Leighton's quarries at what he assured the Morkans was a keen discount and well in advance of other waiting businesses. Then on a Saturday in August of 1884, the Newmans invited the Morkans to town for dinner and what they called "a First Ringing Ceremony."

"Such pomp," Patricia said as she rode in the coach with Leighton. They were headed to Sunken Quarry. "Why could we not 'ring' them from Galway Quarry and assure them we were celebrating in the extreme over our good fortune in knowing them and their telephonic intrepidity?" She feared meeting Archer again for any reason.

Leighton straightened his spine and pulled at the front of his vest. He was spending too much time with Archer in the men's clubs gorging and guzzling. He came home evenings reeking of yeast and hops and grease, swollen like a tick. The dispatch of her duties as a wife grew sadly comical, and some nights she met him with more liquor and feed in hopes that a severe bloat might bed him down for the night, which it often did. A vacation in Joplin's lead districts—a stupefying bore for Patricia—had put even more weight on him. Fidgeting in his suit, he appeared ponderously stout.

"Please, for just this day will you show them some measure of decency?" he asked. His face was red and flushed in the heat. "I can't tally the money that man has brought this family. Now you respect it."

At Sunken Quarry, Archer was busy berating an engineer, poor Edward Woelk, keeper of the phone exchange. Archer's voice rose as the Morkans drew closer. Woelk, with his face as glum and resigned as a raftsman's in a rainstorm, listened to Archer.

Aureole Newman, Archer's wife, waited in the shade of the office and flirted with Gustasson. She had healthy cheeks, a slight double chin, and a body that responded to a corset so naturally she seemed to have a vase for a torso. Leighton bowed to Aureole, then put an arm across Gustasson's back. At nineteen Gus was taller than Leighton now, and Leighton could no longer drape an arm over the boy's shoulders.

Aureole strolled to Patricia, lifted the hem of her dress and dipped her shoulders a bit in a half-hearted curtsy. "Mrs. Morkan, a pleasure."

"The pleasure is to me, you should know." Patricia did all she could to make Aureole believe that her English was weak and that she had difficulty conversing. If she remained a Dutch embarrassment in public, then maybe Aureole would avoid associating with her.

Aureole moved uncomfortably close and spoke very slowly. "I must say, Leighton has grown so pleasingly fleshy. You must keep him very happy at home."

Doctors were injecting dead bugs into people's blood and the bug corpses absolved the blood of disease. Bottled voices from city blocks away came to your ear by wire. Almost all the buffalo had thankfully been eradicated for the greater warmth of the nation. But still men had invented no cure for abrasive and crass people. What is enlightenment worth if one must still battle fleas and stickleburrs?

"He is happy, I can say. How happy are you?" She said this with a smile as backwards and innocent as a wooden shoe.

All along the dusty cliffs Negro workers broke into song. From the four towering cylinders that bristled with ladders, pipes, and ramparts there rose columns of smoke thick as rolags of wool, and this made the high sun seem even more sweltering. Aureole blinked her eyes, exasperated at Patricia's broken English. Behind the handkerchief Patricia held to her lips she fought back laughter.

Leighton distracted Archer with a drinking story so Woelk, the phone engineer, could make his final adjustments without Archer's advice.

Woelk led them from the dust and noise of the quarry into the gritty heat of Leighton's tin-roofed office. For Patricia, the curious thrill of exploring the domain of her men vanished the instant she lowered her head to enter the white-seared, clapboard office. Across puncheons blanched from years of lime, two gray-crusted easels tottered, one for Odem, another, she knew from her son's stories, for her boy. To think of her son, so bright and articulate, hunched there before ledgers and notes from semiliterate contractors set her teeth on edge and made the old wound in her jaw ache. Leighton's desk, its top warped like a riverfront doorway, crowded the room. In the center of the office, someone—Archer Newman likely—had set a pedestal on which rested a dripping bucket of ice chilling four bottles of champagne. The one-armed accountant Odem rose from his easel, and Patricia went immediately to his side.

"Emil, how are you?" she asked, stroking his shoulder where the arm vanished in an orderly cuff.

"Mrs. Morkan, always enriched by your presence," he said, with a quick, warm smile. "But the check I'll be cutting the phone exchange," he whispered to her, "gives me no pleasure whatever." They shared a fetish for frugality and sighed together now at the lack of it rampant all around them.

Odem put a hand above his mouth and whispered to her. "I tell you this is a waste, these here phones. Mr. Morkan ought to be more worried about the damn labor recruiters coming back here from the smelters in Joplin. The wages they're offering!" He rolled his eyes, and Patricia gripped his shoulder in sympathy, and they both groaned in mutual and delicious agony at one more occasion in which the universe seemed construed to sop money from the upstanding and the hardworking.

"If you folks will gather round," Archer said dramatically, though in the tight quarters, the group of them could not band much closer. Archer strode to the wall behind Leighton's desk. There the telephone glowed, the only item clean of lime dust, its two brass bells shining like eyes above its ceramic snout.

Archer plucked the receiver from its hooks. "Let me show you all how one of these works." Flaring his cuffs with a flick of his wrists, he demonstrated the crank and held a little ceramic vase to his ear. "Central? Let's give 49er a line check. What?" He moved closer to the phone as if he might smother an answer from it. "Come again? Oh, yes. Much obliged."

He set the receiver back on its hooks, stuck his hands in his coat pockets. "Now, the etiquette of answering." Rising up on his toes, he bobbed his eyebrows at Patricia.

With that auburn hair and sharp chin, the tan bowler cocked just right, he was solidly attractive. She imagined for a moment that she bore Aureole's breasts, that she was Aureole, voluptuous and fertile rather than tall and barren. She imagined Archer's lean face staring deeply into her eyes while his hands gripped her corset creased waist.

And he was staring into Patricia's eyes now. Then suddenly a profound change came over him—his chin, his jawline went slack as if he were stunned, and he seemed to know something of what she was thinking.

Bowing her head, her face burning, she burrowed the toe of her shoe against one of the lime-hardened puncheons of the floor. Both Leighton and Gus watched Archer intently, waiting for his demonstration of the phone to continue. Aureole yawned and stared out the window.

The bells on the phone rattled. Archer held up a finger. "You must first identify yourself." He recovered his showman's swagger. "The ring is a question asked at you from beyond. From South Street, from the state of Delaware, maybe one day from the Belgian Congo!" The phone rang again, and he lifted the receiver. All but Aureole craned their necks his direction.

"Newman at Sunken Quarry," he answered, and shifted his shoulders, cramming the black receiver against his ear.

His rump was so much more compact than Leighton's, and he must have had his coat and pants tailored to pique this aspect. Patricia blushed again, thinking this.

"I appreciate that a great deal," Archer shouted into the mouthpiece. He replaced the receiver and turned to them. He bowed low. Aureole rolled her eyes at Patricia.

"Champagne," Archer exclaimed. He took a bottle from the bucket and began wrenching the cork from it.

"Well, before champagne...." Woelk began.

"Nothing before champagne," Archer interrupted, popping the cork. A cascade of white fizz flowed at the tip of the bottle. He pulled one of the ceramic beer steins from a hook on the wall and poured, then handed the stein to Patricia with a slight bow. "Details later." He poured a stein for Aureole, then for Gus and Leighton. Odem and Woelk declined.

Aureole bonked her stein against Patricia's, and their drinks crackled as if topped with sparks. "We should enjoy ourselves, my dear," she whispered. "As fully as their little world can afford." She nodded to the men.

"A toast, then," Archer said. "Today Sunken Quarry and the Morkan family enter a new territory," Archer continued. "In this very office, a nation at the height of its learning and power is inventing itself." He raised his stein. "We are at the epidermis. We are the frontier, where the first cells are forming. We are the skin of a country where the rules of living are ours to make."

"Here, here," Leighton said, though his forehead creased in puzzlement.

The champagne was bright on Patricia's tongue, and for the moment it helped her revel in Archer's bluster.

"I really do think someone ought to try the connection to the kilns before we celebrate much further," Woelk said. A Dutchman, he raised his eyebrows to Patricia and moved close to her, as if wishing she could make these clodhoppers see reason. He smelled mightily of sweat and his skin shone as if dusted with copper filings.

"Ah, sad is the voice of reason that thinks a drink will stand in the way of human progress," Archer said.

"Gustasson." Leighton pushed himself up from the chair behind his desk. "Let's ring your lovely mother from the kiln." He touched his stein to Patricia's.

"Oh, may I come along?" Aureole asked. "I would so love to see the Morkan men in their element."

She grabbed Gustasson's elbow before he could offer it. Woelk followed them, leaving Patricia with Odem and Archer.

When the door had shut, Odem excused himself to tend to business and left the office. She and Archer stood alone for some time in awkward silence.

He smiled and removed his hat. "My dear Patricia, it has been too long," he said in perfect German.

She curtsied very formally. "Believe what you like," she said, in English.

"If I may be so forward," he continued in German, his voice lowering to a register Patricia did not expect. "I have always envied Leighton his learned and practical wife." His speech was both tender and alarming. "Not coveted, for that degrades us. But sincerely envied."

To her relief the phone rang. When she moved for it, Archer blocked her way and held up a finger. "Always let a phone ring at least once more. The operators may now and again send a call to a number in err and correct themselves before you answer." The phone rang again, but still he blocked her path. "Not unlike life we find ourselves connected in long conversations with what was probably the wrong number."

It rang again, and he stepped aside with a gallant gesture ushering her to the apparatus.

Flushing, she lifted the cool receiver in her hand and pressed its cold circle to her ear. There was a rattle of static, like hail cracking on a tin roof, then a swirl of sound as if she held a seashell against her ear, a back bay's windy inlet of noise. "Patricia Morkan," she said, bending to lower her lips to the snout of the phone. "At Sunken Quarry."

"*Meine Liebe,*" Leighton's voice began awkwardly. "*Es ist eine neue Zeit.*" He spoke each syllable as if reading from a slate. He must have practiced for weeks. "*Wir würden uns alle sehr freuen, wenn du mitkommen würdest.*"

Smiling, she blushed deeply and felt sweat itch at her hairline. Her eyes grew wet. Then from the corner of her vision she caught Archer's face. His eyes had narrowed and his jaw tightened. What an intruder he was on this loving moment, this precious evidence that her brute of a husband could surprise and care for her. Shivering, she reminded herself that Archer also was once the White Knight, a killer of killers.

"*Wollen wir mal sehen,*" she said softly into the snout.

Leighton said something more but this vanished in a crash of static that coincided with a rail car rattling above the mill.

Then his voice was lost in the shirring of a vast ocean. What had he said? Was it a protest? An affirmation? A question? A whisper of endearment? "Leighton? Leighton?" she called. Then with care and some disappointment she replaced the receiver on its hooks.

"Impressive, is it not?" Archer asked.

"Oh, yes." Were she younger, she would have told him the hard truth. But where would the truth lead them? She moved to the glassless windows shuttered with wood so gray and dry it could have come off shipping pallets. She pushed a shutter wide open. Beneath the stacks of the kilns, Gus, Aureole, and the sweating Woelk were listening to Leighton pontificate. If she were not Yankee Dutch, if she were not battered and ugly as a boot, would Leighton drag her through details like this, grit like this, stinking men and rattling hardware? "How many of those little rail cars run past those mills in an hour?" she asked Archer.

Archer moved so close to her, she could smell the hint of jasmine in his hair. He feigned a look out the window, but his eyes were not on the mill. They were on her arms and dress. "Right many, I'm sure."

Leighton waved as he and his party approached. She waited until Leighton and his group were almost within earshot. "Why on earth would you covet me, Archer Newman?"

Archer turned from the window about to speak. But Leighton's voice boomed into the office. He was arguing with Woelk in very technical terms. Archer narrowed his eyes on her, then grinned, and she was reminded of the leer on a fox's face just as it outmaneuvered Isaac.

The instant Leighton stepped into the office, Archer asked, "And what is it you desire, Mrs. Morkan?" He spoke with such volume that the party stopped its advance in the door and stood blinking.

Patricia scowled.

Archer kept his back to Leighton, spine rod straight as if he were indignant. To Patricia, though, he showed a cagey smile.

"Mrs. Morkan?" Leighton asked after awhile.

With an extreme show of care, Patricia pulled her gloves on finger by finger, then flexed her hands. "I desire the arm of my husband."

The office remained as still as if someone had pulled a revolver. Then finally Leighton grunted and stuck out his elbow for her hand.

They ate a dinner of wild boar and pheasant in a special reserved dining room of the Carbory, a hotel on National Avenue in the heart of the gaming district, a hotel in which Archer held a silent partnership. The pheasant was smothered in walnut hollandaise; the boar dripped with apple and cinnamon syrup. Aureole and Leighton's eyes glistened, and the two fell into a trance of eating from which they emerged only to purr and adjust the fabric at their waists. If Leighton were alarmed by the scene with Archer, he did not now show it. For a time, Aureole's eating fascinated Patricia, it was so like a man's. But as their mutual gorge continued, the spectacle became nauseating. Leighton's plump fingers and lips glistened with grease and his shirtfront was showing in ovals between each vest button. Aureole's face had flushed and her eyes bore the euphoria of a morphined invalid. Patricia quit eating entirely. So did Archer.

The little fruit and melon balls served between courses swam in rum, and within two bowls, Gustasson was asleep in his chair. With a wobble of his head Leighton finally sat back, his stomach rounded like a pumpkin in his lap. Beneath the tablecloth, she pressed her open palm to it— under his soft fat it was like a sheep's side nigh to blasting. She gave him a worried look. "You'll make yourself ill," she whispered.

His lip curled at her. And then he grunted, sat forward and began tearing viciously at the pheasant again.

The dessert was some sort of cake set on fire for a moment, a fire that, when extinguished, left a sweet smelling, blackened syrup. Aureole ate so much of this Archer turned his chair screeching from the table and sat with his back hunched, smoking cigarette after cigarette, crushing each out on the heel of his boot. Aureole ate with loud smacks and exclamations until her face glowed and sweat shined along her cheeks.

Archer glanced at Patricia, who raised an eyebrow and stuck her chin at Leighton still straining. She shrugged and shook her head. And then there passed between her and Archer the mutual commune of old spouses, eerie to Patricia. It was the signal to take leave before things deteriorated further, but here the sign was shared and comprehended outside marital bounds. The affinity was suddenly as deep as it was frightening.

"Oh," Aureole husked. Both Patricia and Archer sat up alarmed.

She was bent over her plate, her face red. "You really should try this, Leighton. It's better the more you have." The fork trembled entering her mouth, and she swallowed the hunk of cake as if it were plaster. Archer drank brandy straight from the bottle.

To her surprise, when she managed to get a catatonic Leighton to his feet to take leave of the Newmans, both Archer and Aureole jumped from their seats and joined hands. "Oh, you cannot go," Aureole said, glowing and trembling.

Patricia glanced at Leighton and was alarmed to see hesitation cross his face. She pulled on his hand.

"Well, Gus has his horse, but Patricia and I ...."

"Oh , send the driver home and back tomorrow," Aureole said. "Or we'll stand you the livery fee."

Leighton looked at Patricia, his eyebrows rising slightly, a frown forming.

Patricia pressed her toe against Leighton's boot but found it too thick and Leighton too dull. "I really must beg pardon for time at home," she said.

"We'll all feel more comfortable after a rest," Leighton said firmly, smiling at Aureole. "We'll stay the night. We'll get a suite."

Patricia felt her breath escape like vapor from a kettle.

They took rooms at the Carbory and though they attempted to turn in at nine p.m., they found the streets did not sleep. They stood on the balcony amazed at the city still roaring with life, astonished at the hissing gaslights and the golden glimmer of phone and telegraph lines that partitioned the skies. Traffic thinned but was far louder—gunfire and jubilant whooping, curses and accordions, insults, bugles, bells on dashing bicycles, horns on clopping, mule-drawn street cars, dogs yiping and gnashing their teeth. The Carbory was the most humane hotel in Springfield's rugged and gaudy gambling district, which ran along National Avenue to Sunken Quarry, then up St. Louis to Dollison. The Carbory and many hotels in the district bore Archer's high-faluting style, prows and cupolas and ornate trellises.

281

And Patricia knew from Gus's rants that much of Leighton's work sparkled around them as well—mortar and whitewash, the stone foundations, the white sizzle of the gas lamps, the lines to which required Morkan lime to keep the pressure steady. Watching Leighton and Archer, she sensed the giddy expanse of their power. They were building a city, and it made her heart dizzy. If the traffic paused below and the street rowdies cooperated, Patricia thought she could just hear the whir and plock of the little ivory ball bounding along the roulette wheel down below in the hotel casino.

Gus was long since asleep. Patricia stood at the balcony finishing her own bottle of champagne, which she hid behind the rail. Leighton and Archer sat smoking, and Leighton drunkenly showed Archer how the end of his pepperbox could be greased so that all the barrels would not fire at once. He was so bloated only his round arms moved while the rest of him kept still as a boulder. Archer had his derringer out as he watched Leighton touch the grease to the muzzle. What could Archer, so thin and composed and fit, think of his gluttonous companion? Worse, what could he think of Patricia who had to bed down with such a *Fettsack* every night?

Aureole, who had already been ill after dinner and declined to stand, lay on a lounger recovering beside Leighton.

Down below, four Negroes stepped from the back door of the Carbory's gambling room and lingered in the puddle of gaslight there waiting for someone. They each held foam-topped glasses of lager. Across their chests were sashes painted with the words, "Eleventh Hour," the name of a lead mining company in Joplin. So a recruiter had been around. Then there he was, stepping into the sallow light, a White man with shoes the gloss of which Patricia spotted from the balcony.

"Say, look it there," one of the Negroes hollered. "It's Mrs. Morkan on that balcony." The Coloreds were drunk and emboldened.

"Sure enough," said another.

Maybe they were laborers from Sunken Quarry. She raised her gloved hand and gave them a little wave and felt girlish when they all lowered their heads and removed their hats.

"Hey, c'mon fellas," the recruiter said scowling up at her. "None of that."

"We work… used to work fo that family," a Negro said. "It's all right. She a fine lady." Then to the recruiter's horror they all four locked arms over one another's shoulders and began to sing, eyes turned up toward Mrs. Morkan.

> What a fellaship, my love, what a joy de-vine,
> Leanin in your everlovin arms.
> What a blessed dove, what a peace is mine,
> A'leanin in your everlovin arms.

"Who's down there?" Leighton asked. He strained his neck to see over the balcony's railing.

The four singers wore tattered coats, the tails of which were stiff with lime. One wore a new top hat that was bright green.

"Is that an old hymn they're ruining?" Leighton asked.

> O how sweet the walk when you go my way,
> Leanin in your everlovin arms.
> O how bright the path grows from day to day,
> A'leanin in your everlovin arms.

Archer shook his head. His eyes were pinched as if he were in pain. With the care of the very drunk, he forced the derringer back in his coat pocket. Patricia's palms were braced against the railings, and she was leaning beyond them with a smile that surprised Leighton. The night sky was crimson and black, like iron cooling. A fingernail of a white moon hung above the yellow pools of gaslight. With the lamp below blurring their vision, maybe the drunken singers thought Patricia was a beauty. She arched her back, her arms quivering, and for the first time in his life, Leighton saw his wife in unfeigned ecstasy.

"Who is that singing, dear?" Leighton asked.

Archer and Aureole watched her now, too. In their drunkenness the song fell into a chorus that was all vowels, perfectly unintelligible, but the Negroes went on in tune, a harmony bounding and falling so naturally Patricia felt her heart clench

283

with joy and rapture and a terrible sadness. These Negroes were headed for the smelters at Eleventh Hour Mines in Joplin, and there they would lose eyebrows and appendages, all the hair on their bodies, they would tremble and suffer the flux from zinc poisoning. Most likely, they all four would die.

"Patricia?" Leighton asked.

One Negro's head drooped, and his singing fellows held him up.

"Patricia Weitzer Morkan, are those my men singing?"

"Will you shut your mouth?!" She swung the bottle toward him. The champagne pinged inside it, then fizzed from the top. "It is a love song. Please."

Leighton felt his face grow warm, and he forced a laugh. "Sounds like an old coon shout call to me."

Patricia stiffened for a moment, and he could see rage in the arch of her neck. She was about to speak when Archer touched Leighton's shoulder. "By God, old man, it's rather good."

Patricia glanced at him. In the flickering light, she saw at first only cunning in the lean cut of his jawline, the superbly trimmed red sideburns. But here he had affirmed her, defended her. That sense of eerie commune crept over her once more, but rather than fright, she felt a caress in Archer's gaze. With the rush of the newly drunk, she abandoned herself to this, the rail seeming so thin, the night sky so filled with fracas.

Eventually Leighton sat back, the wicker chair creaking. Patricia shook her hair down as if she stood in radiant sunlight. The song swelled to its close. Many dozen times the Negroes bowed. Patricia Weitzer Morkan applauded long after they were gone, the silk of her gloves swishing and popping.

Even at 3 a.m. the gas lights remained on. Patricia slept, breathing softly, her mouth a dark oval. Leighton stepped out on the balcony and smoked. The moon was gone, and the stars truly appeared to be the millions of miles away accorded them in Gus's science quarterlies. He remembered resting during the war in the madness of the guerilla-infested wilds under the trillion stars that were no higher than clouds, so tangible their trails hissed when they fell. Hardly a mile from where he now stood there had been only forest and scraggly oak savannas. Now roads etched the landscapes. Flagstone walkways bordered brick and mortar shops and warehouses. Thanks to him and Archer, a city was conquering the woods.

He smiled as the gas light flickered, and he imagined the pressure stuttering somewhere deep in the maze of pipes, regained by the seal of his lime rushing into the gap. He and Archer and Patricia were no longer just survivors. The war was gone, and by dumb luck they had triumphed. But what an empty victory. Here he stood, near forty years old, one of the richest men in Springfield, capable of lavishly providing for his family. And what lay behind him, snoring with her horseshoe stiff chin bobbing, her long white legs thin as the blades of shears? A wife he sometimes loved no more than a man can love a worn saddle or a pistol that no longer fires, but has seen several fights.

And who was he, and what would he ever accomplish worthy of these stars and this city? He would die of a busted gut or an exploding vessel while aching still for a fat old Negress. And he would leave nothing to remember save for holes in the ground and scalding, teal pools.

Beside him, Archer sprawled in the lounger Aureole had abandoned. His mouth was open, his eyes rolled back in his head, the whites quivering. The weight of the derringer pulled his coat wide revealing his rumpled shirt. Archer appeared as if some thief had given him a rough search.

Leighton knelt to him. He snorted, but choked back a laugh. "O, Great White Knight," he whispered, "O, Vagabond's Bane, High Templar of Vengeance." He bit his bottom lip.

But then, in the gaslight, Archer's yellow teeth shone, and Leighton recalled Archer threatening him just as the tracks were finished at the quarry. With a pang he heard the tremor in Patricia's voice when she related the story of the intruder on the balcony at home. He took the pepperbox out, ran his thumb along the fluted grooves of its stubby barrel. As if his hands weren't his own, he pressed the muzzle to Archer's temple. Transfixed, he rubbed the black grease along the ridge of bone above Archer's eyeball and into the soft reddish hairs of his eyebrow.

His name was whispered. Past the open French doors, back in the suite, Patricia's form moved to the foot of the bed. "*Mein Gott,*" she said. "Leighton!"

In the gaslight, the pepperbox was as dark as lead against his palm. Slowly, he opened his coat, dropped the pistol down in its pocket.

"Please. Come away from him," Patricia said, her voice thin and high.

He slipped off his coat, sat on the edge of the bed. Though the mattress was soft, he could feel her trembling.

"The doors, close them," The she whispered in German, "What horrible people!"

"We'll manage," Leighton said. "Keep in mind, he still is who he is, and that means money." He stripped down to his bedclothes, lowered his head to the pillow as if the fabric were made of eggshell.

With great care she placed her fingers on his shoulders, then wrapped her long arms around him. "I'm awful," she whispered. "I almost wished you had shot him."

He rolled toward her, lifted her nightclothes, and mounted her. She placed both hands at his meaty sides, not pushing him away, but holding him in place, then stroking his heavy chest and thighs to hurry him along, whispering to him in German, her eyes closed tight, her forehead creased, her breath sharp, not from any pleasure, he was sure, but because she was being crushed. His mind felt afire, as if he had never been so awake, never thought so clearly, yet all he wanted was relief, madly wanted it, then sleep. He felt large, larger than the room, larger than the hotel, larger than the block of National Avenue the Carbory squatted on. Yet inside, as he rammed her, he felt he was a mere filament of wire. Still drunk and dizzy. His mind dithered and told him something about skunks in the ventilation shafts and how the Negroes routed them out with live electric cables. Patricia's face was a fist of pain, but she gripped his flesh and pulled him to her, urged him on. At last, he gave up, and lay panting.

For a long time, Patricia did not move. Then she slowly inched toward him. It was so late, she thought. The hour of truth came round, the few precious beats of co-existence, so often after love but just as often after a struggle, when spouses were equal and could speak.

"You are killing yourself, Leighton," she whispered. She rested her head against his shoulder. "You work these Negroes like chattel. You're getting so fat."

"I know," he said, his mouth pasty, his voice rough. "I don't understand what I do. It's as if I want everything. All of it. To devour it."

She lay there stroking his arm until he slept. Then she wrapped a comforter around her and stepped painfully to the French doors to let the breeze carry away the stale smell of his cigars and bourbon, his sweat, and the lime. On the balcony, Archer had curled his legs against his chest. If it weren't for the well-tailored clothes, he would appear like any deadhead in a rail car, sleeping one off. Above him, the city sky was webbed with telephone lines that glimmered like strands of gold where the lamplight struck. She imagined the tired young operators connecting and connecting. Such confusion. When the wind stirred, she smelled jasmine in his hair, and clove from his cigarettes. Even beneath his trousers and coat, she could see the lean ripples of an exquisite musculature. O, appetite, be gone. O, what might be. What should never be! Over the golden lines she knew there came the empty roar of the new ocean.

III

STEAM DRILLS CAME TO THE QUARRY AND LEIGHTON dropped his weight. Steam swept over his face and left his beard soaked and clammy. In the shaft, the air turned to a milky vapor. In puddles of lantern light Negroes forced the rattling drills against the stone. Leighton shuffled over the hissing lumps of asbestos tubing that issued from the steam plant far across the lot. A lamp bobbed towards him. When it passed, he saw only the gray-coated black hand on the lamp's ring. Black-gray fingers gripped his shoulder, and suddenly a face lurched before him, all gray, but with a broad nose and yellowed eyes. In the steam, the lime dust coagulated into a liquid fog of gray and cloaked every man with a new skin of gritty sludge.

"Pardon, Mister Leighton. Mistook you fo…." The name the man spoke was lost in the hissing and thumping of a drill. His face and hands vanished.

Leighton shuffled onward, grabbed the shoulders of Negroes as if their bodies were a ladder's rungs propelling him deeper into the shaft. There was a lull in the drilling. Walking backwards, a Negro bumped into him, then moved aside. He and a partner were carrying a third Negro, overcome, holding the bow of his body by its armpits and knees. Leighton pushed beyond them.

"Miasma," he called. He whistled, but the sound disappeared as if into a cotton blanket.

"Here, sir," Miasma's voice answered.

Running his fingers along the wall, Leighton led himself forward until the stone became more jagged. From a single fat worm of asbestos, steam lines spraddled out. A driller knelt resting his head on his arms, which were draped over a drill. Mounted on a tripod like some terrible piece of artillery, the

288

drill shuddered and vented squirts of steam, then grew threateningly still as it took on pressure. Leighton was still amazed that sloth could so grip a man as to allow him to rest if not sleep soundly on a spitting, smoking machine. Miasma and three other Negroes tamped sticks of dynamite into the holes.

The driller jerked awake at nothing in particular, then scowled at Leighton. "This ain't a'workin, boss. We got men dropping by the minute."

There had been a lot of this harping lately. Several progressives across the state circulated petitions and met with legislators to discuss the outlaw of miners being paid in kind at such stores as Leighton's. All this would have bothered Leighton no more than an abolitionist pamphlet on cathauling had bothered the old Morkan, except that Shane Peale, still sheriff off and on at the whim of the electorate, took to interviewing miners and their families and cataloguing their plights. Despite the wind of reform along the Mississippi and Ohio Rivers, the notion of the Ozarks sheriff in his rain-splotched Stetson spitting tobacco and asking Negroes about their woes was at first laughable to Leighton. Very early one rainy March morning, Leighton swung the Percheron into an alley to light a cigar. A wet wind whooped and pounded, making awnings thwop and glass shudder in its frames. He almost missed the twang of Peale's voice coming toward him down Jefferson Avenue. A tablet of light gray sky speckled with dark nodes like cinders hanging in cheap soap capped the alleyway.

"So how do you describe your troubles with this pay scale?" Peale asked.

"Ain't got nothing to do with scales. Work's too hard and it takes too long."

Leighton heard Peale's boots on the boardwalk about to turn the corner. Leighton murmured to his big Percheron, a dapple gray with a black mane, and pulled the reins. Swinging its head side-to-side, the brute finally took a few mincing steps backwards. As Peale and the Negro passed, Leighton pulled his derby forward, leaned his face against the horse's mane, which smelled sharply of hay and shit. Peale was writing on a clipboard. The Negro bit fiercely on a twist of jerky.

"Fact, Sherf Peale, quarry work made me lose my faith in God. Ain't no God in the world would let there be work like that for men to do."

Peale's interviews with the Negroes had them asking tiresome questions of their own—"Mr. Leighton, what if the store got nothing I need?" "Mr. Leighton, how come the hemp's all been wet?" "Mr. Leighton, why can't the store stock primers for the children?" Faced with such questions, Leighton rose up on the balls of his feet, clenched his fists and shouted, "The store is the store!" To him a Negro child with a primer was as foolish as a woman memorizing tables for steam giving factors. Excess knowledge only served to confuse the mind, concern the individual with elements beyond its ken. He told his critics, look at Holy, who daily jeopardized himself and other miners with his woolgathering and literary outbursts and his own annoying questions.

"What?" Leighton asked the driller.

Balls of gray sweat crawled like lice down the White driller's cheek. The White miners were far more emphatic in their demands, and Leighton often had a notion to sack them all and replace them with Negroes. He was getting too damn old for such grousing.

"What's that?" Leighton asked.

The driller stood. "I said, you're a son-of-a-bitch, and you're treating every man down here like a Nigger." The driller swallowed. "And if you don't pay us by what we're worth, you'll pay for it in a hole worse than this."

Miasma moved beside Leighton.

"Miasma," Leighton said, "take this man to Mr. Odem and have Mr. Odem pay him his day's coupons."

Holding pressure, the drill shook on its tripod, its copper and brass sides crawling with gray streams of slurry. The driller cowered back with a snarl on his face. His vest hung heavy with gray water, and the steam matted his shirt as if the fabric were foil. "Don't you touch me."

When Miasma plucked him by the arm, the driller swung at Miasma. With a forearm, Leighton caught the driller's neck and slammed him against the wall, squeezing until the driller gagged.

"Don't harm a man in my employ," Leighton said, then slowly let the driller free.

The driller crumpled to his knees, holding his neck. Miasma yanked him up and dragged him away into the curls of steam.

When the two disappeared, Leighton told one of the Negroes to pull his gloves off and tear down the drill. He worked alongside a Negro then, stoking the drill holes with dynamite.

Miasma returned bearing the blasting wire. Gus came with him and gripped Leighton by the shoulder. They walked the tunnel together in a quiet tension that puzzled Leighton. When they emerged into the shafts of sunlight at the tunnel mouth, Leighton noticed Gus's jaw rippling side-to-side.

"What's the matter?"

Gus pulled Leighton away from the shaft into the shadow of the cliff. Behind them a rail car banged into its queue. "Peale's gone to Jeff City with his interviews and his petition. Three thousand signatures."

"Where else would he go with it?"

Gus waited for a pair of White foremen to move along. Gus was twenty-one now, a citizen to Leighton's mind. Drury College had even hired him to teach surveying and basic German for stints in the evenings. A teacher like his mother. An accountant like Odem. What if any imprint of Leighton's was there? Gus's hands were the Weitzer's, long fingers, veins so thick and blue it appeared you could pluck them from the skin. "But what will you do?" Gus asked.

Annoyed, Leighton waved this away and headed for the blast retainer. As they walked, Gus's face hardened and his gaze followed the movements of Negroes jerking the hoses and hustling equipment from the shaft. His gray eyes narrowed like his mother's. Fixed above a face so honed and pale, so akin to the dead Morkan's, those eyes gave Gus a predatory appearance, like a copperhead ready to lunge. Emerging from a fog of weariness and noise, the thought crystallized in Leighton's mind: This is the man I will give this quarry over to, work of my hands, my father's hands. And it troubled him that today he felt no satisfaction in this but instead bitter rancor.

Settled behind the retainer wall, Gus stared at the ground and away from the tunnel. Miasma was the last out of the shaft, calling cover, then fire in the hole.

Everything human became still. Eyes all around them stayed wide, or crimped tight; not a soul blinked. In the morning sun, stumps on the red hills east of the quarry shone like stubble on sunburned cheeks, and the willow beside the quarry office shone white as if frozen in years of dust.

The blaster's whistle shrieked three times. Beneath them the ground thumped and each man felt in his chest a blow that made his breath stop, then gasp for a cadence. Eventually a black and yellow plume of smoke rushed from the hole. Gustasson's eyes watched Leighton as the two of them waited for the whistle to sound all clear.

"What more do you want me to do?" Leighton asked. The stone and debris of the berm that created the blast retainer dug at his scalp through his old Federal campaign hat. He felt as if he and Gus were down in a trench, discussing something none of the other troops should hear. "I paid the damned senator, what's his name, from Louisburg. And paid a mountain to that mine lobby who was supposed to bribe them others."

Gus scooted closer. "I can imagine we might want to run some numbers and consider dropping the store altogether." His whisper made his voice seem fierce.

"My God. You, too. A reformer?"

Gus's face turned red and his lips pursed so tight they lost their color and became pale. "I haven't run the figures, but by all I can reckon you'll still be ahead. Why not take it quietly and gracefully?"

The all clear whistle pierced the lot.

"Squandering your legacy? Impoverishing your mother and me? I'm to take that gracefully?"

Gus's brow and jawline grew flat and serious. For the first time, Leighton saw contempt in his son's eyes.

When Leighton arrived home, he slumped in the mud room with his brogans undone. His back throbbed in places he could diagram in his mind, and every so often a pain struck a rib and wrapped about it, as if a tether were trying to jerk the bone from his side. Gustasson sat down, was out of his shoes and gone so quickly he had hardly taken a breath in the room. Leighton stared at Gus's shoes, the brass brads, the leather hardly cracked. Gus kept brogans at the quarry and wore slicks to the saloon, used all the newest adjectives and exclamations like "Catch!" and "Gads!" Young whores begged him to buy them drinks, and then wouldn't drink from the mugs for many minutes, holding them as if Gus had kissed their rims. When Leighton brushed the front of his dungarees with his palms, cement ticked on the stones and bench. He felt he was a thousand years old.

Holofernes stood at the door with a notebook.

"Oh, Christ," Leighton said.

"You did promise, sir." Holy watched him with slim eyes. His nose was round, flared like Judith's. The sides of it and his cheeks shone orange in the candlelight.

"Get me an ale and some bread and butter," Leighton said.

Holofernes left, then returned with bread, a mug of ale, and a cigar.

Holy asked to sit, and when Leighton nodded, the Negro took the bench opposite Leighton. Holy dabbed his pen in the inkpot. "Please tell me about St. Louis, Mister Leighton."

Leighton drank and let out a weary breath. "It was a muddy river town, and we were Micks and were despised by everyone but our fellow Micks and the railroad people."

Holy scrawled, the pen making a noise like a bug burrowing. "Did you work on the railroad?"

"No."

"Why not, sir?"

"Too young."

"How young, sir?"

"Very young. Holy, this is a waste of your time. Why don't you interview Judith or Johnson? They'll be able to tell you things that will matter later on." He rose to leave, but felt a pang of remorse. With his dark eyes imploring Leighton, Holy seemed much older than Gus. Like Leighton, Holy was in the stone every day, while Gus was often in the office with Odem much of the week. Lime had already dried the corners of Holy's eyes. His fingers, which had been plump and soft were now cracked, the insides of his palms now crusted like Leighton's.

"Sir?" Holy blinked up at him. "What about you won't matter for me?"

"Holy. Please." Leighton left him sitting. He took the stew and bread Judith had left him to the library. There he ate among books so dusty and sun blanched, their spines seemed to be made of oak leaves.

A knock and Holy stepped through the door. "Mister Leighton? I do understand you."

Leighton stopped eating. The lamp's flame shimmered in the window.

"I have your story, Mister Leighton, a part of it from every person you knew."

Leighton lit a cigar from the lamp and began drinking the ale. "Holy, what in the world have you been doing?"

"Long time ago, Miss Patricia say 'Choose a chore for to write about.'" He crossed the study and stood near a chair opposite Leighton. He opened the notebook. "And I have written about you, what people say about you."

Leighton stared at the notebook. "What does our friend Gus say of me?"

Holy pulled each page and held it from the notebook's spine. It was a lovely notebook with parchment-style end sheets and heavy paper. But it had gotten wet; its pages were wrinkled and inflexible. "This is Gus speaking," Holy said. "'My father was a soldier, but will not talk of this unless he is among other soldiers, and then they talk for a long time, not about battles, but about other soldiers and where they have gone to and what line of work they are in, how they make their money and how much.'" He read each word as if no word had any relation to what followed or preceded. "'If a soldier is from the east or fought out east, then some long stories of battles are tolerated, but if all the soldiers are from the Ozarks, no such stories are told.'" He glanced at Leighton, then looked down longingly at the seat, then the floor.

Leighton nodded, pointed his cigar to the floor. Holy sat Indian style on the cold limestone.

"Go on," Leighton said.

Holy cleared his throat, straightened his spine and held the notebook out. Leighton could not decide if Patricia had turned the boy into a trouble maker or a fool. Outside of the quarry his habits—speaking his mind, speaking out of turn, reading, reciting—could easily pit him against the local rubes. Listening to him read, Leighton was struck with a pang of worry and doubt. "'Father is a man,'" Holy read, "'who acts rather than speaks. It is more natural for him to offend than to negotiate. He does, though, brood privately and over-sent-a-ment-a-lizes stones and family objects.'" Holy turned the page and squinted at it. He frowned. "Here Mr. Gustasson says several things in German which I must ask him about."

Leighton nodded.

"So, Mister Leighton, will you help with your story?"

"What? After having been pegged a man of action rather than a man of words? Holy, I'm through with your journal and you should be, too, especially if I'm all that's to be in it." He stood.

Holy watched him. "May I stay here, sir?"

"Yes. Fine. But leave the books on the shelves."

When Leighton left, Holy set the lamp beside him on the floor and read again the passage where Gus told the second-hand notion that his father was difficult in bed and had appetites for dark women, and this Gus had learned according to a barmaid, which had to be the skinny old blonde Danny who sometimes brought ale to Gus and Holy at the back door of Shulty's and whom Holy intended to interview within the week. He shut the book and tied its ragged purple ribbon.

Patricia was attending a late lecture at The Women's Lutheran League, and Gus was courting one of the Evertz girls, so Leighton hurried home before sunset, eager to wrestle somewhere with Judith. But Holy was poking around the upstairs, and Judith would not send her son away.

Leighton ran his knuckles along Judith's round cheek, then stroked her coarse hair. Stout as ever, she rested her bulk against the doorframe in the kitchen and closed her eyes, pushed her cheek against his hand. She was growing old, Leighton knew, but he had no way to measure it other than her girth. The black gloss of her skin vanquished any crows' feet at her eyes. In her hair, short as a hound's, there was a twist or two of silver, but in the evening twilight, with only the stove's flicker in the kitchen he was unsure of what he saw. He cupped the back of her neck in his hand and kissed her lips, something he rarely did. The touch of her lips, their fullness and warmth coupled with the jet black of her skin was as disturbing to his mind as the sparks that leapt off a detonator battery when the wire to the charge was mislaid.

Tenderness, he knew, aroused her as much as it annoyed her, so he continued petting and kissing her in his own combination of lust and childish play. And he was sure she let Holy uselessly thump around upstairs only to heighten the tension.

He kissed her again, and she held his face to her for a moment, her rough fingers crackling in his beard.

"Why you do this to me?" she whispered.

"What's that?"

Her eyes sparkled in the light of the stove. "Make me love you, when you know, *you know* she coming home?"

Her voice held in it a yearning and sadness that undid him, and his heart stirred warmly, though his face flushed with guilt.

Holy's heavy steps made the ceiling above them pop and creak. They both held very still. Then they moved separately, as if watched, to the library.

"We just being cruel to each other anymore," she whispered. "We ought to stop." But her hand reached under his coat and stroked his chest beneath his shirt.

"I hear at market some of what they say in town." She touched his shoulder, stroked his arm with a tenderness meant only to comfort him. As her warm, broad hand pressed his arm, as her skin whispered down the wool of his jacket, it struck him that Patricia had seldom touched him with only comforting him in mind. Patricia's touch always demanded something: Stop. Hold me. You are wrong. Move. Ravage me.

Judith wanted nothing now. There was not the least hint of desire in the yellow and black of her eyes. The warmth he had felt for her in his heart earlier in the kitchen cracked open like a seed. He turned to her, planted his hand on her shoulder, and leaned his forehead against hers, which was soft and oily.

"Why don't you change, Leighton?" she asked after a bit. She stroked his hair as if combing it into place. "That war's over. You won everything back. Why fight another one? Just pay them people."

He moved his thumb in slow circles across her shoulder, and the skin beneath her dress felt ashen. When his hand moved for her breast, she said, "Please. Don't."

When Holy left, it seemed too near Patricia's return to start anything, for Leighton took his time now, and Judith told him plainly that once she got all her stuff out, it took a job of work to cram it all back in. They sat together on the library sofa for a long time, resting against one another. The April wind stirred at the window, and far back in the forest the first tree frogs clattered like river stones knocking together.

"Why did you have to be a Negro?" he asked.

She snorted, then fell to laughing, but covered her mouth with a hand when she saw how earnest he was. Her eyes widened.

"Why do I have to be what I am?" he asked. "And love you?"

Bowing her head, she trembled. The room stilled as if a quilt had been thrown over it. "That sound like young Leighton. My Leighton. Used to worry so much over his soul." She shook her head. "My Lord, back then I wanted you so often, I about clobbered you to put up with that worrying talk."

He rested his head against her shoulder, and the nut and yeast smell of her flesh filled his nostrils.

"Come here," she said, gripping his shoulders. She hoisted a leg up on the divan then made him turn and rest the back of his head against her belly and bosom and stretch his legs out. Folding her stout arms over his chest, she sighed. "You know," she said, "some time I think I see a long ways ahead, like the way you feel hearing footsteps coming up the stairs and knowing who it is." Her voice fell to a quiet register, yet against the back of his head he could feel her words hum deep in her chest. "Some day I see, it's just us, like in the war, and everything proper don't matter, and want don't matter, and who you is don't matter, and who I am. Nothing but us."

"That sounds like the old Judith, all magic and the seer's future, water that talks, the jungles of Africa." He waved his fingers like a magician. "My Judith."

Judith snorted, then stroked the top of his hair, which was graying, she just now realized. Silver sparks showered in all the black, and it was not lime. "I ain't from nowhere but here, and I figured out more since coming to that than I ever will listening to water." She thumped him in the back of the head. "Don't make you no better a man, though. Cruel, cruel, cruel."

They sat that way a long while, her holding him in the cool night, both listening to the clatter in the woods, both listening for the hooves and the rattle and creak of the Dearborn bearing his wife come home to part them.

After a day of newspapermen calling, legislators wringing their hands, and laborers grumbling, Leighton plodded home on the Percheron. In his head he chanted Our Father so that no other noise could rattle him. Gray as a ghost, he leaned on the doorjamb to the kitchen. "Judith, get."

Judith ducked her head, and he let her pass at the door. Patricia rose, holding her coffee to her chest. She walked to him with her head bowed, but she could not remove the smile from her face. She touched his filthy coat. Lime crumbled like sooty snow falling from a chimney.

"No one to teach, old girl?" he asked.

She leaned very close to him and whispered, "Maybe I want to teach your little fing." She pushed her hand against his crotch and began stroking. His forehead wrinkled and his eyes popped at her in mock surprise. Within seconds, she had him following her up the stairs dropping his coat and vest and shirt behind him while she taunted him in German.

Once they had the bedroom door shut, they did not see Judith stooping with a sour face, gathering the filthy coat, the wool socks as wet and rank as bread gone bad, the dungarees stiff with lime. As she worked, Judith stared up at the bedroom door, remained still for a long time, muttering foul words to herself. At one point, she thought of kneeling to the keyhole, but she shuddered. What a blow it would be if she saw him pleasuring Patricia, or worse saw Her Leighton taking pleasure from the Dutch himself.

Afterwards Patricia and Leighton lay together in the bed. They heard the slicking of Gustasson's shoes on the stairs. Though it was late, he was humming. He must have repaired things with the Evertz girl—an off and on romance he had running—and Leighton smiled to think this.

Patricia had been talking a long time on an airy subject, but a change in the tone of her voice, the real hint of pain made him listen. "I just don't want to go through my life and die and become dust and know we have never really had the love we could have had," she said. "I want that love for us, or else I will look back on the whole of my life and say, I believed in nothing and I had nothing. Do you see, Leighton?"

"Yes," he said. "Of course."

She was quiet for such a long while he worried she knew he had not been listening. He really had no idea what she was after. How could she look around her and say she had nothing?

"Don't you ever think of your soul, Leighton?" Patricia asked him in German. She began stroking his chest, and the fingers that had once been at least soft, now seemed sharp to him, wrinkled and steeled.

"Mmm?" He understood her perfectly, but hoped she would drop it.

"Your soul," she said in English. "Working men that way. Paying them at the store as you do." She leaned up on her elbow, making the bed rustle. A thump, Gustasson shutting the door to his bedroom. "Do you think of his soul?" She stuck her anvil of a chin toward Gus's room.

Leighton feigned sleep.

She grabbed a handful of the hair on his chest and pulled. "*Antworte!*"

He snatched her wrist and squeezed it until she loosed him. Then he slipped out of bed and downstairs to the library where he curled up on the old divan. With his nose and cheek against the upholstery, he could swear he smelled Judith's sweat even above the dusty reek of his father's old books breathing in the moonlight.

299

At the quarry, Archer brought Leighton the news that Peale was back from Jeff City. Old Ziggler, who had rankled Leighton so long, was dead, but Ziggler's son had accompanied Peale, and their reception at the capitol had been cordial and warm, and three legislators had formed a committee to begin drafts of a bill banning mine labor from being paid in kind or coupon. The legislators, none of whom Leighton had been able to pay or bribe, were leftover Radical Republicans looking for attachments. *The Daily Leader* ran a long retrospective of the quarry, including all the dead Ziggler's columns. In Gus's bedroom, the sewing room and nursery where Holy learned to read, Holy now pored over the articles. Slicing each piece from the paper with the German pocketknife Gus had given him for Christmas, Holy pasted the articles in his journal.

Leighton penned Peale a note:

> I THINK WE NEED A HAIRCUT.
> PLEASE MEET ME AT JACK THE BARBER'S,
> 4 P.M., SATURDAY.

Peale answered him:

> OLD FRIEND,
> I GOT ME A NEW BARBER WOULD LIKE TO MEET
> YOU. 3 P.M. SATURDAY WHERE MONROE MEETS
> THE JORDAN.

Leighton arrived at three, but was hesitant about the address. Negroes scuttled across the streets toward Happy Hollow, the neighborhood where most of the Negroes in town lived. The smell of wood smoke and garbage fumed from every alleyway. Possibly the barber shop had closed—it seemed to Leighton that no business of substance stayed long in Happy Hollow. But there where Monroe meets the Jordan was a small red shop and above it a sign that said "Money and Henry's A Barber." Leighton stepped inside.

Three Negroes stood from their card game, wiping their knees with their hands, adjusting their coats. Across from the card table and its cane chairs were two barber's chairs. Back behind this was a partition where the stove was smoking. From behind the partition, a sewing machine whirred and thumped.

A tall Negro in an apron stood and nodded to him. "Mr. Mo'kan," he said, his voice so deep and soft it took Leighton a moment to register what the Negro had said.

It was Darnit, from Jack the Barber's. "Well, sir, I am pleased." Darnit grinned.

"Darnit," Leighton said, nodding.

Darnit cocked his head at him. "I change my name, sir, to what it really is—Money, Money Henry. And this here's my cousin, Henry Henry."

Leighton shook Henry Henry's hand and stared at Money. The Negro wore a red-striped, collarless shirt and a brown apron with streaks of shiny soap and green and blue spills across his waist.

"I tell you, sir! If I may," Money said, "let me please cut your hair."

"I'm waiting on someone."

Money frowned and nodded. "Less he's a barber, he won't be no help."

"But when he arrives," Leighton said, "you certainly may, Money Henry."

Money brightened.

Peale stooped on entering the barber's door. He removed his hat. Along his face ran wrinkles burned from riding hours in the sun. His bottom lip and his teeth were stained brown.

"It is good to see you." He extended his hand.

He and Leighton shook hands, then sat down in the barbers' chairs. The black men who had been absorbed in cards stood and tipped their hats to the Henrys, nodded to the two Whites, and left.

Money caught Leighton's eye. The Negro raised his eyebrows, glanced at Peale. Then Money grinned at his fellow barber and set to work on Leighton's hair. Peale watched with a bemused smile.

"You look right well," Peale said.

301

"I appreciate that." Leighton eyed him in the mirror. Peale was thin now, more gawkish and intense than when he was a young man. Leighton felt sweat ball and itch at his armpits. Money, then Darnit, had been gone from Jack the Barber's for some time, but Jack had never said to where. Peale had pulled an excruciating trump. Leighton waited for Peale to speak. Clearly working with a familiar client, Henry Henry finished Peale's hair in a couple of minutes.

After combing and snipping meticulously, Money finished with Leighton, and swooped the cape around. He nodded, and his forehead wrinkled with pleasure. He rang a little bell.

A stooped, thin Negress entered, but when she glanced at Leighton her eyes widened. She glared at Peale. With her head bowed, she began scooping hair into a basket. Leighton stared. Her face made his mind grope backwards.

Peale cleared his throat, and Leighton's heart dropped. "Old Friend, let me introduce you to Mrs. Miasma Sullivan."

The woman froze. Her dress hung off her bony frame; her arms were thin; the bones of her wrists shone like musket balls. Her shoulders formed a stiff arc, and the knots of her spine poked up through the faded cloth along her backside.

Leighton stood, and after a moment, he bowed.

She nodded, her arms trembling.

"It is a pleasure to meet you once again," Leighton said. "And if Miasma hasn't thanked you for us, then please accept my thanks for the lovely wreath. It lasted us many years. My wife still cherishes the memory."

She nodded, but remained staring down at the pile of hair in her basket.

"Mrs. Sullivan, please tell Mr. Morkan what you'll do with his hair."

She cringed. Both barbers bowed their heads. Leighton glared at Peale.

"Mrs. Sullivan, the work you do's nothing to be ashamed of. Please tell Mr. Morkan. He's certainly a friend and benefactor of your family."

Mrs. Sullivan was shaking, her eyes growing wet.

"Peale," Leighton said.

The sheriff's eyes were cold as the heads of nails.

Leighton paid quickly, and nodded to the door. They went outside, walked from the shop past their horses and into an alley that met Monroe Street. Leighton faced him. "If you have an issue with me, take it up with me directly, instead of grinding down a poor Negro woman. That was the most despicable thing I've seen a man do."

"Couldn't you say this in the shop?" Peale said. "Or did Money Henry learn English?"

"What do you want, Peale? My Negroes have worked just fine, without a gripe for years. What do you want them to have, a forty-five hour week? All of Saturday off? Cash to burn? They get into enough trouble on what whiskey they can get."

Peale shook his head. "You shamed that woman, Leighton. You shame her with every coupon you cut in your damnable store. I'll see that she sews you a hairpiece."

Later that next week, Leighton had Gus and Odem click numbers at the abacus to discover what the shape of the finances would be if all the miners were paid cash. Odem cursed and spat, and Gus snorted with laughter as his old mentor grew exasperated.

"This is serious, you peckerwood," Odem hissed at him. He was growing old now—his face seemed drawn close to the bone and his hair, once so blond, was waxy and graying. Worse, he was subject to the fantods if he did not have laudanum for his arm before ten a.m. "We give this money out and they'll be madness in the streets."

The postman and his laden donkey arrived. The mail brought the city's list of building permits, four letters postage due, circulars advertising dynamite and steam generators, misdirected R.F.P.s for the Galway Quarry, shipping bills, and a box from Shane Peale wrapped in brown butcher paper.

Leighton fingered the box as Gus handled his petty correspondence. When Leighton opened the box, he sat back with a start. Inside was a gray and black mouse strangled in twine all about its body. Then, on closer examination, he lifted the bundle of hair, undid it, and found it was a half-finished hair piece, each black and gray hair fastened to a canvas mesh as if threaded by a needle.

A note inside said: "These are the straight hairs of White men, so this goes at 13-½¢ per. If Ms. Sullivan makes and sells five in a week (no small undertaking that), her children can have a meat dish at Sunday dinner. Happy Easter, Old Friend."

Leighton pushed the hairpiece in a circle. By the color and texture alone, he could tell it was a combination of his and Peale's hair mingled with others.

Odem and Gus stared at him.

"What the hell is that?" Odem asked.

"The start of a hair shirt," Leighton said. Once the abacus resumed its clicking, he tucked the hairpiece into his coat pocket and kept it there for a week. It left black and gray fragments on the ivory butt of his pistol that seemed never again to come clean.

IV

OVER THE YEARS ARCHER NEWMAN INSINUATED HIMSELF into the Morkan family with a steady insistence. With Leighton and Gustasson at lunches, with extra lecture and theater and concert tickets for Mrs. Morkan, with gifts attached to no holidays, dinner offers at his hotels. If there were a civic event of any import, the Leighton Morkans found their invitation secured. Only later did there come smooth reminders of fortune's source.

To Leighton all this kindness assured him that his rival and conspirator, his old vigilante comrade truly was a friend, not unlike a brother one might fight furiously and then embrace and drink with long into the night.

To Gustasson, these associations were horrifying and insidious. When he confronted Leighton with a dossier of Archer's faults and craven habits, Leighton exploded. Father and son were silent for weeks. The City Engineer's constant presence—so often without his trollop of a wife—confirmed for Gus that his father was getting soft in the head and mushy in the heart.

For Patricia, the frequent spectacle of a sophisticated, dangerous, superbly built, nattily appointed man became a thorn in the flesh so deep it could stop her in mid-stride. Pushing the sheep into the shearing corral, hearing their bleating fear, she caught her work glove on a splinter, and when this obstacle tugged and halted her, she was consumed, ecstatic, by the image of Archer bending down for something at Doling Park, a ribbon his ditzy wife had dropped. Such power in those thighs, in that glorious rump. The image of him thrusting forced all the air from her in a gasp that sent Isaac hurrying to her side. The ram's gooey, black eyes followed her the rest of the day with sure animal sympathy. After spending her passion atop Leighton that night, she cried, and prayed, and read the Letters of St. Paul till dawn.

Patricia poured Archer a glass of burgundy and glanced upstairs where Leighton's boots thumped to the side of the bed. Leighton was retiring for the night and yet Archer, their dinner guest, had not left. Even Judith looked sidelong at the City Engineer as he ran his finger along the rim of his glass. He smiled at Patricia.

In her annoyance, she muttered, "So glad you could stay."

"Actually, I have a particular piece of business I wish to discuss with you," he said in German.

Patricia lowered herself into a chair at the table and could not decide whether to compose her hands in her lap or upon the tabletop. Finally she rested both hands palms down next to her glass. Where was this man's wife all the time? She wondered if toting huge, fat breasts around made one despondent and unsociable. It certainly did Judith.

Archer had taken age better than Leighton. Where Leighton's face was gray and scarred, Archer's was ruddy and lean. In the strands of Leighton's hair a brittleness crackled, as if all across his scalp the mane of a horse had grown out and stiffened. Yet Archer's hair waved red and full, with just a touch of white. She imagined Aureole's hands coursing through it. She raised her shoulders. "What business could you possibly have with me?" She strained to smile.

"To be in truth I am here to pillow a blow." His German remained quirky, old and literary, and contained none of the American simplifications of St. Louis *Deutsch*.

Judith's shadow lurked just inside the ell to the kitchen, and Patricia felt the old Negress move like a comforting breeze through the air. "What blow could that be?"

"I am about to acquire a great deal of your past. Or at least propose the sale of it."

Patricia sat back slowly, drawing the wine glass with her, watching him.

He shifted his shoulders. "I have not come to Leighton with this, but have first come to you out of deference...."

She cut him short. "What of my past would be worthwhile to you?"

His forehead wrinkled. Gazing at her, he stilled. Finally he spoke in English. "Patricia, I don't mean to be bold or prying, but surely Leighton has told you the value I place on the heritage of the German people, on their remarkable contributions to philosophy, theology, pedagogy, warfare, engineering, and physiognomy?"

Patricia stiffened a bit. "Leighton and I find very few occasions to talk about the German people and even fewer occasions to talk about what *you* think of my people."

"I saw something quite astonishing yesterday," Archer went on as if sensing none of her growing irritation. Even his English was pompous. Rutgers, she figured. Blue-blooded, Northeastern, Emerson-addled bullshit. "On a jobsite of ours, a red-skinned Negro named Holofernes happened to be working in a crew with four other Negroes bringing cement to a very complicated machine called an extruder."

Moving her hands to her lap, Patricia endeavored to calm herself. Archer knew every string to pull. And somehow, hearing him speak Holy's name drew her taut as a gut thread stretched in a suture.

"Correctly operated, the extruder produces, I would say even births a street curb as honed as a steel rail from the white of lime and gravel combined with elemental fire and water. But on the day this mildly black Holofernes was there, something went drastically wrong, and the curb issued forth scorched and with a great divot scored in it."

Archer removed his pouch of tobacco from his coat, and began rolling a cigarette, watching her as he did.

"None of my crew were mechanics," he continued, "and of course the other three Negroes with Holofernes were dumbfounded."

She could feel her frown flatten her chin. Some of her tension subsided. But, as Archer lit his cigarette and Judith's shadow inched forward, Patricia sensed the encroachment of something truly bitter in him. A whole reservoir of bile, black as the wool of her old Rambouillet. This was the man who made a partisan of her husband, and just then, with the match flickering against his sharp face, she saw the predator in him.

He rolled his cigarette between his thumb and fingers, making some weighty evaluation of the tobacco and paper. "To my amazement, Holofernes commenced to recite the process by which the steam pressure could be relieved, the plates released, the slag wire adjusted—in short, as if channeling another's spirit, as if possessed of some homunculus not of his race, that young, fair Negro described exactly how the problem could be alleviated. Though a bit at a loss, my men eventually did as the Negro outlined, and had the assembly dismantled and the problem fixed within the hour."

Glancing up from the cigarette, he eyed her intensely for so long, she felt she had to speak.

She nodded. "That's all very wonderful. I'm sure Holofernes Lovell, Judit's child by the way, has learned a great deal working alongside Gustasson and Leighton."

"Judith's child? Your Negress here?" Archer watched her from under a rumpled brow, his face fixed and incredulous. "A remarkable boy, indeed."

She frowned. Knocking on a door I may not want opened. "I would rank him merely attentive."

Judith slammed a cabinet in the kitchen, and Patricia fought the smile that ached at the corners of her lips.

Archer drew on the cigarette. "Well, on asking him I discovered that he had read the manual that morning while we were waiting for cement to make. *Read* the manual. A Negro! And within that one reading he had the thing memorized." Smoke curled from his mouth. "And that all this is a skill he learned from you. The reading. The memory. The recitation."

She raised her chin and felt a warm droplet of pride form down in her chest. She said in German, "Holofernes speaks the language better than you do."

Archer smiled at her, his eyes bright in the kerosene lamp. She longed for the gaslights of a boulevard, for they made eyes seem hollow, black and the skin jaundiced. Under kerosene the world showed its truths too closely and searingly. And in lamplight Archer was intolerably handsome.

"You know, I will mince no words," Archer said in German. "I truly and deeply admire you."

Her mouth fell open a bit, and her jawbone ached. She wished suddenly to be veiled head-to-toe like some Berber's wife.

"In a chivalric manner of course. The courtly way a fellow knight would love, admire, and protect the wife of his closest brother in arms."

"Whatever I have that you want must be quite something."

His eyes fixed on her, but she did not look away. Strange that it was Holofernes's halting, emotionless voice that came to her as he read, "Horse can read fear in the rider and will know instinctively when the rider can be lead to ruin."

"Yes," he said. "Yes, it is."

She felt her throat tighten.

"The old Weitzer house," Archer said. "Leighton's rented it to Italians?"

"What?" she asked.

"Italians. Wops. *Maurers.* Those brickmasons." When she said nothing for a long while, he leaned forward, and his brow creased in what she took for a kind of concern. He stood, and out of instinct she stood as well, but found herself shaky.

"I wish to buy it."

"Well, ask Leighton." She steadied herself with a hand on the table.

He moved very close, so near that when he blocked the lamplight, she felt his shadow consume her chest like sudden, numbing ice on a winter pane. Standing he was truly irksome, for the cut of his trousers, which were a dark jade, rounded at his thighs and along the teardrop of his calves. His face, though hatchet-like, could have passed for an idealized portrait of what Habsburg princes wished to be, predatory and commanding.

When he reached and touched her hand on the table, she was too transfixed to move it. "He will only say yes," Archer said. "And he will not consider what his wife's desires might be."

She was frozen now, and infuriated with herself. On the back of her hand, she felt the scratch and draw of a callous like Leighton bore on his palms. The room seemed to tilt a notch. His lips were small and thin and curved as if written in pink calligraphy.

"Purchase it. Whatever you want." Her voice was a whisper, and for a moment, when neither of them moved, she wondered if she had actually spoken. She removed her hand from under his with great care.

He smiled. "That is exactly what I wished to hear," he said in German. He bowed, then called to Judith for his coat.

Both Judith and Patricia saw him to the front door. He had another cigarette lit by the time Issac had his horse ready.

She and Judith stood on the porch in the brisk February air. Out in the moonlight, the hillside and ridge, cleared of trees for the kilns at Galway Quarry, rose as if the ground glowed from within.

"Judit?" Patricia asked. "What do you think of that man?"

Around Judith's face there hung a silver sheen. "He look a little like the old Morkan, but not half as much as Gussy do."

"Old Morkan was a very striking man, wasn't he?"

Judith pursed her lips and squinted at Patricia, a face Patricia had often seen Holy make. "No'm," she said. "He never lain a finger on me."

Riding home, Leighton had to shake his head to clear it from the blather of the modern quarry. In a year price for crushed quartz had doubled and the bits played hell and stuck without it. The quarry drills were now entirely air powered. At Sunken Quarry, most of the scaffolding and rails on the cliffs were dismantled and three shafts plunged into the rock. Long rails extended below, lime in ore cars climbing subterranean depths then up to the kilns. From these tunnels, gray miners trooped, shoulders and backs laden with bits, hose couplings, gaskets, wrenches, their helmets glaring with a Cyclops eye, their overalls glittering with quartz and mineral oil. So much noise—the yellow dolomite—what to do with canary—the gaskets on three intercoolers blown in two days. For blocks every shop owner on National blamed the quarry for chaff in his water pipes, and two homeowners phoned him each morning the instant blasting began. Leighton opened a third quarry near a place called Doling Park, where a railroad magnate had built long wrought iron fences to surround a wide lake and creeks, a mule-churned carousel, a Ferris wheel, and a roller coaster that hurled scream-ing citizens along its tracks. A mile drive of the new quarry's best stone led carriages and foot traffic into the park and paved every walkway. The blue-white of it was so striking the amuse-ment park became commonly known as Dolomite Park, which was the name of the quarry, the Morkans' third.

That spring of 1898, Archer bought most of South Street's houses for a song, old Weitzer's place included. He condemned the houses and knocked them down using city laborers, then retired as City Engineer. With Leighton's stone, he started construction on a mansion set far back on the Weitzer's newly cleared lot. The mansion became the pattern house for every lot he owned on the street. No longer would there be the blocky 18 X 18 rooms, the vernacular squares. There would be instead prows and parapets, steeples and iron, rooms of all sizes and newfangled purposes, even rooms dedicated for particular bev-erages—absinthe or Turkish coffee.

South Street was an ideal area. Workers were erecting poles and cable for one of the new electric trolley lines, which would run from North Town through the square to well past the Na-tional Cemetery. Its stops would be near enough for residents to reach with ease but far enough for home life to be quiet. In ad-dition, owners of the great houses adjacent to the line could have their pride swollen and their extravagance justified by admir-ing riders. By August, Archer capped the façade of the model mansion with turrets and a ceramic tile roof, copper gutters, and on Leighton's insistence two wrought iron weather vanes. All Leighton could get were the sort he had seen on barns—two cocks crowing, but he assured Archer weather vanes had to sit on each turret.

"These people used to be bumpkins, Archer. What you must do is bring countrified ornamentation to the point of audacity. Ozarks Gothic. Imagine a cathedral built entirely of bois d'arc." He was going to miss working with Archer everyday, and of course miss being the exclusive quarry on every city contract. Archer had become a more faithful friend than Leighton ever expected. Archer and Gus were constant, red-headed pillars of his daily life. Archer had become almost an uncle to Gus, or so

311

Leighton liked to think. And Archer happily maintained very cordial relations with Patricia, despite razing the house of her birth and childhood.

Archer, whistle clean in his suit, patted Leighton's dusty shoulder, then climbed on his horse and rode for a lunch with Gustasson, served by Patricia.

They ate on the back porch, a pleasant change after a wet winter and eating inside. To Patricia, Archer's constant presence made him no longer as alarming, no longer an intruder. As if she had been forced to live with a panther in her parlor, his fangs, his panting, his watchful glance, all banal. So long as her son or Leighton sat with them at mealtime, all seemed like cordial business.

The air in the yard sparkled with lacewings and insects that gleamed yellow in the sun and milled in pursuit of wanton creation. In German, Gustasson and Archer were discussing Prussia without Bismarck. Gustasson, Patricia could see, admired but distrusted Archer. Her son was that way with all people, engaged with them, witty, sardonic, but wary. Beneath every conversation with Gustasson there seemed to be a joke to which only he was privy, as if the world were bound to fail him, and he was wise enough already to know mirth was the only answer to darkness. Only with Holofernes did he seem at ease. To think of Gustasson now in such finished terms made her lurch in fear—she could still sense in his adult features the tender visage of his childhood, and she could hear in his voice the boy's mischief. The conversation turned to some new philosophers Archer admired. With each name and its attendant palaver, Archer raised his eyebrows at Patricia as if he wished her to affirm something about these Berliners and their noteworthy ideas. She simply smiled—Archer carried a sump pit of the Western world between his delicate ears.

Did he know she had never in her life seen Germany? Had only twice been north of the Missouri River and never south of the Arkansas line? Listening to Archer's prattle she was swept away with the notion that he might think her worldly and traveled. She longed to touch her brow, deep in thought, and say knowingly, "In the bank lobbies of Frankfurt, commerce is conducted beneath gasoliers designed by Immanuel Kant's son."

312

But to what end? There was nothing constructive in all this posturing knowledge men stored up then gassed over cognac.

Gustasson, half listening with his sarcastic smile, pealed the skin off a peach with his pen knife. Finally, he begged his mother's pardon and had Isaac fetch his horse.

"Shall I have him fetch your mount?" Gustasson asked Archer in German.

Patricia caught the mockery in the elevation of Gus's diction, but Archer did not seem to notice. *"Ach, nein, danke schön. Magenverstimmung is meine Fluch der meinen Eltern."*

"Mother?" Gus asked.

Patricia rolled her eyes then shrugged. Hesitating for a bit on his horse, Gus squinted at Archer then rode off in the dazzling light.

As Judith was gone to market in town, Patricia cleared the table herself and Archer followed her inside.

"Wie geht's mit deiner kleinen Musterstadt, Archer Newman?" she asked him. She had come to enjoy conversing with him in German. With Leighton, she could say almost anything in her language now, but beyond simple inanities, he never answered back in kind.

"Was ist eine Muster Stadt?" Archer asked.

She shook her head, turned to him and leaned against the slops trough. Years this man had been entangled with her family, a nemesis, a familiar, dangerous, handsome, the channel of riches. The kitchen seemed bright and tightly organized as if Judith had thrown a fit and cleaned. Smiling at him, she crossed her arms at her chest. The light made her feel lithe and young rather than tall and old and cronish. "Archer Newman, you know, your German really is ridiculous at times," she said in English.

To her surprise he paled a little and pulled at his bottom lip.

Moved, she stepped before him and touched his arm. "I'm sorry. I didn't mean to be cruel. It's just that sometimes your German sounds as if it came from an old book of manners." She smiled and laughed. "Please, don't be hurt. I think it's charming, but I just wanted you to know in case you ever employ it...." Gripping his arm tighter, she managed to pull his hand from his lip to rest at his side. His face remained rigid, though it reddened slightly.

Quietly, she fell into German again. "I've come to care about you." She looked into his eyes. "I would hate for you to make a fool of yourself somewhere. If you found yourself among Germans, other than Gus and me."

When he stroked her bare forearm, she felt no hint of the old fear. Instead, to her dismay and sorrow, it was as if the sunlight coursing through the window were electric and drove every small hair on her to attention. The panther in the parlor suddenly rose and planted its claws around her head. "Before you," he whispered in German, "I feel like making a great fool of myself this very minute."

He raised his head slightly. All the passages in all the romances she had read of the war blanched in the awful clarity of this moment. Heroines and heroes, grand, chaste lines proclaimed over plains laden with bravery's carnage paled and crumbled away like the dead vines of ancient ivy on a rock wall exposed to a booming sun. She could push him away, or lean to his embrace. And she saw, then, her green, vigorous will climbing free of the gray, winter plateau her life had become. Maybe the simplest way to dispose of a bestial desire was to let the panther and the hind clasp just once?

The kiss that fell between them was wet and tasted of the meal's wine and far off tobacco smoke. He pressed her bottom lip in his teeth for just an instant, squeezed her shoulders in his powerful hands.

What struck inside her was like the mad oscillations of a spring finally released, wobbling and shuddering. She took a huge breath inward, so sharp and high, it echoed off the stone floor and down the ell.

Archer's eyebrows rose, and his forehead wrinkled slightly. At such a fiery moment, when she felt her heart finally opened, she had squealed like a girl! Flushing, she laughed and lowered her forehead to his shoulder, which smelled of new velvet and a touch of rose water. He laughed as well, a deep laugh she had never before heard from him. He stroked the long back of her neck with his hard fingers. The velvet of his lapel was warm with sun.

She raised her head slowly, ran a hand through his hair, and its red and gray strands were as soft as the pelt of a setter. "This is not right," she said. "Not at all right."

He kissed the palm of her hand, and watching him do so, watching his slim lips purse and touch her skin made her heart founder, as if in her homeliness, her ganglyness she had never been an object of such passion. "My God, Archer," she whispered urgently, her voice high and small.

He looked her square in the eyes for a moment, then, to her amazement, he lifted her off the ground, cradling her in his arms like a new bride. He carried her powerfully through the ell and to the stairs, but caught one of her feet on the railing, grunted and nearly dropped her.

She laughed the old ringing laugh from long ago, the laugh of a girl hoping for love. "Put me down."

Frowning, he acquiesced.

She smiled. "Don't you think we are old enough to take these stairs without any courtly flourishes?"

He bowed low, raised his chin. "Once again, I am...."

She touched her finger to his lips, and he quieted. With her heart racing, she took his hand and led him quickly up the stairs.

Leighton rode through the square where workmen were erecting what the papers called "The Gottfried Tower," a steel construction four stories high on top of which would perch a replica of the Statue of Liberty.

A massive, stiff-legged derrick rumbled and waited beside the construction. The derrick was larger than was needed for the job, but this undertaking was more a daily public event than a building site. Crowds gathered to gawk each morning. Even the mules attached to guy wires on the peripheries had red, white, and blue ribbons at their bridles. Uniformed policemen and sheriff's deputies were busy clearing foot traffic. The bells of the old mule-drawn streetcars bonged and bonged for the crowds to part.

The derrick grunted, and the final section lofted in the air and swung slightly, then was righted by the scrambling of men, mules, and shifting guy wires. Slowly, with much shouting, cursing and pointing, the workers and the derrick eased the section into the waiting hands of riveters who were strapped to the tower by leather harnesses. In the wide, muddy square, the intricate steel of the tower shone. Leighton patted the neck of his horse to calm it as one of the new electric streetcars came banging and sparking behind him. Lady Liberty twirled from the derrick's lanyard and was finally set to rest at the apex of the tower. Cheers and laughter broke out below.

Isaac met Judith at the bottom of the trail before she turned for the house. She slowed the horses and scowled at him.

"You need to get up there and get her out of trouble. Don't you take nothing to the spring house till you do!"

"What for?"

"I still got Marse Newman's hoss. And they's laughter upstairs in the bedroom."

Judith sat up straight, and a smile crept over her face. "Well, that Marse Newman a very funny man." She grunted, heaved her large body around and began rummaging in one of the parcels behind her. "I do think I have me a chaw of tobacco right this minute."

"Judith!"

She spun around glaring at him. "What make you think I give a damn what she does to ruin herself?"

Isaac's toothless mouth hardened, his chin pressing forward. "Remember, my dear wife, that they ruination is our ruination." He stalked off cussing, shaking his head.

Judith sat for a moment, sweating, the reins in her hands. In the light shimmering through the trees, with nothing to stop it but the faintest yellow-green of newborn leaves, she saw shining on her wrists the two bands of scar where Old Charlotte Morkan collared her hands with lead weights to keep her from reaching into cabinets above her head where the sugar was. She watched her husband's bent form tottering back up the hill to the white mansion. Oh, watching him made her feel ancient now—her father dead and buried, her boy a man, her husband a toothless scarecrow. Closing her eyes, she saw the lanky Dutch woman's back arch up like a bow, her flat, ivory stomach and long arms trembling. Judith rested one of her wrists atop the other and held the leather reins tightly.

Patricia lay in bed, exhausted. An exquisite kind of pain emanated from her groin and spread all over her body. Archer was a great deal more stout between his legs than Leighton, and that fact struck home again, and made her shiver. Like a fool, she had asked him if something was wrong when she saw the size of his prick. "*Entzündung?*" She asked touching it gingerly. "*Infektion?*" He laughed tears into his eyes, and laughing they had coupled. With that, the whole episode had seemed a thing of joy, innocence, and now a sweet, parting melancholy swept the room as if carried on the breeze, laden as it was with rosebud and honeysuckle. She watched him now as he carefully fastened each of the studs in his white shirt, his fingers as precise as a woman's.

He cocked his head, smiled at her. The gyrating feeling swarmed over her again, a surging of the heart she did not want to feel, not now, not so late. Something else touched the air, cloves and jasmine—his cologne. Oh such a delicious mistake this!

And then it blazed before her suspended in the air like a gem cut from perdition's fire, the vision of real, purified temptation. One could be loyal and faithful and true all one's life and strut the world self-satisfied in righteousness; but, O God, to be put to the test before the flaming brilliance of this exquisite, flawless desire. It rent her flesh, and her eyes and mouth numbed in animal want of what she saw sparkling and turning, red and ice blue in the air before her, perfected, a form of a form, and from Hell.

"Mademoiselle Weitzer, I'm hoping we can cure my indigestion again very soon."

Slowly, she drew herself up on her elbows in the bed. "Oh." It took all her strength. "Oh, no, Archer." Aching. It was not what she wanted to say, but what she had to say. She felt as if she were clutching the precipice above a chasm. "It would be wrong. We have done wrong." The gem still hung before her mind's eye, scorching, beautiful.

His face hardened. "You can't mean that."

She choked a moment and was unable to speak. "No, I can't yet mean that," she managed. "But that is what I believe. And that is what must happen."

He stood, pulled on his pants roughly. "So you would be loyal to him, and deny yourself a love you deserve." He tucked his shirt in as if he meant to stab something beneath his belt. "Even when you know, you have to know, he has not been loyal to you."

"What in the world are you talking about?"

His eyes narrowed on her. "Holofernes Lovell. Or is it Morkan?"

She pulled the sheets toward her, and sat for a moment in silence. The fragrance of the air became suddenly oppressive, as if she'd drank a glass of syrup all at one swallow. "There is no way to tell if that is true." She turned away from him to the window. Far off in the blazing azure sky she could see a trail of white smoke rising from one of the kilns at the Galway Quarry. "And even if it were, it was an indiscretion of youth. A mistake made by a boy forced too long in close proximity with a beast of the field, a mere semblance of womanhood. A mistake never made again." The gem, the vision, dissolved, and the air it had occupied became firmly once more the puncheons and plaster and ancient bedspread of the Morkan bedchamber.

All through this he had been noisily strapping on his shoes, fastening their buckles tight, breathing hard. "Is that what we are then, a mistake? Two left too long in close proximity, eh?" He halted, looked at her for a long while, and his chin trembled. Was it anger? Was it remorse? Was it, God forbid, love? "You know, I used to envy Leighton his wife's great intellect. But now that I feel it at work, I am not so sure."

He pulled the door, his face an angry knot, his coat wadded at his arm.

"Archer?" she said, and shot her hand out to him. In the light her arm seemed terribly thin and long.

Holding the door, he turned, regarded her, his eyes crawling her open palm and forearm with contempt. "What?" he asked. His face darkened.

When she said nothing, when he did not kneel to the bed and take her hand to his lips, all the grandness and passion evaporated. She sobbed once. He slammed the door and descended the stairs.

† † †

In the dappled light at the bottom of the trail, Judith watched Archer Newman approach on his black horse. He stopped next to the wagon and stared at her, then at the goods waiting in the wagon's bed. His coat was rumpled, and between the index and middle fingers of his right hand, Judith spotted a shadow of red. She had always imagined him to be hung like a horse. There was the specks of blood from inside of the Dutch after their romping to prove it.

"You such a handsome man, Mister Newman." Judith said. She spat chaw at the ass of one of her team and the horse shivered and flicked its tail. "You ought to get you a pair them kid gloves."

She hawed the team, and before the Devil could speak, they pulled her away.

The Morkans' lawyer, a stout, gray-haired man from North Town was already in the office when Gus arrived. "Gus," Leighton said, "Lawyer Dean has a contract for you to think about. Here's what it does—splits everything I have right now down the middle. I own the Galway Quarry, you own Dolomite Park, we co-own Sunken Quarry. All existing equipment, payrolls, debits, accounts receivable, etc. at Dolomite are in your hands. But here, you and I make decisions together. Come outside. Let's make this one our first."

Leighton gathered his miners and told them they would be paid in cash every two weeks for their dozen days' labor. It was a full quarter of an hour before he and Gus could get any of the men back to work.

319

V

On September 23ᴿᴰ, 1899 Colonel Phelps's son, now the mayor, decreed an electric lighting ceremony. Invitations circulated for a private soirée, and Archer managed to get Leighton and Patricia invited, though several on the city's lighting committee hinted that Mr. Morkan's presence, while not unwelcome, might not be widely appreciated.

Just to irk the lot of them, Leighton put in a great sum of money for the fireworks display, doubling the railroad's portion and ensuring that the name Morkan & Son Quarries appeared on every advert and poster and handbill. An hour after dusk, the rockets launched, booming mortars flashed sending up cascades of green and red, light blue, a golden eagle that floated down and fell burning. Explosions thumped against Leighton's chest and addled his breath. The constant thunder was mightier than cannon at the Battle of Springfield.

Near the close of the fireworks, thousands of flickering missiles traveled and opened brilliantly above the crowd in such great numbers that Leighton could clearly see the shadows of wrinkles about Patricia's eyes and lips. For many seconds, the world shimmered in a blue light, and she seemed frozen and unreal to him as if she were an image flashed in the artificial intensity of a stereopticon. Her jutting chin and long features—in coruscating light, she was both regal and hideous. Blinking and turning from the bombardment, she smiled at him tenderly, mistaking his dismay for desire.

"We can't be satisfied with stars, Archer," Leighton said as the smoke settled around them. "We have to declare ourselves into a sky that won't take us. The soul, the afterlife made phosphoric!"

That started a discussion they carried on at the party and dance on the square. With the century turning there was much ink in the papers devoted to healing magnetism, to mediums who claimed to be in regular contact with the dead. The millennium held wonders and mystery, mesmerism, spirit knocking, cries of coming Armageddon and promises of a kingdom come.

Coloreds and poorer Whites followed the rich carriages downtown after the fireworks. The uninvited stood drinking beer from taverns and vendors. A milling mass, they watched the rich and powerful at their dancing and dining and were kept back by a vast circle of broad-shouldered thugs and concrete barriers donated by Morkan & Son. Potted shrubs of thorny Abashag threatened between the barricades. In the gas light the slick, green elegance of the thorns, the lime gray of the leaves, and the blue iridescence of the concrete gave the plaza and its swirl of music a funerary seriousness. Centered above all the gaiety and pomp, the Gottfried Tower soared, waiting to see its promise kept. Over each gas lamp loomed an iron pole topped by a globe of glass bright and thin as a soap bubble. Thick black wire ringed the square.

At midnight, the mayor rose from his dignitaries' table. He held a brass servant's bell above his head, then rang the elites to attention. Except for the murmur of the common citizens milling outside the square, the revelers stilled.

The mayor raised his hand, brought it down. Each gas lamp waned and finally was extinguished. The square fell dark. Only the Tower glowed above them, a ghastly green in the last reign of moonlight that would ever fall unadulterated on Springfield's square. After humming and popping, the wires began to shower sparks that rained down on high and low alike. Then, inside each globe, a red worm glowed, became orange, and finally white. The square blazed in a steady white glare. Those near the poles shielded their heads and scuttled for safer tables. Everyone free of the sparks applauded.

The mayor held up his hands for silence again. He had old Phelps's same gray beard, and the Colonel's long, proud face. He raised his hand in the air, and with a hiss and a flourish of fire, a rocket shot into the sky and ended in a disappointing blue puff. With a crackle, an immense bulb on top of the Gottfried Tower lit up, and there in a white halo of electric light was the brass Lady Liberty.

"The promise," the mayor began, but his timing was too quick, for his words were drowned in a standing ovation that lasted for a full minute. Blushing he gave up and resumed his seat.

When they all sat again, Leighton leaned to Archer. "See, Archer, even this is the same sort of stuff. The sun is not enough, so you build suns to signify, 'Here we are!'" Leighton lifted his glass of whiskey punch and toasted the lights. "And after the lights go down, what is there left?"

"You talk as if not a one of us had a soul to save. No breath of the Divine," Archer said. "All we have are popping lights and pretty buildings, eh?"

"Well, tell me about the soul Archer Newman." Leighton cringed a little at the sarcasm in his voice. It was too strong, and he was tired and his lungs felt taut and heavy.

At the band shell near the mayor, a new set of musicians tuned up, a family of four with a bass, a fiddle, a guitar, and a mountain dulcimer played by an elderly woman. The mayor rose again to speak. "The band from St. Louis will soon arrive, I promise. Meantime, some local entertainment."

The fiddler waved beats with his bow, each swoop matching a tap of his foot. At his bow tip, one gut strand frayed loose, floated free in a golden filament. At eight counts, the four leapt into "Run, Johnny, Run." The elderly woman played the dulcimer with great accomplishment and often the band dropped out entirely and the dulcimer swished and rang in the band shell. At times the tan wood of the instrument hummed and echoed as if it were a bag pipe, the notes of the melody unfolding like a road through the hills with twists and beautiful vistas. Leighton thought of the hills south and east of them, the Ozarks Mountains blue and black in the night. Always they would be hunched in his mind, cool lime and red clay, bristling with oak, hickory, and cedar. Dark mounds of green in day, violet in twilight, they surrounded him, protected him with a spell more powerful than a circle of salt. He thought of Galway, and the quiet of eventide, and peace and death. On the dulcimer the old woman's fingers walked like a long-armed man in miniature, stumbling, coursing, skipping from end to end of the fret board as if down a familiar slope, her other hand swishing a pick across the strings.

Without accompaniment she played "Bonaparte Crossing the Rhine." Patricia's leg pumped in time to the music. Patricia's long neck was no longer gawky, but was elegant, touched with a speckling of brown Leighton had only just noticed. Her chin rigid, her eyes intent. Moving to the music, her thigh was brushing Archer's trousers with a swish, swish. When Archer inched away from her, her leg stopped. She blushed.

When the musicians rested, Leighton resumed his talk, though Archer had his arms crossed tightly over his chest. Clearly the music was foreign to Archer. "With each day, the only thing I can imagine lasting of the soul after death," Leighton said, "is simply the story that men and women stick on that soul and it carries on in story for however long everyone's memory lasts. I used to think deeds had something to do with it, but they are subject to such distortion. One could go through life and commit nothing spectacular and the soul might be better off." He cocked his derby forward on his head and held his arms out as if reading from a newspaper. "He was a quiet man who lived a nothing life in a dull town, and his death, like his life, was uneventful and swift."

Patricia scowled at him. "You've certainly botched zat prospect." With the four punches she had finished, her accent had thickened, and after a pause, she laughed as did Leighton and Aureole. Patricia calmed. "One need only read the newspaper's cruelties on Leighton to see story sticking everywhere and mucking up real life."

Leighton squeezed her shoulder. That Lutheran Women's League had resurrected her assertiveness, and so long as her assertions were in agreement with him, he enjoyed having an advocate. She was still demanding in bed. Seeing the tan spots on her neck, the wrinkles at the corners of her lips, Leighton wondered with all her copulating whether she were trying to recapture an old love or propel a new one. Why hadn't he really looked at her lately, seen her age, these lovely spots, the earned creases of worry that never left her forehead? They had just made love that after-noon, and yet he could not conjure an image of her lying in the bed, could not even picture her gray eyes. In fact he remembered nothing about it save that afterwards she helped him find an old tie clip. How could they make love and then simply forget bliss and go on about their dressing for this occasion, which was noth-ing but foolishness and flat beer, weak punch, sulfurous smoke, and the smell of carbon amid palaver and posturing?

Archer shook his head. "There's no foundation in it. You're just mangling theology." He spoke with such flourish that Leigh-ton paused for a moment. "How can it be words or a story?" He sounded like an Easterner. "To be honest with you, if anything, this is a great big cosmic joke. Consciousness, progress, it's all a ga-lactic ultra-maroon." Archer's gaze was on Patricia as if he awaited her approval of his wit. And it struck Leighton that Archer's talk might be only histrionics meant to impress Mrs. Morkan.

A light crackled, and its wire shot fiery sparks. Archer stared defiantly at Leighton, and Leighton felt that old thrill of rivalry.

"Recall Pentecost, Archer," he said. "What was the first thing that happened to the apostles after Christ brought them the Holy Spirit? What did they do?"

Aureole rolled her eyes. "They had a cigarette."

Archer glared at her. After she stared blandly at him a mo-ment, he dealt his wife one of the pre-rolled cigarettes from his case. Patricia took one also and twirled it in her palm, blinking at it. She whispered something to Aureole, who shrugged and lit the cigarette for her.

"The tongues, Archer. They spoke in languages they never thought possible. Their souls were on fire with the very flame of eternal essence. Words, Archer. Story."

Archer waved to a waiter and had another round of punch brought. The crowd was stirring. Archer stood and shook the hands of two city officials, one of whom winked at Leighton and patted him on the shoulder. The other trotted on snoot high. Patricia's chin slid back and forth in anger.

Nearby, Constantine Ziggler was talking loudly to a group of men, most of whom were craning their necks and shoulders for a chance out of Ziggler's circle. Ziggler yammered about the *Daily Leader* and how it had contributed the money for the potted, thorny Abashag, and how the lights would attract business to downtown merchants. When much of his crowd slipped away, he excused himself for the dignitaries' table. In his hurry, he hooked his toe on Patricia's chair and stumbled.

Leighton stood, steadied her chair, then held a hand out to Ziggler. Several tables grew silent and watched the two adversaries. Leighton noticed how the electric lights cast shadows immovable as stone, and Ziggler's bearded face, his brown curly hair appeared odd in the electric light, as if someone had bothered to put whiskers on a mannequin.

"Leighton Shea Morkan." Ziggler shook Leighton's hand. "I have to tell you," Ziggler began, he looked all around him with the easy grin of an orator. He wore a ridiculously bright tie on which an angel was painted holding a lightning bolt, the symbol for the Electric Company. He raised his finger. "And I am an lover of honesty and plain talk, aren't you?"

Leighton stared at him, and said, firmly, nothing.

Aureole sniggered. By now the tables around them had unabashedly turned their seats toward the two old enemies.

Ziggler nodded. "Well, I speak brash and honest, and despite the risk of our guests insinuating anything, I must say, no matter what you do, Morkan, you make one hell of a story. Whether you're paying Negroes or enslaving them, enabling their savage criminality or riding in torchlight justice, you couldn't do a quiet thing to save your life."

"Glad you've been here to make sure people know just what to think about me."

"Well, I'm an honest man, and I honestly vent my feelings."

Leighton bowed. "We are all in your debt."

There was a little laughter, but the tension around them caused some of the men to lower their heads, and watch with eyes askance. Leighton saw Patricia grip the crenelated edge of her dress.

Ziggler leaned very close to Leighton. He whispered. "You really don't need to screw with me. We'll all go on making money. It's all just bluster to get the citizenry mad as hell and on its feet." His voice rose and he patted Leighton's shoulder and smiled at him. "And of course buying the *Daily Leader*."

325

He vigorously shook Leighton's hand again. Then he hustled away, waving to someone who ducked from his attention.

The Morkans and Newmans sat in silence for some time. Scowling, Patricia smoked. Then her gaze fell on Archer and she looked at him so languidly and for such a long time that Leighton sensed something strange, like passion coming from her. When Archer caught Patricia's glance, the look of sympathy that came over his face was so tender and so unlike Archer that Leighton felt his suspicion confirmed.

Coloring slightly, Archer leaned to Leighton. "You were saying, Leighton, what a soul was?"

Aureole nodded, hopeful that the festivities wouldn't be quashed.

Leighton took a deep breath. He let it out, lit a cigar. He could feel them all watching him with pity and sadness after the brush with Ziggler. And he detested their pity, though he let them sit that way for a while.

Finally he placed his palms on his knees and cleared his throat. "The only thing I think the soul can be is the imagination. Only in imagination do the word and the object the word embodies directly bond, and the word is so strong, we can say heaven, and the imaginative soul fashions the image." Leighton turned his tumbler against the table. "When we build, we imagine the word first—light. Then we pass that word to others and they construct, and the souls are made manifest, made flesh I guess you would say."

"What if I build a guillotine?"

"Then you have a butcher's soul."

Archer smirked.

"All right," Leighton said. "Take the Tower of Babel. All the people were of one language, one supreme set of words. All souls imagining at once in the same color of stone: 'Go to, let us build us a city and a tower.' Their souls made manifest to make them a name, an afterlife. And it is the one time God expresses a real fear of man."

Archer raised his eyebrows. He waved a waiter down for another round.

"Indeed there is the verse," Patricia said: " 'Now nothing will be restrained from them, which they have imagined to do.' "

Archer shook his head. "There is another. 'And God saw that every imagination of the thoughts of man's heart was only evil continually. And it repented the Lord that he had made man on earth.'"

Leighton squinted at him. "That proves it even more clearly. There's God fretting again about the imaginations of men. I didn't say He had to like the set up."

Archer finished his punch and added the glass to the glittering set accruing on the table. "So in the soul God granted," Archer began, "he gave us the capability to imagine wrapping a man's head with a rope and yanking him up into a tree until his neck breaks." Aureole punched him in the arm.

Leighton was silent for a moment. Maybe Archer was drunk enough to think that the past was the past, and a lovely one at that, one you could brandish at table in public. "Who cares what the fact is when we have made a constellation of it to hang in Heaven an immortal sign?" Leighton quoted Emerson back at him from their youth. Archer's mouth hung open a bit, and his eyes, their silver, seemed to cloud and fade. "It must be that evil is the simplest to imagine and make manifest. Look how crude are the articles for chaos and destruction—the meat ax, the lead ball, the pike. The rope. Maybe it takes a second store of imagination to act for the good opposing evil, to ignore bombast and glory mongering and focus on a better light?"

In their pause, Leighton surveyed the crowd. With their dark suits and bow ties, the scarves and shawls, their glittering earrings and cufflinks, they appeared to be good citizens on the whole. Then he watched Archer and Patricia again. What if for a long time, for as long as he and Judith had been wayward, what if Archer and Patricia had been together and unfaithful? The thought made him shudder and look once more at the crowd. Decent men and women, many of them unschooled, hardworking men like him. Yet they led hidden lives, sordid and secret, passions that meant more to them than any of this surface light. We spend so much time and energy in this sort of faerie glow, yet this pantomime is not what we crave, not what we hold dear. As the lights sparked, he gazed on the cruel and lovely thorns, the Abashag where darkness circled and the rabble waited. Judith's dark softness engulfed his mind and held him in rapture for a moment.

"I don't know that there's a man here with the imagination to do good," Archer said. With a mournful expression he lifted an empty glass. "To be honest, Leighton, in all this signifying, you have a distinct advantage." Then his eyes held Leighton in a malevolent gaze, the old look of the wode. "I'd give anything to have even part of one of those quarries. You are making the world they live in. And you hold a mighty son to leave it all to. Let them deride and lie about you all they want. You've mortared every joint around them, when all I have done is make airy promises, and brick façades." They all sat in silence. "I would gladly trade you places," Archer said, but he was looking intently at Patricia.

"Archer." Leighton put a hand on his shoulder. He narrowed his eyes on his rival and friend. With Patricia, he thought. Surely not. Madness! Would wonders never cease?

Voices at the tables continued in their happy murmur. Leighton sought to lose himself in the chatter. But he was aging, and the mind once locked on trouble turned the danger all about like a jeweler hunting flaws in a diamond. There was laughter, the sound of dinnerware tinking against plates. A few tables over, bearded old men were involved in a heated argument concerning the details of some Cumberland battle. There was a smattering of applause as a fiddler took the stage. But all Leighton could manage was the one dark gutter of thought—Patricia with Archer. As the fiddler tuned up, Leighton took Patricia's hand and rose, and Archer and Aureole rose with him. They stepped onto the sanded dance floor bordered by small electric lights fronting the whitely lit band shell.

"Thank God," Patricia whispered to him. But then the mayor interrupted everything and begged the fiddler's pardon with a hasty announcement of an award for some painter or bell wright or maybe some fellow named Bell Wright, who cared, after all? It was time to dance, at last! "Such philosophizing." She smiled, but then seeing his expression, she touched his cheek. Oh no, the mayor had fetched prepared remarks.

"I am fine," he said. "He's a newspaper hack like his father."

"Words, though!" Patricia said, bobbing her eyebrows and smiling down at him.

Lord, she was smart. "Have you ever. . . have you ever loved anyone else?" Leighton asked. In the fierce, faerie light from the new electric bulbs, redoubled by the white clam of the band shell, the two of them seemed suspended, removed, protected in a bright anteroom. "Patricia Weitzer Morkan, have you loved anyone besides me?"

She looked down at him with her juniper eyes trapped in their crescents. But settled in the rumples of age, her once incisive, penetrating eyes seemed tender, delicate, and suddenly far away. The mayor droned. "Oh, there was a fair one. Long ago, Leighton. An invalided soldier, almost my age, in the hospital, the old *Turnverein*. He was doomed. That kind of childish, girly love. Pure and outrageous. Unrequitable. Doomed."

He sighed dramatically. And she sputtered a laugh, then made a loud raspberry with her thin lips pursed together, a mouth noise Holofernes used to make, farting like a kazoo up and down the halls seeking his hidden chum, Gustasson.

She shook herself; the insulted award recipient, this Mr. Bellwright, frowned severely her way. Stroking Leighton's lapel, she whispered, "And you, Leighton Shea Moorken? Have you loved anyone besides me?"

While there was still much to hide this late in their lives, tonight, in such new and scalding light? "Long ago. You already know. After the war ... and doomed. Doomed."

Scowling, not meeting his eyes, she was very serious and still for a long while. Behind them the mayor bestowed a plaque on the beaming painter. While the fiddler drooped, Mr. Bellwright went on and on about what he called Practical Christianity. The drunken elite held their temples, grimly awaiting the freedom of a little music.

"A cosmic speech," Patricia said in a low voice like the gypsy impersonation from years past. She took in a small breath, and looked him over as if settling something at last. "We are fortunate to have tolerated each other so long and so ... bearably."

"Indeed." He felt warmed almost to laughter and tears.

Exhausted by the platitudes, the crowd did not even clap when the painter, who sounded Eastern and appeared educated, thanked Jesus, and his Dear Ozarks.

The fiddler craned his weathered neck as if the honored painter might never take a seat. Relieved, he grinned. "This first tune has got to be sung, but I'd be surprised if you city folk can do her. Yankees, let's not even try!" He winked toward the safely departed painter. Then he began to saw a tune Leighton remembered his parents dancing to. He recalled his mother singing it to him in a carriage above the hum of the wheels, and in the fiddle he heard her voice, and the memory of it made his eyes ache and his heart pound.

A few singers muttered the old words from the corners. Patricia gazed on them with a smile. Her arms guided Leighton in the dance, and yet she could watch the scene, while he had to watch her or her feet. Most of his life he had been in the presence of this graceful, worldly woman, and he had abused her, cheated her, condescended to her and her people, when all along he could have truly loved her and reaped a wealth of love in return. Of course she would stray—who wouldn't? The thought struck him with the force of a lead ball, and he missed a step. She pulled him true with a lift on his lower back from her long hand. "There, there. You'll do," she said in German with sweet assurance.

All around them beyond the halo of light, the thorny shadows of the Abashag tore a fierce barrier between the magic of the dance floor and the tribulations of the poor on its rim. More than a dozen couples worked a circular reel, but he and Patricia and a few refined others were dancing halting waltzes to the ancient tune. Their feet whispered and scuffed over the sandy puncheons. When the words of the song welled up in him, he blushed. But his voice rose, raw and nasal and fitting with the shuffling feet.

> Ah, Sister Phoebe, how merry are we
> As we all sit under the juniper tree.
> Put my hat on your head to keep you warm
> And take a sweet kiss. T'will do you no harm.

The fiddler nodded at him, grinning, and many of the dancers awoke, male voices croaking the old Ozarks love song. Such a blend, smooth baritones, wheezing monotones, drunks shouting the words, all following Leighton's own voice. Patricia blinked at him. And as she laughed her old ringing laugh and led him, it seemed the dark world they populated had finally turned the corner and passed into cascades of permanent light.

Judith rested her arms on her breasts and watched Holy where he sat against the rail of the Morkan front porch writing in the notebook. One of Isaac's retired hounds sighed and trembled. Over the yard, the moon was a sliver, and the stars were out in the thousands. Pops far away to the northwest, and the glitter of the fireworks spangled the air. Then she saw a perfect square of light hanging on the horizon, above the city, Leighton's city glowing as if he had cracked the ground open and starlight issued.

"Mother." Holy sat up. He turned the wick of the lantern up, brightening it. "I want to finish this journal. Never got to talk to Johnson again, but I get to talk to you."

She nodded. The journal moved her. She often opened it to hear it crackle and spent many minutes running her hands over the black indentations. When she was sure she was alone, she buried her forehead down into it, and prayed for a long time, prayed all the muttering prayers Mrs. Charlotte had made her and Leighton learn—Have Maria, Save Regina—hoping that when she raised her head, Holy's marks would make clear sense. But still they remained as meaningless and mesmerizing as frost on a window.

Holy opened the book, dipped his pen. "How many times did you lay with Mister Leighton?"

Stunned, she stared at him. The dog for some reason looked up at her alarmed, its eyes red and gooey in the lantern light. "What you mean?"

He paged through the journal. "Says here, Johnson claimed Leighton invented a garden and other things for him to do so that the house could be cleared and Leighton could lay with you as he might a White woman at his will."

Back in the trees, a whip-poor-will piped so full and hurried that whip poor, whip poor was all he told. The dog's head bobbed with its panting. A stream of drool thick as an icicle hung from its mouth. The creature seemed to be waiting for her answer.

What she was about to tell him he clearly knew. But it would shatter the mirror of glass she used to encircle her world the instant she spoke the truth. She took a breath.

"The first time was in a cave down by where they bury Johnson." She watched the wind make the turned leaves in the few oaks shimmer like flecks of gold in a dark river.

"Did he kiss you and touch you like he might a White woman?"

This was not the voice of her son, but the voice of a constable or a revenuer, polite but fast at its questions because they were all memorized and thought on a long time.

"He looked on me like he might the most beautiful White woman on earth," she said. "They was a time when his eyes said he love me. And he plow me like the fields."

She told Holy of all the years up to now, of a love that was love and not love, because it happened only in the dark or only when she and the master were alone. And she told him that he was a child of this darkness, this sweating and longing. He was a curse and a blessing. "With so many paths in life, Holy, you find you want love, and fear love, and hates love, and walk that path of love with gladness in your mind and gall in your heart. I am sorry," she said. "And I am not sorry at all."

Holy wrote biting his bottom lip, his chest not moving, as if his breathing had ceased. He looked up at her for just a second, then his gaze bore down on the notebook as on a Bible full of solace and right thinking.

I have lost my son, Judith thought. And gained what by it?

"Momma? Does it still happen?"

"Breaks my heart like you breaking it now."

332

Book 4

Easter 1906

I

ALL AROUND SPRINGFIELD AND MOON CITY, IN BUILDINGS
Archer Newman designed and built, he left himself a cubby, a
flop, or a loft, and stayed silent on this deviation from printed
plans. He trusted and used only three contractors, all matricu-
lated as lads from the last days of masked riding, and they hung
on Archer's every word and vested his secrets like acolytes before
Nikola Tesla. Buried in the real estate contract, the codicils describing dimensions, access, and ownership of these niches were
sometimes overlooked by faraway or careless landlords. Careful readers of abstracts, usually hired attorneys, called these to
attention, crossing out the strange descriptions and initialing
alongside, or circling and flagging with a waxed sliver of ribbon. Then the transactions languished until buyers' representa-
tives could corner him. He smiled and said blandly, "Another
purchaser can be found." Never did he telegraph, write, or telephone so that outside the abstract—eventually tucked away in
the courthouse, which like so many in the Ozarks might any
day burn to cinders—no other written record of these spaces
came to light. On the surface, it would seem easier for him to
retain ownership of a building and do as he pleased with all its
square footage. But then others might readily find him and he
might be held responsible to someone! In this way Archer Newman retained many options of ducking complications or making
liaisons on the quiet, such as today's with the rowdy agitator,
the blacksmith Doss Galbraith, who hated the Negro and held
many potentially useful opinions.

Archer waited in one of his favorite of these nooks, in a
foreclosed building between Moon City and Springfield, The
Chesapeake it was called, one of the owner's many follies. The
confusing, irrefutable, and infungible presence of Archer's anom-

alous walk up on the far northeast corner of the four story brick building ground a bank sale of the property to a halt. When the bank failed soon after, the Chesapeake became just one more empty shell following the 1901 panic.

His favorite smell, as it preceded a system in collapse—the agitated, cordite-like unseen fire of blocked rotors humming in a St. Louis electric motor. At the Chesapeake, Archer kept a veritable museum of electric engines, specimens ranging back to Farraday's Mercury Rotator, Double Barlow Wheels, a Sturgeon's Interrupter, and forward to Tesla's Coil and Edison's Rotors. On oak work tables the zinc electrodes, copper coils, rotators, stators, and commutators ensnared one another in hedgerows of experimental brush.

His favorite sound—the low moan of the wind caused by a window not properly framed, never completely to be shut. Winter wind circulated furiously against an ell he created in the Chesapeake. His favorite sound because when the North wind hit at anything above ten miles per hour, that skewed window moaned like Aureole the night he first discovered her. A whore in Providence. Some sailor had beaten her unconscious. Archer watched the assault from a closet where he had crawled in to sleep off the brothel's dreadful gin. With scientific detachment, he witnessed the Briton gag then pound her and stumble away. Fascinated—this would be the first human he witnessed in the act of dying—he observed her rib cage rise and fall and then diminish. Such a waste, she bore high, round cheekbones, a doll-like face, tremendous breasts, and now she would die. A pity. But after an hour of insensibility, she used both palms to push herself off the hard-swept puncheons. Scanning around with wet, brown eyes, she realized she was not in Heaven, not dead. And, naked and beaten, seeing where life had at last taken her, she made the terrible low, winter moan coming from the window now.

His favorite sight—out the window near Fassnight Creek clung a forest copse on undeveloped land that still retained the wild look of the Ozarks woods. And, even now in winter, staring deep into the tangle of oak and hickory and cedar and poison ivy and sumac and creeper to the shadowed point that from chaos truly formed the wode brought his mind's eye closer and closer to that moment of blank, black void where there was no one and nothing but only his own mighty, whirling, vicious conceptions.

In every of his secreted cubbies across Springfield, he kept two trunks beneath the panels of the floor or resting upon deal wood nailed between rafters in the attics. In each trunk two locked compartments. In the compartment oriented northeast, patents of which he proudly held several, other pending or failed patent applications, journals, sketches, drawings, and plans. In the compartment facing southeast, a duplicate set to the undiscerning eye, but, upon close inspection, falsehoods, flaws, fatal turns, mercury added befouling formulas.

His least favorite sight now came into the window that looked out on Fassnight. He reached to turn down and then extinguish the lamp. Leighton Shea and Gustasson Morkan strolled West Grand in clear, exultant communion, the father guiding the son in some matter, the son absorbing, relating back, and delighting Archer's aging rival. In the dark of his warren, Archer brooded on their promenade—were they meeting with Phenix Lime and colluding; where were they strolling? How had fate dealt him three unmarried daughters that floated like swollen airships from room to room, from bakery to café to dinner club to church then weeping to the confectionary with no callers or prospects? He had, after all, rescued a whore from sure death and an unmarked grave! O, to grip a son's shoulder with that exuberance and point to some future that was his, that was theirs together, the power of the gesture mightier than a standing wave in the lee of a mountain! And not just one son, but two, the secret son Archer knew in the Negro Holofernes Lovell. Bundled like a deadhead against the chill of the otherwise abandoned Chesapeake, he did not register the St. Louis motor's final kick at the screwdriver he had jammed in it. And in the ascent of the Morkans along Grand, he could not relish the rise of smoke and valence from the cataclysm he had made of a perfectly sound little system.

337

When he heard boots scraping the stairs, he wondered how often Doss Galbraith had thought of Leighton Shea Morkan, who loved the Negro race so well.

Leighton held the bridle to a shining Missouri mule while Holy drew a brush through its coat. Over its back rested saddlebags branded MORKAN HARDWARE, and strapped there were new rakes and shovels, leather gloves, and one of the ancient Belgian smoothbores glowing with oil.

The employees of Sunken Quarry gathered and the yards idled save for the kilns where smoke curled into the blue April sky. The Negroes and Whites waited for Leighton to name the workman of the year, a tradition just before Easter.

"Day's wearing thin, Mr. Leighton," Holy whispered.

Leighton smiled. "I don't see too many more of these for me, Holy, so I'll savor it, if you please."

Light was growing in the afternoons, lasting longer—Easter soon, though the miners shivered when the wind rose. Leighton beamed to see them, eighty-nine men in dungarees and hard-hats, machinists in their denim coveralls, firemen with bulky as-bestos gloves and stiff cloaks, blasters and powder monkeys with rubber gloves jiggling below their bristling vests and goggles set like glowing tumors in their wild and lime-ridden hair, stone-cutters in their skullcaps and long aprons, the lime casting all but the blacksmiths in gray hard skins like some dime novelist's feverish depictions of a new, space-faring navy girded for war with Mars. And that's how he saw them—warriors in a frontier war that was nigh unto won, the city makers.

In Galway, Odem was awarding a mule. And across town Gus was making a similar presentation at Dolomite Park. Leighton was proud to think that this traditional incentive passed from father to son. And there was a secret pride to stand there with Holy. When Leighton was young, Gus was his bright satellite; now in Leighton's dotage, Holy was his warm shadow. Holy whispered something to the mule and it straightened its neck to look even more a prize.

"Well, my dear lads, another year's come round," Leighton began in his booming voice. They all closed in and looked on him with affection, anticipation, and a touch of fear. He was still solid, eyes bright and slanted, beard sharp and groomed and now gray. Tucking the brush in his vest, Holy clasped his arms behind him and raised his chin, solemn and pleased to be on the platform with Leighton. "1906. Who'd have thunk we'd live to see these wonders? Man has taken flight. Man drives in carriages without horses. Man runs drills without steam. It always gives me a pleasure to point out one of you all as an exemplar. But this year I'm moved to give this mule, stores, and hunting gun to... " He paused to let them ache awhile. "Pony Dalton, Blast Captain."

The Negroes cheered and the Whites clapped politely.

Pony Dalton stepped up on the platform, clasped his hands above his head and shook them as he danced a quick victory jig.

"Hooraw, Pony Dalton," the Negroes hollered.

Pony stepped up to Leighton and settled himself, imitating Holy with hands behind his back, but his smile couldn't be fought down.

"Pony Dalton, first Negro Blast Captain at this quarry, you have proved yourself. In 1905, waste debris is down. And expense on explosives is down as well." Leighton regarded Pony head to toe. A tall Negro with smart, clear eyes and skin so black it seemed made of blue steel, a full nose and solid lips, probably not a scintilla of White in him. "But most importantly, under this man here, in 1905 there was not a single injury to any miner or powder monkey during a blast." He grabbed Pony's arm and raised it. "This is a captain who takes care of his own." Leighton handed him the bridle to the mule.

"Hooraw," the Negroes hollered once more. "Speech."

Pony held up his hands and they quieted. "All's I can say is, I ain't walking the tracks home no more. Hooraw, Leighton Morkan."

"Hooraw!"

Holy gave Pony the livery fee to stable the mule till evening, then he followed Leighton to the office. "Can you take it for the day, Holy?" Leighton asked. "Just get them settled down and back to work. And remind Pony late in the day that it's a whole new year. I don't want to see him resting on his mule."

Holy nodded and was about to go, when Leighton held up a finger. "Something for you, Holy." He reached in the desk and pulled out a hard leather box. The metal brand on its corner read DIETZGEN.

Opening the case, Holy paused and his face grew darker as he admired the engineering tools.

"Made by Germans," Holy said. "Mister Leighton …."

"Never have given you a mule, Holy. But you have become invaluable. And I'm hoping with the right tools, you will toss out the notion of literary journalism and become a true creator, an engineer."

"I ain't been to school like Mister Archer."

"And I thank God for it every day. I can teach you what to know, same as I taught those Adams boys, right?"

"I would sure cherish teaching from you." The Negro said it with such emotion and in such a quiet voice that Leighton's heart bound tight.

"We'll start," he said. "You have my word. Now get after 'em. You'll have to be me all the rest of today, you hear?"

Holy made a fist and pounded it against his open palm, an old symbol between them. In their world rock defeated paper, there was no overcoming stone.

Leighton hustled onto the boardwalk to avoid the storm of a cabriolet barreling up Summit from National. Its driver, a young Negro in a brown coat and starched shirt, was drinking whiskey from a bottle. Next to the driver another Negro in the same cut of coat and shirt swooped his arm around a busty Indian woman whose black eyebrows and cherry red lips were painted atop a caking of white powder. The two Coloreds were clerks at Hardrick's Grocery downtown. It was evening, the first Monday in April of 1906. In the hint of warming air, drinking songs already floated from the Quarry Rand. From Peale, Leighton had heard of a blacksmith name of Galbraith who was railing about gallivanting Negroes just such as these, and Peale said Galbraith sounded a lot like Leighton and Archer so long ago when they rode and lynched and roared about justice.

The boardwalks became flagging closer to downtown, stone mined just after the war, in places so worn from rain that only

340

the whitest of fossils remained joined in spectacular webs. Many of the wooden buildings had been replaced by brick and stone, though some of these bore Archer's façades, brickwork backed with cheap wooden clapboards, and pine wood frames as anterior. All down Summit he could see Archer's handiwork, could see women hustle from Archer's doors, their enormous bustles trailing, the hems of their dresses swishing.

Within a block of the quarry, the street was jammed with carriages and horses, street cars ringing and clacking as they sparked down their wires. Men wore their mustaches short now, their beards cropped as closely as his had always been. Clothes fit poorly now since the duds of city folk were store bought and made in factories instead of spun and sewn at home. Derbies were on almost every head, and the errand boys scurried in knickers and dusty coats. So many faces—Springfield was now a city.

In the square, horses and wagons were gathered at a corner smithy, where the shadow of the Gottfried Tower stretched on the Macadam. More men were drinking and jawing than having work done. Several contractors were there soliciting laborers for the next day's work. There were no Negroes. A high voice was engaged in a tirade.

"And it is certainly a fine thing to see them zipping around in carriages, screaming drunk, fondling White women. Ain't enough that they take our work and wages, but for Niggers to take our wives, why gentlemen, it's a blessing!"

There was laughter, beer mugs held high clanking together. Archer stood among the men gathered, laughing as well. A man of leisure now with time on his hands, Leighton mused. Archer's hair bore strands of silver among the red, and he waxed this as if to emphasize the silver, like fluting in garnet. Some of the men quieted as Leighton moved through them.

The tirade spilled from Doss Galbraith, who sat in a cane-backed chair. With a pocketknife he was carving an apple into crescents. His arms were knotted with trembling muscles. Galbraith rarely had soot on him, and spent most of his time at the bar he and his wife ran. His eyes widened on seeing Leighton. A slice of apple tumbled off the end of the knife into the dust.

He whistled low and long. "I don't believe you'll be needing any smithing done here this evening," he said to Leighton. "Nor any quality, White, Scots-Irish to labor."

Leighton pulled the cigar from his mouth. "Didn't come here for anything but the humor, Galbraith."

Galbraith popped a slice of apple in his mouth and pointed at Leighton with the knife. "Standing right before me here is a man who made more of our problems in this fair city than even that Jew judge and his railroad boondogglers. And to think, I read where he was the son of one of the best men that ever quarried or owned a slave, and now his son and grandson stoke the fire and tend the hearth for a quarter of the Niggers in this town."

Archer's face grew grim and he worked his way through the crowd and took Leighton by the arm. "What do you want to hear this for?" he whispered.

"I should ask the same of you," Leighton said with a smile. Frowning, Archer stepped away from him.

When Galbraith was silent, the crowd of men, sooty, dusty faces hardened from a long day at work, looked expectantly on Leighton. Some may have sided with Galbraith, he could not tell, but most he knew just wanted to see a tussle. "Niggers, Niggers." Leighton said. "Why is it always some Nigger's fault that you aren't earning your rightful chunk or missing some fun. Two years, Galbraith, you been singing this same tune."

"And why should years change me?" Galbraith asked, flushing. "They are the same in days and nights as ever, and injustice to the working man is the same as ever." He looked all around him at the men listening.

Crossing his arms over his chest, Archer raised his eyebrows at Leighton.

"Well, I forgive you then," Leighton said. "For how can a man judge himself over time?" Leighton peered at several of his listeners, then Archer. "Who here hasn't looked in the mirror and wondered at the old crow staring back?"

Galbraith stiffened. "I ain't sure what you mean. But I don't like it."

"I mean, Galbraith, pissants like you come and go. Old stones, like Mr. Newman there, and me, we are long-lived monuments."

Archer slowly uncrossed his arms as eyes in the crowd turned to him. Leighton waited for his friend to speak and even hoped he might leave the circle now and come along to have a drink.

Archer raised his chin slightly. "Though he is right that some of us stones stay long, Mr. Morkan forgets how some of us need to roll along and so avoid getting buried."

From Archer's lean features and sullen glance, Leighton gathered nothing certain. But as he tipped his cap and wound his way through the grumbling, parting crowd, he worried Archer might relish leading men to justice once more.

Gus arrived at the Galway Picnic Grounds driving one of his wife's surreys. Beneath the dining tent, Patricia lifted the flap to watch him help a pregnant Gretchen Evertz Morkan from the carriage. She had gone to finishing school in Chicago, had studied philosophy and botany, could quote Nietzsche and sometimes Gregor Mendel. Her figure was so slight, her upper body reminded Patricia of a kestrel's wing. And her second pregnancy put no weight on her save to round her stomach. With her riding goggles in her hand, she was a new age woman, her dress white with navy blue trim at the neck and sleeves, all flat, no frills, no bustle.

Leighton shook his son's hand, but only nodded to Gretchen. Patricia strode to them from the gaggle under the tent. Gretchen squeezed her hand. Little Karl, Gus's five-year-old son, leapt from the surrey and into Leighton's arms. Leighton blinked and laughed, but put the boy down too quickly, hardly knowing what to do with such effusive affection. With menacing grimaces and manly gunslinger nods, Karl and Leighton went through the motions of tugging their coat sleeves, straightening ties, combing their hair. Then with much flourish, they slapped hands against their hips, and thumbs and fingers became pistols. They blasted away at one another until Leighton clutched his heart and staggered back. Rushing to him, Karl latched onto his legs squealing with delight.

Galway was now a retreat for parties of Springfield's well-to-do. They came in a long rattling train of polished vanity, and left by dusk, their horses and brass-trimmed carriages touched with a chalky film of lime. They sat at long tables arranged under the sycamores by the creek. This being the first warm evening in April, they were out in droves. The little Italian, Domino Danzero, was wandering around with his tripod and black-cowled camera. Ziggler was there, as was the owner of the three big livery stables, all the Pearsons of Pearson's Tack, the Quinns, such a big family of Catholics.

With the house so close, Patricia ordered Judith and Holy to help her down the hill with dinner, no need for a carriage. Mother and son, servants still, sat facing the creek, their backs turned to the tables of Whites, who were eating and laughing.

Patricia brought seltzer in white bottles and whiskey, fried mutton rolled in bacon, potato salad, and a Waldorf arranged on thin crusts of pastry. She produced each from her wicker basket and set them in carefully arranged servings on china. They were devoured without pause or comment. Gretchen drank only the soda and nibbled at the Waldorf, which Patricia had topped with a sprig of mint and delicate beads of peppermint icing. Even on Gretchen these niceties were lost. She squinted intently at the conversation that passed between Leighton and Gustasson. Gustasson was discussing a group of men from a company called Marblehead of Chicago. With Archer Newman as escort, they had visited the Sunken Quarry that morning while Leighton was at Galway Quarry. They were offering a substantial sum for just the mine.

"They were surly," Gus said. "But the offer was preliminary, or that was Odem's impression."

Leighton scooted a piece of bacon around on his china. "We can clear that much in just a single shaft down there." He squinted at Gus. "Four of them in from Chicago." He shook his head. "And Archer Newman. Why didn't you ring me?"

Gus's jaw set, and his cheeks reddened. "I thought I'd better just deal with them. They seemed in a hurry."

"People from Chicago are always in a hurry," Gretchen said. She fixed Karl a cookie with butter swirled on it.

Leighton scowled at her. Patricia made him another whiskey and soda and set it before him.

He nodded. "She's right. They are. Did they visit Dolomite, or Phenix? I can't imagine them not falling for Phenix, or even Eastgate if Griesemer will part with it." There were half a dozen new competing quarries around Springfield, mostly small time operations, save for Phenix. Many of the managers and owners were here today under the sunny tent, posing, hoping to be noticed, and watching the Morkans. They had come to town from Ohio, New York, and Illinois, from Ilasco and big plants out east. On first impression, the city slick managers thought the Morkans to be eccentric hicks, but every contract lost to one of the three Morkan & Son Quarries quashed that. Soon they all wished their operations ran like a Morkan Quarry.

"I don't know," Gus said. "I'm flattered they were there anyhow."

Leighton snorted. "Did they leave a card? Where are they staying?"

Gus shook his head. There was a long pause between them. Karl's little eyes flashed between the two, and wrinkles of distress rilled his forehead. At the far end of the table a music box pinged a waltz by a Russian.

Leighton rubbed his napkin over his beard, wadded the napkin and dropped it on his plate. He squinted at Gustasson. "You appreciated their offer enough to consult Odem, but you did not keep a card?"

Gus stared at him, crossed his arms over his chest. "They'll come back."

After a moment, Leighton stuck out his bottom lip and nodded. "Fine then. Call me if they do." He drank the whiskey. "Archer Newman! 'To be honest with you!' I would never leave you out of something like this." He meant for this to sound reassuring, but it came out wounded and vindictive.

Gus excused himself to "stroll off his dinner." Gretchen followed.

"Tell me you didn't hear all that," Leighton snapped at Patricia once Gus was out of earshot. "Have you ever? That is what is wrong with today's businessmen. Insolent. No protocol. Half cocked. Ill-informed. And why would a person want to walk off a dinner good as what you just served, I ask you?"

345

"Pah," she said. "The Weitzer groused the same way about another half cocked, ill-advised, young billy goat I know. And it was not me making dinner. I showed Judit what to make. And he is forty."

He slapped his hat against his thigh and yelled for Holofernes.

Later, Patricia cleared and called to Judith. Judith trundled the basket to the house, while Holy and Karl stayed by Leighton who was shooting skeet with a dozen other men in a meadow that had been the Weitzer's. Gretchen and Gustasson walked by the creek. She was arguing with him, jabbing a finger at the palm of her hand. Patricia sat and poured herself a soda, the miraculous bubbles rising like dashes of quicksilver. She wondered if something in the soda ate at the bottom of the glass to create the bubbles. How otherwise could such fury be convinced to remain in water?

In the meadow, the men at skeet dwindled. Leighton handed the shotgun to Holy, and Patricia set the soda glass down. The palms of her hands grew chilled and wet.

"Pull," Leighton shouted.

The remaining men were staring at Holy, then at Leighton. After some hesitation, the pigeon boy yanked his string, and the clay pigeon arced from the catapult. Holy fired and missed. Karl clapped his hands.

Leighton held Holy by the shoulders, pointed down the meadow as he instructed the Negro, who still held the shotgun up, its point wavering. The other sportsmen turned away, but Leighton continued. Patricia saw the white diamond of Venus above the house, which was dark gray nestled in the trees. A tired ache glowing like sunlight filled her chest and stomach. Their lives had achieved such a lovely arc. For all his violence and insolence, Leighton had come to at least indulge her, if not love her. And he had been faithful, save for a youthful indiscretion, something more than many wives at the Galway picnic could claim. When he took off his coat, his gray pants were molded to his strong rump. She thought of him working atop her, and her cheeks flushed.

The sportsmen all lighted cigarettes and their arms crossed waiting for Leighton and Holy to leave the meadow. Negroes. He had no notion of his own society's queer, new-fangled necessity of absolute separation from them.

The skeet arced. Holy fired. The pigeon shattered. She decided she would demand her husband make love to her the moment they arrived home. Surely Gretchen would want as much. Surely the sad, plump wives fidgeting with untouched desserts would wish to feel the surgings of a rump like that.

At Alf Adams' home, Negro businessmen gathered for a dinner to honor the Morkans, Gus and Leighton. Though some of the Negroes had gained starts working at the Morkan quarries, Leighton sat glumly at his separate table in the dining room and felt unwelcome. Two Whites, two seats to their table. The Negroes assumed these two Whites, even as invited guests, wished to be treated like members of a separate and superior clan. Leighton had eaten at table too long with Judith and been covered in the equalizing gray slurry of lime working alongside Miasma Sullivan and Pony Dalton too many times to condone the new credo. Such separation efforts were more clear indications to Leighton that the end times neared once more. His Republicans recently determined that they no longer needed the Colored vote to win elections. It was time to rely on bigotry, fear, and division, just like the Democrats! Gus circulated among the crowd and received cordials due a visiting potentate. Despite Leighton's anger with him over the visitors from Chicago, pride in his son and in the young man's grace overwhelmed him, and he felt his eyes sting.

The guest list demonstrated the impressive rise of Springfield's Negro community and would have set Galbraith to pointing and squawking. With Adams were his brother Mose and nephew Walter, stonemasons Menzardo had trained, now artisans in their own right. B. F. Adams toured the rooms as well—he published a newspaper, *The American Negro*, which Leighton advertised in and read. Dr. Clark, the pharmacist; McAdams, principal of the Negro high school; Campbell, the Negro mortician; Bland, a shoe store owner; Graham, a restaurateur; the Hardricks and Tindalls and Julian Stemmons, grocers; old Will Gatewood, a freight hauler and politico; and Walter Majors, the Negro cyclist and tinkerer who built and drove his very own automobile—all wore sober dark suits and bow ties. They never

left Leighton unattended, one by one stooping to him and praising him and his son and the quarries, which were to their minds
the first major White businesses to employ the Negro and teach
skills that became opportunities. The Adams brothers had even
opened a quarry and Leighton had advised them and sold them
aging equipment. Still as they praised and thanked him, Leighton watched their full pink lips, their eyes dark as the flanks of
horses, their yellow teeth, and their wet pink tongues and felt
he was being spoken to by men from the moon. Springfield's
Negroes had nothing but usury and terrible wages for which to
thank him. Maybe he should have felt a condescending, fatherly
pride? Maybe that's what Gus was feeling as he shook hands
and nodded and squeezed shoulders? But he could not feel a
lie, could not see himself in some benevolent light. He had run
a company store, for God's sake! When had Leighton Morkan
helped any one of them save when he was forced to by law, by
guilt, or by his ache for money?

After dinner was served, B. F. Adams tapped his fork against
his wine glass and rose from his seat near the head of a raised table.

"I desire to say a few things in behalf of the better class of
Negro citizens of this community, so many of whom I see here
with us tonight. The better element of our race can easily be
distinguished from the low, reckless, ignorant, and lawless. We
stand for good society, reputable homes, good citizenship, and
service to church and city."

There was a tense silence, as if these were not words taken
up before the likes of the Morkans.

"But this recognition is slow in coming. So we honor the
Morkans, who have granted many among us a trust hard-
earned. They were, my kinsmen will attest, no easy taskmasters.
Theirs is a cruel work for hard wages. Meaning no disrespect
to Leighton and Gustasson, but change and justice took long
learning and association, times that were not always an advantage to our people."

Scowling, Leighton pulled at the callus on his palm. But
he admired Adams' frankness. He glanced at Gus, who was in
raptures at what Adams said, his mother's crescent-shaped eyes
falling softly and appreciatively on the tall Negro.

"What will it take for this recognition to become widespread? I know it will take more time, more association, even possibly more suffering of injustice. We toil for this recognition when the Negroes of Springfield have no leaders. Every fellow is his own leader. This, too, is not a credible state of affairs."

Adams raised his glass. "For now I must put my trust, guarded though it may be, in men like the Morkans. And soon I hope at such a place as this, in so fine a home, we will herald together leaders of both races and thereby help to, 'Ring out the old, ring in the new, ring out the false, ring in the true.'"

Many drank and called hear, hear. But Leighton did not. He rose and held his glass. Gus watched him with a pained expression. "I salute Benjamin Franklin Adams. I salute old Will Gatewood and Alf. I salute Principal McAdams." He pursed his lips, took a deep breath. "But I can accept none of this honor. I know what I am. I know how I employed you. For too long it was men like me that kept an Adams or a Clark or a Stemmons from becoming the leaders you call for, B. F. But now I don't know what keeps you from having leaders." He raised his glass a touch. Gus was holding his temples, his fingers so tense Leighton could see the knuckles whitening. "It is your people we should honor, for I have seen you in my lifetime sweat your ways from illiteracy and root conjuring to doctoring with science and publishing newspapers. The worst among my people, the ignorant, the vigilantes, the fearful and the fear mongers, the rabidly righteous, they have a great deal to fear from you. Let them fear. I hope you will heed my example, and take from them as I have taken from you. Show them the hard turns of commerce's wheel."

He drank his wine down, crossed his arms over his chest. Gus glared at him and gripped the edges of their little table. There were no cheers, only stupefied stares and grayed cheeks. Several tables over a white-haired gaffer with a sun-blasted, charcoal black face leaned to his dapper, stunned comrades and shouted, "There's times I'm mighty glad we can now keep them assholes separated from us generally by law. Huh? What?"

349

Inside the carriage home, Gus waited until the horses were clopping, then spoke up. "That was the most ingracious, ill-mannered thing I have ever seen you accomplish."

"One day, Gus, you, too, will become an old blowhard with no tolerance for anything but your own version of the truth. Remember me then."

As Gus stepped down from the brougham, he managed a long, calm look at his father. "Those people didn't need your truth or anybody else's. They needed a little peace, a little uplift, a little gratitude, which requires a little fabrication. After all, they were honoring us." He shut and latched the door with careful contempt.

II

BACK FROM MARKET, PATRICIA CLINCHED HER FISTS IN frustration and let fly a sound like a teapot's squall. Upstairs the beds were unmade, coffee was left cold and spilled, shirts and linens and nightclothes remained in piles.

She found Judith downstairs asleep on the library couch, so stout now she filled its end. The Evertzes were due for dinner, led by Gus and Gretchen. Though a roast was started, its fragrance gripping the downstairs, the rest of the house was dusty and cluttered, moist and mildewed.

"Good God!" Patricia hollered. "Throw open these windows at least. We don't pay you to sleep, Judit."

Judith held a hand to her eyes. "I had me an episode on the stairs."

"Of course you did, so fat." Patricia heaved up a window-pane as if she meant to flip it into the yard. She stood with her hands on her hips. "Judit, I have trouble pitying you. I have seen your gluttony." She pulled at the high lace collar of her dress and went on a rant, her voice gratng. "Leighton and I are so happy, Gus is so happy, and yet you put us in turmoil and make vis house a disgrace because he will not dismiss you out of stupid sentiment. Well let me tell you I am so mad I can't see straight. If you have exceeded your use, then a pension is arranged, and *auf Wiedersehen*."

Pacing like that and clutching her lace collar beneath her big crusty chin she reminded Judith of a snake mad to shed its scales.

"Meanwhile a beautiful piece of meat is roaring away in the oven without any basting. This house will be cleaned and cared for whether I have help to do so or not." She stopped and paced. "This is my house, Judit, and you are not well and are too old and

351

infirm to care for it, and I am too damn proud of it to let you sully it like this anymore. I cannot count on you any longer!" She tore out of the room.

Judith heard upstairs the hamper bumping and drawers chuffing open and slamming shut. Rubbing her face with the heel of her hand, she stared at the lowness of the sunlight outside. Days were slipping past. Judith grew older and fatter, and the Dutch grew so thin now she was like a young boy again, with fight in her, no end of energy, and mother fits like that one. And she took away Judith's place in the house. Oh, the Dutch was an even more nettlesome bitch when she was right. Judith was too old. Her body stunned her as if it all were some strange float bladder expanding and gagging her. She was in the house not for money—through thrift she had saved in an old hackberry's cavity enough money to buy her another house and maybe the land again if she needed. She was there because she wanted to see Leighton every morning, and see him home at night. And she wanted to spite the Dutch, who did not now how little she mattered to Leighton. If there was one thing she was going to ask God in the end days, which were soon coming, it was what in the nation were You thinking when You conceived them Germans? Her greatest fear now was that she would pop her heart while scrubbing something of the Dutch's rather than burst it in pleasure like she wanted with Leighton on top of her. She closed her eyes and imagined cradling Leighton's tired head in her lap.

After the Evertzes had gone, Judith was gathering ashtrays and wine glasses in the study when dead Michael Morkan appeared in his old armchair. He blinked at her behind icy blue spectacles and stroked his chin. He was wearing Johnson Davis's coat and a favorite black slouch hat. Three train tickets stuck out of his pocket.

"Come for my grandsons, Judith," he said.

She dropped an ashtray and fell back against an end table, toppling a lamp. She spun and grabbed the lamp, righted it. He was gone.

She backed out of the room and shut the door. It was Thursday evening, guests gone, dinner finished, dishes cleaned and put away. She bunched her dress and struggled up the stairs to find Leighton and tell him of the appearance of his father and the awful sign he bore. Leighton would take ken to it; the Dutch would call it nonsense. The door to the master bedroom was shut. When she rested an ear against it, she heard a soft moan. Slowly, she lowered herself to her knees, hesitated, then placed her eye at the keyhole, and peered grimly through. Patricia and Leighton lay on the bed, Leighton on top of her, his arms planted beside her. They were both nude and covered in the flood of sunset through the western windows. The muscles of his ass bound and quivered. Patricia grabbed him by the shoulders, and with a grunt he rolled off of her. She crawled on top of him, planted her long, pale arms on the sheets. She arched her spine and threw back her head. Judith's heart bunched like a fist—every meal she ever cooked was in those two cavorting, all the water she brought, the hogs she slopped, the linen as clean as they thought their hearts were, all of it from her, and there they moaned into each other, in a room brighter and more sturdy than any she had ever called her own. The motes that rode the air about them were gold and ruby, sapphire at the edges of the sunlight. She wadded her dress at her groin and pulled, her teeth set in a snarl. Patricia shivered, and Leighton, whom Judith had swaddled and cleaned of filth as a newborn and eventually brought into her own thighs as a man, gurgled at the Dutch like a babe. Judith eased away from the door. She released her dress. Then, touching her finger to the sweat beaded below her nose, she clumped down the stairs in broken jolts.

In the yard bathed evening pink, the oaks drizzled pollen that dusted her skin yellow. Birds bantered in the trees. Frogs chattered and whistled. At her cabin, she took Holy's journal, lately neglected, for he thought it finished. She tucked it under her arm and went back to the Morkan house. In Gus's old room where Patricia had taught Judith to spin, Judith opened Patricia's wicker sewing basket. She scattered fabric on Patricia's worktable, dotted the fabric with spools of thread, some of which she tore at and unraveled. Then she placed the journal in the basket so that it stuck out from the lid.

† † †

Patricia woke late, dressed and wandered the house cradling a cup of coffee to her chest. A wonderful soreness ached at her groin and made her shy away from the blocks of white sunlight blazing from the windows. The vessel of her heart was as warm and delightful as the cup she held. If she paused and leaned against the banister and closed her eyes, she could imagine and relish Leighton's hip bones which she had found last night among all his meat and muscle. She had cupped them like two geodes. Below the staircase, from the stone floor came a cool, lime-laden wind that was rich and wet, and she could smell him and touch him. She adored those gray lumps below her, a floor she detested as a young bride. It smelled as he did at night, as his breath did in the morning, as her arms smelled after a day in the house. She leaned hard on the banister, the wood popping pleasantly, and stared down at the stone landing—such sinister gray lumps they had been, but no longer. She let the draft dampen her cheeks and fill her nostrils.

How he had shivered and grimaced, enamored with her body, hers! All thoughts of Archer she wiped away, as if happiness were a warm, wet cloth and life a chalky slate. Strange that so late in life she and Leighton would find such bliss. She was fifty-four, yet she desired him with an appetite greater than ever before. Surely the rise of these appetites must be a secret among women. She thought of marriages among her peers, couples who had grown contemptuous of one another—Archer and Aureole especially. What a pernicious trick God played. Just as a woman's skin begins to wrinkle and sag, the man becomes wizened, distinguished by his gray, and desirable. And just as the woman's appetite trebles, the man's turns itself away. Except for her Leighton. From an open window came the sound of a robin cackling across the yard.

Leighton's desire kept pace with hers. She was never refused. Even now, sore as she was, she would be brought to ecstasy to hear the front door slam, to hear him call her name, to hear his brogans on the stones. She found her eyes full of tears and laughed at her gush of sentiment.

354

In her sewing room, Judith had strewn spools and fabric all across her worktable. Taking a seat on her stool, she shook her head, began winding thread back onto the spools. When she had them all arranged in a row and all the fabric folded once more, she lifted her basket. Resting it in her lap, she removed a book sticking from its lid. Judith's silliness, she thought. Or Holy? The book, a tattered old Morocco binder, was Holy's journal, the one she had asked him to keep when she was teaching him to read and write. She turned it over and over. It had been brown, but was now green and black, water marked and battered. When she opened it, it crackled, its pages brittle with the imprint of lettering. She smiled, spread the book on her lap, smoothed her fingers over her student's writing.

She pressed the page again, flipped several, found the title page—A JOURNAL OF INTERVIEWS CONCERNING MISTER LEIGH-TON MORKAN AS TOLD TO HOLOFERNES LOVELL.

Above each entry was the date, time, and place of interview. The respondent was then listed and underlined. Each entry was titled in block letters. The titles were intriguing: "MISTER LEIGHTON MORKAN DEFENDS JOHNSON DAVIS FROM TEXANS BUT JOHNSON SAYS IT DON'T SIGNIFY." She sniggered. "MISTER LEIGHTON MORKAN MURDERS A HORSE." She read a little of this one. It was a confusing story of moving some freight or other with burnt horses and Leighton stealing a gun from his father to put a horse from its misery. She smiled at this noble, sad ending.

She found an entry called "MRS. JUDITH MORKAN LOVELL TAKES MISTER LEIGHTON MORKAN TO A CAVE." Intrigued she read.

> HE WAS WATCHING. HE WAS WATCHING EVEN AT TIMES HE DID NOT KNOW, BUT HE WAS WATCHING JUDITH. I COULD SEE IT FROM THE DEW ON STONES AND THE SILVER OF THE CREEK. SHE SHIFT IN THE CHAIR. AF-TER THE BATTLES, IT WAS LIKE A HARD WIN-TER IN THE MIDDLE OF SUMMER: THE WHITE MORKANS WAS ALWAYS HOME WITH NO WORK, LAZING AROUND, RIDING INTO TOWN TO SEE HOW FAST THEY COULD GET BACK TO MAK-

ING MONEY. THEN MOST ALL THAT WAR DEAD
MISTER MORKAN WAS AT PRISON AND IT WAS
JUST JUDITH AND LEIGHTON MAKING HOUSE.
WE WERE LIKE ANY TWO MARRIED FOLK
WHAT SHARES THE SAME PROBLEMS AND JOYS
AND COURSE THE SAME ITCHES. I TIRED OF
ALL HIS LOOKING. THEN HE MARRIES THAT
DUTCH FOR NOTHIN BUT HER DADDY'S LIME
AND LAND AND NO LOVE. YET HE STILL LOOK-
ING AND I DECIDE IF I TAKE THAT BOY TO
THE CAVE AND LET HIM SOAK A LITTLE AND
GIVE HIM WHAT HE'S LOOKING AFTER, THEN
I DON'T HAVE TO WORRY WITH HIM LOOKING
FOR MUCH LONGER. WELL, I DONE EXACTLY
THAT, AND LET ME TELL YOU, THEY WORK
THE SAME AS US IN MANY SPECKS SAVE JUDG-
ING. COLORED MAN, HE KNOWS WHEN A MINE
IS PLAYED OUT. WHITE MAN, HE COME RIGHT
BACK TO THAT OLD MINE. FACT, JUST LIKE A
WHITE MAN, HE FELL RIGHT IN LOVE WITH
ME AND HAS STAYED THAT WAY EVERY DAY
IN HIS LIFE, EVEN NOW, SPITE ANYTHING BE-
TWEEN THE TWO OF THEM.
MISS JUDITH WHISPERED THIS LAST AND
THIS THE ONLY TIME THE INTERVIEW HAS
HEARD HER WHISPER.

Patricia paused and read again, her mind parsing the words
as it might figures on a merchant's bill that ended with an unexpected and colossal sum.

WASN'T NO DUTCH SITTING UP FEEDING HIM
LISTENING TO HIS PALLABER ABOUT THE
NEGRO WHEN THEY TWO HADN'T SPOKE SO
MUCH AS "OUT OF MY WAY" TO EACH OTH-
ER IN A YEAR. WE WAS SOMETIMES IN THAT
ROOM WHERE THEY NOW PUT UP THE CRIM-
SON SASH; WE WAS SOMETIMES IN A TOOL-

SHED, ONE TIME JUST OUT IN THE FOREST,
MANY TIMES DOWN IN THE CELLAR FOR
YEARS AND YEARS CARRYIN ON. LEIGHTON
BROUGHT A WORLD OF SORROWS ON HIM-
SELF. TO LOVE ALL THAT TIME AND HAVE NO
WAY TO SAY IT ALOUD.

It had to be a lie. She ran her fingers across the page.
The ridges in Holy's script seemed ragged like the serrations
along a file. Surely Judith could not say such things to her
child. Holy invented them. But then Holy memorized most
of what he knew. That was why she asked him to interview
and handwrite in the first place, so that he could increase
his practice and repetition of handwriting skills without
the necessity of invention, but with no model to mimic. His
handwriting in exercises did improve, and so she had seen
no reason to read the journal. So far as she knew Holy was
interviewing Colored house hands and she could not fathom
there being substance in what they said.

She flipped forward, stopped. The sunlight that had been a
lovely square on the floor now fell like a yellowed shroud across
the hardwood, and in that square every blemish shone—gashes
and scuffs from brogans, pitchers dropped, divots where the
spinning wheel had been exercised. The pages crackled like a
stoked, steady fire.

MRS. JUDITH MORKAN EXPLAINS MISTER
LEIGHTON AND THE ENERGIES: HUMORS
WITH SPIRITS
I MADE FOR HIM A PROBLEM. HE COULDN'T
KEEP UP HIS FASCINATIONS IN BED ABOUT
THAT SKINNY DUTCH WIFE THAT WON HIM ALL
THAT LAND.

The sob came from her as if something had landed suddenly
on her from above. She did not hear her cry, and was aware of
only the spearhead of heat and pain that gripped her neck and
spread down her sternum.

WHAT WAS BEHIND THIS PROBLEM WAS OUR
TIME IN THE CAVE AND ME THAT HE STILL AT-
TACHED ALL HIS VISCOUS ENERGIES TO. HAVE
THEY EXPLAINED THE ENERGIES TO YOU? I'M
SURE THEY HAVEN'T. THERE ARE THREE SORTS
OF ENERGIES—VISCOUS, WHICH IS BOTH OR-
NERY AND CRUEL AND VERY FLUID. SPIRITU-
AL, WHICH IS BROUGHT OUT BY CHURCHING
OR SOLITUDE. AND MINERAL, WHICH CAN BE
DRUNKENNESS FROM ANY SPIRITS OR ILLNESS
FROM BAD FOOD, AND SUCH LIKE. ANYHOW,
LEIGHTON STILL MAY HAVE NO VISCOUS EN-
ERGY TO SPARE HIS OLD WIFE. BUT I TOLD HIM
THAT ALL HE HAD TO DO WHEN HE WAS SER-
VICING HER WAS TO CLOSE HIS EYES, THINK OF
ME, AND IT WOULD RISE LIKE THE SUN, DIDN'T
MATTER WHO WAS UNDER HIM. WELL, YOU CAN
TELL BY LOOKING AT HIS FACE, THERE ARE A
SHIMMY OF WORKINGS ALWAYS UNDERWAY
BEHIND THEM EYES. AFTER SOME YEARS, HE
LEARNED ONE OF THE DARK SECRETS, I RECK-
ON, AND YOU MIGHT WRITE THIS DOWN, BOY.
HE STILL HAS LOVED ON ME EVEN THIS YEAR SO
LATE IN LIFE. YOU CAN LOVE ALL YOUR DAYS
SOMEONE WHO'S NOTHING BUT A WORKING
OF YOUR MIND, AND BECAUSE IT'S YOUR MIND
THAT DOES ALL THE LOVING, YOU MAY NEVER
NEED TO LOVE THE REAL PERSON ANY BETTER.

Pushing with her thumbs, she eased the journal away from her until it fell, chattering and open, to the floor. She sat blinking at the folded fabrics and rows of spools, the silver needles. All that wool she and Judith had spun together. She could see in her mind's eye Judith's plump and pale palm, the part of her skin most like Patricia's, but anointedly oily, perfect for the binding of old wool with the new. Oh, God, how Patricia had tried and then taught the son... and now this. She plucked a size three needle, which she had used to mend denims. It was machined so that the inner lip of its eye held a sloped edge that was blued like the end of a chisel. A diagonal stripe of light crawled along its silver skin. She knocked the ball of a tear from her nose and sat back. The needle stood vertically between her thumb and index finger, its eye framing the sage-colored pages of the journal on the floor into a delicate fang. Her life, all her passions, what she had built, taught, spun, and woven, ceased to make any sense. She felt as if she had rushed into a room with great purpose, then after a long time standing hopefully and eagerly she found she had no answer for why she came there. And that superfluous visit was her whole life now. Her mind stuttered like a wheel that's thrown its band, and when she awoke, as from a stuporous dream, she had no idea how much time was passed.

Downstairs Judith was scraping something from a pan in the kitchen and the noise sizzled along Patricia's spine. At the banister she hesitated and considered what an astonishing spectacle she would make if she threw herself down the stairs, a tall tree flipping down a mountainside. Not at the house at least and not such a mess. Jesus.

"Judit," she said, crossing the kitchen. The Negress's back grew stiff.

Patricia held the journal up. "You left this. You've made a mess in the sewing room with the basket."

Watching Patricia, Judith released the handle of the skillet as if she were relinquishing her hold on a weapon. She rubbed her hands in her apron.

"My boy sure can write, can't he?"

"Why, Judit?" She paused, her mouth dry. "When you were getting away with it, eh? If you love him, if he loves you, truly? Well then, haven't you ruined it all by bringing the wife to understand?"

"I am old. Ain't you said so? Pretty soon I be too old and fat for loving. For laying in pleasure with My Leighton." Judith whispered it, and her words hissed like a knife through paper. "I just wanted you to know, since you so keen to have old Judith sent home, who really has been in charge of this house, who made it go."

Patricia set the journal on the kitchen table. "And to think, I worked past misgivings and my own bigotry and taught you to spin and weave and sew, and taught your Holy to read and write. Now see how I am repaid."

Judith tilted the old skillet. The bottom, from so many burnings, was brittle and oxidized and held now a caldera of molten lava fissures in an oil black sea.

For just a moment Patricia thought Judith might come at her with it, and then Patricia wished the Negress would.

"I ain't about to let you take the one truth I know away from me, and that's his true love," Judith said. "You ain't really loved nobody and nobody has loved you." She let the skillet drop with a clatter. "I wish I was sorry for my big part in that, but I just can't bring myself to care no more about it. Your life's been a lie you didn't even know you was telling."

Down at the riverfront the German nurses and teachers would take their lunches where the Roma performed puppet shows. Soiled puppets battered and tricked one another, and a music the gypsies made came grinding up from a music box their greasy daughters turned and turned. That music fluttered across Patricia's mind. Metal teeth down in the hurdy-gurdy so out of tune that the puppets all seemed inebriated weaving to it. Patricia imagined sinking the needle or better a knife deep into Judith's stomach from which Holy sprang, marker of Judith's truth. "You are through for the day, Judit. I want you to head home."

Judith blinked at her. "I ain't through. Got dinner to make."

Patricia shook her head. "Not tonight, Judit. It is Good Friday, and I feel like cooking our Leighton his dinner."

Judith's eyes widened and she looked Patricia up and down. "You know I'm right, now, don't you." she said. At the back stoop, she glanced once more at Patricia, who shut the door.

Patricia watched her from the kitchen window, then from the front porch until the Negress unlatched the wrought iron gate at the bottom of the drive. The stones of the living room floor humped in gray mounds. Nights when it stormed, she came downstairs and set a low-flamed lamp in the midst of this floor, like a sea roiling, in their patternless landscape of large and small, ovoid, square, and circular. Only an Irish mind could envision such primitivism and make it function. Where had she failed him?

When she boarded the streetcar, she walked down the aisle, her hand passing from rung to rung. She sat and folded her arms on her lap. Sparse were the passengers, farm help off early for Good Friday going downtown. They stared at her, though she couldn't fathom why. Her, an old Dutch woman with a jaw like the heel of an infantryman.

Tidy white clapboard houses became brick façades—Archer's work—two-story, then three, and four, high glass windows, smokestacks and water towers, wall advertisements that touted powders, pianos, Widbin & Fox, the Evertz stove. At the many stops there boarded onto the car white-crusted plasterers, pimpled lard refiners, molders black with foundry sand, carders smelling rich with lanolin, the paper curtain hanger, deaf millers from Schmooks, glaze-eyed reelers, yeasty brewer's apprentices, gritty broom makers, the aparian. What lies were they telling their loved ones, their mothers and wives and daughters? Where were they spending the Friday dollars crisp and secreted in their pockets? The young wheelwright there with a bouquet of flowers in his lap. Were those bachelors' buttons, mums, and lilies for a love recently kindled or one he was about to extinguish? Rather than one youthful indiscretion, why not tell a lifelong lie? Why be faithful to a barren old crone when you could carouse all night with a fat and randy Nigger servant?

She looked down at her hands, at the old work dress, the one speckled with all the colors of mordant and dye—that was why the farmhands stared. Changing from her peignoir at the house she did not recall, and why did she chose this? One farm hand pushed up his new straw hat with the nub of his arm, the rest of the arm lost to some accident. With a pang, she remembered Theodor, so long ago. What chance had she at true love now? She had made full confession to the Church of her one transgression with Archer. Yet now that healed wound seemed like life's one great missed opportunity.

The streetcar halted at the North Springfield train depot. All gathered their truck to depart, yet she lingered.

361

"End of the line. Pardon and rise," called the glum, little conductor stalking the aisle in his blue uniform. "Pardon and rise. End of the line."

When the car cleared of all but her and the conductor, she stared as he slammed the benches forward. How they pivoted so smartly on their rockers, seats becoming backs, bottoms becoming tops! The oak slats, shiny from the comings and goings of so many souls, dove and vaulted as if life could go that way—suddenly, officially, end of the line. Pardon and rise. And then all a change of direction and back toward the start.

"Tokens and seats. Make yourselves to home. South Town—Division, Calhoun, St. Louis, Mt. Vernon Road, Rockbridge, Galway—South Town Springfield, all stops."

In front of Patricia, he held his hand out for a token. His hat was so big on him, he appeared to be blinking from under a blue boxtop.

Near the benches for the St. Louis-bound trains she bought a copy of *Anzeiger des Westens*. The gray type might as well have been Cyrillic for all she could focus on it. She noticed an advertisement for a nurse at a Lutheran hospital in Grendel, Texas. A locomotive chuffed twice, building steam.

Across the platform, Archer Newman smoothed the collar of a tan greatcoat folded over his arm. A heavyset man in a black suit was jabbing the air with his cane. He had no coat. A Northerner, for him the occasional April chill was no menace. Archer placed his hand, those long, lovely fingers over his chest, and spoke words of honor as the steam jetted at his feet. He bowed, then helped the heavyset Northerner onto the train.

"Patricia?" he asked. "Or should I say, 'Mrs. Morkan.'"

The newspaper rattled as she tried to fold it. Her eyes burned.

He sat down quickly and dropped the greatcoat over her shoulders. "What in the name of heaven?"

"Not here," Patricia said. "I must go."

"What's happened? You're dressed like a gypsy. What's all this?" He plucked the shoulder of her many-colored dress.

"Archer," she said. She took his hand and squeezed. "You have a carriage? Not here." She released his hand and shielded her brow. She began to weep.

362

He pulled the coat close to her, glared at people who began to gawk.

Wasn't that the old Dutch, Mrs. Morkan? Crying at the train station in Mr. Newman's coat? And handsome Mr. Newman holding her two shoulders as he led her to his wagon? Holding them tight as if that lank old Dutch could crumble like ashes and sticks? What could be wrong, maybe her husband? Judging how we saw him a'shouting at his Coloreds at the quarry just this morning, surely not? Or maybe? And where was Mr. Newman and Mrs. Morkan headed? Driving like mad Kansans for the gambling district?

At the Carbory Hotel's back door she could hear ragtime music playing inside the saloon. There were two Negroes smoking cigarettes under the red awning where rotting wooden tables were set for Coloreds to get refreshments. These two wore straw hats and brown vests and trousers with spats. Giving Archer half a look they kept at the pair of dice they were rolling and rolling.

"Say, Bristle, get Big David for me, will you, and two whiskey coffees?" Archer requested. He rubbed her shoulders tenderly and the great coat sagged a touch. "Is this okay, dear? Big David will have us a suite and we'll talk with no one to bother us." As he spoke he shot a glance down the alleyway and clutched her close to him as if he wished to hide her.

Bristle tossed his spent cigarette in a high arc and bolted into the Carbory.

In the suite Archer did not light a lamp. Instead he let the late afternoon divide the room into swaths of yellow crossed with gray velvety shadows.

A knock and the coffee arrived and Archer set this aside. Patricia hunched in an overstuffed green chair that smelled of cigars and vegetable soup.

"Now. What is the trouble?" Archer asked.

Below them, a dealer called out a large bet and crooned the possibilities. "Bet the hardways. Acie Deucie, nice and loosey."

I am sitting in a suite above a gambling hall, she thought, where harlots have fornicated and fools have passed into eternity drunk as lords and children have been misconceived. It has come to this.

"Leighton has ... I have found something."

"Something more than what you already know? What could be more a thorn than that half breed stumbling around reciting everything he reads?" His eyes narrowed. "A woman of your ability and family. How have you ever endured that walking humiliation?"

She shook her head but shuddered at how clearly Archer saw this, likely felt it all along. "What Southern woman hasn't put up with such? So many families with Black help, you know there are Patricia Weitzers on every city block. The mind can talk the heart through acres of male weakness. "

Archer frowned at this.

"What I know is worse."

"Well what, then?" Archer asked sitting on the bed and placing a hand on her knee. There was care in his eyes, surprise, and concern even.

When she said nothing he handed her the coffee and she held it in her hands against her chest. "All along." She stopped, held the cup to her lips, then lowered it. "All along he was, even in these last few months, he has been carrying on with that old cow Judit as if she were a White woman, one to have an affair with." She steadied. "Beyond an affair. Archer, they were in love. They *are* in love. I was nothing in my own home."

Archer removed his hand and leaned back. "I see." He watched her as her hand trembled holding the coffee. "Isn't that a ripe state?"

She sipped, then gulped rapidly. He handed her his own cup.

"Archer, my life up until this point has been a lie that I lived out as truth with all the conviction my heart could muster. What would you say to that? To such a state?" She drank deeply of the second cup.

He crossed his arms over his chest. "It strikes me that some time ago I offered you a chance at living a richer life, one maybe even more full of love. But you said that was folly." He sat forward, leaning into the light made a gauze by the curtains and crimson by the sun traveling down. Before her was the young Archer Newman, shrewd, with a hatchet-shaped face, auburn hair, and a powerful body.

"Don't be cruel. Not now. Please, Archer."

"You refused me. You let me love you, and then refused me in favor of him." Archer paced with his hands locked at his back. "He has taken a lot from me, you know. Your Leighton. There was a time when I protected this city, when my word meant that trade could go on, that building could commence, that peace and ease was assured for law-abiding citizenry." He counted these on his fingers. "He took that away. He dealt with the very devils that built Moon City under my nose and erased what I was as city engineer, made me jack fixit of a town nearly gone to seed. He took all that away."

She set the coffee aside and watched him as he raved. There was in his eyes the same delicate fang of hate she saw through the needle in her sewing room. He hated Leighton. Down her ribs a cold ball of sweat fell like an ice crystal.

"And then he took you away."

She hid her face. "When you were with me, were you merely striking back?"

She heard him stalk across the room; then he stooped to her and raised her chin to force her to look at him. "God damn." He released her, then touched her cheek. "I have never met a woman like you." When he saw her expression unchanged, he waited. Very softly he spoke. "At first my want was revenge, you are absolutely right. But then as I came to know you, I realized just how fortunate Leighton Shea Morkan really was."

He knelt, hesitated. To her shock, he buried his head in her lap. "I have wasted my life," he said.

For a moment she sat stiffly. And then her hand fell to stroking his hair. A smell from its strands, fennel and claret, some cologne of his, rose up in a wave.

"My God, Archer. Oh, my God."

They stayed that way for a long while, until the electric lights snapped on, until the noise of merriment downstairs subsided and the piano player stopped his raucous plinking. Giggling, cursing, clattering, rustling below—the dancers readied. Soon cabaret!

He raised his head, and she cupped his cheek in her hand.

"How did you find out?" Archer said. "Tell me you didn't witness...."

"Ssh," she said. She ran her thumb along his jawbone and felt the crackle of stubble starting there. "It is the silliest and saddest of things. I read the journal of Holofernes Lovell, the boy I taught to read and to write. It was all in there. Years of it." For just one moment, confessing all that to another, she felt lifted, free of it, like a lark over a sunny mountain, and no failing in the valley below was greater than a speck.

"Holofernes," Archer said the word low in his throat.

"Yes," she whispered. It all came crashing back. "What do we do now, Archer?"

He was still. She let her hand fall.

"Where were you going?" he asked. "At the station this afternoon?"

It was not what she expected. She wished him to say, Well, I have a plan, now that we know you do not need to be loyal to him for certain. "I was thinking of throwing myself under a train," she said.

He frowned. "See here. None of that," he said sharply. "You are free. You can go anywhere. St. Louis. Freistatt. Hermann."

She plucked his shirtsleeve. "You will go, too?"

He shook his head. "We had a chance, and that is over, and we are old, and we have squandered." Reaching for her face, he touched a thumb to her tears and they vanished in his dry skin. "Let me take you to the station. I will pay for whatever you like. And I will tell him only as much as he needs to know."

Below the room, the sish, sish, sish of the cymbal recalibrated time. A trumpet began, like a small animal crying inside the walls.

"Archer, that is not what I want." Feet pounded, and men's voices roared.

He gripped her arm. "Come. You are tired. If I cannot take you to the station at least let me take you to Vanderhaus at the synod office and he can shelter you. It is a reveler's Friday. Listen to them."

Music erupted once again and the craps dealer called, "We got a debutante and we're having a comin' out party. Roll 'em, toots."

She did not know the streets the wagon was taking, but the way Archer hunched as he drove told her he did not wish to be seen. A horse blanket itched at her arms and shoulders and she pulled it close.

"Which is it, train or the church office?" he asked.

They were north of old town nearing the tracks, coursing into a grove of ash trees that whispered in their uppermost leaves newly unfurled.

"I don't want to go anywhere without you," she said plainly.

He took his eyes off the team and stared at her.

Before he could speak, a black shadow dropped from the tree and onto the lead horse. Another shadow fell between them onto the seat, then yanked Patricia off the wagon. She hit the roadbed hard and shouted. Another bandit dropped from the trees onto the wagon, which Archer urged on and sent barreling away. She screamed. And the bandit on her grabbed her by the throat and tumbled with her into the brush along the railroad tracks. The bandit, with his black, enormous hands, pounded her against the gravel of the rail bed, then thumped her head once against a rail tie. The gypsy's music whirled with the ragtime.

Next she found herself walking along the railroad tracks, but to her horror, the low amber glow of the city was behind her. She lurched. Surely, she thought, the tracks went north and to the station and to help. But she had come too far and nothing but darkness lay ahead.

She was cradling her numb arm, and she could feel her lips throb, massive and swollen. The back of her head felt as if some-one had emptied a pan of warm grease on her scalp. She turned to where the sky yellowed up above the lights of Springfield.

Walking so long it seemed. There were the ashes. There was a dark rider on a horse stepping towards her. The flash of a star on his chest. Poor Archer. She had only once failed Leighton Shea Morkan, and then never again. Even after she learned what real temptation meant. And Leighton and that beast had made her life one long lie. Moaning, she could not yet make the fist her mind conceived.

"Oh, God. Here she is." The policeman dismounted and gripped her arm.

Other policemen moved their horses near and overshadowed her.

"Is it true, Mrs. Morkan?" one asked. "Was it Holofernes Lovell?"

Wind through the trees, hot, gusty, wet, like blood on the breath. In the lantern light, the verge shivered, and on one branch of a rowdy Ozarks chinquapin bobbed the grackle, lit and vigilant. There are two paths, up or down. His violently purple head curved to turn upon her one onyx eyeball circled in the most perfect halo of copper. What surged over her she knew was her mother's vision, at long last.

Two paths!, commanded the wind. You know the right. Obey!

The Holy Spirit lifted all the new leaves of Easter in one single, shirring note.

Repay the love of your Lord. Forgive and turn away from sin.

A rider, a mounted shadow, void against the lanterns the officers held. "Who was it, Mrs. Morkan?" A black fang with the copper light of Springfield blazing round him, offered himself. The needle's eye. One dark rider of vengeance opposing the wind, defying the light. "Who?"

"It was he," she said. "Holofernes Lovell."

III

LEIGHTON STABLED HIS OWN HORSE. ONE OF THE CORRODED hinges to the barn door was holding on by the grace of a single square nail. He leaned on the door, loving the creak it made. All at once he longed for the house and Patricia's touch, the hurried kisses she gave if Judith were present. Johnson Davis dead. Gus married. Holy grown. Judith an old woman. After all this time, sentiment could warm him and make him feel he and Patricia had really achieved something like love.

At the ell of the house there were no lights lit, and there was no smoke from the kitchen stove. He opened the door and called for Patricia. Chill air crossed the mud room and touched his neck and face. He found the house empty and most of the windows still shut as if it were morning. On the kitchen table was the old journal Holy kept, his literary pursuit of Leighton Shea Morkan. The handwritten book was open to a page on which someone was very vividly describing Leighton's fornication with Judith.

He flipped pages until he found the beginning of this. It was dated seven years ago. If it were Holy interviewing Judith, then he certainly captured her voice, her mystic nonchalance, her sarcastic sensuality, her honest longing. The more he read, the more he was sure the writing was from an actual interview. And there were other accounts of recent frolics and assertions of his love for the Negress. Holy had questioned Judith; Judith had answered; and now Patricia had certainly read this, an account of how a Negress taught him to tolerate making love to his wife, and then how a Negress kept his heart all the days of his marriage to Patricia. Inside he felt a jolt as if some cable tethering him together snapped, jangling as it unwound. He stared for a long time at the pages, wishing their presence were some nightmare, and he might arise free and into the waking world so sweet and safe moments ago.

Where would she go after reading this? To the church? To the quarry? He should have passed her on the ride home. He went to their room, paused at the bed, slid the rug about with the toe of his boot. Last night, Maundy Thursday, they had loved there.

As he rode through town, the darkened windows of shops glowered down on him. A streetcar dinged past, and in it, the receding passenger stared at him as if Leighton were someone the passenger knew. Sparks exploded from the car's pantograph illuminating the façades of buildings for an instant. In the blue flash, the walls and windows of the flickering buildings created a decrepit canal in which only the wooden car moved like a river ferry run from its cable. The passenger's face brightened, then she was borne away.

He entered a street where electric lights hummed from black iron poles. A deputy on horseback galloped by, saw him, then swung his horse around. He rode up and removed his hat, scraped it against his thigh.

"Mr. Morkan?" He leaned forward. "Let me take you to the Sisters of Mercy." He swallowed, the Adam's apple bobbing on his gray neck. The Sisters of Mercy was a hospital downtown. "Your wife's been attacked by Coloreds."

"What?"

"We're out looking for them. They'll be in jail before the night's over."

They rode at a clip for the hospital. Groups of men with lanterns were roaming the streets. Some had cudgels; a few had drawn weapons. Those that recognized Leighton removed their hats.

"Is she alive?" Leighton asked the deputy.

"She's hurt, sir. It's a bad situation. The doctor will explain." He nudged his horse. "And Galbraith and Mr. Newman got the whole town in uproar over this."

At the hospital, a policeman took the tether to Leighton's horse. The deputy who had escorted Leighton bowed his head. "I promise we'll get them, Mr. Morkan." He rode off toward Happy Hollow.

A nun led him to an office where a doctor and the sheriff, Shane Peale, were waiting. The doctor cleared his throat. "Mr. Morkan, I won't mince words. Your wife's likely been violated." His brow furrowed, and he took Leighton by the elbow and led him before an armchair. "I am terribly sorry."

"I thought she was attacked, robbed, whatever." He did not sit and shrugged the doctor's arm away. The room was dark and the air close. It smelled of alcohol, quinine, and urine.

Shane Peale stepped beside Leighton. "She was attacked, Leighton, and Mr. Newman along with her." His sideburns were gray, and his face was a reddened map of exploded veins stretched thin down to his sharp jaw. He had been elected term after term on the notion that he was a war veteran and a great Federal scout. Whenever a juicy case went unsolved, he was defeated, then re-elected when it remained unsolvable. "Near the northwest tracks. Over the Jordan."

"With Mr. Newman?" Leighton asked. "Why were they out there?"

Peale raised his eyebrows at Leighton but gave no answer.

"Take me to her."

A long open breezeway with a high ceiling housed the ward. White partitions created an aisle and beneath each partition were the wooden feet of bedposts and the foggy hems of habits passing. Along the walls, a system of steam radiators clicked and popped. As the doctor led them across the ward, bands of heat gripped their cheeks, only to be blasted away by cold drafts.

"You see them spiders, sister?" A drunken voice croaked from behind a partition. The doctor muttered something to himself, wringing his hands. The back of his neck beaded with sweat, and his crumbling collar was a dingy yellow.

In the far corner, the doctor paused and held back the curtain to a partition. "Mrs. Newman is with her," the doctor said, "for strength."

Patricia's face and neck were so pale they appeared blue. She held herself rigidly, one arm in a splint. Only the animation of her eyes broke the illusion that she was a corpse. A crust hung at the swollen corners of her lips.

"I've given her a good deal of laudanum," the doctor said.

Leighton nodded and stood beside her bed. Patricia blinked, laid her head to the side so that she could see him better. Her lips retained a flat line, and the way she held her chin reminded him of the haughty girl who had ridden an oxcart to the Morkan house long ago to beg.

He removed his hat and knelt at the bedside. "No need to speak."

She stared at him, her eyes narrowing. Her face appeared thin, the skin of it stretched so that the nose was sharp, the eyes sunken.

"Nod if you feel well enough to have me here," he said.

She remained stiff, staring at him. An ache spread under his Adam's apple and his eyes itched. After a moment, he raised his hat, paused and watched her, hoping she would stop him from leaving. He placed the hat on his head and made ready to go. When his hand shook, he clasped the edge of the bed.

"Leighton?" Aureole whispered.

She was sitting in a chair by the bed, her hands clasped in her lap. Her color was rosy, and Leighton wondered if this peril set her to running a fever.

She looked up at him, her big eyes blinking. "Have they caught them?"

Leighton shook his head. "They don't know who 'them' is." He waited wondering how indelicate he could be. "Is Archer here?"

Aureole lowered her gaze, then shook her head quickly. She glanced at Patricia. Patricia's eyes were wide, her forehead creased as if she expected something more, something painful, not of Leighton, but of Aureole.

"I have to tell you," Aureole said, still watching Patricia, "Holofernes Lovell was among them."

Patricia closed her eyes, the lines of her forehead creasing even further.

"Holy was attacked as well?"

"No," Aureole said, her voice pained and sharp. "He was her attacker."

"Can this be true?" Leighton asked Aureole. "Who says this?"

She glanced at Patricia again. "Patricia recognized him."

372

"Is this truth?" He asked Patricia, still gripping the covers and mattress.

She remained rigid. Then she nodded, and turned her head away.

When Leighton faced Aureole again, she cringed just enough to make the shoulders of her gaudy dress rustle. The radiator hissed and popped as hot water filled it. The air in the partition tightened.

"Why was Archer with her? And where is he now?"

Aureole looked at him, her face doughy and crowded with wrinkles of pain. "Archer found her at the train station and was taking her home."

"Patricia. Holy was on a delivery, for Strafford. Are you certain?"

Patricia remained with her back to him. The part in her hair formed a pale blue worm, like an old scar. Beneath it was the sure answer, untouchable, irretrievable unless she spoke.

Slowly and loudly, Leighton repeated, "Are you certain?"

"You have no rights to ask anything of me any longer," Patricia said, the laudanum dulling her tongue but intensifying her voice.

Holy had never once been violent around him. Addle-headed, gentle, he fainted when Johnson died, shielded his eyes when calves and colts were birthed.

The curtains parted and Gustasson entered. Gus touched Leighton's shoulder. He wore a broad-lapelled spring suit of light tan and was dressed for the gentlemen's club. "It can't be Holy, not like Peale says." Gus's voice was an urgent whisper.

"Let's let them discover that," Leighton said. He raised his hand, but then refrained from touching his son.

Gus removed his cap, knelt to his mother's bedside. "I'm so sorry."

She did not stir.

"Let's let mother rest," Leighton said.

Gus gripped his mother's bed sheet, then nodded and stood. Taking him by the shoulders, Leighton jerked his chin at the partition. After a second look at his mother, Gus followed his father.

Peale stood when they entered the breezeway. He moved apart from them, kept his head bowed. But Leighton could see him lean toward them as they began to talk.

"Listen," Leighton said to Gustasson, "I want you to go to Odem and get Holy's whereabouts all day long. Take the sheriff with you. If Holy's innocent, Odem is where to start. But it's time we leave your mother alone."

Gus's face darkened.

"Mother says this was Holy?"

Leighton nodded. He confirmed all of Gus's questions, yes, Archer Newman was with her. Gus muttered, his eyes ranging about.

Leighton touched his arm. "Are you up to this? The sheriff can go alone to Odem's, but," his voice dropped. "I want one of us there."

"Why don't they start by grilling Mr. Newman? How do they even know it was a Colored man along those tracks?"

Peale had his arms crossed over his chest, his head still bowed, but his eyes caught Leighton's. He raised his chin and faced the two Morkans.

"Sheriff?" Leighton waved him closer. "Can you answer that?"

Peale nodded. He licked the tips of his teeth as he took Gus by the arm and led the Morkans far away from the partition.

"The deputy of mine that got to the scene first found Mr. Newman a good deal away from Mrs. Morkan and beat badly, but standing walking around his carriage, which had throwed a wheel and lost the team." His lips flattened in a thin line, and his eyes dulled. With such a slim mustache, his lack of expression made him appear as if he were reading from a page. "Mrs. Morkan came a'walkin' from the tracks, very disoriented and very far from Mr. Newman. Mr. Newman had no other names for the Negroes and had no number he could put on them but three, and the one that attacked Mrs. Morkan he insisted was Holofernes Lovell. When questioned, Mrs. Morkan confirmed." Blinking, he gripped his jaw, moved it side-to-side. "Meaning no offense to you, Leighton, but I can't see how any man who worked even a few minutes at your quarry could leap on a woman and crack her head good, wrestle with her, yet leave not a speck of lime on her." He nodded at Leighton, who had not changed his lime-crusted coat since leaving the Galway Quarry.

Gus dug his heel into the floorboards. "So what really happened?"

Peale shrugged. "Someone beat your mother."

"And so you are looking for Negroes based on the testimony of two citizens, one who has had her head cracked and another who should be keenly embarrassed at being with then abandoning a married woman to wander the tracks?" Gus asked. "One of these Coloreds you suspect is as close to us as family." Gus leveled his eyes at Leighton.

Peale sucked a tooth. "You been out this evening. You seen your townsmen. Galbraith's got them all riled up. They're out with pistols and their meanest hickory. We're going to have to bring in some likely suspects or it's going to be a long night."

"That's preposterous," Gus said.

Leighton touched his elbow, shook his head when Gus glanced at him.

"Peale, who gave these men authority to be armed?" Gus asked.

Peale wrinkled an eyebrow at him for an instant, his lips and face flat. "Some are deputized to find the culprits. But you see Archer Newman has deputized some on his very own." Peale stepped to one side and spat a brown squirt pinging into a bed pan. "Welcome to democracy, young Morkan." He fixed his Stetson on his head. "I'll wait in the priest's office for whichever of you wants to go chat with Mr. Odem."

Gus glared after him. Leighton nodded his head toward the exit, and he and Gus stood on the steps facing the Street. A knot of men tromped past. They were drinking from bottles and shouting at one another. "We won't stand for it!" "It stops here!"

"Gus, you need to get a hold of yourself or you'll make a worse mess of this." Leighton dug in his pockets and found his last cigar. "Peale knows what he's doing. He's a smart man."

"Whose mind is right in tune with the mob." Gus's jaw was thrust forward, his teeth clenched. Under the light on the building's exterior his skin was pale, dotted with freckles of red. He was a man now, broad-shouldered, a slight double chin since his marriage. His gray eyes were pinched.

"He has the testimony of two witnesses," Leighton said.

"I don't trust Mr. Newman."

"I don't trust him either, but it was your mother identified Holy as well."

375

"Mother is a woman."

Leighton glared at him. "Your mother has been assaulted." Gus's eyes dropped. Two deputies on horseback cantered past. "Let's take Peale to Odem's. I imagine it will be morning before we can take mother home."

Patricia had closed her eyes when Leighton returned to the partition. Aureole looked up from hands clasped as if in prayer. What does a whore pray for, Leighton wondered, and how does she pray? For I could use the guidance about now.

"She sleeps," Aureole said. She stood and gathered her dress and walked to him. Watching Patricia from the corner of her eye, she spoke softly, "Leighton, you know all my days in Springfield I have been faithful to Archer."

He watched her face closely.

"Leighton are we …" her voice quieted, " … are you and I being lied to?

He touched her shoulder. An old woman now. All played out, heavy and sagging, and likely her husband, whom she had long tolerated and pampered, had rewarded her by rollicking with a gawky, dry, old, Dutch biddy. "I aim to discover the truth. And thank you for staying with her. She never gave you your due."

Before departing, Leighton slipped a policeman a fiver to keep watch on them.

He and Gus and Sheriff Peale took a streetcar to Locust Avenue in North Town where Odem lived. His shirt collar undone, his white chest hair bristling, the old accountant told them Holy could not have reached North Town and the bridge at Jordan when Mr. Newman claimed he had. Odem did not have his prosthetic attached. At the bottom of his right sleeve, the broadcloth was folded in a neat closure like an envelope.

Peale rested his elbows on his knees, locked his hands together. Leighton marveled at his hands, long fingered and corded with veins close to the skin. He recalled those same fingers clasping a trigger, recalled the gun snapping at bushwhackers running through the dark woods when they were drunk with bloodlust. When they were just boys.

"The receipts will bear it out," Odem said. "He'd of had to have a team of thoroughbreds at top speed. For two hours."

Leighton sat at the edge of his cane-bottomed chair.

Peale nodded at him. "What are you thinking, Leighton?"

With the palm of his hand he ground at his chin, and his whiskers rasped on his callous. "The truth in this…." Leighton began. Blank tired faces stared back at him, waiting. "I feel like I've put on a pair of busted spectacles. Everything's mirrored back at me. No light forward."

Odem and Gus frowned. "Meaning what, Papá?" No answer. And then for a full minute they sat in a tense silence turning all the terrible news in the hearts.

Peale's gaze scoured each of them, their shoulders, chests, and faces tan in the gaslight spilling in from the street. "Mr. Odem, can I have your promise that you'll talk with no one concerning the nature of what I've asked you, most importantly, no attorneys and no journalists?"

Nodding, Odem looked at Leighton, then looked away.

Peale sighed and rose to stand at the edge of the porch. The streets were quiet. "There ought to be music from down on Commercial. On a clear night like tonight you can stand on Bolivar Road and hear pianos." He turned to Leighton. With the city lights behind him, the sheriff was a black void that blocked out the tan street, the twinkling gas lamps, and electric lights.

"Leighton, I don't have to tell you how important your own silence is. And Gus's. Please understand." He removed a kerchief, blew his nose, and stuffed the kerchief in his back pocket.

"There is a lot of this that's beyond our control," Peale went on. "There's folks roaming the streets. Even my deputies are pretty hell bent. And you know what the papers will be full of tomorrow."

Leighton strained to listen to the night beyond the porch. Only the happy noise of robins in the soft maples. He imagined the men he had seen stomping around with bludgeons and lanterns. He could invision them in their saloons, under the fitful light of corner booths, tumbling the word *Nigger* between them until it became a sharpened spike. These were the contractors

377

and workmen who came to him every day, negotiated in something near good faith, built the city's buildings, walkways, and culverts. They were the day laborers, hostlers, the stablemen, mechanics, linemen for the power and light.

Peale asked if Mr. Odem would take Gus in and wait for a spell. With a dark glance back at Peale and Leighton, Gus followed Odem inside the house.

The railing creaked as the sheriff leaned back against it. "Leighton, why is your wife claiming that Holofernes Lovell assaulted her?"

The question made him catch his breath. Leighton pushed the toe of his boot hard against the slats of the floor. "Recently, a family secret was revealed to her, one from long ago, an indiscretion she found painful, I'm sure. Involving Holy. And Holy's mother, Judith. I have no way of knowing for certain if the two incidents are connected."

Peale pulled something from his shirt, and Leighton saw the flicker of a pocketknife carving tobacco. Holding the black lump of tobacco against the steel with his thumb, the sheriff lifted the blade to his lips. He chewed for a moment, watching Leighton. "If you see Holy before I do, what will you tell him?"

"What do you want me to tell him?"

"To leave town."

Beyond the porch rail, the city's stillness was palpable and thick as if a tremendous snow had fallen.

"What will you do if you find him before I do?"

"I'll have to arrest him." He moved off the railing and stood at the stairs leading to the street. "I'll do everything I can to protect him, but…" He gave a dismal laugh. "Not long ago, I would have feared repercussions from you and your night riders." He stood with his head bowed. "Does this have anything to do with that?"

"I doubt it very much."

"What are Newman and your Patricia hiding?"

"I am not sure what to make of their being together."

Peale spat, and the holly tree at the porch's edge rattled.

"Are you hiding anything for them?"

"Peale, I don't understand this well enough yet to hide anything."

"Fair enough." Peale removed his hat, ran his fingers through his hair. "I pray you find Holofernes Lovell first."

Leighton watched him leave, then stepped back inside Odem's house. Gus was standing with his hat and coat on. Odem had his head bowed, a fresh drink in his hand. Leighton apologized for Peale's briskness, but Odem waved this off.

"He's a lot sharper than he was when we were young," Odem said.

Leighton and Gus said goodnight and thanked Odem, then took one of the mule trolleys that ran after dark. Gus sat across from Leighton who insisted on seating in the very back of the empty, eight-bench trolley. He gripped the bottom of the trolley bench, his arms stiff, his shoulders hunched.

Leighton cleared his throat. He spoke at a whisper so low he had to lean toward Gus to communicate. "Gus, the sheriff understands your concerns."

"From what I've heard, my concerns are pretty well founded."

Leighton nodded. "This is your mother, Gus. Let's not talk outside of the family."

"Holy is family to me."

"To me, too, but…"

"Don't give me that."

The mules clopped. The city crept past. The driver hunched to light a cigarette.

"None of them are family to you," Gus said.

"Where do you get that idea?"

"You fucked Judith like she was a sheep, and the seed you left forced her to marry Isaac." His whisper was sharp and voluble, like filthy water slapping distant flagstone.

Leighton stared at him. From under the canopy and columns of the trolley, gaslight swept in squares that expanded, narrowed and vanished in perfect intervals. They passed a gaslight, and Gus's face shuddered in a slow, bilious yellow strobe.

Leighton watched the back of the mule driver's head for any sign of listening. Blue tentacles of tobacco smoke probed around his ginger hair and crimson cap. "How do you come to know this?"

"Holy shared everything with me. Including his journal."

The black windows of buildings gaped like abscesses in a cavern wall.

"I don't ask you to do anything for my sake," Leighton said. "But for your mother's sake, please trust me that Peale can and should handle this. It will be resolved. For your mother, Gus."

"My mother is a neurotic from a failed family whose marriage left her so confounded and alone, she looks to a madman like Archer Newman for comfort."

Leighton felt his chest and arms tremble. He clenched his fists, waited for a moment. "Will you please let Peale handle this?"

Gus glanced at the road, then the trolley's floorboard. "If I find Holy before Peale gets him, I'm going to tell him to leave town."

"Well, stun me like a beef, Gus Morkan," Leighton said. He crossed his arms over his chest. "As if I won't tell him the same."

Gus stopped the driver. Along South Street, the panes of mansions glinted yellow in the lamplight. Gus stepped down from the trolley, paid the driver.

"Holy didn't do this," he said, turning to Leighton once more. "That much is clear to you, isn't it?"

"It was clear even before we talked with Odem."

Leighton watched him walk alone under the lamps, beside the looming turrets of the still mansions. Out in the night, he could hear the weather vanes creaking and yawing like the wood and metal of spectacular riverboats edgy at their moorings. That street his son ascended, that formidable wealth, he and Archer had built that whole luxurious world there framed in the gaudy, tasseled canopy of the trolley and lit in gaslight's sallow splendor. And Gustasson strode up a street that was about to be ripped asunder in riot and hate, and Leighton in his exhaustion saw the whole landscape of his Springfield afire, just as the fire-eating bigots running the newspaper desired. Howling at every crime, they stoked a blaze knowing but denying Pierce City could happen again. Weather vanes and mullioned windows and Italianate stone arches, vanity of vanities. Rejoice in thy wife in this life of vanities, all the days of thy life. O, God, that and many vows he had failed.

Leighton eyed the driver and stepped down from the trolley, the iron step creaking. "Who are you? And how do you vote?"

The mule driver turned wide blue eyes to Leighton and removed his boxy, crimson hat. "I am Pole from Chicago. Down on train." His accent was very thick. "I come here, work for strike. I don't care where I take you or who you are speaking to. I am nobody."

Leighton tipped him handsomely. "Now, to Happy Hollow, and don't spare 'em."

The Hollow, normally rowdy with music and block-long parties on a spring Friday night, was silent. Doors and shutters were fastened. Negroes in the streets stole along with backs hunched and purpose in their gait.

He stopped the trolley at Tiny Dalton's, a two-story prow house with a porch neat as a Dutch garden. Pony Dalton answered the door, which opened into a dim parlor. There by candlelight with sticks and knives in their hands were Tiny Dalton, Miasma and Prism Sullivan, George Tyree, and Brim Coker, all Blacks, all big men, the best of workers.

"You sure got great big old balls coming here," Pony said.

"Sure as I'm living."

After hesitating a moment, Pony pulled him into the house. He removed his hat. The Negroes began folding and sheathing their knives, hanging the cudgels on the loops of their overalls. On a little card table square in the midst of the parlor there was a bottle of bourbon glowing by a black candle, bourbon opened but none of it drunk, its amber light bobbing in the room and coloring their skins as if the candlelight sent out waves of syrup. A pyre of huckleberry leaves smoked steadily, and dice were down, a one and a five up, an inconclusive answer.

"If you here to get us to help you catch anybody," Pony began, "you best turn around and head back."

With his bottom teeth showing, old Miasma shot Pony a look that would have stopped a hound on the trail, but Pony kept his eyes on Leighton.

"Holy is innocent. You all know that same as I," Leighton said.

They gaped at him.

"What I'm about to ask you, I want you to keep close to the vest. Do not take to the streets armed. This is no night for posturing."

381

Grumbling and accusations, but Leighton held up his hand. "What I'm asking you to do is save Holy, please. Find him, shelter him, then get him as far out of town as you can. You understand if the police find him he will go to jail and so will anyone with him. They will say he is safe in jail, but boys, I fear my townsmen ... I fear there'll be a mob. You remember Pierce City." He paused, then added quietly, "Holy is very dear to me."

When his voice wavered, they all froze, and their faces changed from hard and clenched to looks of shame and blank surprise. They glanced at Pony.

Pony stood undecided. On the card table the huckleberry leaves sputtered and an orange ember flared and circled. Finally he said, "We do that, Mr. Morkan."

Near the hospital a deputy stopped Leighton in the street.

"Sir, there's newspapermen from both papers and a couple from the St. Louis paper's bureau at the front door. Do you want to avoid that?"

Leighton thanked him.

To dodge the press, the deputy led him two blocks around and they entered through the back of the Sisters of Mercy. And there Comstock of the *Daily Republican* was waiting. Leighton tried to bull past Comstock, but the burly journalist clutched Leighton's coat. "See here, Morkan. I would hate to holler out and bring them out of town boys." With his mustache and round face, Comstock always reminded Leighton of Teddy Roosevelt, happy to be furious.

Leighton stopped. "Comstock. My wife. This is family."

"Yes and she's changing her story around or the police are doing it for her. Police are saying it appears she isn't dead sure it was Holofernes Lovell but she knows it was a squat, yellow-skinned Negro." Comstock waited. "Don't let the jackleg police write this story. Bunch of sore Democrats! Let me talk with her, and I'll write the truth, Morkan."

"You'll play hell," Leighton said.

Comstock raised his eyebrows. "Refuse and I will play hell indeed."

In the ward, he asked an orderly to wake the livery boy, and he rented a surrey. He bundled her in every blanket the hospital could spare. Outside, she shivered. He paid the driver double the fare even before they'd left and told him to keep it slow. They rode without a candle in the cab. And Leighton stepped his horse alongside, watching his wife tremble through the carriage window.

At the house, Judith helped pull the blankets from the surrey with a frown that was practical and glum, as if this were nothing more than an annoying late night arrival.

The laudanum and the ride put Patricia to sleep, so Leighton slung her over his shoulder. Through the ratty old work dress, his hands touched the knotted bones of her spine. Her head and torso bounced as he walked. In their room, he laid her on the bed. Then he fired the stove and worked the coals furiously until it blazed. When at last he turned from its orange light, her eyes were on him like two ovals of galena.

"Will you tell me what has happened?" he asked.

Her eyes closed.

He sat on the bed and brushed her hair back from her eyes. "If you do not clear this up, Holy could very well be lynched." He listened to her breathing, then he squeezed her arm. "Patricia, do not punish him. Punish me."

Her eyes popped open for a moment. "*Reue empfinden*," she murmured, and he did not understand. Her arm was small and cold in his hand, the skin soft and loose and aged. In the flickering motions of the coal fire from the stove's grate he felt the world humming around him, spinning from a hub of sin he had crafted. Consequences whirled above him and bore down. In his hands, her arm seemed slack and dry as a rope.

In the kitchen, he found everything straightened, and Holy's journal gone.

Outside, Judith stacked wood near the back door, carrying just a stick in each hand. Sprigs of blue hair escaped her bonnet. Wrinkles crossed her cheeks and eyes. She was puffing and sweating, steam rising of off her.

"There was a notebook in the kitchen," Leighton said. "Where is it?"

Judith stared at him, her cheeks glistening with sweat. "Took it home."

"Did you set it out? For her to see it?"

Around her eyes, the whites had become yellowed, even brown in patches. She looked ancient to him standing with the stove wood in her hands.

"Why did you even have it out?"

"Learnin to read."

Leighton snorted. "There are hundreds of books in this house."

"Ain't but one book written by a Negro."

Leighton clinched his fists in his pockets. "Can you read it yet?"

Judith looked down. "No. But I will. I will read it. It's by my own son."

"Your words are in it. You know what the hell it says because you told him." He pointed back at the house. "And she read the damned thing."

Judith held the two sticks of wood like cudgels.

"And now Judith, your boy ...." He stopped. "Our Holy may end up in jail and it's entirely likely there he will die lynched by a mob."

Judith did not move but looked down on him with her eyes wide.

He stepped close to her. "Understand me. Holy is in a great deal of trouble. And you are to blame."

She rose up on her toes when he neared as if ready to clobber him. "What once go in the dark has to take its turn in the light."

"Well, stand there and blow, will you? Your boy may just die, and I hope you'll still feel risen up and righteous about the truth and all the magic future you can see then."

"I didn't ride me into town. I didn't find me Archer Newman to lay with." She set the firewood. "And I ain't the one holding out a lie on what happened."

Leighton clasped his hands before him, and for the first time in a long while Judith saw him worry. "You realize our Holy is in mortal danger?"

She scraped the bark from her apron. "For something he didn't do."

"Do you know where he is?"

"Likely with them boys from the Transfer Company. Running, hiding."

"Good," Leighton said. "I will do everything in my power to keep him from harm."

"You had better." She lifted a lantern and walked slowly for her cabin.

IV

WHEN LEIGHTON ARRIVED AT SUNKEN QUARRY, ODEM WAS already there, stove lit, electric lights burning, newspapers spread. Odem had disconnected the phone, too, leaving the tar-covered copper wires to sprout from its back.

"Come here, Emil," Leighton said, pointing to the chair and the child's wagon where the old, sun-yellowed prosthetics waited.

Odem complied, and Leighton sat slowly, rested his forehead against his accountant's shoulder. Catching a whiff of lye and the sour hint of last night's bourbon, he took hold of the prosthetics. Odem must have slept late, for he had neglected to saddle soap the leather straps this morning, and they were brittle.

Odem sat stiff in his age-old position of need. Working the small brass buckles with his crusty fingers, Leighton tried to find calm. But peace was nowhere—there on the table the newspapers were spread, their ink staining the air. When the cold hasp wouldn't meet the hole punched for it, Leighton's hands began to shake and his vision blurred. A sigh escaped, one he was not even aware of. And it shocked him when Odem, always so still and mortified when assisted like this, raised his good hand and grasped the back of Leighton's neck and pressed his aged employer's forehead to his shoulder.

They sat that way for a long time, Leighton choking and weeping and Odem holding him firmly with his good arm, not speaking. And then Odem released him and pushed him back gently as if to say, "Enough." Breathing deeply, Leighton returned to the task, forcing the hasp through its lime-crusted hole and pulling the strap to. When he straightened his back, their eyes did not meet.

"I thank ye," Odem whispered.

"And I you."

"There's the papers."

Leighton glanced at them. "You know, Odem, all these years I read them things, eager for business, jealous at another's fame. Feel like I passed through a veil."

His head bowed, Odem lifted the *Daily Leader*, then, beneath his whitened brow, looked up at his boss. "Afraid?"

"Dismayed."

"There a difference?"

"May you never know the difference."

With his forehead creased Odem traced the *Leader*'s story. Then he looked up at Leighton. "Holy's your son, ain't he?"

On the cliffs one of the Negroes rang a hand drill at the stone, and it was a tentative, lonely, expert peal, the search for the seam. "Yes," Leighton said.

"It ain't any of my business but that must be something awful for Mrs. Patricia to understand."

"I reckon." Leighton stared at him coldly, but Odem did not turn away and looked at his employer with entirely new eyes. In his firm, old face was a new challenge. "Odem, I know full well I own a lot of blame for all this." Leighton looked down, and his hands were clasped before him. With his back bowed, seated there, he was suddenly reminded of confessional in St. Louis long ago. "A body can live in lust, practicing that sin so frequent that. . . well, it no longer becomes sin. It becomes routine, like talc in the hair, like oiling a gun. But then there rises something to question you, and you look on the whole of your life." He opened his hands, peered at them. Only the rumpled gray.

"What do you aim to do?"

It took him a moment to answer. "When we hit starting time, I want you to pay the men a day and send them home save for Junior, Calvino, Scheer, and Kelso. Have them load the train with that Bolivar order and send it. Then arm them and guard the gate."

Odem stared at him. "Pardon me, Leighton. But don't you want to head home? Forget all this. We'll handle it."

"There's no good at all in me being home. Let's leave it at that." His shoulders slumped. "Send Menzardo's boy to find out where Archer Newman and Galbraith are." Then his voice fell. "If mob's start out there, Odem, we have to keep hold of the powder and dynamite at all costs. That goes for Galway and Dolomite as well. Call Galway and Dolomite. Make sure every boom shack key is in our hands. None leave. Clear?"

The walls of the tunnel glistened with water. Leighton sat on a square slab of stone. A lantern flickered on the spot where the gray faded and became the ugly red of worthless chert. He had to decide whether to abandon the tunnel for a new one or blast onward. And a problem such as this was a blessed diversion. He could roam the streets and outskirts looking for Holy. But he knew the Dalton brothers, the Sullivans, the Negroes he met last night were the best possible huntsmen. His fingertips ran across the fan of a clam shell in the stone, lines so perfect the fossil seemed to be a machined decoration. Harder and far less friable than lime, chert held its fossils like a stubborn man clings to every grudge. In the light from the tunnel's mouth, a shadow closed on him. He hoped it was Menzardo's boy or Odem. The shadow hesitated.

Leighton turned. Peale stood in the water holding a mining lantern. His shirt and the front of his pants were wet with gray muck as if he had fallen. The open end of the tunnel was a blazing yellow square.

"Holofernes Lovell is in the jail house. And two other Negroes," Peale said. The whole tunnel quietened and closed, and the surface world, its light felt far away.

"Who's with him?"

"Deputies I can trust."

Leighton snorted.

"Leighton we have until the evening papers to get you and Mr. Newman to drop the charges on Holofernes and get him out of town."

"I drop them now. I dropped them last night."

"Well, to the courthouse, let's go."

Menzardo's boy, big and olive skinned like his father, came striding down the tunnel splashing. "Newman is preaching fire at Doss Galbraith's."

Peale looked down. In the water around his pant legs, rings the color of tarnished silver hovered. "Is Patricia well enough to come to the courthouse or the newspaper?"

Leighton shook his head. "To hell with the papers. I drop the charges, and we get Newman to do the same."

Peale's voice fell. "All of Odem's testimony checks out. The fellows at Strafford confirm it. And Cooper at Pickwick Transfer is right adamant that his boys weren't anywhere but at work. But Leighton, there's city cops involved, who don't give a shit 'cause they're gone with the new mayor. The heat is on me. Otherwise I'd run Holofernes and them boys to Christian County and keep them the hell away through the 4th of July. We need Patricia to change her story, loud and fast."

"Well, one at a time. Newman first."

At Galbraith's, men were drinking and looking grim. With their brows mashed they reminded Leighton of disgruntled children whose fathers have clamped a hand to their heads to steer them. From the back, all their hats, yellow new straw, created a shoal of pebbles in a creek bed. They milled like children, their attentions wavering from one red-faced orator to the next. In their center, wooden crates, upended, improvised a stage.

The crowd, almost all White, bottled up traffic, women in floating bustles and severe traveling dresses, clerks and laborers with their coats off, their suspenders pinching the backs of their white and tan shirts into billows. Leighton forced his Percheron into them, and they parted grudgingly.

"When will there be justice?" Archer called out. "You have read the papers, citizens. It's all indecision and excuses from our city police and election pandering from our sheriff."

Peale moved his horse alongside Leighton's as the crowd grumbled.

Seeing Leighton, Archer crossed his arms over his chest and raised his chin. The crowd quieted, some glancing over their shoulders at Leighton then back at Archer sensing the troubled polarities between. Young boys scurried about, elbowing each other and pointing. "That's him," one exclaimed. "That's the fella whose Dutch got it." "Hush," said another.

389

With the crowd a little quieted, Archer's tone fell less strident. "When a brute, White or Black, attacks and ruins the life of a White woman, we believe in swift justice."

Cheers. Amens.

"Courts mean only indefinite delay and fail to protect defenseless women of the South against such outrageous crimes."

Listening to Archer's words, watching the crowd's brightening eyes, Leighton sensed that old, terrible current, still intense. Archer held them spellbound. Already from their newspapers they were filled with terror at the criminal, animal menace of the Negro. His words incited a well-worn chorus already croaked in Fayette, in St. Louis, in Pierce City, a noisome, pedestrian ballyhoo for blood in defense of Southern womanhood, in the name of order. Yet that was their magic—they were not Archer's words alone. Instead they were as well the prayer of a multitude of Whites, the psalm whispered when wells of fear and stores of simmering hate conjoin. Archer, still bearing a black bruise beneath his eye, a cast on his wrist, was the mouthpiece praying out loud the rage the crowd stoked in its heart. Rage of the laborer and clerk—Archer gave them trajectory and blinded them to their real enemies, all for power.

"We are beleaguered, beset by a barbarian already inside the gates," Archer crowed. "We are no lovers of violence. We are lovers of decency."

These citizens were not the fringe. They were the button stampers and die cutters, wagonwrights and farmhands, charcoal sellers and butchers. And some were his own White quarrymen. This was Springfield. These were his townspeople, the men and women he did commerce with every day of his life, and Archer could herd them as easily into a mob as a drover drives his oxen to water.

"There is nothing left for Southern men to do except to handle the guilty."

A shout hurrah from man and woman alike. Hats ripped from heads and swirled.

Peale leaned from his horse. "No ground to gain here."

Leighton edged the Percheron forward so slowly its steps became regal. Parting, the crowd fell quiet. "It's Morkan," someone said. "Let him talk. Let's hear Morkan."

He fixed his hand on his hip, raised his old frame erect in the saddle. With his gaze he dredged the crowd. The bone-gray crescents burned beneath his eyes. Solid ovals of meat and muscle crystallized under his coat. He knew full well the figure he cast. Here was the Nigger-driver, the tyrant, the old Federal, the company-store miser, the lover of a Yankee Dutch, a Black Republican hammerhead mounted atop a horse fit to drag swords from stone. He let the image work on them.

"If we were truly Southern men," he said, turning slowly to Archer, "I would call you out and shoot you in the street like a dog, Archer Newman." Dead quiet from the crowd. The elders drew back. "But this is no Southern city. This is Springfield. We are Ozarkers. We know where the hell we are."

The crowd stared.

"That man on that crate has been wronged, sure enough. But the Negroes he has accused, those three in our jail, weren't anywhere near him last night. Nor were they anywhere near my wife." Leighton brought his fist to his chest three times as he said this.

"You weren't there. How the hell do you know?" Galbraith hollered.

If this were a wrangle in the quarry office, there was reasoning that could be done, facts laid out, logic to follow. But this was a mob starting, and they wanted banners and hoods and pomp and slogans. They wanted to be told that the hate they were feeling was not just right, but righteous. They wanted ivory heroes and undeniable victims, villains of irredeemable blackness, white knights on gleaming horses.

"Would I stand before you, would I raise my voice against a friend, against my own wife, and call them both liars if I didn't know?" Leighton nudged the horse, and it snorted into the crowd, pawing the ground. He stared out at them, blue eyes slanted above the gray crescent scars. They looked on him, their mouths screwed tightly in resentment. Some bore looks of shock, mouths hanging open, eyes wide. He was ruining a real good time. "Go on about your business. Then go home," he said. "Easter is coming. You have families. Love them. Go to them."

There was a long pause. Brows that had been crimped and intent, became flat and puzzled. Men removed their hats and women gazed at their gloves and handbags.

"What kind of man," Archer began, "would sully his own wife's reputation? In public? Before you? Ask yourself why Mr. Morkan would be so concerned with three Niggers when his wife lays abed suffering from an attack at the hand of one."

"Yeah. What about that?"

That quickly he brought the mob back.

Archer stepped to the edge of his crate. "Mr. Morkan, tell us. Let's be honest. Do you bear some special connection to any of these Niggers we ought to know about?"

The question resounded like a tear in cloth, a seam rended.

"One of the Niggers, the very one that assaulted your own wife, he's awfully high yellow, isn't he?" Archer asked. "Slant-eyed? Might mistake him for a Chinaman?"

The crowd stirred and murmured. It was not a long walk to the realization of who Holofernes Lovell might be.

"Or an Irishman," Archer added.

Even the dullest among them caught the gist now. The crowd swelled at one hundred or more, policemen dawdling and bored along its edges. And it was then he heard in the low murmur of their voices that whisper of a sound very old, very intimate. In the sun that touched his face, in the rich Spring smell of wet limestone Macadam on the road was the presence of another, of Judith very near him, pleading, urging him, her hands clasped at his ears, the murmur there. With any word he spoke, he sullied himself and destroyed his wife. He pictured Patricia's face as it appeared after the bushwhackers robbed her long ago—the bulbous, shining purple chin, the agony of her wired jaw, the heartache of knowing what little beauty she held was shattered. How she clung to him, aided him all these years, endured the fear of vengeance shadowing her home and her child. Yet again his waywardness was leading her to destruction.

He jerked the horse squarely to face Archer and stepped it toward him. "Holofernes Lovell did not touch my wife. She has lied. And you, Archer Newman, are lying." He turned into the crowd. "And I leave you, my people, my Ozarkers, my townsmen, with that fact. The man whose wife was assaulted came before you this day and told you directly you were lusting for the blood of an innocent Negro boy. From here on out, your sin is your own."

In the wake of their silence, he rejoined Peale. Some of the crowd dispersed, and others pooled to whisper together. A sad pride filled him. Maybe he had broken the spell.

The crowd began to shout and wrangle. "Well, that's one Nigger-lover's word, don't mind it!" "I've heard enough." "One innocent shouldn't spoil nothin." "Morkan's right. Go on home."

Peale took him by the arm and whispered close to his ear. "Let's get to the jail and get them boys out of this county."

He turned in the saddle and eyed the crowd, some of which followed him with looks of wonder, even pity. "Peale, you do that, soon as it's dark, soon as you can. I believe I'll go home, and we'll see if we can't get Mrs. Morkan to recant."

Peale's gaze darted among the crowd. He scanned the policemen with contempt. Every one of them was a lame duck, and as soon as the new mayor was in, they were out. What did they care if the city burned? "Leighton, you may have bought time. But people forget real quick."

He rode alongside Leighton, peering urgently at him. His small horse bounced giddily to match the plodding of the monster Percheron. When they left the crowd and Leighton turned his horse for Galway, Peale clutched Leighton's coat. "I am sorry you had to do that."

Leighton bowed his head.

"I'm sorry for you and Archer," Peale said. "I'm real sorry for Patricia."

"Maybe it's over now. I read somewhere after lynchings that if one man had stood against the mob, it would all be quelled. Don't you feel we just done that?"

Peale watched him for a long time holding his arm. Then he patted his shoulder. "That's for novels by great writers who are far away and aren't Ozarkers. Get Mrs. Morkan to recant. I'll be here."

Judith was stoking the stove in Patricia's room. Patricia was sleeping with the covers pulled tight under her chin.

Judith looked up. "Holy's caught, ain't he?"

Leighton nodded. "Has she been awake?"

"Some," Judith said. "Ain't as weak as she was. She ate."

"I'll see you downstairs," he said to her.

Judith frowned and watched him for a moment before leaving.

He knelt at their bedside. "Patricia."

Her forehead buckled.

"Patricia." He pushed her arm with his fingertips.

Her eyes opened and she blinked, then stared at him. Though the room was bright with afternoon sun, her face was gray.

She blinked and her lips smacked as they parted. She swallowed. "Have they caught him?"

He kept his hand on the bed, his fingers touching her arm. "Patricia, Holy wasn't with them boys. Odem, the contractor at Strafford, the dispatch at Pickwick—all account for him that whole evening. He was nowhere near. I want you to tell the newspaper that."

Her chin quivered as her jaw clinched. She moved her arm away from him. He was silent for a moment.

"Patricia, unless you recant. .... Archer is whipping people into a mob. There may never be a trial. You know what they'll do. It'll be Pierce City all over again."

She was silent and her eyes seemed scalded, the skin around them pink, the pupils withdrawn.

"Patricia, I saw Holy's journal. That is something between you and me."

She sat up, her knuckles trembling where they held the sheets.

"That was long ago," Leighton said.

"Long ago? Bastard!" She slapped the frayed comforter and the burnt smell of dust rose in the room. "It is right now, even today. You took me to bed and have taken me to bed without any love for me." Her eyes bulged. "Only lust for a servant. And still you lust for a servant. You made me live a lie. My life amounts to nothing but falsehood."

He gripped his temples, rubbed them. "Holy will hang unless you recant. You and I can live with everything that's happened. What's about to happen I cannot live with. Now, I want you to tell me the truth."

"You want me to tell you the truth. That's rich." She crossed her arms over her chest and clucked her tongue. With a crunch, the coals in the stove shifted. "Here's truth—a stout, short, yellow Negro jumped on me while I rode in a wagon, broke my arm, beat me, and robbed me. Your inbred, jackass townsmen, your loyal hooded riders would come lynching some Negro or other after this no matter what. Let them spend themselves on one, then, I say. Too bad if he is your own blood."

Leighton stood slowly. "So you know it wasn't Holy?" he asked her, hardly believing the words.

She glared at him. "You have made a fool of me. When I thought I had your heart, I had nothing and no one." She breathed sharply, her voice growling. "And I loved you." It was a shout that rang through the whole house.

Downstairs water slapped stones, and an iron bucket gonged as Judith tossed it aside. Leighton clasped his hands before him so fiercely that a pain shot up his forearm. From the window, the afternoon sun was swallowed in a cloud's shadow and the room dimmed abruptly. His reflection hovered in his mother's ancient oval mirror with all its tumors and islands of purple and dusky blue. For a moment, in the tense set of his jaw, he saw his father's face, and he heard old Morkan's voice in his own. "Gus, our son, is going to have to live in town after this. Either in bearable shame, or in unendurable infamy. Either with a mother who lets an innocent man die, or a mother who is the victim of an attack, but woman enough to withdraw a lie."

He watched her for awhile hoping to see some effect. She remained rigid, her back so straight he could see the knobs of her shoulders rising beneath her blue gown. "An innocent man. I only ask this because I know you to be a bigger person than me, a better person." He waited. "What will it be?"

"Suddenly they are 'men' now, these Negroes," she said. "Has the Negress Judith earned the status of 'woman'?' Is she a woman like her boy Holy is a man, deserving that I make public sacrifice? Was she so privileged as to wear the name Morkan and the Christian protection and approbation of marriage while she bore her carnal burdens? Did she know enough to refuse you? Could she have refused you and kept her living? A Nigger then to you like any other farm animal, kept ripe and fat and always ready for a quick fucking. How fortunate this animal accommodates its keeper so well!"

He turned to her, breathed, made a fist, but kept it at his side.

"So is it this drop of White blood that makes Holy one I should shame myself for?" She asked. "One drop? No. Holy is his mother's son, a Negro good as any other." As she spoke her face flushed red and her chin thrust forward. "You have taught me too well. They are not my own. They are not my equals." Her eyes shone like beads of steel. "I will not be put off my pleasure on account of bettering the lot of any Negro."

"Well, then," he said. A calm came over him as if some contract had settled, some long-awaited forecast had transpired. It was a peace, resting like Odem's warm hand on the back of his neck, so forceful and all encompassing and so sudden that he questioned his reasoning and worried that he was coming unhinged. "You sit in your pride, then, and you'll reap judgement for all of us after Holy's hanged and dead."

"Judgment?" She choked, then swallowed so deeply her neck arched. With her arms crossed, she spat on the comforter. "Descend to your promised land, Leighton Moorken. On hands and knees it waits scrubbing your floors."

He left her glaring at him, the covers knotted in her fists.

At the bottom of the stairs, water sparkled on the stones of the floor, but Judith sat in the library on the couch. She held her face in her hands, her elbows stabbing into her thighs. In one of her hands she clutched the boars hair brush used to scrub the stones. Though its bristles dug into her cheek she made no move. He watched her for a moment, and light from the water batted against the mottled walls.

"Leighton, I weeped till I can't even weep no more."

396

He knelt to her, then took the brush from her hand. He clasped her hands in his and they rested in silence.

"Save my boy. Please."

"She won't recant."

She ran her fingers through his hair and gave him a look of pained amazement, her brow bunched, eyes squinting. "I wouldn't neither," she said finally.

"Well, I leave you with her," he said. He touched her knuckles to his lips—after all what was left to hide? A fool's passion swept over him, then just as suddenly turned to anguish. "I imagine if you had wanted revenge, you had all morning to get it."

Judith shook her head. "I ain't touching her. Fault don't matter no more. Sin don't matter. Go save my son. Please, Leighton."

In town, balconies and porches were decked in blue and white, clots of yellow daisies with black middles, ribbons draped together joining each façade. People jammed the main streets, so he coaxed the horse through criss-crossings of back alleys until a throng blocked him at St. Louis Street. It was the finish point for the parade that had ended now, just before Easter vigil began. Bandsmen in bright red and brassy epaulettes milled about. They unstrapped their instruments and braces, ran white chamois over the brass of their horns. Some held foaming bottles of beer in one hand, timepieces in the other, watching for seven p.m. when they could end their Lenten vows. Many were already drinking. A trumpet player lit a cigarette, smoked, and shivered, craning his neck in ecstasy, his forty days over.

He scanned the crowd. In the lamplight, their faces shone. A man near him gripped a woman's waist with such ardor that her bonnet shifted. She caught it, glared at him and whispered something sharp to which he grinned. On a bandstand, a large podium of pine wood had been erected and above it hung a banner that read: "Constantine 'Little Lou' Ziggler: Grand Marshall 1906 Easter Parade." Criers in knickers and dusty coats were shouting and distributing copies of Ziggler's *Daily Leader* while others scrambled to sell the rival *Daily Republican*. As Leighton rode for the jail he heard Ziggler's speech begin, the crowd shouting for justice.

At the jail, young boys in knickers and overalls were chucking pebbles at the lower windows where Leighton was sure Holy and the Coloreds from Pickwick were incarcerated. As Leighton approached on the Percheron, the street cleared and the boys hustled off to sulk in alleys.

A deputy led Leighton through a cluttered, dusty office, which bore the spermy smell of stale spittoons. The deputy fiddled with his key ring, then down the stairs they went into the mud-bottomed cellblock. Two lanterns lit a single hallway of iron bars and packed dirt. Leighton brought his collar to his face. The stink of urine and sweat were strong, though the draftiness of the room chilled the air and fought the odor down.

Near the end of the hall, Gus stood with his hat off, his reddish hair streaming down. His forehead was pressed up against the bars. Then as Leighton descended the last step, he saw Holy behind the bars. The Negro's fingers were stretched through the iron to touch Gus's shoulder, and Holy's face was right close to Gus. Holy was whispering and looking very reassuringly into Gus's downturned face. Gus was shaking his head, grinding his forehead against the greasy black iron. His pale cheeks were wet. Leighton stopped to steady his breath. Two men, banded together now as they had been in childhood when they were inseparable playmates, pretend bushwhackers, pirates of the high seas. These were his two sons suffering and in fear, and he had no remedy.

Though some of the prisoners craned their necks or stood to see who was coming, Gus and Holy did not break their communion. It was Holy whose eyes first flashed on him, whose face lit in a smile.

"I knew you would come. I knew it," Holy said.

Gus raised his face from the bars, which had pressed two trenches of purple into his forehead. "Father," Gus said.

"I sent for Peale." In his throat his voice felt brittle as an oak leaf long into winter. He struggled for a moment. "I want him to take you to Christian County when dark falls. You'll be safe there."

"I thought you said he would be safe here?" Gus asked.

Holy's eyes were wide now.

Leighton took Gus by the shoulder and tried to lead him away and tell him of the mood downtown when Holy reached out from the bars and gripped both their lapels. "Stay here a spell, will you? I just want to look at you both now." He patted their arms, squeezed their coat sleeves. And suddenly his face, which had been smiling and confident, grew slack and pale. His brow creased with worry. "Two Morkan men," he said. "Two good Morkan men."

Gus closed his eyes and bit his bottom lip. Steadying himself by gripping Holy's arm, Leighton cleared his throat. "Look here, Gus. Won't you give me and Holy a minute?"

With a glance at his chum, his half brother, Gus fixed his hat on his head and walked toward the stairs.

Leighton turned to Holy. The redbrick wall back of him was poorly mortared, a yellowy goop with chunks of aggregate like beans in tan soup. Even the bricks were substandard, greasy and black with too much ash. The city had skimped—this was nothing Morkan Quarries would have sold. Staring up at the ceiling the two boys from Pickwick rested on the floor behind Holy. The bars shocked Leighton, and he touched them as gingerly as he might the wire to a failed charge.

"What a God damn mess, Holy," he said.

Holy nodded.

"I am so sorry," Leighton said.

For the first time in Leighton's memory Holy looked on him with skepticism, with one eyebrow cocked high. "Why you letting her say this about me? Was you found out? Does she know now I ain't no child of Isaac?"

"She did find out. But I'm not *letting* her say anything. She's saying it, and she won't take it back."

Holy stepped away from the bars for a moment, his lips drawn into a tight frown. "She means to say that of me, knowing it's a lie." He bowed his head.

"Please understand, Holy," he began, then he didn't know what to say. "She's disturbed, distressed. By the time the trial comes, well, maybe she'll have come around."

Holy looked up at him, waited. "What am I supposed to understand?"

Leighton leaned his forehead against the bars. The ammonia and dirt closed around him and he could feel the grit of rust falling on his lips and beard.

Holy put his callused palm against Leighton's knuckles, then clasped them. He whispered, "They always said I was a seer, Miasma and them. Want to know what I see?"

Leighton raised his eyes.

"I see you and me in Glory."

In the lamplight outside, when he stood with Gus and gave his son news of his mother and her stance, the rust tainted his hands the color of old blood. Once he noticed, he hid them behind his back. They split up in search of Peale.

Later that night Holy took off his dungarees and sat in his underclothes on the jailhouse floor, his right side pressed tightly against the bars so that he could get as much light on his legs as possible from the lantern hanging outside the cell. He was searching for deer ticks, had snatched four already. The two boys from the Pickwick Transfer were arguing about Mr. Pickwick's clout in the city, whether or not he could get them free of this trouble. One of the boys had not even been with Holy on the trip to Strafford, but had been at the Transfer's stable the entire afternoon. Two cells down from them were two Negroes accused of a tailor's murder. They were on trial, and court resumed Monday. Whenever they talked, they assured Holy that he was a dead man and would hang. But the boys from the Transfer promised the two killers were only grousing and bragging because they had no alibis of their own and were dead guilty.

Holy felt the hard knot of a tick stuck to his groin. He pinched it, felt his skin pull with it. He and the boys were full of them. They planned to hike to Fairplay to a farm owned by a Negro friend, but the roads were busy with vigilantes. They hid in a burr-choked cedar glade until a farmer and three coon hounds had flushed them out early the next morning. The two deputies that brought them in were punch drunk and laughed the entire way into town, said they expected to be made heroes and be given a plaque on the courthouse wall.

Holy sat apart from the Pickwick men while they finished their slops. Outside, the sheriff's dogs began barking. When the noise increased, Holy stood carefully on a cot to peer out of the barred slot at the ceiling. Lanterns bobbed, hundreds of them, yellow and green. The chains holding the sheriff's dogs lashed and hummed as the animals rushed again and again to the ends of them. The people holding the lanterns made no noise as yet, but their feet in coming made a murmur and scuffing. In the lamplight, their faces shone and vanished, white with black eyes, white necks and chins, white cheeks and ears.

One of the Pickwick men smacked Holy's leg. "What them dogs after?"

Holy shook his head.

"O my God," one of the tailor's killers said. "Look what you Niggers done brought on us."

"What?" The stable boy jerked at Holy's leg. "What the hell's going on?"

The dogs were showing their teeth, their noses peeled back. The people were skirting them. In their hands, they had pistols and cudgels, ropes looped into nooses. Holy stepped down from the cot.

"Motherfuck," he said.

The boys from Pickwick scrambled to the slat but toppled the cot. They cursed and the stable boy threw a punch at his partner, which knocked him to the floor. Lantern light, then a white face glowered from the ceiling grates.

"Here they are, you men! Here's our Niggers!"

Scrambling, Holy could not find his dungarees. The bars of the cell were frigid against the backs of his thighs. The iron pulled at the hair on his legs.

Down the hall, the tailor's killers were rattling the bars so hard, the metal behind Holy shook. There came a pounding at the jail's outer door. The Whites were shouting encouragement to each other like old hammer crews at the quarry. The

401

lanterns made the bricks of the window slat glow yellow and orange as if a fire lit them from inside.

"Gentlemen! Gentlemen!" It was Sheriff Peale's voice. "This is not Taney County. This city will not tolerate this. I want you all ...."

"Bugger off, Peale," shouted a voice. Laughter and shouts followed, then the Whites were rooting for someone to "Come on, get him! Hit him, Fisher." A huge cheer erupted, and after some moments the pounding continued.

The door from the office to the jail cells slammed open. The sheriff's wife in her nightclothes hustled through, pushing her fat daughter before her. The wife's eyes were wide with fear, but the daughter wore an impish grin. When the wife stopped down the hall, Holy and the Pickwick men crammed their faces against the bars, screaming to be released. Holy could see her shadow by the cell of the tailor's killers—the bars raked his face like the teeth of a saw. The daughter was grunting, "Come on, Momma. Let them Nigras be." Outside something smashed against the wooden door to the sheriff's office. Mother and daughter left through the back door; then the door to the cell of the tailor's killers clanged open. Both the tailor's killers bolted out, left Holy and the others hollering after them. There came a crack, wood being smashed, a great hurrah.

The Whites poured in like hornets streaming from a nest, one, ten, then twenty. Their faces were whiskery yellow and gleaming with sweat. The smell of beer and fagged clothing collared Holy's throat. The Whites growled and gnashed their teeth, cursing, spitting through the bars. A glob of sputum caught Holy in the groin and hung there warm and slick as blood. One White man grabbed the bars, then a dozen latched onto them; they rocked at the bars downward and back with all their weight, propping their brogans and boots at the bottom of the bars and hanging by their arms like apes in a menagerie. As mortar rained from the ceiling, they grunted and heaved. Holy and the Pickwick men cowered in the far corner of the cell. Above them, through the slat, a boy of not more than fifteen was screaming "Whoopee, Niggers! Whoopee!" One of the Pickwick boys was weeping and imploring God.

Several workmen pushed through, one a foundry man Holy knew. These produced hack saws, picks, files, and sledges. In the wicked speed of their industry, in their mashed brows and determined lips, Holy saw the locusts raining down on the Egypt of Mrs. Patricia's Bible.

One tall man in an ivory jacket emerged from the sheriff's office with his hands raised. He elbowed through the crowd of Whites. From one of his fingers, a ring of keys spun. It was Archer Newman, Mister Leighton's friend, and for just a moment Holy thought he was saved.

"Let me unlock the door, you piss brains!" he shouted.

Their brows scrunched; they blinked for an instant then cleared him a way to the cell door. Twisting the key, he jerked the door open and stepped inside, waving behind him to have the Whites hold back. They waited, goggle-eyed as steers at a trough. The skin of Mr. Newman's hand that held the keys was a pink sort of white, like the color milk takes after running with strawberries. His eyes were the silver of old coins. The Pickwick men backed away from him. He was broad shouldered, muscles making ovals in the ivory sleeves. He reached to Holy, grabbed him by the ear. Mr. Newman's chin was slightly rounded. His hair, neatly greased, was a shade Holy knew only on women, a yellowy red, the most thoroughbred White man Holy had ever seen.

His smile showed teeth that were straight and gray. His fingernails biting at the back of Holy's ear, he shook Holy's head. The Whites behind him were still and quiet. "Look, gentlemen, at the broad, ape-ish nose, muted somewhat, thinned as if our blood were somewhere behind him. But still ..." he jerked Holy toward the bars "... the broad primate forehead on which God has written nothing but Rape and Steal."

The white faces stared with wide eyes and gaping mouths.

He jerked Holy's head up until they were nose to nose. The end of Mr. Newman's nose was as dry as a scab. "Well, gentlemen: Vengeance is mine," he said, "and I *shall* repay."

The Whites shouted, slapped the bars, stomped their feet, shaking the jail.

With his free hand, Mr. Newman opened his white coat and drew from his belt a rope that ended in a noose. He dangled the

403

rope above his head, the noose swinging like a pendulum. "To the Tower, gentlemen."

Cheers and thunder.

From the corner of St. Louis and National, the crowd became almost exclusively male, overalls and dungarees, smudged, reddened faces. Still searching for Peale, Leighton negotiated past them with his head down. Some held *The Leader* rolled like clubs in their fists. Many were drunk, shouting vowels and nonsense, but most frightening to Leighton were the clear-eyed men—the hog reeves, the wrights, the mechanics, and the clerks—men Leighton was sure came straight from work, had not had time to visit a saloon. Their eyes were narrowed, their shoulders stooped, their lips wet. They bore the look of sober, calculated hate that has gained complete focus and is near its goal. It was dark now. When they passed under the lamps, their skin shone a pallid blue.

At the jail, there was a mob of men gathered and cheering. Archer rode on his black horse. Behind him muleteers led three mules and on each a Negro swayed, Holy in front, hands bound behind his back. Holy was stripped of his shirt, wearing only his underclothes. His cedar-colored skin appeared red under the lights. The men waved lanterns and jabbed torches in the air.

Archer led them south to the broad, open square decked with Easter crepe and American flags. There the Gottfried Tower hummed in a halo of electric light. A trellis of white steel was draped in wilting Easter lilies that drooped from the ground to the top where iron lady liberty thrust her torch up.

Leighton swung his huge Percheron in front of them, and Archer halted for an instant, the mob jostling and shouting then stopping in a ragged semi-circle around the two of them.

Leighton stood high in the saddle. "You know who I am, all of you."

Archer glared at him.

"You know these boys stand accused of an assault on my wife."

"Out of our way, you old bag," someone shouted.

He drew out the pepper-box, held it high. "I swear by God these boys are innocent, and you are about to commit a terrible sin."

Murmurs, then more shouts for him to move. "Crazy old man!"

He turned in the saddle to cast a glance at each man in the mob's front rank. "Which one of you fools is wanting to kill enough to be killed right now." There it was for them, the equation that would stop them. Leveling the gun, he looked for Archer. "You there, McKenzie. Is this the last Saturday of your life?"

Men in the front ranks ducked and pushed at their neighbors. But those free of his aim shouted and snarled. Something had snapped in them. The crowds that had milled toward the jail early in the evening had no more spirit than boys at a charivari. But these. Though they were men he knew, he never expected the knots along their jaws, the dark sickles of their brows, the blue serrations of their knuckles holding torches in their fists.

And he wondered, then, how he had looked to the men he had ridden down and hung. "I have four shots. Four of you ready to die right now?"

A stone whizzed by his ear. The horse took quick steps back, its head rolling. A lantern crashed on the ground, flames whirling around it. The mob surged forward, and he could see Archer's grin. He fired the pepper-box, all four barrels spouting. From the crowd a second pistol cracked and a bolt of fire and searing pain exploded in his left shoulder. The pepper-box twirled from his hand, his fingers outstretched. The pepper-box disappeared into the rush of men, and they had him off the horse, which plunged and rose, churning its huge forelegs and hooves. Revolvers snapped and the huge, gray animal went down screaming. Four men slammed Leighton against the boardwalk outside the Springfield Cigar Store. They pummeled his face and chest. Let it happen now, he prayed, now if it has come to this.

"Let him be!" Archer wrestled one of Leighton's assailants aside, and the others raised him up. Leighton's jaw burned, his left side ached where a fist had caught him. Blood oozed and weighed down the hairs of his beard and stuck his shirt to his back. A bore of fire like a blazing hot rivet burned in his shoulder.

405

"All these years, forking money to the Niggers," Archer said loudly so the crowd could hear. "Well, let's let Mr. Morkan witness justice as it ought to have been done from the start."

They cheered, waved their hats. One man leaned in to spit on Leighton. The drool slid down his neck and dipped under his collar.

Archer bent close and leered at him. "This time I win," Archer whispered.

He told two of his men to bind Mr. Morkan's hands and gag him; then he tipped his hat. The rope bit into Leighton's wrists as his captors tied him, his shoulder flaring, and the rolled, stinking handkerchief tore at his lips as they bound the gag.

The mob proceeded to the Gottfried Tower, and soon the three Negroes were standing on the platform beneath it. The ropes, noosed at their necks, draped over the steel high above them. Crews of men eagerly gripped each rope and tied them off to the three mules the Negroes had been forced to ride.

Leighton's captors followed Archer to the tower leading Leighton along behind. The mob was growing. Leighton estimated the square was almost full, maybe two thousand or more men. Lantern and torch light bathed the platform in orange brilliance. Moths and lacewings swirled about the Negroes heads, which were all tilted slightly, their faces darkened, mouths gasping. Whites kept the ropes as taut as they could be without yanking the Negroes off their feet.

Leighton's captors grabbed his arms and hoisted him up to stand at a far corner of the platform. Archer stepped up on the platform, and the crowd cheered and whooped. He raised his hands, his white coat billowing. He bowed his head. They fell silent. Leighton saw Holy's eyes narrow to watch Archer.

Archer raised his head. "When, in the course of human events, it becomes necessary for one people to dissolve the political bands which have connected them with one another." He paused and took a deep breath that made his broad shoulders swell. "When in the course of human events, a government becomes destructive of the ends of life and liberty and the pursuit of happiness, it is the right of the people to alter or to abolish it." He spoke slowly, shaking his head and closing his eyes in a reverie of verbiage. His voice carried, rang off the brick buildings on the far side of the square.

"In the history of man, no set of words has produced more trouble and more truth. The world waited time immemorial for those sentiments so purely thought, and finally they came from an American. An American. Tonight, gentlemen." He rolled his eyes. "Tonight we fulfill them."

He paused, and they whistled and clapped. Above them all, lady liberty glowed in her pool of promised light.

"Tell me, my people, has not this government allowed the trial of the tailor's killers to wane and wallow in delays when any set of jurors in the county would convict?"

They grumbled, shouted Yes.

"And what of these men. A woman says she has been attacked, and identifies this one by name." He popped Holy in the chest. Holy's rigid body wobbled on the rope. The Negro's eyes bulged. "And yet, we come near to an act of clemency on the word of a man who should have made sure his wife was safe, was at home, was taken delicate care of? A man who hired Niggers over Whites to work in his quarry as a practice? You see, here is a man who is a force in the very government that balks at justice." With each word, his open hand bounced and pointed to Leighton as if he were presenting him. "Have you not seen him parade his Niggers out to chat your streets, to lay your walks, to pave the road to the memorials beneath which our fathers and his own lie a fathom down, dead from a war that was nothing if it was not about these Niggers?"

Archer crossed his arms over his chest, surveyed the crowd nodding with a smug frown as they answered him with *yes* and *amen.*

"Tonight, gentlemen," Archer said. "Tonight we take our city back!"

He raised his hands to quiet the cheers. "If we are to truly be free, what would our mercy encourage: the perpetuation of weakness! And clemency, fair trials for the obviously guilty: the possibility of escape for a criminal race! Tonight, gentlemen. We make our new nation tonight! A nation

407

where the word of a woman is golden and true enough to condemn. A nation where men can live as Thomas Jefferson intended, live off and on the earth, as merchants and miners, bankers and braziers, cobblers and artists. Look around you. Look for what prevents such a life? Is it our wives and their petty desires? Our land, our methods of living? No. It is the Negro scourge visited upon this nation, mistaken for labor, and it now must be removed. Lincoln knew it, spoke openly of it. Yet here the problem remains and has festered, spread from our saloons and alleys into the very parlors of our homes. We must tie it off." He ran a hand along the rope and noose tied at Holy's neck. "We must lift it out." He grinned, pulling on the rope enough to make Holy's back arch. They roared.

The mob closed on the base of the platform. Torches among them threw off orange sparks that rose and whirled in the strong night breeze. Row on row of faces, bearded, clean-shaven, derbies and Stetsons, foreheads glowing in the orange light, faces so crowded together they appeared as myriad as the surface of dolomite, a sea-floor grave where a thousand on a thousand similar and gray have congregated, drawn by current or sunlight or a warm fissure there to become stone. The teeth of the souls—Judith had called the fossils that in the cave where she and Leighton had lain so long ago. Even then, the cogs and wheels, the fangs of sharks and skins of lizards had clashed in Leighton's mind, whirled and gnashed in a frozen moment of death and life, joy, appetite and hatred. Archer's voice held these faces like no other he had witnessed. They were about to crystallize as one. And they were wrong. Their prophet lied.

Archer raised his hands. "Gentlemen, there will be those that assume this stage tonight in fear of their own weakness, in fear of your censure, or for their own fleeting gain. To be honest, I take this stage for no reason save this: look at my skin." He rolled back the sleeves of his coat and showed his hands and forearms. "Look at these eyes. This hair. Gentlemen, I take this stage most importantly for you. Look at this skin. I have heard you and spoken your words. Gentlemen, tonight, White to the bone, I am all of you."

They surged onto the stage, some embracing him, a group holding him high while the muleteers held tight to the mules and Archer protested until the jubilation subsided and he descended to stand among them.

He was right in that more took the stage to speak— a mayoral candidate who had lost, a man who expressed his stern wish to become sheriff, two ministers, a son of a veteran of McBride's battalion who thanked all assembled, then wept.

Archer stood before Leighton while a fire and brimstone preacher raved. Archer's eyes caught the torchlight as he gloated. "You had everything didn't you, Leighton? Wife. Home. City. Grand Business. Son. Well, sons. A mistress." He smirked. "Say goodbye to all that now."

Leighton lunged, but his captors had his arms. A bolt of pain shot from his throbbing shoulder. Blood cupped his armpit in a warm sluice under the weight of his coat. The knot of his gag tore at his hair.

Archer glared at him. "I can kill you, you damned fool," he said. "But I want you living for years after this." Archer put his arm around Leighton, gripped his wounded shoulder so that he cringed. "Thine eyes will see the glory," he said.

The mob was chanting something which became, "Now! Now! Now!"

Out among them, Leighton thought he spotted Peale. He shivered and goose pimples pricked at his back. His teeth trembled against the gag, and would have chattered. The sheriff forced his way near the tower and was shouting something that went unheard.

Archer flinched. His eyes widened then narrowed on Peale, with his arm in a sling, moving toward the platform.

The preacher rose up on his toes. "Did not Elijah strike the children with a beast? Did not the Lord punish even Moses and withhold him from the Promised Land!?"

"Do it now," a little man with a woolly beard shouted. He pounded his fist on the platform and tried to reach for the preacher's feet. Peale was caught in a shoving match with a member of the crowd. Then fists flew at him, and he was overcome, swallowed in an undulating mass of pumping arms and shoulders, stamping legs. Deputies fought their ways toward him.

Archer whistled at the muleteers. "Hee-yaw!" he hollered.

The muleteers shouted men aside, yanked the bits and hauled the somnolent mules forward. The ropes wobbled taut. The crowd exploded in one solid guttural vowel. Then from them there came every kind of sound: "Praise God! Damn! Jaysus! Raise them Niggers!" Weeping. Shouts of agony and joy.

Though Leighton's captors gripped him fiercely, a struggle began until one of them clobbered him with an elbow to the back of his head that crushed him to his knees.

Holofernes rose off the platform his legs kicking, eyes, black divots in yellow, bulging and turning to Leighton. His eyes jittered and with the rope slowly turning him it seemed he was being roasted, his face deep red and glistening. Eyes that had devoured manuals. Lips that knew reams of animal husbandry and mechanical shortcuts. Hands that had comforted and served Leighton and Gus. And Patricia. The rope turned Holy once more to him and behind Holy's throbbing eyes, Leighton could see his son's mind scrabbling in terror for any escape.

The other two Negroes rose, the ropes catching, then bumping taut so that the three of them ascended in jerks. Leighton could feel each successive jolt in the wood beneath his knees, a rumble and vibration as the Negroes rose against the trellis's friction. He felt it in his smashed shoulder, in the tips of his knee caps. Kneeling and his world was ending, kneeling as he had a thousand times on the stone, but now anarchy around him, murder above him.

Holy stiffened, urine coursing down his leg, dribbling from his toe onto the platform. He spun, his neck stretched, his face darkened, and the light left him.

Leighton turned away, and more forcefully than before he heard the rancorous, joyous murmur of the mob, that shirring, oceanic sound between Judith's fingers cupped at his ears. From that one moment, all was undone. The mob roared. He saw Gus emerge at the front of the crowd, struggling, men restraining him. Gus's mouth fell open, his face went entirely red, and he screamed, Leighton was sure, the name of the young Negro, and that name was lost in the din. Men lifted Gus by the arms, carried him back through their midst away from the tower. Leighton lurched to his feet in fear for him, but one of his captors smashed him to the platform with an elbow to his neck. Gagging, he thrashed and knees and fists pinned him. Finally he gave out. For a moment his eyes stung and blurred with pride that Gustasson also had fought. He wanted to rush to his son, embrace him, urge him on. The inappropriateness of the affection sweeping him made him shake his head to regain his wits. In the faces around there shown a mix of hatred and jubilation, glaze-eyed zeal, and even in some the ashen white of horror. Three Negroes swinging in the first moments of Easter in the first of a new century. What the hell was appropriate? These were his people, and they were gone mad. The bottoms of Holy's feet were pale pink. His bare legs shone and pulsed.

An unshaven man leapt to the platform whooping and spinning with his arms extended. In each hand he held an open jar of kerosene. The unshaven man spun, and the silver-yellow kerosene twirled and spattered on the wood of the platform. Archer stepped off the stage and with a glance back at Leighton he disappeared into the crowd. His captors jerked Leighton to his feet.

The unshaven man loped about, his long arms swinging. He wore only overalls, and his sun-burnt skin and knobby arms marked him for a farm laborer. A hill person in town for a drunk. His loping became a dance, and soon the crowd had picked up the rhythm of it, and was pounding its hands together as he jigged and flung his kerosene. Some of the crowd was trickling away. One of Leighton's captors was gone, the other intent on clapping with the mob. Leighton stumbled toward the back edge of the platform. The three Blacks twisted on their ropes.

Leighton felt fingers grip his arms. He whirled and there stood a young boy, his brown hair matted to his sweating forehead. A knife glinted in his hand. Leighton closed his eyes. Then as it was, is now. Ever shall be. He winced when he felt the warmth of the boy's body press against his coat. He took a breath, and felt the old tightness in his lungs, the white clutch of fibrosis the lime had long burned there. He steadied himself for the knife's entry. Without end, Amen. Killed by a mere boy. Of all the luck.

The blade was cold against his wrist. It pulled the rope deeper into his skin before slicing the rope. The boy unwound the rope, and Leighton's fingers erupted in needles. When his left arm fell free, he stumbled, opening and closing his numb hand.

The boy grabbed his good arm and led him off the stage. He glanced all around them. There was a whoosh of air and fumes, and flames rose high on the platform. The boy slipped the cold knife against Leighton's cheek, cut the gag in two pulls.

Leighton clutched at his cheeks. When he straightened his back, he had to grip the platform's ledge. The boy was gone. He raised his head and felt the gunshot wound sizzle in his shoulder, then throb with redoubled intensity. On the platform, the crowd was flinging boards, chairs, wagon seats, newspapers by the hundreds, hats. The fire whirled and took the feet of the Negroes, singed the bottoms of their feet, but rose no higher. After several bottles of kerosene produced nothing but billows of black smoke, the muleteers untethered the ropes from the saddles. Holy dropped, and the freed end of his rope leapt into the air, then swung to a stop where the end of it dangled across the trellis. Following him down, the other Negroes plummeted into the flames. The ocean roared.

A booze huckster who had made what he called his Easter run let Leighton hitch a ride from the square out to Galway. The huckster talked the entire time about how Lent was such a profitable idea, took no notice of the glistening, growing patch of crimson on Leighton's shoulder or Leighton's silence or the fire that lit the sky behind them. Leighton could see the huckster's bottom lip shining plump and wet even by starlight. Eventually he closed his eyes and slid sideways on the seat. Leighton took the reins and kept the horses on the road. He left the horses and wagon tethered at the gate to the house, the huckster snoring.

Standing on the hill near the house, he could see an orange ball of light in the middle of town. A door shut behind him on the porch. Judith moved to the railing under the lantern she'd kept burning.

He ascended the stairs. "I did all I could do. Almost died with him."

She bowed her head, her jowl swelling. Her eyes watched him. "They's a lot of almost in your life."

"Forgive me, please."

Judith reached and grabbed him by the arms, and he thought she might toss him down the steps. She pulled him to her, cupped the back of his head, buried his face in her chest. "I ain't never going to forgive you, long as you live, never, never."

His throat ached. His lungs moved like sacs stiff with cement. After a moment rocking there against the Negress's bosom, locked in her embrace he knew he was damned and hoped for nothing better.

V

LEIGHTON ENTERED THEIR BEDROOM WHERE PATRICIA slept. "Get dressed," he said. He leaned on the bedpost, gripping and shaking the quilt near the ridge of her feet. "Easter clothes."

"I'm ill." She blinked at him. "Have you been out drinking and fighting?"

"Get dressed or I will take you as you are to see your city."

She narrowed her eyes at him. "You are still drunk. Judith!" she hollered. "You are mad." She tore at his hand as if to scrape it from the quilt.

Judith stepped in the room, arms crossed over her chest.

Patricia blinked at her. "Help me!" Her fists pummeled his arm and wrist.

He remained, a mass of scar tissue against searing morning light.

"Which dress you want to wear, Mrs. Morkan? I get it ready." Judith spoke in a voice like a sleepwalker's.

Patricia sobbed.

An hour later, Judith was helping her down the stone front steps. Patricia wore a black dress with broad shoulders, a frilled bonnet and black veil. Leighton donned a crimson suit from New York, one his new tailor created for Easter. He wore a reddish suede derby with a silver band to match. A yellow and green checked vest completed an outfit he had hoped to feel like a hundred bucks wearing. Instead he felt like a dirty Claibe Jackson fiver that has lived in some whore's garter through a long occupation. Beneath his coat, holstered, he wore his father's old navy Colt for the first time in years.

Patricia stared at his suit, her lips screwed tight. "That is hideous."

Judith helped her into the surrey, and Patricia wedged herself far back in the corner. "Look to the time. What service do

414

you intend to make it to? You aren't doing the favor of taking me to the Lutheran service this late?"

"Giddap," he said.

The sun beamed on bows of foaming purple redbuds and white, promising dogwoods, service berry blooming and cheat greening. Silver winged ants frothed from every nest. Wrens warbled maniacally. They passed the yawning chasm of the Galway Quarry, its cliffs now every bit as sheer as those at Sunken Quarry.

Another couple passed in their wagon, the plump father pulling at his tight waistline. His wife spotted Patricia and turned away. The man saw them, removed his hat to Leighton, but urged the horses on.

Patricia fidgeted, lowered her head so that the brim of her hat covered her face. "Did you spring him from the calaboose?"

"The issue has been decided."

They passed a Baptist church where the bells were ringing and brightly dressed men and women were ascending the steps. The streets were crowded with wagon and horse traffic, and people scurrying in to the church. Some stopped and glanced at Leighton, who sat far forward on the seat, all but his back in the sunlight. Even with the sun on his suit, he shivered now and again with a chill he was sure came from the wound in his shoulder. Patricia remained wedged as far back in the surrey seat as she could, a wool blanket clutched at her knees. She cut her eyes at wagons and people that passed, especially anyone who stopped to gawk at them.

"This is appalling," she said. A woman swung a parasol up after recognizing the Morkans. "Why can't you sit back? Is this some kind of display?"

"I'm cold."

"You're gray as stone. Did you lay in some gutter all night?"

"I did not. I was on my knees."

She squinted at him. "What's wrong with your eye? Your cheek is swollen."

"There was a riot last night after the parade." From the Episcopal church, an organ was blaring. He was taking a long way around, avoiding prominent homes.

"A riot?" She sat forward. When he said nothing she slapped the cushion with her palm. "Don't lie to me."

At St. Agnes's, the parishioners were descending the stairs. Many of the women had taken lilies from the pews and these were twirling in their hands. A little girl with an armload of the white flowers ran past them, laughing and screaming through the sunlight, though no one was chasing her.

He turned on Walnut, then on South street toward the square.

"You've missed your muttering Mass. I want to know where you are going."

"I have something to show you."

Where South entered the square, a crowd had gathered around a young news crier who waved his paper and hollered, "Three Negroes Lynched By Angry Mob! Three Hung Minutes Into Easter!"

Patricia stiffened. Her eyes widened and cast among the crowd—brown checked suits and pants, bowlers and top hats sparkling with quicksilver, yellow vests and ivory-tipped canes, bustles and crinoline, bosoms rounded above the armored corsets, sweat on plump, white cheeks.

"Give way here," Leighton hollered. "Give way for a lady."

People parted with annoyed glances at him. Those who recognized Leighton and the tall, dark shadow of a woman with him stepped aside with mortified looks, mouths dropping, whispers starting.

He pulled the carriage into the square, drove diagonally across the open dirt toward the Gottfried Tower. The crowd thickened. The flowered ribbons were now only frayed strips waving in the breeze. Beneath the tower was a black pile of rubble. Peale was picking about the perimeter of it. A young deputy followed him with an open sack. Following Peale and the deputy was a reporter in a cheap brown suit with rounded tails and a dusty hat. He carried a notepad and asked questions neither officer answered.

A few in the crowd stood aside, and Leighton drove until the horses' noses were almost touching the platform. The horses stamped and nickered, backed away. A blue-gray smoke hung about the charred heap, and in this was the twisted, ash-blue figure of one of the Negroes, his shining skull dotted with swirls of wiry black hair and oozing tufts of scalp. A single length of rope, singed at its bottom, dangled from the trellis above.

Patricia let the blanket drop. It was a blanket of wool she and Judith had spun and woven. Leighton watched its slow surrender to gravity, its crumpling like parchment in a consuming fire. She touched her lip with the tips of her gloved fingers. Her face paled.

"Holofernes Lovell," Leighton said, his voice rough. "And two other Negroes."

She shuddered. Her long neck stiffened. "You saw this done?" With her chin trembling, she seemed to be striving for that old façade of pride.

He snorted. "The newspapers reported your story with extra zeal. The good townsfolk took it to heart." He stared at her until she returned his stare. Her chin remained haughty. But when her hand dropped from her mouth to her lap, he could hear the crinoline shiver as her hand shook.

"Pray," he said, "that the Lord may accept the sacrifice at your hands."

"*Verdammt!*" she whispered. "Take me away from this."

"Why? It is what you willed," he said. And then her eyes widened and her back bowed as if he had hung round her neck a great and everlasting weight. He felt no joy, no satisfaction. Only a flat, final horizon, devoid of hills, leaden with cloud.

Peale approached the wagon just as Leighton was coaxing the horses to yaw back. Leighton relented. Peale's hair was matted, covering his forehead. His sling was far more sturdy than the one he had worn to the tower last night. With his good eye, he stared at Leighton, then Patricia; his other eye was purple and swollen shut. His nose was puffy and black along its sides. He glanced at the platform, and back at Leighton. Then a frown pulled down the corners of his lips.

Peale removed his Stetson, and, as if the Morkan's rig were the forecarriage in a funeral procession, the deputies and nearby men in the crowd also removed their hats and stood blinking, holding their hats against their chests, none exactly sure of why, but comforted in acting as one, respectfully, and seemingly at peace.

Peale leaned inside the cab, spoke quietly to Leighton. "There are bands of men out posing as militia. McDaniel has armed them, from his hardware stores. They're threatening Happy Hollow, and I hear there's a lot of Blacks leaving town." He

417

looked around him. His good eye was bloodshot, a black lip of fatigue hanging under it. "I have posted some of my own men at Dolomite Park and at the Sunken Quarry. I think it best that you take Mrs. Morkan home. Now that church has ended."

"Could you spare a deputy to ride home with her?"

Peale glanced behind him. "I might could."

Leighton bent close to him. Off the sheriff's coat, Leighton smelled the rankness of the fire. Patricia smelled it as well. Her nostrils flared, her neck stiffened, driving her hat and veil crackling against the awning. "Shane, Mrs. Morkan would like to know why that boy up there is dead. Why isn't he safe in jail? Why isn't he in Christian County?"

Peale stared at the two of them, his jaw working in agitation. He breathed deeply. "Because we failed. The both of us failed. The three of us failed. And a lot failed with us."

Leighton seized up and coughed into his hand. "I appreciate your deputy's time," he managed, his breath tight.

He turned to Patricia. "The deputy will take you home." All in black, her spine rigid, eyes on the platform, the charred body. Her hands were clasped so tightly together Leighton could see ridges of black silk bunching along the wrist of her gloves. "Judith, I'm sure, can help you rest."

Chin thrust forward, cheeks placid, forehead smooth as the globe of a lamp, she turned slowly to him and spoke as if in the throes of laudanum again. "I thank you for all your kindness." She met his gaze for some time without flinching or even blinking.

When he stepped to the ground, he turned again to her, and her gray eyes held him steadily, devoid of their dour scrupulousness, as if all had been asked, all had been answered, and nothing but smoke and dust remained between her and her husband. The deputy climbed in the cab, nodded to Patricia, whose gaze was once more fixed on the ashen body twisted in the rubble.

The deputy turned antsy horses back, then headed them for home.

Peale's neck and ears were red as if they had seen a lot of sun. Sweat soaked a gray serration into the top of his collar. When the carriage left the square, he cleared his throat. "How could you bring her here?"

"If you had asked me that just as we came up, I would have told you it was the easiest thing I ever did."

Peale stared at him, the one eye blinking, the other fluttering like a fledgling trapped in a black egg. His bottom lip wormed around his chaw. Near them, men and women were murmuring that the sight was horrid, unthinkable. They were well-dressed, and many had likely not been with the mob last night. Leighton watched closely for any man he recognized from the lynching. He saw two, and they were both pointing at the tower, giddily, proudly describing a story to their wives and children.

"I'm going to see that every fool in this pays for it," Peale said. He spat.

Leighton wished him the very best of luck.

He went to the livery and finally raised the stable boy. The boy stared at him with bloodshot eyes. His flannel shirt was unbuttoned and crammed into his dungarees. His matted hair still bore a ring where his hat had been. After a moment staring at him, Leighton recognized him as one of Archer's muleteers, one of the three who had led Holy and his companions to the slaughter.

"Hard sleeping?" Leighton asked.

The muleteer smirked. "Slept like a babe."

"Really?" They walked down the row of stalls. "You look like you wrassled all night with an Angel."

"If I did, he's bested." He looked Leighton up and down, put his hands on his hips. "I won't take no more bull off you, Morkan, but your money."

Leighton rented the biggest horse in the stable, a 17-hand chestnut and went straight to Sunken Quarry. The Percheron, dead along the street in all the rubble and mess!

Miasma's son, Young Sullivan, was standing at the quarry gates when Leighton clopped toward the lot. Odem waited with his head down. He nodded when he saw Leighton. Two deputies were nose-to-nose with Young Sullivan arguing, but they stopped as Leighton slowed his horse. Odem moved beside him.

"He's fine, friends," Leighton said. "Let him be."

The deputies backed away. "Well, how could we have known?" One of the deputies had a cut on his chin. Their coats were red with dust. The rims of their eyes bore greasy black shadows, and

419

they kept their arms stiff like men accused. "McDaniel's given out rifles and shotguns and ammunition. Everything's turned on end."

"I called them here, Leighton," Odem said. "The dynamite."

Young remained fixated on Odem while the accountant shook his keys from his coat pocket. The Negro's collar was stiff. He wore creased pants, yellow suspenders, the best suit of clothes Leighton had seen him in. Young pouted and ran his starched shirt cuff under his nose. Sweat from his chest and arms had made his dress shirt a translucent pink.

"Sure am glad you come along," Odem said. "I'm figuring we will see a lot of our boys today, maybe for the last time."

They stepped into the office, and left the deputies, who sat on the ground with their backs to the gate's arches. Leighton expected Young to speak up, but the Negro did not. Instead, he stood with his back stiff, his fists clinched at his sides. He pouted out the open door, and by the intensity of his stance, he was ready to leap through its opening.

"What can I do for you, Young?" Leighton asked.

He blinked at Leighton. "I'm here to get my milling bonus and my daddy's if I can."

Wagons rattled into the quarry lot, and both Young and Leighton turned to the door. Several Negro miners were stepping down from their rigs. A few wagon beds were already stacked high with trunks and rockers, bureaus and tables tied down with rope.

The sun seared through the slats and placed golden bars of light on Odem's shoulders. "May not have the cash for all them," Odem said watching the Negroes gather.

"Holy didn't do nothing, did he, Mr. Morkan?" Young asked in a loud voice, as if no conversation existed between the White men at all. Across his face, the noon sun threw a jaundiced swath.

"He was innocent, Young," Leighton said. "He died an innocent man."

"Ain't going to be many folks stay around." Loud again. Young worked in the smithy, and the anvil ruined his hearing.

The red fury of Young's eyes made Leighton drop his gaze to the slat floor.

One of the deputies rapped on the door frame. "Mr. Morkan, what do you want done? This is a pretty fair amount of Nigras pulling in here."

"Let them come. You leave them be. Tell them come right to this office."

The Negroes began to file into the office. They were all dressed in crisp coats and slacks. Some had on spats, which they had dirtied, ascots, cufflinks soiled, scratched. They removed dusty felt top hats. Their outfits were unsettling, humorous to him when the first few of them entered the office, but when twenty of them had crowded in and stood in their Easter Sunday best, he felt sad and disquieted, as if they had all lined for a picture at a memorial. Their cheeks and jaws were tight and set. Almost every face bore a rumple of fatigue, or maybe it was a squint of suspicion. He never knew.

A wagon swung to a stop before the office; driving it was one of Dolomite Quarry's White firemen. The fireman balanced a repeating rifle with the butt against his thigh. Someone climbed down from the surrey, head and shoulders wrapped in a woman's shawl. It was a man, judging by the trousers and patent leather shoes with gray cloth tops. It was Gustasson.

Gus removed the shawl and stepped into the office. His face was full of scratches. Yellow marks of iodine salve left a patina that made him appear ill. He wore a teal coat with padded square shoulders. His ascot tie bore a teal swirl on a silver background. It was wide and gaudy as a table napkin.

"Gus," Leighton said. "Thank God."

Gus glared at him.

"Last night," Leighton said. "When they carried you off, I thought …"

Gus interrupted him. "I didn't come here to reconcile."

Leighton paused. "However you came, I am glad."

"Your indecision already killed Holy," Gus whispered sharply. "What else?"

Leighton pressed his palm flat to the desktop. Young Sullivan was by now scowling at him, tapping his hard leather soles on the slat floor.

421

A driller named Chalmers stepped forward. He glanced at Gus, then at Odem and Leighton. "I'm sorry to ask this so sudden, sir." Chalmers cheek bore a gash from his cheekbone to his chin, and the wound still glowed pink.

The other Negroes milled in more closely. There was no timbre of violence in Chalmer's voice, but Leighton unhitched his coat button to reveal the Colt.

Chalmers licked his lips, watching Leighton's belt. "I'm taking my people out of here tonight, and I was wondering if I could please have my millings bonus for Monday."

"That's what I'm here for, too, sir," another miner said. "Don't know if I be back."

Leighton raised his hand. "What cash I have here I can give you. But when it's gone, you'll have to take notes."

"Who gonna cash a note for a Negro in this city?" Young Sullivan asked.

"What the hell else can I do? Banks are closed."

There were mutters. Some of the Negroes scuffed the floor with their dress shoes. Chalmers frowned, then stuck out his hand over the desk. Leighton shook with him. Chalmers leaned in close. "Mr. Morkan, could you hurry? They's folks out armed at every road to get us. They's men a' roaming, talking about how they gone burn down Happy Hollow, just like they done us in Pierce City."

Leighton scanned the faces of the Negroes. Their lips were set in grim, flat lines. He could see their jaws clench, the muscles beneath their cheeks shift and bind. Chalmers could hand drill a block hole with a beveled interior so angular and perfect the other Blacks would run their fingers up and down its insides and make lewd faces before they set the gas drill. When the coke was at full heat, Thaddeus Stumph could sharpen twenty-five bits an hour, and had once on a dare finished a flawless thirty-four without a helper. The brawny nipper, Bradford "Bar" Clay, who insisted on hauling bits exclusively for White foremen, kept a deceased foreman's finger curled in his shirt pocket. In his last will, the foreman had mysteriously left his nipper the ghastly relic, and the nipper refused all questions of why.

These men were already gone to Leighton. Holy was dead, his son, who could recite a client's billing and credit history after a single read through his file.

Among the Negroes he sometimes counted himself in the simple communion of a little rebellion against Springfield. But in the sum of suffering life, such easy commune amounted to naught. With a few smart lies, he knew anyone could rearrange his story. His life up to now could affirm what all long to hear: My people, All your wars are good and glorious; all your heroes brave and charitable; all your sagas end in happy marriage; and your lives lift inexorably upwards to salvation. One champion can stem a tide of cowards! And, even if the worst prevails, keep one rousing, exemplary legend, and you are absolved.

Balderdash. In everything he had done, he had perpetuated the Negroes' slavery while he satisfied himself with these easy, universally loved dodges of usury and greed. A wind moaned at the flue of the stove and blew the stink of ashes into the room.

The door slammed shut, and the Blacks parted. Miasma Sullivan and Pony and Tiny Dalton pushed to the front. They were smeared with soot, their clothes torn, eyes glaring from the sores of fatigue puckering them. On their overalls foundry sand sparkled.

"Mister Leighton, we come here asking only out of respect." Pony stretched out his hand and placed on the dry, splintered desktop one long, iron key.

All the Negroes drew forward and their eyes widened on seeing the key. Pony kept his fingertips on it as he spoke. It was a duplicate of the key to the boom shack where the dynamite waited. There hung an ancient iron lock requiring a skeleton key like few others. Only Gus, Odem, and Leighton were to carry a copy. "If they don't leave Happy Hollow be, we gone blow up Walnut and South Streets and burn them mansions down."

Several Blacks at the back glanced at each other, then fixed their hats on their heads and slipped out the door.

"You intend to take the dynamite?"

"If you don't give it," Miasma said.

Leighton rubbed his brow. His shoulder throbbed and he could imagine the bullet in it, hanging in a sack of blood and pus. His left hand was numb and tingling. "Miasma Sullivan," he said savoring the name for one of the last times he would say it. "If you go out in the streets and threaten Archer Newman and Galbraith and McDaniel, do you know what that will do to me and my son? Do you know what you are asking me to do?"

"Another mob's a'starting," Miasma said. "Ask me what I'm losing."

Pony Dalton drew the key back.

Gus put a hand on his father's shoulder and squeezed, and Leighton could sense the situation lurching out of hand. His lungs felt as if they were cemented, and his heart thundered in his ribs.

He straightened his back, rose up in the chair. "You men, listen. You will get your millings bonus. But I want you all to step outside a minute. Leave us with Miasma and the Daltons here."

The remaining Blacks glanced at one another. Murmuring, whispering, they replaced their hats and stepped outside. The office grew still.

Gus sat down on the desk and faced his father, kept his back to Sullivan and the Dalton brothers. Gus's face paled, and with his chin raised a bit, he suddenly looked very much like his mother. He leaned close to Leighton, very close. And Leighton recalled the tender feeling of the boy, so sharp at mathematics, touching his small lips to Leighton's ear to whisper and warn him of a pitfall, to urge him toward a price with a brilliant margin. "This will ruin us both," Gus whispered. "Think about this. Holy is dead. This will not bring him back. Think about my wife. Think about little Karl."

"It goes beyond Holy. Beyond all that," Leighton said. He gripped Gus's arm, kneaded the muscle of his forearm. "You would have died for him last night, Gustasson."

Gus stared at him for a long while.

Outside, tack and leather rang and snapped and wagons creaked away.

At last Gus stood behind Leighton with his hand on his back.

"Pony. Set that key on the desk," Leighton ordered. He tapped the desk.

Pony's brow furrowed and his eyes thinned with suspicion. The Negro glanced at his companions. When Miasma nodded at the desk, Pony fished the long gray key once more from his overall pocket. He placed the key on the desktop and stood back, clasped his hands behind him and stiffened as if ready for a lashing.

Retrieving the key, Leighton held it up in his fingertips, turned it over and over in the light. Dark oil from a lathe mingled with filings to sparkle down the iron. The turning was not skilled—the chisel had missed and drawn craters and curls all along the shaft. At the tip, a tine was overly soldered to add what had been hammered too close. Leighton sat back slowly and pulled a massive key ring from his pants pocket. On the ring, the thickest, longest key he isolated, then set it alongside Pony's key. He ran his fingers down the two of them, leaning over the keys with a pout like a jeweler's, his bottom lip shining.

"You done this from memory?" Leighton asked.

Outside a mother hushed her child. Some of the Negroes began arguing.

"Yes, sir." Pony answered, his voice dry. "Would it of worked?"

Leighton held Pony's key up for them to admire. Despite the rustic tooling, it was a work of handcraft and they were all craftsmen enough to recognize the many hours spent and to honor its fearsome symmetry when Leighton held it to the light alongside his own. Odem lifted his copy on its ring to make sure it was still safely his. At a reputable quarry, no key was guarded more closely than this one. Loss of it was a disgrace that meant sure dismissal for the manager, and likely withdrawal of the quarry's blasting permits. Its theft alone might keep a manager from working in mining again. Such a release meant mayhem, robbed banks, even toppled governments. "I reckon the one time you needed it, it would have done the job."

"One's all it would of took," Pony said.

Leighton nodded. "Odem take your key off'n your ring. Gus, you too." He pointed at the desktop.

With a deft flick of his wrist, Odem slipped his key from its ring and cast it across the desktop. Gus set his alongside quietly.

Frowning Leighton pulled his key from the ring and set it down. Four in a row. For each one, a doorway opened to rubble and rebellion. A long time ago the old Morkan sat down with Confederate generals across from him. And the

Confederates wanted the equivalent of what rested on the haggard, lime-crusted desktop here now.

"Gus. Odem. Does either of you two good men want this quarry to stay out of this?" he asked. "We can let these three Negroes go with just a reprimand and a fare ye well."

Pony flashed a glance at each of the Whites. After a moment his mouth fell open and a look of final betrayal came over him.

Slatted across the white, dusty office, the sun froze the place as if in some ancient and spoiled tintype—the Negroes halted, jaws locked, Odem and Gus stared at Leighton, their lips tight, eyes wide. White-haired, white-bearded now, Miasma stole a small breath.

"Per the usual," Odem began, "I got no idea what in the hell you are fixing to wreak on us."

Relieved for an instant, the men laughed sharply, and Gus smiled at Odem, his old mentor. Outside Negroes were quarreling and a dog barked furiously until a thump sent it yiping away.

"I come this far with you," Odem said. And they all quieted.

"*Ja*," Gus whispered. "*Geh weiter.*" And Leighton heard the fear there.

He breathed, and his lungs felt as if they were coated with plaster drying, thick and heavy. He inched forward in his chair.

"Miasma. Pony. Tiny." He nodded at his key, and Gus's, then Odem's. "Take them."

The Negroes hesitated. Then each stepped forward and bent to take one of the White men's keys. The iron dragged and scraped across the dried wood, a sound as if an ancient and terrible door were already opening.

Leighton sat back now, his head bowed. "Those bear our mark."

The Negroes turned the keys and at the bottom of each, where the shaft met the flattened base, the iron bore the prominent stamped initials MQ.

"None will mistake it."

Leighton opened his desk drawer, found his old, mottled Yankee field cap, crusty and hard. He dropped the Negroes' key on the rotting hat. "Those keys will be all you need. You don't need to carry dynamite."

Pony and Tiny drew closer.

"It's madness to think you can set charges under a street in the daylight."

The Negroes scowled.

"But last night you may have." He pulled out a cigar, clamped it in his teeth. "Why during and after that lynching, you had hours on hours to work at such a project. Appears from them keys, you had my help." He struck a match against the inside of the desk where phosphorous had worn a shining scar.

Miasma looked down. Pony and Tiny held the keys in their palms as if each were a delicate, sharp knife.

"Show you a key to McDaniel and to Carson. Show it to each of them at their homes and tell him you already mined the streets." He opened a file drawer—years of ledgers, some bound in morocco like poor Holy's journal. Nothing he needed to hide. "No need to say what streets. Tell them you had my assistance." Leighton watched them for a moment. "Archer Newman. Show him a key last. Tell him if they don't save Happy Hollow, Morkan will blow their streets to high heaven. And then you must leave town."

The Negroes looked at one another. "That going to work?" Pony asked.

"None of them know enough about dynamite to find you wrong. And Archer Newman won't have time to check if he doesn't know where to look. They will believe you. And they will be terrified. Our mark is all you will need."

He cleared his throat. There was Odem, stiff as a sentinel in an ice storm. "Odem, when I leave, have Young Sullivan manage bonuses with Gus. Then, Odem, I want you to ring Governor Fletcher. I want you to tell him that you are the manager at Sunken Quarry, and that your employer has done something that very much frightens you and that you do not agree with. Relate all this first to the operator. Tell her that I have helped Negroes mine the streets and that unless the mob is quelled, I will set the dynamite off. For the civic good, tell her all that, and ask her to raise Governor Fletcher with the utmost urgency. And ask her to ring you here just as soon as she has him on the line."

Odem took a deep breath, then nodded firmly.

"Mr. Leighton," Miasma started, but Leighton held up a hand.

"Leave me and Odem and Gus here alone and go on. You have dark work ahead. And tell them out there we will be ready in a minute. Odem, pay them their bonuses."

Odem paid from the cash box. As the Negroes left, Miasma turned to Leighton just as he was about to shut the door. "I bear this with me and my younguns gone bear this with them and on. I never let anyone forget."

Leighton clutched the hasp of Miasma's overall. "Mr. Sullivan, for once in my life, I don't care if anyone remembers."

When the Negroes shut the door there was a great commotion outside but Miasma's booming voice settled the hubbub.

Sensing his father's fatigue, Gus took Leighton's arm, but Leighton waved him off.

Gus stared at his father a moment—Leighton's skin beneath the black and iron gray beard had turned bluish-pink. His left shoulder was humped, and his left hand appeared swollen and listless. "How do you know this won't send Archer and his thugs rampaging in Happy Hollow with twice the fury?"

"Our mark, Gus," Leighton said. "He knows I have every ground to hate him enough to do this. And he's never been a capable engineer. He won't know whether I did or didn't." He coughed, then touched his lips with the crimson lapel of his coat. "Archer and his kind will believe the Daltons, and certainly the operator on the phone. They'll have guns and men enough to stop a second mob; McDaniel will tell them to; he turns in any old breeze. And the Governor. He will shit his Easter suit when he gets that phone message."

"Well, now you've done something that will always be remembered," Gus said. "No monument could achieve this."

To Gus's surprise, Leighton looked on him with sadness and a touch of dismay. "I am truly sorry for what it will do to you. And Gretchen and Karl. Oh, Gus."

When they were both silent a long time, Odem cleared his throat. "I don't think anyone in Springfield will try hard to remember this Easter. Unless they be bloody-minded race reformers."

Outside, an argument grew to shouting.

Leighton stuck his chin at the door. "Hurry. Let them in. And, Odem, get the operator busy. Tell her everything, and she will reliably tell thousands. For the civic good."

Summit Street was deserted as he rode for South Street and the square. A young boy dashed from the Quarry Rand Saloon, two great buckets of ale swinging and sloshing at his sides. A common family errand, but the cowering boy's face was pale. He ran as if expecting a hail of brimstone.

The square was almost empty. A single deputy dangled his legs from his seat high on the trellis of the Gottfried Tower where he sat dropping lily petals one by one onto the platform. On the slats of the platform, there was still a sluice of ashes, water dripping in black puddles on the surface of which hung a rainbowed film. The bodies were gone. He imagined Peale lifting them, how they were light, as if hollow. He imagined them crumbling into the wagon bed, imagined the eyes of the crowd dropping.

A young woman moved beside him. She wore an apron stained black with what Leighton thought might be coal dust. This she wore over a yellow dress with laced cuffs, which the black had also tainted. She held up a can, rattled it at Leighton. Brass coins shone in the can. Lifting her plump arm to shield her eyes from the sun, she raised the can higher. He took a coin. It was warm. On it, in a circle, someone had punch stamped the words: "SOUVENIR OF 3 NIGGERS BURNED ON THE EASTER OFFERING SPRINGFIELD MO. 4.14.06 SQUARE" He turned the coin—only the rude backwards impressions of the stamped letters.

"You made this?" he asked.

"Me and my Da." She squinted at him. She was Irish by the accent, round faced, brown, shining hair. Solid hips, full chest and plump arms, with her ruddy skin and blue eyes, she was beautiful. Three of the coins hung from her neck on a silver chain. "It's just two bits, a dollar for three. This is history, you know."

He paid her, and she moved on, rattling the can.

The Easter Offering. His townsmen had certainly chosen from among the lambs, the innocent, the ignorant. Holofernes. That voice reciting the proper treatment for hornworms, the recommended packing techniques for Horseley No. 3, sonnets from Old Morkan's library. He gave Leighton the chills at such times, reciting with his eyes lit as if some other spirit blessed and cursed him. Harden my heart, Leighton thought. Harden all our hearts.

As Leighton turned on Center Street, Hurley Wheeler galloped up, reined his horse and parted his vest to show the pearl handle of a pistol. Leighton slowed the chestnut.

"Morkan, you ditch-digging Mick." Wheeler's horse pranced and he had to jerk its head hard to stop it. He owned a furniture store down National from the Sunken Quarry, was likely headed there.

Leighton doffed his derby, then took the reins again and raised them as if he were about to move on.

"Show your face round here after giving them Niggers dynamite?"

Leighton said nothing but kept his eyes on Wheeler's hands and belt.

"Set there like a deaf stone. You know good and well what I mean," Wheeler said. "Niggers are looting in Battlefield and Republic, even your damn Galway, and you set them loose here. With dynamite!" The horse jounced Wheeler about again, and the merchant cursed and ran the animal in a circle.

The Negroes were headed for the train depot in North Town or off for Rolla on Old Wire Road, but not to loot the small burgs around Springfield. The Negro families would be lucky to escape the county without altercation.

Wheeler settled his horse again and touched his pistol. Leighton drew and leveled the Colt. "Ride on or use it, Hurley. Those Negroes aren't looting. They're running for their lives. Now tell your friends to stay out of Happy Hollow."

The merchant dropped his hands at his sides. His face reddened. "It's true, then. You are going to blow up South Street."

With his thumb, Leighton cocked the revolver.

Wheeler ducked against the neck of the horse. "Should have hung you on that tower with 'em." Wheeler slapped the animal's hind end, and rode hunkered without a glance back.

South Street was empty and silent, save for wind that shivered the trees, whistled against the mansions. On the first manse, an iron weather vane creaked as the southwest wind turned it. The drapes were drawn, though the afternoon sun and air were booming and beautiful. Scraps of parade crepe rattled at the lampposts. Broken bottles shone amidst church programs and newspaper circulars. The cables for the streetcars wobbled in the gusty April breeze.

He stopped his horse next to a mounting stone at the end of a drive. His shoulder ached and his eyes itched with fatigue. The walkway tilted, the mansards skewed off center. Hurley Wheeler alone might be enough, but let the rich see him here. The phones ringing. The voices frantic. A rider at the street's end! Morkan! He has mined the street to blow! He cleared his throat and spat. On the stone, blood veined the gray mucous, as if his sputum were a living cell unto itself. Here is the key, they would say. There is Morkan's mark, MQ. An iron key trembling on a Negro palm grayed with callus, looking every bit like Leighton's own palm.

High over the houses the grand weather vanes he recommended to Archer yowled and swerved in the April wind. With the sun setting behind the spires of the castle-like homes, Leighton saw the city he and Archer had built vanquished. In the loaming purple of evening, on the fences and porch rails, on cupolas and prows, whitewash glowed fierce and proper.

VI

ODEM VISITED, BUT LEIGHTON WAS IN A FEVER AND could hardly comprehend. Leighton fell into a coughing fit that shook him until his ears rang and his ribs ached. Judith came in with a mug of tea and the emptied chamber pot. Lowering herself to sit on the bed, she seemed to double in size. She wedged a heavy arm beneath his shoulders, drew his head onto her lap. Somewhere on one of the sleeping porches a chair was rocking and rocking.

"At the quarry," she asked, stroking his forehead, "what you give them Negroes?"

"Nothing." He wheezed. He closed his eyes, and she held him tightly for some time.

Only she saw Patricia stand at the open door for a moment, her hair disheveled, hands folded at her waist. Judith stroked Leighton's hair as Patricia stared. Then the white shrift moved away, and a bedroom door slipped shut.

The doctor's name was Kravatts, and he had treated many of the miners at Sunken Quarry. Odem sent him. He was accompanied by a man who identified himself as a Pinkerton agent. The agent's suit was dusty. He leaned against the bedroom door jamb, scraping his teeth with a toothpick while the doctor listened at Leighton's chest, then worked Leighton's jaw about gingerly. With the calloused nub of his finger, he tapped the wound oozing at Leighton's shoulder. Leighton lurched and grabbed his arm. He tried but couldn't speak, his head sloshing at the sudden movement.

The doctor backed up. "Morkan, you've a tumor, a fibrous-like substance in both lungs." He paused and straightened his coat. His eyes rolled and blinked, his nose twitching. "No need to fool with that damn bullet. I give you two months, then good riddance to you."

432

The Pinkerton man stepped from the doorjamb and took the toothpick from his mouth. He had a square chin and a red mustache. He dropped the toothpick, reached in his coat pocket, then took a long time drawing out something heavy.

Leighton tensed his arms and his fingers spread, yearning for a gun. Shot and killed by a Pinkerton man was a big step up from being knifed by a kid at a lynching.

The agent's eyebrows danced. "None shall know the time of His coming." His hand emerged from the coat bearing iron, and Leighton slammed the chamber pot toward him. With a flick of his wrist the agent cast something at him and it plunked on the bed.

Leighton popped his hand over what the agent had thrown—icy, leaden, slick, metallic. He hefted it from the covers, and held one of the iron keys he had given the Daltons. MQ.

"Lot of fuss soon, empanelled juries and the like." The agent watched him closely. "Folks what hired me are going to be plenty pissed. Respectable town you got here, Bub. Full of some real shitty notions." He fixed his hat on his head. "I admire you some, Morkan. And it appears you won't never be able to do anything that significant again." He nodded at the key. "The Prayer for the Happy Death. I'll be saying it for you."

Early morning, Patricia lay listening to Judith's plodding assault on the stairs, to Leighton and Judith speaking in low tones, to his coughing like corn being shucked. Soon Judith unleashed her customary hailstorm of racket—pans clattering, a spoon scalloping the base of a mixing bowl with such frenetic intensity, it was as if she stood on the top of the stairs to accomplish this.

Today Judith would be obliged. Her lunatic charge would dress her mad self, descend to breakfast, and grace Judith's embattled kitchen with sparkling, maniacal presence. Patricia had the minister's answer in her hand. "The Church may well have a place for you to achieve a kind of peace or at least do no more harm," he wrote.

The edges of the swooping oval mirror, something left over from Leighton's mother, held a purple sheen she could not vanquish no matter how she set the drapes. In the dappled mirror, her face appeared long, and ordinary, like the nondescript faces

433

in tintypes of graduates from the Lutheran School, her mouth a black question, her eyes dull as buttons. Whatever woman could make herself beautiful before this thing? What had Leighton's cow of a mother died of again—glanders, hollow tail, hook worm?

Patricia donned a winter traveling dress with a crinoline shimmer reminiscent of the insides of abalone shells. She lifted the bell at her bedside table, sat down on the bed, and rang. The back of the dress hung so loosely that when she shifted her shoulders the dress shuffled and slipped like the casing of a cocoon. Where had her body gone, the little flesh that held a bodice in place, held a form, made her feel somewhat a woman rather than a gawky girl with an old face? She rang the bell again, and Judith banged something against a table in the kitchen, slammed the stove door and rattled the cast-iron burners.

Normally none of this would have irritated or depressed her; she lived with Judith's delays in the way one lives with excessive dust or the smell of livestock. But this morning, she bit the inside of her cheek and pressed the brass bell so hard against her palm, the bell left a circle of dark red. She rang it again.

Judith stomped upstairs with such fury that the blue mirror wobbled.

Patricia stood and turned her back to the bedroom door. Opening the door, Judith hesitated before creaking across the hardwood floor toward her. "Mrs. Patricia, ain't that dress too winter? And that white slip need washing."

"Judith, please button the back of me," she said in a happy sing-song, as if Judith had not spoken.

Judith's thick, brusque fingers popped each ivory button into place. When the Negress had fastened the last button at the top of Patricia's neck, she paused, pulled one button in the middle and shook the dress side-to-side.

"You best let me take this one in, Mrs. Patricia. You ain't half what you used to be."

Patricia turned, but Judith was already heading for the door. The Negress paused and glanced at herself in the blue mirror, touched her immense buttocks just once as if admiring herself. Then she thumped down the stairs.

"Ready a horse, please," Patricia called after her.

Judith grunted something. In a moment, the back door slammed.

Downstairs, the kitchen smelled of sugar and cinnamon. Three trays of cinnamon rolls were cooling on dishtowels. Judith baked three batches each morning, took them to the Galway Quarry, sold them to the miners, her own business. So many mornings Patricia ate the same breakfast the miners ate, but never paid the nickels Judith asked, reasoning it was Morkan wood that cooked them, and originally it had been Morkan flour before Judith worked up any cash, and the Negress still used milk off the Morkan dairy cows.

Judith returned, shut the backdoor carefully behind her. Her eyes narrowed at Patricia. Then she lowered herself in stages into a seat before the tray of cinnamon rolls and began daubing small pats of butter on each.

"Is there a horse ready?" Patricia asked.

"Am I sitting here? I got things to do, now. You get you own hoss." Judith's eyes were fixed on a glob of butter. "You make a room so cold butter won't even go soft."

Yes, downstairs, we are a different thing. "I suppose I can wait," Patricia said.

"Can and will." Judith lifted a roll, a glue of brown sugar pulling and stretching from the pan to the yellow pastry. Unwrapping the swirled dough in a ribbon, she ate leisurely. "Where you think you going anyhow?"

"What makes you think you can ask such a thing?"

From the tray she set a second roll aside as carefully as one might a hot, dripping saucer. "Your lie killed my boy. Here on out, I ask you any damn thing I please."

In the quiet kitchen Patricia smoothed her dress and her fingers and the fabric made a sound like electricity sparking down a wire. "Indeed, I have wronged you. But, dear Judit, you have wronged me." She placed her long hand on the back of one of the old wooden chairs—how gray her fingers seemed. "I could have lived a life of ignorant bliss, but because you could not share Leighton Morkan, and because you could not abide a comforting and necessary lie, you had to air the truth. I have thought long these last days over the truth, Judit. The truth is not so wonderful a thing."

435

Judith snorted. She split a cinnamon roll in half and began plucking and eating each semi-circle until she reached the largest half ring. "You mean your truth ain't so wonderful a *fing*. How could you do what you done?" she asked. "You taught my boy. And then you lied about him to have him killed. How could you do that?" She commenced eating the other half.

"I have lived a moral life, or one I thought was moral. And then in one stroke I avenged and erased all the good I have ever done before and all after." She smiled tearfully at the Negress, who seemed no longer to be listening but munching away instead. "Maybe I'm not the wonderful and compassionate person you are, Judit."

"Full of shit is what you are," Judith said licking her fingers. "And just cause you killed my boy, you ain't won over me. Ask why I don't kill you now! I'm surely bigger, surely stronger. Crush you like a stick bug. But I am a better human being than you."

With a clopping of hooves and a crackling of gravel, Gus's carriage pulled to a halt in the back lot. Through the kitchen window, Patricia watched her handsome son hop down and jerk twice at the bottom of his vest—a gesture of habit she recalled in Claus Weitzer.

"Yonder comes my victory, Judit. You will never take it from me."

Before she removed to her room to await her son's visit, she took a last look at Judith. Round, jowly, redundant, there was still a glow of triumph about her that Patricia could not reconcile to the scene—an enormous Negro woman seated among pastries shining like studs of armor. As she took the stairs, she heard Gus's delighted cry when he spotted Judith. With the old Negress he was the little boy Patricia recalled but could never conjure. Once again, she thought, I have misjudged what it is to be among these people.

"What do we do about Archer Newman?" Gus asked Leighton. He pulled at his bottom lip. "Or should I ask what will you do?" They sat in what had been Gus's bedroom. There his father reclined on Gus's childhood bed, very likely dying, color gray as spoiled kraut.

Leighton pulled the chamber pot to him, but then collapsed against the pillows as if that one motion sapped all his energy. He stared at a spot on the ceiling, but behind his eyes Gus saw the old fury, his essence roiling there.

"Grand jury's sending subpoenas."

Gus blinked at him. "Have you one already?"

Leighton shook his head. "Pinkerton agent came here, said so."

"Pinkerton?" Gus whispered.

"Gave me this," Leighton said, extending the key.

When Gus did not take the key, Leighton set it on the white coverlet and they both stared at it, Leighton with a strange smile on his face, Gus with a frown and the narrow, crescent-shaped eyes of his mother.

"There are two other keys out there," Gus said.

Leighton nodded. "I don't intend escaping this." He cleared his throat. "Don't know whether to be impressed or mortified ... a Pinkerton brought this. But still, I have no intent on escaping this. I'll testify against Archer, or any one of them lynchers. They can hang me later." He cleared his throat violently and thumped his spit in the pot.

Gus sat forward and put his hands on his knees. It was late afternoon, or so Leighton thought from the sun's amber gauze steaming through the drapes. Forty years old Gus was. Leighton never imagined he would live to see his boy grown into such a man.

Bowing his head, Gus reached a long arm across the coverlet, spread his palm open there. Hesitating, Leighton put his gnarled hand into it. Then Gus clasped his hand with a fierce tenderness.

"I do intend escape, Papá." His voice did not waver, though Leighton could feel the emotion in the trembling of his long fingers. "I cannot ask Gretchen and my children to stay in this city." His hands. So much like his mother's. "We are marked, regardless of what they do to you."

"How can I help, Gus?"

"Let me sell the quarries," he said. "Sell all three to those Chicagoans."

Leighton withdrew his hand. "You sell yours."

"I need all three. They don't want to compete with Sunken and Galway. They want a lock on the city."

"Oh they do?" Leighton pulled the chamber pot to him. "You've been long talking to them, have you?"

Gus clasped his hands in front of him and kept his head bowed.

"Why haven't you been talking to me, Gus?" Leighton said. "You know what I did in the War to keep that one quarry. And I'm ready to admit I married to get another. And what I did to those Negroes bought you that third. That is all my legacy." He coughed until he could feel the cables straining in his neck. A copper taste swept his tongue. "You've spoken for me." His voice rough and thin, someone else's. "And never spoken to me."

"Things progressed quickly. You were ill and in danger. And these men." He struggled with something, his cheeks reddening, his eyes pinched. "To be honest..."

Leighton gripped the sides of his head. "God, not that phrase."

Gus frowned and waited till his father calmed. Then he spoke. "These were numbers men, Harvard and Princeton types, blue bloods, Northeasterners."

"Don't you reckon I've met the type?"

Gus clinched his fist in frustration. "Father, they don't care about history, about what you did to start and keep the quarries."

"I would never expect them to," Leighton said. His eyes felt like they were boiling in their sockets, but he kept them on Gus and watched his son fidget for a while. "Go see your mother, and get along."

Gus rose, his jaw clenched. "I never know what your answers mean."

"I haven't given you one." Leighton pointed him to the door with a jerk of his chin.

Gus hesitated before the door to his parents' old room. His head pounded and whirled. What his father said, the way he said it, made Gus feel like a child again, as if he stood with his head bowed and Odem glum beside him while they took a tongue-lashing from Leighton. In the dim light of the hallway, he looked down at his hands, at the thick stylish cuffs of his shirt, at the length of his arms. It was impossible to reckon forty years to the way he felt inside. So often he still felt like the little boy picking his way through the boulders to follow the white ghosts, his father's laborers. He could not remember a time without lime in the air, billowing thunderheads, smashing and crushing, could not recall a time without numbers and ledgers, without assaying and mucking and channeling and depreciating, a time without Odem. Without Holy . . . riding home with him, his swaying in the saddle, lime pasting his shirts tight to his skin, his back flabby but strong like Judith's must have been long ago. A wave of grief swept him, and he held tight to the crystal doorknob of his parents' old room.

Behind the door he heard something rustle. He breathed, steadied himself. Then he knocked. "Mother?" he asked.

She opened the door. To his surprise, she wore an old violet travel dress and a brown vest with suede traveling shoes he had never seen. Her hair was combed neatly and smelled of rose powder. Though it was gray as lead she wore it as she had when he was young, bobbed like a little Dutch girl. On her face was a calm expression—her lips flat, that long, deformed chin still and redoubtable. Only her eyes betrayed any trouble—they stared out at Gus with puzzlement and effort as if she peered through shattered glass.

"I have somewhere for you to take me," she said quickly. Though she wore a vest and shawl, she snatched a sweater and coat from her rocker, an umbrella, and a brown leather case Gus had never seen, small, like a doctor's valise.

"Mother, I've come ...."

"Hush," she said, grabbing him by the arm with a force he recalled from childhood, her long fingers binding right at his elbow and making his fingertips numb. "This is the last I ever ask of you," she whispered in an old Pomeranian dialect he could hardly parse.

"Mother, we have a lot to discuss," he said, easing her door open again and lowering his voice. "I have hardly seen you and here you wish to go somewhere. Sit down. Settle yourself." He motioned for her to step back in the room.

Using the burl of her knuckles she redoubled the pressure on his elbow. "We will discuss whatever you like on the way," she said. "*Komm.* I have been indoors too long."

He followed her down the stairs, lagging, glancing behind him, his face hot.

439

Judith surged from the kitchen ell when the bottom stair creaked. "All dressed up with an umbrella and bag like that," she bellowed in a voice clearly meant to reach Leighton. "Where you goin? To nurse someone?"

When Gus reached the bottom of the stairs, Judith stopped a moment, her eyes flashing between mother and son.

"Well, Mister Gus, where is it you takin your ole mother?" she hollered.

"To church, Judit," Patricia said, coolly. "Gustasson is taking me to the Lutheran Church." She placed her arm in Gustasson's and squeezed her shoulder close to his.

"I suppose so, Judith," said Gus. "Mother and I will go."

With triumph and fury in her eyes, Judith watched her leave.

Outside, every tree was a vibrant green, and already at ten a.m. the humidity pressed against Patricia's shoulders and chest. Two jays screamed at one another, bobbing on their branches. The air smelled of a dozen new blossoms.

Isaac waited by the carriage. Hunched, he was an old scarecrow of a man now with yellowed eyes. He wore today a dingy purple and black striped suit of Gustasson's, the coat so shiny with the oil of his skin it cast glowing windows of rainbow and gold when the sun struck it. Rolled to his knee, the cuff of one pants leg was tied with a leather thong to show his calf like a bolt of iron welded down into his brogans, which he wore without stockings.

Isaac took her hand from Gustasson's arm and helped her into the carriage.

"Isaac Lovell, what are you doing here dressed so well?" she asked smiling, her voice full of flirtation.

Suddenly she seemed very young at heart to Gus, and this turned his stomach. He sat hard against the carriage seat. One of the roans jerked its head around and flared its lips.

Before he could pop the reins, he was startled when his mother reached out and cupped Isaac's bewhiskered face in her hands. Gus held tight to the leather. From the seat his mother leaned forward. Isaac, who had not spoken, stood still, eyes wide, cheeks tight, as if Mother meant to pull his head from its socket. Then just as suddenly as she caressed him, she released him with a sigh and turned her long face toward town.

Isaac meanwhile touched his own cheek tentatively, as if to reckon what had passed between them. After a second his face grayed. He gave a sharp inhalation and cleared his throat. He spat so hard against Patricia's cheek, Gus felt the spray of it on his forearm after the sputum struck.

Gus rose in the wagon seat roaring at Isaac. The old Negro stood still as a man carved from wood.

Trembling slightly, Patricia pulled the shawl square across her knees and sat up erectly in the seat as if nothing peculiar had transpired. Spent, dismayed, Gus clicked to the roans, snapping the reins on their asses.

They were through the gate before Gus spoke. "That was some fare ye well."

When she said nothing, Gus slowed the two horses a touch. Ashen, the bluish trees of Galway loomed over them and the bright, scalding smell of lime was everywhere. It mingled in the dust of the road as if a hard-blown powdery snow were falling. "Why are we going to church, Mutter?"

Patricia breathed deeply as if she had held her breath from the moment they embarked. "The minister has an assignment for me."

"I see." He clenched his jaw and watched the rumps of the two horses shiver. "Atonement, then?"

"Effrontery!" she snapped, turning to him with the powerful scowl she bore in motherhood.

"There will be no airs between us," he said. "I have no mother now. I have lost a brother to your waywardness. You, a grandmother, colluded with that bastard Archer Newman."

Only the top of her head shook. "I thought to spare my son such tawdry details. I thought we could have a moment's peace. A little ride together."

"Do you deserve a moment's peace?" The hardness of his voice surprised them both. On green leaves of dogwoods blooming, on blue-green leaves of ancient beeches, on young velvet leaves of tremendous sycamores, the lime vanquished all color and life into a baptismal white, weighty and oppressive. The horses' hooves scraped through it, and all the world seemed cleansed and brittle. When an April cloud took the sun, its gray

441

swoop of shadow fashioned the road and woods and lime in an arid tableau of the Lord's heart now that she had sinned so and would be forever away from Him.

Her head bowed. "You sound very much like your father."

"I'm beginning to wonder if that's not a very good thing," Gus said.

"Will you purge me, then? Am I no longer any part of you?" Her voice sounded small and tender. Her gaze was fastened to her lap.

"I don't wish it," Gus said. "But what am I to do considering?"

She gave no answer but touched her fingertips to her eyes, her head still bowed, her neck and shoulders cringing as if something were about to slam down on her head.

"Why were you with Archer Newman?" he asked.

She laughed once, then looked at him, her face long and sad and sallow. "I had just discovered Holofernes's journal."

"And that led you to seek *Newman* out?"

"He was at the train station." As she began to talk, she tilted her head, and her eyes took on a glaze. "All a matter of chance. I took the trolley there." Her speech carried no inflections and she spoke the words in a deep voice as if from a trance. "I wore the dress I used to dye and mordant the wool in—I can still fit it."

Gus stared at her as they passed the first smithies and shotgun houses of the outskirts. In a dirt lot stretching for an acre or more, the derelict parts of failed steam tractors and abandoned wagons listed in the sun. From a shed of blond wood, the sparks of a grindstone vaulted. "Why did you go to the train station? Were you about to travel?"

The light came back to her eyes, and her posture returned, her face remaking itself as if the wagon had passed from a foggy slough into the familiar and comfortable backlot of home. "I intended to jump under a train."

Gus watched her intently for a long while, then he could not suppress a smile, and this pained him. He chuckled.

She grunted. "*Herr Gott*, Gustasson, only you could find humor in this."

"Why at the train station? The trains don't quicken until the straightaways out here in Galway. You would rather be crushed and maimed?" He snorted. "Mother, really. Such drama! Jump under a train? Like one of the great heroines? Is that who you are, Mother, a great heroine of the Ozarks?"

"Oh, the devil with you. I never know what you are talking about."

She flashed her gaze at the sides of the road, irritated at the route they were taking, such a long sweep around town rather than right through the center to the Jordan. "All the heroines I ever knew started religious revolutions or crossed swords with bushwhackers or saved General Sigel's army with some semaphore they sewed. I am none of that."

"Oh?" he asked. He gave a half-hearted nod and wave to a merchant he knew. When the merchant was passed and traffic cleared around them he leaned to her. The ice and venom in his voice made it foreign as if he were suddenly no more relation to her blood than Leighton's dead Irish father. "In one evening's work you have cleansed the Queen City of the Ozarks of the Negro for all time. Hayseeds in all their dumb hatred. Hooded riders in vengeful fury. None before you could achieve such a horrid miracle."

Stock still again, she said nothing. The skin around her eyes reddened.

They arrived at the little white church with its black shutters, its gardens neat as ribbons. He stopped the horses.

"Do you wish me to wait?" Gus asked.

She stared at him, and slowly all sense of pride and all sense of age's superiority drained from her face. She looked on him with an expression of exhaustion and relief. Then a strange smile took hold of her gnarled face. For the first time in his life, Gus felt he was seeing Patricia Weitzer, no longer matron of a leading family, no longer an emblem of German livelihood, only an old Dutch woman outside a churchyard in a town he very much wished to leave behind.

"Gustasson," she said, "I see in you the makings of a good and even a great man. Hear me out, please. I have answered injury with infamy. I have signed away my soul—my life is over." She reached to him, took his hand in both of hers. "Love your wife. Love your children. Love your poor father. Goodbye, Gustasson Morkan." She squeezed his hand once, released it, then turned and hurried through the church's gate and to the door of the rectory and vanished inside.

Madness, he thought, snapping the reins. Such melodrama! His teeth were clenched so tightly, the tips of them began to smart. In two hours I will pick up something from the pharmacy for her, and then have Odem fetch her and take her back home.

Dr. Vanderhaus, the Reverend Minister and her Confessor, held the ebony mouthpiece just below his chin, and touched the receiver to his ear, keeping his gray pinky stiff and airward. His eyes, puckered with effort. Obscured by lenses thick like the bottoms of mason jars, they were slits tiny as thistle seeds his eyes.

He spoke in German to his contact at the invalid home in Texas. "I am confirming the filling of the position by a parishioner of mine, a nurse in the Civil War. Grünhaagen." He paused. "Pomeranian with a Bohemian father, I believe. Very efficient. Yes, bound your way. By train." He listened a long time.

Patricia focused not on the tin voice sniping from the receiver of the phone—the superintendent of the invalid home in Grendel, Texas, a German enclave she read about again in *Anzeiger des Westens*. Instead she listened to the lane outside as if the marching of feet, the crackle of torches, the curses and shouts were coming again, this time for her. She knew full well that outside robins bantered, and rabbits hopped, and the sun nearing Pentecost was booming, and the lane was free of all but a horse or two. And her son, her dear son, was riding away not understanding his mother in the least. Him she would miss, though she doubted the reverse would ever be true again.

"That's just it," the Reverend said. "She will require only room and board where others…. Ah, but this will be a lasting, permanent act of contrition." He turned his back for a moment, then began to speak low in a creaky Silesian dialect she could not understand except to hear the words GRAVE SIN several times.

Her jaw ached as of old, and she touched her chin daintily. The Reverend Minister became still and so quiet she thought he had fallen asleep on the phone. Then to her shock she heard him praying, praying with his contact in Grendel, Texas, and saying, I have failed her, and, God bless you, she will come.

Sighing he turned to her and placed the receiver and mouthpiece on the desk. The base of the phone was polished walnut,
and a yellow fang of light gleamed on its finish.

"Dr. Vanderhaus, that is a handsome telephone," Patricia said.

He took his glasses off and set them slowly on the desk as
if they were a virulent irritant. Free of the spectacles, his eyes
opened. They were hazel, very clear, and stern. "You will have
to learn again to speak only when addressed. You will no longer
be the Mrs. Leighton Morkan, wife of our great quarry owner."

Patricia tried to suppress a look of pride and disdain, maybe
the last one she would ever give. "I hold no illusions. At least,
not about that."

With a frown he leaned forward, and spoke in the familiar
St. Louis German of his congregation. "Fraulein Grünhaagen,
I rejoice that you will devote your remaining years in service to
the Lord. You surely have other choices. But few ministers will
say the truth I am about to say. That night you heard the Holy
Spirit. And you willfully disobeyed."

To her surprise, he drew a cigarette from his desk drawer
then lit it with a match he struck beneath the walnut desktop.
Smoke swirled at his fingertips.

"There are some sins," he said, "for which even the power
of Christ offers no atonement. These are rocks upon which He
breaks His Sacred Heart."

"I have money for the train, Reverend. And I thank you."

Odem returned to the office at Dolomite Park very early, too
early to have gone to Galway and back.

"That minister says he needs to see you, Gus."

"Whatever for? Is mother all right?"

"He wouldn't say." Odem's face was wrinkled with concern,
and the red dust of the road made him seem at the edge of despair.

Gus drove to the church and found the minister standing
in the churchyard by the gate. Dr. Vanderhaus was Gus's grammar teacher long ago. Today he wore a severe black suit and
hat. Scowling at the old master—a black stitch in the dazzling
sunlight—Gus recalled the drills of German usage, hours of humiliation, and the slap of elm switches.

445

Vanderhaus closed the gate and stepped to the carriage then hopped on board. He was as Gus remembered him, expressionless, waxy skinned. His erect posture and dainty hands always made him appear to be in a snit.

"Take me please to see your father, Gustasson."

Gus stared at him. "Where is Mother?"

"I have a sin to confess, and I will say no more until we see your father."

Gus dropped the reins over the brake and leaned back in the seat, then crossed his arms over his chest. And so they waited.

Without taking his eyes off the horizon, Vanderhaus at last said, "I have found your mother a post within the church far from here. Let us go tell your father."

"A post? What do you mean? Where is she now? I'll talk sense to her."

With his spectacles low on his nose, Vanderhaus ran his eyes along Gus from head to toe. His bottom lip, so tense and blue it could have been an earthworm in the cold, stuck out in a frown. "She is long gone, Gustasson. God's will is done."

Gus lifted the reins very slowly, then watched Vanderhaus as he drove.

"I'll have you know my father is very ill." He did not hide his contempt for the old master. "A shock like this could kill him."

Vanderhaus's jaw buckled so that Gus could see the tension run beneath his cheek in a rill. "How fortunate for him that a minister of the church will be there to perform the last rites and hear his confession! And finally, for he never did as he promised, though married in your mother's church."

"You will not speak another word against him."

"Alas. I need only speak *to* him, Gustasson."

Leighton sat at the end of the bed, one blue arm resting on his bedpost as if he were mustering the strength to grip it and rise. He wore a boiled shirt and one suspender snapped neatly to the waist of his trousers. The other suspender drooped against his leg.

"Father, did Mother ever mention the Reverend Minister, Dr. Vanderhaus?"

"Your mother," Leighton said, croaking. "Where did you take her?"

"Mr. Morkan," Dr. Vanderhaus said, "I have here your marriage annulment." He fetched a sealed document from his coat and dropped the contract on the bedspread.

With rage in his eyes Leighton addressed Gus as if Vanderhaus were not even there. "Your mother is not in a state to travel in public," he said. He pulled himself up, bit by bit, using the bedpost, then fixed his loose suspender on his shoulder.

"I'm afraid she *is* in a state to travel in public, and has done so, choosing to renounce all worldly goods, atone for her grave sin, join the church, and accept its sanctuary." Vanderhaus pulled the black bowler in his white hands as if he meant to rend it.

"Sanctuary?" Gus cried. "What on earth are you talking about? This is 1906. We are Lutheran! She's not Elizabeth God-damned Woodville! She's Patricia Morkan of Springfield, Missouri!"

"Dr. Vanderhaus," Leighton began, "will you wait for Gustasson outside, please?"

The Reverend Minister, gray as a corpse dragged from foul waters, bowed slowly and formally, then left, shutting the door with extreme care.

Leighton waited until they could both hear Vanderhaus's small feet on the staircase. "Once again," Leighton said, "you do not consult me. Gus, where is she?"

"I had no notion of this. I thought she was going for a confession. How the church could have taken her anywhere? Sanctuary?" He was so unhinged, he was spitting.

"But *you* did not have to take her anywhere at all! And yet...." Leighton swept an open hand to the wide world as if casting pearls before a champing crowd of swine.

Gus glared at his feet, but his eyes were wide as saucers. "How could I have known? Said she wished to go to church. Lord knows she has plenty about which to pray."

Leighton moved in such slow increments he jerked like a machine without oil. Fetching the annulment, he split its wax seal and ran his eyes over the forbidding German lettering. "You have taken the wife from me," he said to Gus in German. "What more? What more?"

VII

GUS ARRANGED A MEETING WITH TWO VICE PRESIDENTS OF Chicago's Marblehead Quarries to show them the Morkan holdings. He was distracted to the point of madness—his father seemed to be dying; his mother was missing; and Dr. Vanderhaus, Patricia's sanctified Confessor, rebuffed all inquiries, then took an emergency leave of absence. No finding her in the clutches of the church. With poor Gretchen watching behind him he doused his eyes in cold water. "Not long, precious," he said, kissing her forehead, which smelled sweet with sleep. He touched the top of Karl's head, his dear one, five years old now. Karl yowled like a cat. Seated by vandals against his front door, a scorched scarecrow effigy with a charcoal sack for a face and burnt rope at its neck fell inward to Gretchen's panicked screaming.

When he received the Chicagoans at North Town Station, he told them his father sent his regrets and was under the weather. To Gus's relief the national newspapers had ceased to write about the lynching once news of the San Francisco earthquake broke. Even local papers wrote only about the grand jury soon to convene and that carried in small headlines. The Chicagoans, a young man Gus's age and an old Irishman, seemed oblivious.

And they were focused. The young man, thin, precisely dressed in a brown coat and spats, was all business—Princeton, Gus thought. Never once took his specs off. The Irishman, whose ruddy bulb of a nose bristled with white hairs, grunted always in the same key whether he beheld clearly impressive and efficient chutes and air plants or a plainly stubborn chert wall. The young man grilled Gus for figures, for sales models, forecasts, equipment depreciation, for civic attitudes, barrels of lime per day, for labor costs, margins and marketing. At every

stop, Galway, Sunken, and Dolomite Park, Gus worried some
sheriff's deputy would halt them and serve him a subpoena
for the grand jury. But no deputy came, and, with Odem's
tables and his own knowledge, he matched their questions
with informed, direct answers. He led the Chicagoans where
he needed them to go. Yet he always felt on the verge. One
minute he might be praising the efficiency of the blasters at
Dolomite, and the next he felt like turning to these two outworlders and raving: "My mother has gone insane and run
off like a missionary. Maybe she has stolen away with that
wax candle of a minister! And my father? My father would
be seething at me for talking to you two robber barons. And
he's dying. My God! I will have no one to confide in or lean
on save for a tired, old, one-armed accountant." Gus calmed
himself, pinching the cold cylinder of a spent blasting cap in
his pocket. Just as strange to him were his feelings for his father. For so long their lives seemed an opposition, as if father
and son were flipsides to a coin. Always his father seemed
rude, arbitrary. His answers to any situation seemed ill-conceived, arrogant, hampered by misplaced and easily wounded
pride, informed by years of rote drudgery rather than innova-
tion and science. Now, after the lynching and with his world
shaking apart, Gus wondered if life were better met with
Papá's volatility and roughness. The young Chicagoan wrote,
stabbing at a notepad, his upper lip always curled; the Irishman grunted, pounded his derby against his palm when he
wanted his young partner to step it up.

Though he held no conception of what sort of bid they might
make for the three quarries, Gus knew at least that his representation of what the Morkans held was equal to what his father could
have given, if not a touch more dignified and thorough.

When he drove them back to the North Town Station, he
spied Archer Newman laboring alongside two porters. Newman wore no coat and rolled his shirtsleeves high. The porters
strained in drooping uniforms that clearly belonged to Negroes
who had recently abandoned them. Next to the porters Newman looked like a polished carnival showman. The three were
struggling with a great deal of luggage.

449

Shaking hands with the Chicagoans, Gus felt a relief crash over him similar to the exquisite release that swept through him after teaching when a hardheaded class at Drury College ended and the swank ephebes simpered into the hallways.

He shook the old Irishman's hand extra hard. "When you return, Mr. Monaghan, I want you to meet my father. He will like you a great deal."

"Grumph," said the Irishman.

The young Chicagoan meditated on the binding of his notebook.

Gus hurried to the platform where Newman still battled with trunks and cases. Newman stopped when he recognized Gus approaching. Stroking his chin, he glanced down for a moment as if wondering what to do, then strode to Gus and stuck out his hand, smiling, about to speak.

Gus kept his hands in his coat.

After coming up short, Newman lowered his hand, and for the first time in Gus's memory the old killer looked confused. It was an east-bound express he was boarding.

They stared at each other until they grew uncomfortable. In Leighton's day, Gus reflected, there would have been fisticuffs now at the least, or, worse, gunplay. But from his distracted stance, Gus could tell Newman held no fear of Leighton Morkan's son.

"Mister Newman, you were about to say?"

Archer snapped as from a reverie, and his shoulders shivered. "When you are upset, Gus, you look an awful lot like your mother."

With great effort, Gus restrained himself, pushing down hard in the pockets of the coat, fingers searching for the brass detonator cap. "A compliment?"

Newman stepped very close to Gus. Even in his old age, Newman was a striking man to behold, his blue eyes like buttons of ice, his chin and strong jaw smartly proportioned. His few wrinkles and sparks of silver hair made him appear much wiser than Gus knew him to be. "Well, you can hate me, Gus Moorken," Newman said, pinching the seam of Gus's lapel. "But your dear mother, wheresoever she has gone, will not."

Sickened, Gus backed away. That Archer could mock his mother's own pronunciation of her married name and in the same breath hearken to her seduction—How long were they familiar? This man snaked into their lives like a lamprey from some turgid river, sapping all that was dear and proper and transforming it into a slick, green horror.

Newman frowned. "To be honest with you, Gus, I can't fathom your father. All his life he leases his soul to the Devil working Negroes as he did. Then at the end he gives them dynamite, empowers them, saves them. An act that dashes everything he is and everything he's done into the whirlwind of time immemorial. Why?"

Around them, some townspeople stopped, men who recognized Gus and Newman. Gus spoke in German, slowly for Newman's benefit. He never trusted Newman's awkward and quirky *Deutsch*. "Archer Newman, it has long been obvious to me how much you desired to hurt my father, once your friend. But don't think you ride away victorious. You took from Father only things he did not acknowledge and so could not properly cherish." Newman held his jaw so tightly Gus could see the muscles ripple along his cheeks. "You didn't take both his sons. Just the one. What is your victory then, brave, White Knight?"

Only a hint of purple color flashed from Newman's neck and across his forehead. A passerby, a fellow traveler with no knowledge of German would have spied these two and figured them for blood relatives, two Dutch struggling through a formal farewell. "What I don't understand," Newman began. "A woman who most all her life had done good, been righteous under God, in one instant unleashed all Hell. And a man, all his life a greedy pig, in one sacrificial act threatened Hell back into its unholy caverns." When Newman cooled he smiled. "Oh, this God damned backwater! No one will remember Morkan anyway. I need do nothing more. Carry my regards to your dear mother. If you can find her." Then he turned back to the porters who were smoking and dawdling. "Look alive there," he shouted.

At the Lutheran hospital in Grendel, Texas, Patricia was not universally a favorite. Patients complained she was too much like their school instructors or their mothers. A few who craved privacy, though, trusted her above all the attendants and saw her long shadow as a great relief. She was rough, strong. Using her tremendous reach, she hoisted them about with no mercy and no ceremony. They found themselves cleaned and plunked back to the mattress before a word was said and hardly a breath taken. It was the dying ones, old and young in the tubercular wards and elsewhere, that called for her by name, Fraulein Grünhaagen, once the minister had come and gone.

Often in death they told her a remarkable surprise. Holding her hand, old and young prattled for a time, desperate nonsense. But then there came a light to their eyes, a moment of lucidity and soundness as if they never were ill and the ward were a sleeping car where they chanced to meet an old German spinster, who understood and listened. And as they died they told her marvelous things.

"He was my brother. But when I dropped dose boards on his head I knew what I was doing. I knew."

"And I left the babe unter dat Holy vater for hours and she rose and I tell you she breathed and called my name and could walk thereafter."

At times, the commune was so intense, she found herself wishing to say to them: "A whole town riven! By the false witness of my mouth. And three innocents hanging." But how selfish and how useless to break their moments of truth, to impose herself, her story on their last breaths of life. Instead she found a still point and a fulfillment every time she was able to suppress such a temptation and listen exclusively to another soul. Somewhere in each confession she could make a void of her heart and her thoughts until there was naught but that one urgent, truthful voice piercing and distilled by the nearness of its end.

She did this with no promise of Heaven, no sense of these miracles being works *Herr Gott* might score in some book of life. When one defies a command of the Holy Spirit, there is no atonement. As she approached a dying bed and saw in the patient's eyes a story waiting, she was sure, and Dr. Vanderhaus had confirmed, she would roast in Hell all the while adoring *Herr Gott* and singing his praises. And even with fire broiling her feet and sulfur searing her nostrils she intended to sing, *Komm Heiliger Geist, Herr Gott.*

After six months she wrote a letter to Leighton, sent it to Sunken Quarry. One of the young attendants was kind enough to post it with no questions asked and no return address via the Kansas-Pacific. After that one note, she spent years in faithful and silent service, listening. Then one evening an orderly found her slumped dead in a chair next to an old banker. The elderly banker was blinking and purple faced. "Unacceptable! Unacceptable!" he sputtered. "She has died on me just now when I planned to have died on her!"

When Leighton received the letter he knew the handwriting. Holding the envelope in his hardened palm, a cloud came over him and he fought for breath. Odem was in a trance of his last pages, delineating the final divisions in the possible sale of three quarries to Marblehead of Chicago. Leighton had not acquiesced, but Odem refused to be caught unprepared. For a time Leighton watched his accountant work, and a huge affection welled over him. Absorbed in the ledgers, Odem tapped his pencil to his tongue and scratched the perfect letters and numbers, depreciations, receivables, write offs, bad debt, weather damage. Order, order, order in the universe.

Though it was a tremendous waste of time, the testimony before the grand jury revived Leighton. He gave it with passion, his hacking and spitting only emphasizing the urgent need for justice. Negro families returned to Happy Hollow, but many came only to pack. Those who stopped at the quarry to say farewell seemed afraid and shattered.

In the end the grand jury produced a tepid document, and Galbraith went to jail for a month. The rumors about Leighton and the mined streets? No one pursued Negro tales. The system of justice seemed no more effective than in the days before he and Archer pulled potato sacks over their heads and went riding and killing. The two key instigators—Patricia Weitzer Morkan and Archer Newman—were nowhere to be found.

Yet here in his palm was evidence. He set the note on his desk and loosened his collar. Gus was coming with the Chicagoans, and Leighton's mind raced as if he were about to endure an inspection, as if things were not right, could not be set right. Why was his son wanting to "Take him to a dinner"? Gus could be irrationally formal about any number of things, and this meeting Gus arranged by telephone and then sent a card as a reminder. Gus's card mingled in the mail with Patricia's note and a postcard that pictured a Negro in a striped suit and bowler, with immense pink lips and a stupendous grin, yellow spats, a yellow and green-checked vest. The caricature waved a cigar. Beneath him in hickory stick letters was the phrase "RAGTIME LOVER." On the back, the anonymous sender had written, "You, Morkan. And your spawn."

He slit Patricia's note, set it on his desk. It opened slowly of its own accord. He pulled it close in the sunlight. There was no date, no site of correspondence indicated. Even the paper was plain, white onion paper.

FIND PEACE, MY DEAR LEIGHTON.
OR AT LEAST THE ILLUSION OF IT.
—PATRICIA

He smiled. Even in her final words, she gave a command.

Odem was staring at him, pencil still in his hand. Lifting his stump he readjusted the page then clamped it again to the easel with his crusty limb. "I don't ever read your mail, Chief. But is there any news?"

"It is from her," he said. His voice sounded thin in the humid office. "Let's say it's a goodbye, finally."

Odem's forehead wrinkled. "Oh...." A moan from him of sincere, deep pain. "She was such a good woman, Leighton. I am so sorry. I don't understand at all."

Wanting no more uncomfortable sympathy, Leighton rose. Poor Judith, his nurse and keeper, was waiting outside in the October sun. Already it seemed evenings were growing shorter, for the sky dimmed Yankee blue at its edges and burned silver at its center. Seated on the bench outside the office, she had her legs spread wide apart, her hands planted on the round boulders of her knees. She wore a multi-colored dress, one she stitched additions to as she grew. It bore fabric that Patricia's mordanting and dying

454

had tinted, spots of disasters and spills. With her eyes closed and her gray hair kinked on her head, her ebony skin glowing on her arms and neck, she seemed an icon, a statue, some deity's representation beneath which alien pilgrims might leave coins and candles.

Over the quarry, the White work force, almost all White now, was stowing equipment, shedding hard hats, rolling the air hoses. Newly arrived, the night firemen lounged in the wood-piles smoking and pitching nickels.

"Show me something Holy knew how to do," Judith said. She had not opened her eyes. His step or maybe the sound of his breathing with its wheeze and baffle let her know it was he that stood beside her.

He checked the watch in his vest. "Walk with me. If we go down in the tunnel, the powder monkeys should be setting the night blast."

With difficulty, the two struggled to the switching station where the rock cars swung around to return to the maw of the tunnel. The switch foreman's eyes widened when he saw Judith coming, her body shimmying and rustling at every step, hands stretched out at her sides for balance. Hustling, he began to power up the small engine he had waiting.

"Powder monkeys down there, Brake?" Leighton had to shout above the clacking of the engine's pistons.

"Two are, sir." Brake said. He removed his cap. All the men were tense and hesitant, not only because of the lynching and the rumors that continued to center on Leighton, but also because of the possible sale to outworlders, big city people who knew nothing of the Ozarks. "Good to see you up and around, sir."

On half of his face Brake bore a cowl of puckered flesh where a steam drill's gasket failed and scalded him. Blind in one eye and that eye bore a pearly blue film. When he returned to work, Leighton made him foreman of the dwarf engines that bore the miners down into the tunnels and brought blasted rock back out. Leighton gripped the foreman's shoulder, kneaded it. "Lie to me now, will you?"

Half of Brake's face gave a grin. Leighton donned a blasting vest. Brake handed the two of them the hard, square hats tunnel miners wore. Even Judith laughed when she fixed hers on her head. Leighton helped her set it right, running his fingers through her bristle-like hair and pulling the canvas inside the cap close to her scalp. Brake looked away.

The strange company then descended the rails, riding like helmeted children on a roller coaster. Judith twisted in her seat as they passed the maw of the tunnel. The blue, popping haze of lights strung along the ceiling replaced the comfort of the sky. When a caravan of empty cars passed them on the opposite rail, its crusty, white, hollow appearance made her grip the sides of her car.

Leighton poked her in the soft fat of her back. "Set still. Almost there."

At the end of the rails, there was a long flat space of dusty new tunnel. The train's arrival shifted the air so that the floor and ceiling smoked in swirls like the barrel of a gun just discharged. After the tunnel's clean space and its perfect angles, at its terminus, order dis-integrated into a chaos of boulders over which there were no lights. Back in this the shadow figures of two men, the powder monkeys, shuffled like secreted Cistercians behind the altar. Leighton asked Brake to come fetch them in thirty minutes. When the train's rack-et left them, the powder monkeys rose from their work. Recogniz-ing the boss, they touched their hard hats to salute him. On the tops of their hats were lamps that glowed like bullfrog's eyes, and with the lime coating them blue, with their thick gloves and heavy, tool-laden blaster's vests, they appeared like witches to Judith.

Leighton put his hands to his mouth, hollered, "This here is Holofernes's mother."

The two monkeys, both White, glanced at each other and pulled off their hard hats and gloves, then strode over and stuck their hands out. With great solemnity, Judith clasped and squeezed each white, lime-hardened hand.

"Get me a light around here, and I want to show her something."

The monkeys brought a miner's lamp out and lit it.

With the lamp glowing, only a circle of yellow light bobbed around them. Behind them the blue lights of the ceiling faded to a dark violet, then disappeared where the tunnel angled up to the opening. Leighton hooked a wire spool on his belt, and nodded at a box of dynamite. "Pick that up there and you'll be the first Negro I ever gave dynamite to."

She frowned then stooped and hoisted the box up and balanced it on her hip. Leighton picked his way through the rubble of the day's work leading her by the arm. Wire from the spool bounced and twanged. The echo of this resounded like water dripping.

"What kind of cave is this?" Judith asked.

"It's the kind I make."

She snorted stumping along, the box of dynamite balanced at her hip. "No curves. Ain't no cave I'd ever make. So cold down here. Like the grave."

He stopped. Running his fingers along the chilly spool of wire, he measured out what he would need for a circuit. His shoulder ached to the bone at the frigid touch of the wire's copper end. "Walk over to that wall. Take a look at it."

She raised the mining lamp, glanced at him, then set the box of dynamite down and walked to the wall. The cone of the lamp closed down tightly on the lime as she scanned. From where he stood, Leighton could see the glitter of smashed fossils, the white crystalline sparkle of destroyed cogs and rods wherever her light shone.

She touched her hand to the stone, and her shoulders jolted. Holding the lamp out from her, she played it across her palm. She walked back to him, a frown on her face. Tilting the lamp, she directed its eye on her palm, which was dusted white. "You cut right through them. They all dried and gone."

"Think how dry they are when they come from the ovens." He cocked his head over his shoulder to the square of evening light far behind them.

She wiped her palm against her dress, leaving a white print from her stubby fingers. "You still think they nothing but animals from an old dead sea."

"Much more than that. They cracked my hands, choked my ears and eyes; they suck the breath from me even now growing in my lungs. Bastards are plenty alive." He squinted at her trying to interpret her heavy face and narrowed eyes. "They are beautiful, though."

He held the lamp so that it cast its glow down the sheer walls of the tunnel. Tiny crystals winked at them like stars blue and

457

white. What gravestone did she put above Holy, he wondered. Any stone at all? Could he offer one now? He was too ill when Judith made whatever memorial in Potter's Field. There was no forgiving all this. "Can you see now why I want to hang on to it?"

When the wire ran low, they stopped. He nodded at her and she set the box down. He slipped the crate top apart and peeled loose a bundle of six. The dynamite, lithofracteur, was an expensive sort the Horsley salesman had argued against. Leighton purchased a single case of it for sentiment's sake—it still contained Nobel's own Kieselguhr.

Leighton pointed upward and asked for light on the ceiling, which was pitted and fissured where chert nodules occurred or where men were lazy after blasting. He found the drillers holes in the seam that ran above their heads. After peeling sticks from the bundle, he sat on the floor and pinched a stick between his legs. Judith stood blinking at him. "Holy would do this for a whole day if we were short a monkey."

From a vest pocket he pulled the plier-like crimping tool. One of the tool's handles was sharpened to a point as if it were an ice pick. He tore the reddish brown paper on the dynamite, curled it back at the ends and began worming the tool down into them.

"Oh, Lord," she said. She back peddled so quickly the light vanished.

He paused at his work and laughed. "You should have seen..." His throat caught, and he bowed his head, struggled with the roll of detonators in his vest pocket. The wires snagged and resisted. "Holy was awfully quick at this." He cleared his throat. He could see Holy lynched above the fire, a black shadow, like a withered fig hanging before a field of orange. "Get that light over here, or I will blow us to pieces."

She inched forward, and the light circled him. He peeled the paper off the last stick in the bundle, skewered it with the tool.

Leighton removed each copper detonator from the canvas roll that held them like a bandoleer of bullets. Two copper wires like tan legs stuck up from each cap and made the detonators seem like miniature, helmeted men. He shoved their heads down in the tops of the brown lithofracteur. When he finished, he pushed the sticks into the drill holes along the seam. Flecks of lime and asbestos, drops of clay fell and littered his beard. Pinching the copper legs of the detonators, he wired the sticks in a straight series off the lead wire.

With his back arched, he strained, able to use only one arm above his head. His shoulder would never heal. He felt her watching him, straining to see Holy in his gestures. He twisted the last wire in place, then looked at her. His head pounded from the glycerin, but for once, he savored this hindrance.

She held the empty box against her hip. "This how you made these caves?"

"Almost all of them like this."

"Holy made them, too?"

The damp chill of the tunnel bound Leighton's lungs. He had to cough and spit before he could answer. Once he spat and the blood was on the ground in the lamplight, conversation seemed a taxing chore, even with Judith.

"He was very good at it. Very good at anything I put him to."

Out of habit, he patted his vest again to make sure he had restored all his tools in its multiple pockets. "Boys," he hollered at the monkeys. Their goggle eyes beamed up and waved till they found him. "Three in a straight. No clay. No juice. Caps in. Yours for fire."

"Got three, boss."

"Would Holy say that to them?"

"If that's what he had set," Leighton said, and his short breath made him sound gruff when he didn't mean to be. "He was a very responsible workman," he said, patting her arm. "The best one."

She lowered the box of dynamite, then stretched her fingers, her eyes combing the walls. "You brung him here when I asked you to when you could have let him wallow in the nothing at that farm like Isaac done." She gave a deep sigh. "I do love you for that."

What she said shocked him, and he skipped a breath. For months his condition was dire and his tumult over Patricia's leaving extreme. He and Judith had been more chaste since the lynching than at any other time of their lives save childhood. It

459

was October now, and he had recovered enough to feel warmly about her.

He worried her voice had echoed in the tunnel. But in their silence they could hear the powder monkeys starting their chant as they checked charges.

"A2." "Two up." "A3." "Two up. Split." "A4a." "Live." "A4b." "Two up. Closed." "End circuit." "Clay." "Clay."

An old chant Leighton taught them, but the rhythm was Holy's, his sing-song. Leighton's eyes became so clouded and distant that Judith gripped his arm and looked inquiringly at him.

"Judith, if I sell this." He watched the monkeys pick their ways along the wire to the next circuit. "Everything will be stripped from me. I'll fade away. What have I left that anyone will remember?"

Judith released his arm and from old instinct, brushed his lapels and collar free of dust. "You'll have me to contend with. I'll remember you. Even ways you don't want it."

As they watched the train coming for them they could hear the monkeys chanting, and Judith imagined her Holy filling the damp twilight of such a space with his beautiful, technical babble. God almighty, the things he had in his mind and let slip from his tongue after that Dutch taught him. O, where in the wall did he now glitter and shine? She and Leighton both longed to hear his voice just then, and pined together so intensely they kept their gazes fastened on the empty train coming for them and could not even bear a glimpse of one another. Their child was gone.

"C2." "Live." "C3." "Live." "C4." "Cap out. Break in circuit." "Break."

Across the pool blue cliffs soared into the twilight. And Judith touched Leighton's scaly palm, then squeezed his hand until the light and noise of the office grew close.

Odem met them. The office was lit, and a merry music came from its slats.

"They're here," Odem said.

When they entered the office, the music continued at a terrific volume. The recent World's Fair theme blared from a cylinder phonograph churning in the middle of Leighton's desk.

Meet me in St. Louie, Louie. Patricia's majestic city.

Alongside Gus was a heavyset man with gray hair and a bulb of a nose. This would be Monaghan of the Marblehead Company, Chicago. Monaghan wore a three-piece suit in the old style, with narrow lapels and a string tie undone. White chest hair erupted at the neck of his shirt, and his full cheeks glistened. He was grinning at the phonograph. Gus gestured at his father.

Monaghan arched his back a little. Smiling he stuck a thick red finger at the device and rocked back and forth on his heels, bobbing his eyebrows. "Damn thing didn't work worth sputum till your boy lit into it." He shouted, beaming at Gus.

Admiring Monaghan's huge, mirthful spirit, Odem glanced at Leighton, then back at the stout Marblehead boss. The Chicagoan was gruff last time they met, but Odem figured Gus liquored him good this round. What boozy adventure gat them a phonograph?

Leighton beckoned Judith in and she negotiated the door. She stood puffing with wide eyes glancing all around the room—here she had never been admitted.

"My God, you're a great big ole gal, now aren't you?" Monaghan hollered. His smile was too grand to be refused, and Judith blushed as she found her a quiet corner.

"Put that other cylinder on there, Gustasson. Your Da looks pretty glum on this one."

Gustasson bent to the machine, and as he stooped he caught Leighton's eye and cast a glance at the crusty cabinet with its mullioned windows behind which the Scotch waited. With care, Leighton brought the service out—the old crystal bumpers and decanter. So, Gus thinks he's in charge, thinks these are old times, old business. Fetch the Scotch.

Gus fixed a new cylinder on the rotors, gave the crank several brisk turns, and inched the needle to the spinning black. Leighton poured Scotch in each bumper, dousing Monaghan's a touch deeper than the others. After a hiss, Beethoven soared from the phonograph, a piano piece.

"Mr. Monaghan," Gus said. "This is my father, Leighton Shea Morkan."

461

They shook, and to his surprise Leighton felt the remnant of a lime callus on Monaghan's palm. So the old boss hadn't spent all his time behind the desk and on the barstool.

"Shea? And with the Beethoven here? I thought you all was Germans," Monaghan said grinning.

"Irish," Leighton said. "I am at the least."

Monaghan looked at Gus.

"Little of both," Gus said. "Deeply American."

The music unfolded as if troubling questions led the pianist initially to hope but then to even more troubling questions that followed. It turned Monaghan serious, for he drained the bumper as if it were water and listened intently, red-faced. "Now that... is a song." Then he pulled a chair to him and pounded its back with his fist. "Well, let's to business here, gents," he bellowed. "I've come a courtin', Mr. Leighton Shea Morkan."

Leighton lowered himself to the chair behind the desk. "Go and buy Gus's quarry, and I'll buy him out of this one, or buy you out of it if he already sold his half on me. I intend to putter my last here in the place I love."

"Ah. Good man. Work for the firm, then!" Monaghan said, raising a beefy hand and smiling as if the road had been obvious all along.

"I'm not any good at working for another man."

Monaghan nodded grimly. "All three," he said. "Galway, Sunken Quarry, Dolomite Park together. Or none." He pulled a pen from his coat pocket, tapped it in Leighton's inkstand. Licking his fingertips he fetched him a sheet of letterhead, scrawled on it.

He folded the sheet, pushed it across to Leighton.

Leighton pushed the paper shut with his palm. "Did you not hear what I said? There's no need to make me an offer."

Gus leaned both his fists on the desk. "Papá! Look at it. Please."

Leighton took in his son's pained face, then glanced at Odem. The accountant, too, watched Gus, but when he felt Leighton's gaze he turned to him. Odem stuck his chin at the paper. Here were his two lifelong advisors, one-armed Odem, and Gus the echo of dead Michael Morkan. Leighton opened the paper.

The offer was worth every bit of the three facilities and at least two years mining at peak production. "For both halves, I assume. This is for Gus's and mine?"

Monaghan shook his head. "Yours alone."

An incredible sum. What would be his legacy if he let this place go? Why was selling and leaving so easy for Gus? Already they could hear Gus's carriage crunching in the lot. I have failed him, ruined him, Leighton thought. He folded the paper down, passed it back with a spin to Monaghan.

Monaghan scowled, then opened the paper and crossed his bid out. The Beethoven had risen to heartbreaking motions, and Gus reached and carefully pulled the stylus from the cylinder. Writing, Monaghan stuck the tip of his pink-gray tongue between his red lips.

Outside there was a squawk and the door flew open. Gus's son Karl barreled in and jumped on Leighton's lap. The young German nanny stood in the doorway with both hands to her mouth.

"*Mach die Tür zu!*" Gus snapped at her. She shut it slowly.

Karl squirmed back against his grandfather's chest and crossed his arms over his front. With a glance up at his grandfather, he faced Monaghan and frowned imitating Leighton's expression.

"Here's the grand gassun," Monaghan said. "What have I got but a Nigger's Toe for him?" From a white paper bag he pulled the wrinkled black crescent of a Brazil nut.

"Monaghan, you give that to me," Karl ordered.

Monaghan laughed and held his sides. Then settling himself he presented the nut with a flourish. Karl took it then gave a gracious bow.

Karl held the nut up for all to see. He turned it in his delicate fingers. "My Granda, he had Niggers here," he said, all the time rotating the nut around. "They worked like fury, but they got in their wagons and drove away." Still holding the nut in his fingers, the little one looked the office over. His forehead wrinkled with concern—something was amiss; something that he knew belonged here was gone. Suddenly his expression flattened and he looked at Monaghan with Patricia's narrow eyes. "My friend Holy is in heaven, you know."

Judith gasped. All went still. There was his legacy for his grandson, a sterile sameness of white spreading like lime dust over the city, the Blacks gone, Miasma, Prism, the Daltons, Money Henry gone. And the knowledge that they were gone—that, too, was a legacy. Karl's children might not know. For them, all would be White, ever shall be, world without end. But for Karl, Leighton's legacy was clear: "Say, ain't you Gus Morkan's boy? Didn't your grandpappy give them Niggers dynamite?" "Your ole granny, just what was it she done?"

Monaghan glanced at Leighton, and the Chicagoan's eyes were devoid of mirth, devoid of the spark of business. "Keep that, lad." He nodded at the black nut. "You may need the luck." With that, Monaghan cast Leighton the second bid.

It spun before him. But Leighton wrapped his arms around the little one, placed his chin against the warm down of the boy's red hair. Little Karl stiffened, for his grandfather was never one to fawn over him like this. Hesitating Karl reached up, and his fingers touched Leighton's wiry beard. Then he patted his grandfather's scarred cheek.

He whispered. "Granda, you'll get all better. You'll live forever. Mother says we'll never be rid of you."

Leighton laughed, but a cough shook him, and he had to put the boy down. He cleared his throat. Then he opened the new bid. All his life right there in so many zeroes.

"Monaghan, you bastard," Leighton said. But then he nodded.

"Ho ho," Monaghan laughed. "Fine man. Fine! Mr. Odem, you will work it up please? Very good!"

Karl clung to his beaming father, and there were handshakes, backslapping.

They all had a Scotch and the boy showed them a trick whereby he folded strips of letterhead into a lamb lying down, a swan, a cross. It was Patricia taught him all that. Leighton begged their pardons for dinner. The men shook hands once more, and Monaghan left with Gustasson and Karl very merry.

In the wagon Leighton lifted the reins, and for an instant he wished to rush after Monaghan, to call it all back, tear the bid into confetti. The kiln stacks glowed like white fingers. His shoulders sank. Men from Chicago or men from an ocean away, did it matter? He imagined them coming and owning and going and leaving stone and streets, and there was no end of workmen and owners, fossils and dust. Build your city with the teeth of the souls. Offer it up, for you are gone.

He pointed the horses down South Street, where the lights in all the houses were being turned down for the night. As he and Judith drove, the glimmering street swam in his vision. Every sparkle of pavement, the gray lines of mortar tracing every myriad pane and brick had sprung from the quarry behind him, and that was gone. The street rose in a long, lit column of gray and brown as it stretched south, then west toward the purple hills of Galway and home. He breathed, and the horses slowed. They stopped. Behind them the thump of the night blast moved the earth as if, deep within her, a heart was giving one final, emphatic pulse. He handed the reins to Judith.

Judith held the reins, the weight of their leather itching at her fingers. "Hee, horses," she whispered. The horses stepped forward.

The wagon finished South Street, passed the spot where the Daltons were to have set their dynamite. Leighton did not stir. No one would remember properly what really happened here. It was already just a story Miasma's grandchildren would whisper on long nights in lonesome places. Eventually they met the ditches and meadows of the outskirts where night shrifts clapped their tiny stones in everlasting confusion.

Judith shivered. Then after a moment she smiled and saw the dawn in a time not far distant, weeks maybe, time did not matter. Lamplight flickered. It was Leighton Shea Morkan's own bedchamber draped in death's gauzy stench. In the vision, she busied herself about the room before fetching the horse and wagon for the ride into Springfield. She stood with his bedroom door against her back, the heavy bowl of water in her hands, the body washed, all is done. Dawn light, blue and soft, like the far off opening to one of Holy's tunnels, hung in Mrs. Charlotte's ancient mirror. Judith's eyes lingered on the end table, which she had cleared, the sheets, which she had smoothed, the small, blue fingers, which she had folded on the hollow chest of a ravaged body. Judith's eyes held every corner of that room, especially the gray space deep in the mirror where Leighton Shea Morkan's soul crouched easy in the dark and waited to spread itself chattering across the hills and high to every weather vane in the waking city.

Steve Yates

Author's Note and Acknowledgements

THIS IS A WORK OF FICTION. EACH CHARACTER IS FULLY a creation of the author's imagination and no character is meant to represent any person living or dead. With history, the author has taken liberties throughout. The author intends place names throughout to call to mind general locales and a sense of place rather than specific, fixed geographical sites.

Excerpts from this work appeared in *Elder Mountain: A Journal of Ozarks Studies*, in the short story collection *Some Kinds of Love: Stories* (University of Massachusetts Press 2013), twice in *The Missouri Review*, and a novella-length excerpt appeared in *Arkansas Review/Kansas Quarterly*. I am grateful for the patient guidance of editors and staff at each of those journals and at University of Massachusetts Press, but especially for the formative care of Greg Michalson, Speer Morgan, and Evelyn Somers at the *Missouri Review*. Speer Morgan deserves special thanks for the style of the opening chapter, which naturally then shaped the whole.

Translator and writer Elizabeth Oehlkers Wright made echt all the German within these pages, and gave me countless tips on Missouri Synod Lutheranism, including the extraordinary book *Zion on the Mississippi The Settlement of the Saxon Lutherans in Missouri 1839-1841*. No amount of thanks seems sufficient. Gary C. Gebhart shared his store of Nineteenth-century, German-language American newspaper poems saved by his Lutheran ancestors. These are what Patricia sings and prays.

This novel was completed with the generous assistance of two grants from the Mississippi Arts Commission. One grant allowed me time to return to Springfield and study with Dr. Katherine Lederer at Missouri State University. It is Dr. Lederer who planted the seed, the story of a quarry manager, in her lectures. The same grant, afforded me time in The Shepard Room of the

Greene County Public Library, where, as ever, I met with much kindness and invaluable help from the excellent staff.

A library of books should be thanked here, but three stand out: Dr. Katherine Lederer's *Many Thousand Gone: Springfield's Lost Black History*, Kimberly Harper's *White Man's Heaven: The Lynching and Expulsion of Blacks in the Southern Ozarks, 1894–1909*, and Halbert Powers Gillette's *Handbook of Rock Excavation: Methods and Costs*.

In Book IV, Chapter 1, much of the speech B. F. Adams gives comes directly and unchanged from the editorial the real Benjamin Franklin Adams wrote entitled "What the Negro Must Do," published in the *Springfield Republican*, February 13, 1906.

For the steadfast encouragement of William Harrison, Donald Harington, and many other writers I am ever grateful. But this novel would not have come to completion without the hard reading and tough love of writers Matthew Guinn and Paul Rankin.

To my co-conspirator and editor, Donald R. Holliday, I do not know where to begin with the thanks, nor where to end.

About the Author

Photograph by Chris Jenkins, MUW University Relations

BORN AND REARED IN SPRINGFIELD, MISSOURI, STEVE YATES is an M.F.A. graduate from the creative writing program at the University of Arkansas. He is the winner of the Juniper Prize in Fiction and in April 2013, University of Massachusetts Press published his collection *Some Kinds of Love: Stories*. Yates has published short stories in *TriQuarterly, Southwest Review, Turnstile, Western Humanities Review, Laurel Review, Chariton Review, Valley Voices*, and many other journals. His novella, "Sandy and Wayne" won the inaugural Knickerbocker Prize and was published in *Big Fiction Magazine* in a letterpress edition from hand-set type. In *Best American Short Stories 2010*, Richard Russo named one of Yates's stories among the "Distinguished Stories of 2009." Yates's fiction has won two fellowships from the Mississippi Arts Commission and one from the Arkansas

Steve Yates

Arts Council. In 2010 Moon City Press published his novel, *Morkan's Quarry*. Portions of *Morkan's Quarry* first appeared in *Missouri Review, Ontario Review*, and *South Carolina Review*. A novella-length excerpt was a finalist for the Pirate's Alley Faulkner Society William Faulkner / Wisdom Award for the Best Novella. He is assistant director / marketing director at University Press of Mississippi in Jackson, and lives in Flowood with his wife, Tammy.

CPSIA information can be obtained at www.ICGtesting.com
Printed in the USA
LVOW11*2229120315

430367LV00005B/11/P